The Traitor's

Eleanor Swift-Hook

© Eleanor Swift-Hook 2022.

Eleanor Swift-Hook has asserted her rights under the Copyright, Design and Patents Act, 1988, to be identified as the author of this work.

First published in 2022 by Sharpe Books.

Table of Contents

County Durham, Late September 1642
Chapter One
Chapter Two
Chapter Three
Chapter Four
Chapter Five
Chapter Six
Chapter Seven
Chapter Eight
Chapter Nine
Chapter Ten
Chapter Eleven
Chapter Twelve
Chapter Thirteen
Chapter Fourteen
Chapter Fifteen
Chapter Sixteen
Chapter Seventeen
Chapter Eighteen
Ryedale, Yorkshire, Early October 1642
Author's Note

County Durham, Late September 1642

Howe Hall was hung with black.

Black cloth curtained windows and covered mirrors. To Sir Nicholas Tempest, it seemed to swathe the very air he breathed.

The darkest room was one that was normally the most brightly sunlit. Today its wide windows were hung with a gauze of black silk making it gloomy even in full daylight. At the centre of the room, surrounded by candles in silver candelabra, stood an elm coffin. It was painted black and lined with lead and satin set over a layer of bran. Within it, wrapped in linen and black camlet and sprinkled with rosemary and lavender from the gardens, Sir Bartholomew Coupland lay dead.

It seemed incredible that less than three weeks ago, Sir Bartholomew had ridden out of the gates of Howe at the head of the men he was taking to the Earl of Newcastle to fight for the king. He had been in his usual gouty ill-temper, adjuring Nick to be diligent in his task of rooting out the traitor Philip Lord who was known to be somewhere in the area. Two days ago, Sir Bartholomew returned, at his own ferocious insistence and carried in a chair over the threshold of his home. Placed in his high bed, he had gripped Nick's hand with a claw of incredible strength, glared at him with fever-bright eyes, and spoken in a voice hoarse with pain.

"Get rid of them all, their long faces and wringing hands. Tell them they can come back and mourn me tomorrow." The dying man didn't release his grip as Nick gave the needed orders. But a superstitious part of him wanted to break the grip so he wouldn't be pulled down into death himself. Once the bedchamber had been emptied, Sir Bartholomew began speaking, his voice and grip growing weaker with each passing moment.

"My will and full instructions for my funeral are in my cabinet. My personal bequests and other matters, those I would not trust to public view, are in a small drawer in the document chest. You'll not discover it until the whole is emptied and the false bottom removed. There are instructions that you *must* follow. The Covenant will demand it." He broke off, the strength that had been sustaining him gone. Releasing his grip on Nick's hand he lay back on the pillow, eyes closed, chest heaving.

The Covenant. Nick felt sick when he thought of it. The mysterious conspiracy that had shaped his life and that of his family from the shadows for three generations. A conspiracy which had as its unwilling focus Philip Lord, traitor, mercenary commander, and sworn enemy of the Coupland clan. Sir Bartholomew had left Nick in Howe instead of taking him to join the Earl of Newcastle's muster so that he could hunt down Lord, ensure his death and free them from the yoke of the Covenant for good.

The hard eyes snapped open again.

"Do everything as I have asked. Everything. And Howe is yours to enjoy." Sir Bartholomew's voice had become little more than a thin thread of air. "Fail me, and Howe will be your doom. The marriage must stand."

"Marriage?" Nick asked, puzzled. He had waited a

long time for a reply before he realised the glaring eyes no longer held any awareness.

The irony of it all wasn't lost on Nick. No glorious wound taken in battle had killed Sir Bartholomew. No defence of realm or right. Nothing to inscribe with pride in the pages of history about how the last Coupland fell. It had been a tawdry way to die. An accident the day before Sir Bartholomew had arrived in Newcastle. He trod on a rusty ploughshare when a horse startled as he dismounted. The spike had sheared through the leather of his boot and the flesh of his foot. The wound, untended, had festered and poisoned his blood.

Looking at the diminished man as he lay in the coffin, waxen features surrounded by wisps of grey in the all-cocooning black, it reminded Nick that even the greatest plans can be brought to nought by ill chance. Something he promised himself he would not forget. If his uncle had taken the time to have the wound looked at, perhaps he might still be alive, snarling his frustration at being unable to ride for a few days.

At least now Nick wouldn't have to face the old man's fury for losing so many of the men left for Howe's defence and admit his own mistake had led to a disaster Howe would feel in the years to come. And at least now the mill ruins, within spitting distance of Howe, where Philip Lord had squatted with his ragtag band, were now empty. Lord had gone who knew where.

As much as Nick had respected his uncle and even held him in affection, his overwhelming emotion as he looked at the still figure in the coffin was relief. Shamed by that realisation, he left the dead man alone in the darkened room and went to set the affairs of Howe in order.

ELEANOR SWIFT-HOOK

That evening, in the torchlit dark with the lych bell tolling, he walked in the procession that passed out of Howe Hall bearing his uncle away from his home for the final time. In the little church built from the same stone as Howe, the curate spoke the obsequies that committed Sir Bartholomew to eternal rest in the family vault.

"Man that is born of a woman hath but a short time to live and is full of misery. He cometh up, and is cut down, like a flower..."

Nick found it hard to concentrate. Lit by the flickering torches and the silver candelabra that had accompanied the coffin from the house, the inside of the church with its unfamiliar opening into the crypt below, took on a preternatural feel. It was as if the whole building had slipped from this world to become a gateway to the next. The words of Dante Alighieri came unbidden and unwelcome into Nick's mind.

Per me si va ne la città dolente...

Through me you go to the city of pain, through me you go to eternal sorrow, through me you go to the lost souls...

They clashed in sentiment with what the curate was saying. "In the midst of life we are in death: of whom may we seek for succour, but of thee, O Lord..."

In Nick's mind, those words of consolation were faint compared to the grim and daunting message delivered by the open entrance of his uncle's tomb.

Flickering light painted animation on the stone walls as though the flames of hell were licking at them. The dark orifice into which the dead man was delivered became the first descent into an infernal underworld. The shadows and the bitter smoke from the torches reached up from the darkness below like the grasping talons of some predatory bird.

Abandon all hope, you who enter.

Nick suppressed a shiver and told himself it was because of the cold. Once the coffin with its silver embroidered mortdrape had been lowered into the crypt and the final words of bleak condolence uttered by the curate, he escaped. Cutting short those of Howe's tenants who offered condolences, he left some small purses of money for the poor of the parish on Sir Bartholomew's behalf and strode from the church.

The old man's insistence on a nocturnal funeral meant no one expected there to be a gathering after the internment, for which Nick was grateful as he returned to the hall.

Tomorrow he would examine the papers he had found in the secret drawer.

Tomorrow he would discover the extent of his uncle's legacy.

Chapter One

I

Had Gideon been in Germany, the Low Countries or Italy, the sight of a company of soldiers on the move would have been commonplace.

This being England, it was not.

But even before the King had raised his standard at Nottingham a month ago, the movement of troops of all kinds had become increasingly familiar.

The company Gideon rode with numbered around sixty people, including women and children. There were over forty fighting men, most riding horses trained for war. All, including Gideon himself, bore swords that had drawn blood and taken lives. They marched in a disciplined column escorting the lumbering carts and wagons which carried their possessions, essential supplies and two pieces of field artillery.

This being England, the roads being poor, and the season being autumn, their progress was slow. Every hour or so, it seemed to Gideon, they had to stop to free a foundering wagon or repair a wheel. On one unpleasant occasion, it had been necessary to kill a horse that broke a leg when the front of a wagon collapsed. Unable to salvage the wagon, they had abandoned it together with a dismantled bed frame, a pile of pallet mattresses and three firkins—one each of vinegar, wine and butter—for whoever might chance upon it to their benefit.

THE TRAITOR'S APPRENTICE

For a week they had been travelling, making ten to fifteen miles in a day from Weardale down through the palatine lands of County Durham and into Yorkshire. Following a drovers' road meant there were sheltered stopping points, wayside inns and places where they could buy supplies at need. That meant he journey wasn't as arduous as it might have been even on the chilly and beautiful Yorkshire uplands.

Although Gideon was willing to help when needed, he had an injured ankle that was still recovering so there wasn't much he could do. It meant he had a lot of time to think.

Three weeks ago, he had been Gideon Lennox, an upcoming London lawyer, with a promising career ahead of him. He had travelled north in the early summer on the promise of a profitable undertaking on behalf of the Hostmen coal cartel of Newcastle-upon-Tyne. Unfortunately, a mix of their unreasonable expectations and his own inherent integrity had doomed that to failure. Having been dismissed, he was offered another well-paid commission—to deliver a message on behalf of Sir Bartholomew Coupland. His employer had neglected to mention that the man to whom he was to deliver the message was the attained traitor and infamous mercenary commander, Philip Lord, known to his men as the Schiavono. He had also neglected to mention that he intended Lord to kill the messenger.

Instead, Gideon had accepted employment with Philip Lord and been given the name 'Fox' by the men he rode with. It played both on the colour of his hair and that he had used what they saw as his 'lawyerly cunning' to save some innocent women in Weardale from false accusations. The name was a mark of their respect for that—and for his killing a man in defence of one of their own women.

Zahara. There Gideon's thoughts always ended in a mire of confusing emotions. Slender and straight, she rode pillion further ahead of him. Her hair, kept hidden beneath its coif, was the colour of fresh peaches, her skin like an English rose and her eyes a brilliant kitten-green. She was wise, courageous and kindhearted—as unreachable as the sun and able to bestow as much warmth with a single smile. And she was not a Christian.

He still hadn't come to terms with that, but it only troubled him in her absence. When she was with him, she became the answer to every issue he had with her origins, and her religion mattered no more than the date of her birth, or the place—Aleppo. The man she rode behind was the silent Shiraz, who protected her as a brother might his sister or a father his daughter, dark gaze missing nothing. He was one of the most dangerous men Gideon had ever encountered and seemed as loyal to Lord as he was to Zahara.

If Zahara was a mystery to Gideon, then Philip Lord, with his white hair and brilliant turquoise eyes, was an enigma. Before they left Weardale, Gideon had been with Lord when he made some startling discoveries about his heritage. Things that suggested he might be descended from royal blood. Part of the reason Lord employed him was so that should documentary proof of that ever come to light, Gideon could apply his legal skills in determining its veracity.

"I wonder if our valiant commander has any specific destination in mind, or if we are merely moving away

THE TRAITOR'S APPRENTICE

from retribution." The speaker, riding beside Gideon, was Anders Jensen, a Danish physician-surgeon. He was the one man with whom Gideon had formed a friendship in this alien company, although Anders had problems of his own. The Dane had suffered a false accusation of malpractice—of causing the death of Matthew Rider, an officer the men had held in high regard and Philip Lord had called his friend. But Lord's continuing endorsement meant most still welcomed Ander's presence.

"I have no idea of his plans," Gideon said. "Since we left the mill, I haven't heard more than a dozen words from him and those were mostly orders to keep out of the way."

"He seems preoccupied with military matters," Anders observed. "We are not in favour with the Earl of Newcastle as he is friendly with Sir Bartholomew Coupland. I wonder if we will seek out Lord Ferdinando Fairfax, who I understand, is organising for Parliament in these parts."

Gideon's grasp of leading figures and politics more than a few miles north of the Thames was shaky at best.

"I think we can take it as a given that Philip Lord will stay away from any friend of Coupland's," he agreed. "Though where he intends to go, I couldn't guess."

One of the men was riding back along the route of the march towards them. Gideon lifted a hand in greeting as he recognised Roger Jupp. Jupp had been one of the first in the company to accept Gideon, even giving him a red coat to match his new name. Jupp rode up and grinned, nodding at them both, then addressing Gideon.

"The Schiavono wants to speak with you, Mr Fox. He's up ahead."

ELEANOR SWIFT-HOOK

Leaving Jupp with Anders, Gideon pushed his chestnut mare into a canter and overhauled the rest of the train.

Two mounted men were visible on a rise of ground away to one side of the road. Philip Lord was distinctive even from a distance. His hair, unfashionably straight, stark white against the dark blue of his cassaque and doublet. He wore a wide-brimmed hat that had a white plume curling from the band and looked more a gentleman than a commander of mercenaries. The man beside him, clad in a buff coat and pot helm, looked the part better. He was the man whom Gideon—and most of the company—knew as Mags. A mercenary commander once of some repute himself, he now held the place left vacant by the death of Matthew Rider, that of second-in-command to Philip Lord.

As Gideon rode up, the two were looking at a large house that lay a mile or so away and seemed to be partly surrounded by water. There was an orchard and a walled garden. A dovecote stood beside the orchard and smoke curled from the tall chimneys of the house.

The heart of the house was an old peel tower. Once it would have protected the local community on those occasions the wild Scots ran over the border and made it past Durham. It was built from solid grey stone with narrow windows. The top looked as though someone had placed an extra battlemented layer to enhance the defence.

At some point, the owners must have decided the risk to life, limb and property was no longer so great because they had built out from the tower on two of its adjacent walls. One wing was in an older style with wooden beams visible in the lime washed walls, but the other was modern and bright, brick built with large windows. To Gideon's urban eyes, it looked prosperous, and peaceful—everything that England should be, but which was fast slipping away between the grasping fingers of the iron-plated gauntlets of war.

"...and ripe as a plum for the picking," Mags was saying as Gideon reached them. "It's shameful to see."

"*Thanne shaltow come to a courte as clere as the sonne, the mote is of mercy. The manere aboute, and alle the wallis ben of witte to holden Wille oute.* What do you think, can it keep us out?" He was addressing Mags, who looked thoughtful.

"They could, if they had the men or the means. But I saw neither. The only shell that sweet little nut has at the moment is yon tower."

"And if we knock politely and offer, as tradesmen might, to put the place in good order for these times?"

Mags laughed. "And who do we turn away when they come calling asking for plate? The king's men or those who follow his parliament?"

"Right now," Lord said, his tone considering, "I would say either or both. Although I am content to at least consider the wishes of the householder on the issue."

"Whoever that might be."

"That would be the fourth Baron Belamy of Wrathby," Lord said. "Who, they say, is a man more concerned with husbanding his crops, his flocks, his kine and his wife, than pushing his nose into politics of any description."

Mags gave him a narrow-eyed stare. "You seem to know these parts, then."

"Not too well. I inquired at a drovers' inn."

"Canny lad," Mags said. "I just heard the manor was

ELEANOR SWIFT-HOOK

cursed or maybe haunted, depending on who you talk to."

"That could explain the run-down look of the place," Lord observed, then turned to Gideon.

"You see our problem?" he said as if he had just been explaining something.

Irritated because he had no idea what he was being asked, Gideon shook his head.

"Do you mean the problem of who to declare for in this war? If so then I would agree that asking an invested individual who has given the matter many weeks of thought, weighing up the arguments, is better than opting for whoever pays most."

Lord laughed and produced a silver penny, holding it up to catch the autumnal sun.

"I was thinking to flip a coin. If it lands so he looks back at me, then his majesty has my support and if he avoids my gaze, then I should oppose him." The coin spun and Lord caught it on the back of one gloved hand and covered it with the other. "Shall we look and see?"

Gideon bit back the words he wanted to say. He was wise enough now to know when he was being baited.

"What is it you want me to do?" he asked instead.

Lord lifted his hand and peered at the coin.

"Heads," he said and put the coin away. "Well, it's good to have that settled at least."

Mags gave a scoffing laugh and shook his head.

"Your task," Lord said to Gideon, "is to ride up to that *'courte as clere as the sonne'* and help explain to the fourth Baron of Wrathby that we would like bed and board for fifty-six and a half people—Gretchen is pregnant. In return for which we are willing to do the place up a little. Add the odd earthwork behind the

THE TRAITOR'S APPRENTICE

orchard, extend the moat, repair the walls, that kind of thing. We will even be willing to help train up whatever men he might have so as to hold the place in an adequate state of defence. It is, you can see, a most generous offer. *And in the same house we shall remain, eating and drinking such things as they give: for the labourer is worthy of his hire.*"

Gideon looked over at the tranquil house.

"And if he says no? We leave them in peace?"

"We leave," Lord agreed. "But they might not find us peaceful."

"You would plunder them?"

"In the German wars we'd have pulled them all out like winkles with a pin, taken everything worth the having, and burned the place," Mags said helpfully.

"This," Lord said, his tone one of mild reproof, "is Ryedale and not Rheinfelden. Besides, I am confident the fourth baron, who anyone can see lacks an adequate means of defence, will welcome us with open arms to be as protectors to himself and all he holds dear in these troubled times. And, no doubt, be more than grateful enough to share roof and board with us in return."

"What if he stands for Parliament?" Gideon asked.

"Then he will need to have us there so Royalist commissioners can't steal the family silver. But there should be no issue. Yorkshire has set itself on a path of harmony and there is to be a treaty of neutrality. Both factions will embrace as brothers and live in county-wide concord whilst war and chaos reign all about their borders." Lord looked thoughtful for a moment then nodded towards Mags. "Perhaps it will be worth mentioning that we are in company with nobility. Name dropping is always a good tactic."

Gideon wondered what he meant, but. Mags was grinning.

"I can go and *impress* this baron if you want." He hawked and spat.

Mags? *Nobility?*

Then Gideon recalled a conversation he had with Roger Jupp a week ago when Mags had first joined them. What had he said? Something about Mags having been granted lands and title somewhere abroad, before losing them again when the tide of war and politics flowed against him.

"I think it might be better if your name preceded you," Lord said.

"Which name is that?" Gideon asked.

Mags made an imperious, mock bow in the saddle towards Gideon. "Graf von Elsterkrallen," he announced, as if presenting someone at a formal gathering.

Gideon, who was aware that his knowledge of both the German language and the geography of just about anywhere in continental Europe was lamentable, echoed it back as he heard it pronounced. "Graf von *Elsterkrahlin?*"

Mags nodded. "Near enough. Small place. Doubt many will ever have heard of it. But it was mine for a time." Gideon wondered if he imagined the uncharacteristic wistful note. Then Mags laughed. "I had to marry a hideous old besom to have it, mind, but there were compensations."

"You just miss your *jus primae noctis*," Lord said.

"True. Though some of the lassies there I'd take the merchet instead."

Gideon hoped they were joking. The practice of a lord

taking a woman on her wedding night before her husband or paying a fine to avoid it happening, was so barbaric he was sure it must no longer be allowed in any civilised nation. But then he had no idea what was permitted in German lands. English law was more than enough to master. He let it go and focused on what he was being asked to do.

"You want me to ride up to that house—"

"Wrathby."

"Ride up to Wrathby and tell the owner that either he lets us move in and improve his defences or you will despoil his house and lands?"

Lord thought for a moment.

"That is, in essence, what I am intending," he agreed.

"I won't do it. I am a lawyer, not a brigand." Gideon closed his mouth and tightened his jaw.

"There's a difference?" Mags asked.

"*Woe unto you also, ye lawyers, for ye lade men with burdens grievous to be borne, and ye yourselves touch not the burdens with one of your fingers.* I think," Lord said, "this is a burden that grievous or not you must touch. Look at it this way: whether you go or you do not go this will happen. You can help ensure it happens in a way the occupants will find more—" he broke off as if searching for a word, "— more congenial."

There was something else in the steady turquoise gaze, something Gideon wasn't sure he could understand.

"I would," Lord said, "rather it was you than Mags, and I suspect the inhabitants of Wrathby would as well."

"You could go yourself," Gideon pointed out, aware of the acid in his tone.

"That is and has always been, my intention. The issue at stake is who should accompany me: a man of law or a man of war? Which would you prefer were you living in Wrathby."

"If that is your thinking," Gideon snapped, exasperated, "why not take a physician?"

Lord considered his words. "Now that is an excellent idea. Who could mistake my good intentions if I am flanked by two men devoted to the weal of humanity?"

Of course, Gideon went. Riding one side of Lord, with Anders on his other side and eight men, armed and armoured, behind them as an escort. From the appearance of the eight, they had been selected as being the best groomed and least mud-splattered that day.

"Have a care, gentlemen," Lord called as they rode along the track that led to the gates of Wrathby. "Close your files. We are on display."

Behind him, Gideon saw the horses pull closer together and something shifted in the posture of the men. Instead of appearing as a group of well-armed riders, they were now a cavalry unit. Glancing at Lord, he saw a similar transformation had occurred. A man dressed like a well-to-do gentleman had metamorphosed into a military commander, by altering his posture and demeanour.

Gideon recognised with regret that he himself was not doing as good a job of looking like a lawyer. His clothing was ill-matched as it had all been borrowed or donated. He glanced over to Anders who had one hand gripping his hat and looked equally unmilitary. And that, Gideon realised, was the impression Lord wanted to convey and was the reason he and Anders were there.

Closer to the house, Gideon could see small signs of neglect. It was far from falling into ruin, but not being stewarded as required. Their approach took them by the remains of a moat, clogged with weed and granted a view of the church beyond. The church was a small rustic building with no steeple or tower, which looked as if a part of the old house had somehow escaped and cantered off to stand in a field nearby.

The wall that encircled the newest part of the house was designed for decoration, but it met an older wall that ran from the end of a stable block to where there was an impressive gatehouse. The gates themselves were high and strong, which would have posed a real obstacle to anyone determined to enter had they not stood open and unguarded.

The small troop slowed as they approached the gates and Lord gave a brief laugh.

"They are fortunate it is we who come by and not someone with nefarious intent."

If he was being intentionally ironic, Gideon missed it in his tone. But as they rode through the gates, and then along the short track from there to the first of the buildings, it became clear there was some kind of disturbance going on. Much of the household were in the courtyard which was separated from the stable area by a row of outbuildings, and either talking in low voices, wringing hands, or standing around looking uncertain.

One man noticed their approach and stepped forward, calling out as he did so.

"Have a care!"

Other men glanced over and moved to stand with the first. One pausing to pick up a musket left leaning against the wall. He held it as if unsure whether or not he should be pointing it at the approaching horsemen.

By the time Lord lifted a hand to bring his small troop

to a halt, there were eight men ranged in a line behind the man who had first spotted them, and the musketeer was busy checking his priming powder.

"Who are you and what do you want?" The man who spoke was better dressed than those who flanked him, and his voice had both a hint of Scots and a strong overlay of educated English. It was an accent very familiar to Gideon. Many of his friends, who like himself were the children of the Scots who had followed King James to London, spoke in such a way. That he didn't himself was a cold witness to his poor relationship with his father. The expatriate Scottish community of London was not a huge one and even if he didn't recognise this man, the chances were they would have acquaintances in common.

Philip Lord seemed unperturbed by the brusqueness of the greeting and spoke in a voice that had acquired a marked French accent.

"*Je suis* Philippe Blanchard, brother to the Vicomte de Coeurlain and I am here to offer the compliments of Graf von Elsterkrallen to Lord Charles, Baron Belamy of Wrathby."

"I'm not sure he would appreciate them. He is asleep in the nursery and at four months old, is scarcely aware of more than his mother and his nurse."

The speaker, standing behind the men, was a well-dressed woman with striking good looks, her dark hair in fashionable ringlets.

"The fourth baron has…?" Lord lowered his head as if in pain and sympathy. "*Mes condoléances.* I am so sorry. My condolences, *madame.*"

"You knew my brother?" The woman sounded surprised.

"It is my regret that I never had such a privilege. He was in amity with *mon seigneur le graf*. I know *le graf* had hope of renewing their friendship and of offering his assistance in these troubled times."

Gideon was willing to bet good money that until he had heard the man was dead, Lord had no intention of claiming any prior acquaintance. The sheer gall and effrontery of it was incredible, but the professional lawyer in Gideon had to admire the smooth aplomb with which it was achieved.

"You need to speak to my sister-in-law," the woman said. "But she is preoccupied as our housekeeper has had an accident."

Anders stirred in his saddle.

"An accident?" Lord echoed, tone redolent with gallic drama. "*C'est terrible!* How terrible, but most fortunate that I have a physician with me. *Mon seigneur le graf* will be pleased if we can help."

"I rather think," the woman said, "that she is beyond such assistance. But, why not? My sister-in-law is the one more in need of your physician's care."

Lord dismounted and gestured to Anders and Gideon to do likewise, handing the reins of his horse to the nearest man in the human barricade. Gideon dismounted with care, favouring his recovering ankle and entrusted his own horse's reins to the mounted soldier behind him, then followed Lord on his supremely confident path.

The three of them were shown across the stableyard by the late Baron's sister. The man who had first spoken to them followed behind.

They were taken into the brewhouse. An open floor above the brewing area offered storage for sacks of malt and hops. A stairway led up to it, and at the bottom of the steps lay the sprawled figure of a woman in her middle years. Anders pushed past the small group of people about her with a polite apology and knelt beside her.

"Who—?" One of the women there, marked out by her finer dress, turned in confusion.

"Elizabeth, this is Monsieur Philippe Blanchard, he knew Charles and he is here with the Graf von..."

"Elsterkrallen," Lord provided and made a slight bow.

"Graf von Elsterkrallen. Thank you." She smiled prettily at Lord before completing her introduction. "Monsieur Blanchard, my sister-in-law Lady Belamy, widow of the fourth Baron and mother to the fifth."

The woman she was introducing had a haunted look that Gideon felt was more a part of her nature than caused by the present tragedy. She was plainer than her sister-in-law, and her brown hair was put up beneath a neat lace cap.

"My apologies, monsieur." Lady Belamy's voice was quiet and unshed tears were visible in her eyes. "You have arrived to find my husband has died and now another tragedy. Alice, will you please take our guests to the hall where they can receive some refreshments and I will come as soon as I am able."

Alice gave a tight smile.

"I am certain the physician will do all that can be done. Why not come with us and leave the matter to Mr Muir? He will make sure all that is needful is seen to."

As he straightened up, Anders' looked grim. "If I may suggest in my capacity as a physician, that is the wise course, Lady Belamy." His voice was at its soothing best. "The unfortunate woman is, I am sorry to say, deceased and there is nothing more you can do for her by remaining here."

His words released the tears that the mistress of the house was fighting to withhold. She buried her face in her hands and gave a heart-rending sob.

"What do I do now? No one will take Ruth's place as housekeeper. They are all too afraid in the village. They say Wrathby brings bad luck to those who work here."

"You can see why," Alice said in an unhelpful stage whisper directed at Lord. He ignored it, turning to the baroness and offering a small bow.

"It may be impertinent of me to suggest such, *madame*, but there is a woman who travels with myself and the graf who is skilled at such work. If you are in need, I am sure she would be willing to assist, should you find her suitable."

"Ruth wasn't suitable," Alice said, putting an arm around her sister-in-law and guiding her towards the door of the brewhouse. "She was a lazy slattern much of the time, with a tongue too sharp for her station." There was a sharp gasp at her words from the other servants present but she seemed unconcerned. "I know one should not speak ill of the dead, and it is, of course, sad she has died, but I think few will mourn her."

Lord lifted a curled fist to his mouth and cleared his throat, before following the two women. Anders walked beside Gideon and spoke in his ear.

"That woman may have fallen down the stairs, but she was struck before she did. This was no accident. It was murder."

II

The morning after the funeral Nick sat in his uncle's cabinet, the room which held all the books, ledgers and important documents, trying to get used to the fact that he had every right to be there. After all, Howe and all its many possessions were now his—or should be, but from what he was reading, it wasn't as clear cut as it should be.

As he already knew, there was a fee tail upon the house and its immediate lands which meant that only a male heir could inherit. Special provision had been made to permit that to be passed through the female line to Nick, and letters patent issued to that effect. Of course, he would need to be confirmed in the baronetcy, but that was only a legal formality.

Howe Hall was now his. But the hall and its immediate estates were not the prime source of Coupland wealth. If anything, the opposite: it was the wealth that supported and maintained Howe. Most income came from such things as the Coupland interest in the Weardale lead mines and lands leased from the Bishop of Durham. Nick would have expected such to be settled upon him as well, to sustain Howe as it needed.

But what he read gave him the same sepulchral chill he had felt in the church the previous night. As if the hands of his uncle were reaching across the threshold of death and still shaping his future.

Those leased lands, the interests in the mines, indeed every aspect of Coupland revenue not bound into the entail, was left to him conditionally. And if he refused to meet the condition then they would be bequeathed to others.

But that had not been the biggest shock he found in the papers his uncle had left.

The biggest shock had been discovering that since his seventh birthday he had been betrothed. A detail affecting the entire course of his life that neither his father nor his uncle—both of whom must have signed the betrothal agreement—had troubled to tell him.

His uncle's handwriting said little that was helpful.

This betrothal to Christobel Lavinstock must stand and should the marriage be rejected by Nicholas Tempest, the unentailed portions of my estate shall be disposed of according to my will, the full version of which is held by James Stott of Durham. However, if the spousal is completed, Nicholas Tempest shall inherit them in full. Until such time as the marriage is completed, all monies from the unentailed estate shall be held in abeyance.

For Nick to claim he had never given a thought to marriage would have been disingenuous. Of course he had. What young man didn't? But never with any sense of urgency. Marriage was something that would happen in five or ten years when he was portly and middle-aged. When having someone to look after him and his house and provide the essential heir might look very different to how the prospect stood at twenty-one.

But if he refused, he would be left with the unavoidable burden of Howe yet lack the means to support it. His life would become one of endless struggle striving to sustain the stones of Howe on a pittance. The one way out of that would be through marriage to a woman of wealth at some point anyway. And the delay would mean material damage to Howe and his own prestige. Added to which, his uncle was the kind of man who would have tightened every loophole into a noose. Nick didn't enjoy the sensation of having a curb bit forced into his mouth by hands now beyond the grave.

The trouble was he was sure this was not just his uncle's and father's doing. This would be something to do with the Covenant. So he would go to Durham. That was where his uncle's man of law was based and where the originals of the will and the betrothal document were to be found—and where he could discover more about who this Christobel Lavinstock might be.

Chapter Two

I

Somewhat to Gideon's surprise, the occupation of Wrathby was rapid and unopposed.

Lord was so convincing in his assurances to the distressed Lady Belamy, persuading her Mags had been bosom close to her husband in his youthful military adventures, that she insisted they stay. Zahara had been taken on as her housekeeper after a private conversation from which Gideon had seen the mistress of the house emerge more thoughtful and less despairing.

Gideon had no idea how Lord managed to ascertain that Charles Belamy had spoken German, but that the baroness, and indeed no one in the rest of the household, could do so. Under strict instructions, Mags admitted to no more than a few halting words of English, making it impossible for anyone to interrogate him further about his relationship with the dead baron. It also, Gideon noted, meant that Lord kept control of the company's relationship with the household, even though Mags was supposedly his commander. Though why Lord wanted things set up in such a strange way, Gideon had no notion.

The main part of the company was installed in outbuildings on the far side of the stableyard, which included a large barn. Lord, Mags, Gideon and Anders were accommodated in the old wing of the house which stood out from the tower by a short adjunct. Lord and

Mags had rooms of their own, at either end of the older wing. Fifteen-year-old Liam Rider, son of the dead Matthew Rider, had a truckle bed in Mags' room. He was to be Mags' body servant, an accoutrement of rank Lord declined for himself. Gideon shared with Anders, in a room between the two.

It was a pleasant room lined with dark oak panels. There was a small hearth and the window looked out over the walled garden, the orchard, and its dovecote beyond. The bed was well appointed with hangings to keep in the warmth.

But Gideon had little inclination to appreciate any of it. His mind had been preoccupied since their arrival. Anders had said the housekeeper was murdered. As Gideon saw it, if one housekeeper could be murdered, then another could be. So as Anders eased his boots from his feet, he received the full force of Gideon's pent-up anxiety.

"What do you think happened? Can you be sure it was murder? What if whoever did this killing does it again? You must tell Lord—"

The Dane dropped the boot he was holding on the floor with a thump, holding up a hand, as if warding himself from physical assault.

"Save your blows for your enemies, my friend," he said.

Gideon drew a breath to go on, then realised Anders was right and closed his mouth again.

"I have already spoken to our Lord and master," Ander's went on, working at his second boot. "I told him that I could see no way the injury to the back of the housekeeper's head could have occurred through the fall she suffered, although that is the explanation accepted by the household here. Our patron seemed unconcerned in the extreme about the matter."

"Unconcerned?" Gideon echoed, outrage returning, and he strode over to the fireplace. "A woman is murdered, and he is *unconcerned*?"

"That was the word he used," Anders replied, setting his boots aside. "He told me that he considered it a matter of little consequence to our stay here. It was, he said—and I use his words—most likely an extirpation of an unpopular tyrant amongst the household servants. Thus, it was unlikely, in his opinion, to pose any hazard to anyone else." Anders finished undressing, then clad only in a nightshirt, set his clothes to air in front of the hearth. "He forbade me to speak of it to the men or the household and concluded that he found it unsurprising someone was pushed to such an extreme since the lady of the house refused to hear a word against her housekeeper. The real problem, in his view, is the inability to employ good and effective staff here due to local superstition."

"What if Lord is wrong? What if there is another motive for this murder? What if…?"

"And," Anders went on as if Gideon had not interrupted, "Shiraz is to be about the house posing as a servant to keep Mistress Sara under his watchful eye."

Gideon felt the wind taken from the sails of his fury.

"Why not tell me that from the first? If you had..." He drew a breath. "I'm sorry. I have been taking my frustration out on you."

Anders pulled back the covers and climbed into the bed.

"We have a saying in Denmark—better a bite from a friend than a caress from an enemy. Now let us get some sleep. Who knows how long we may enjoy this kind of comfort before our whimsical patron decides it is time for us to move on again."

The comfort was welcome, and Gideon slept well despite his turbulent thoughts. It meant he woke with a clear mind and a firm determination. As soon as he was dressed, he sought Philip Lord and found him in his new quarters.

This room was much larger than the one Gideon was sharing with Anders. It was well lit with two wide windows that shared views over the walled garden. Some chests containing Lord's belongings were installed along one wall and Lord's travelling desk had been set up in a corner beside the bed.

But the centre of the room was dominated by a trestle table where Lord stood with Mags. They were pouring over charcoal-sketch plans of Wrathby and its lands. Lord was adding notes, new lines, symbols and diagrams in his neat hand. He looked up as Gideon closed the door behind him.

"*How he is metamorphos'd. Nothing of Lawyer left, not a bit of buckram.*" Lord looked at Gideon speculatively. "But maybe still within there beats a heart of law? If so, I assume you are here to chastise me for my failure to seek an inquest over the accidental death of the unlamented housekeeper? There. Your expression betrays you."

Mags grinned and Gideon bit down his annoyance. He didn't like to think he might be that predictable.

"Unfortunately for your legal sensibilities, the local justice is away to war," Lord told him. "It was a tragic accident and Lady Belamy will pay a generous fee to the housekeeper's family to ensure she has a worthy funeral."

"Gideon baulked at that. "Anders told me she was murdered. Someone hit her from behind before throwing her down the stairs."

Mags looked at Gideon, and Lord's eyes narrowed. "Then Jensen will need to explain to me why he felt the need to share information I had told him to keep to himself. I trust you, at least, will be more discreet."

Gideon felt his cheeks redden. If anyone had cause to know that he could keep confidences it was Philip Lord. "Anders didn't go against your orders in the matter. He had already told me of his suspicions before he had the opportunity to speak with you." It was stretching the truth, Gideon knew. He realised belatedly he should have thought this through before speaking out.

"Murdered?" Mags gave a brief chuckle. "No wonder you told the Dane to keep it quiet. Let's hope they don't notice."

"Fortunately," Lord said, "no one apart from Jensen has suggested it might be anything other than an accident. This tale of a curse means people here are quick to put anything down to that."

"The woman was *murdered,*" Gideon said in exasperation. "That means there is someone in this house who killed her. Someone willing to kill a harmless woman."

Lord looked thoughtful and for a moment Gideon believed his point might have struck home. Until Lord spoke.

"I think she did a lot of harm. By all accounts she was malicious, bad at her job and good at blaming everyone else for her own mistakes and shortcomings. She even managed to get one of the best-liked maidservants turned off last week, which seems to have upset everyone."

Mags coughed hard, fighting a battle against mirth.

"That means it is all right for someone to murder her?" Gideon felt as if he had stepped into a shallow puddle, only to find his feet treading water with no solid ground beneath him. "I don't see—"

"No. You wouldn't," Lord agreed, cutting across him. "Because unlike myself and Mags here you are a decent, law-abiding member of society, who inhabits a pleasantly ordered world in which killing someone for anything other than strictly judicial reasons is anathema."

"And you think it is acceptable to—?"

Lord made a dismissive gesture with his hand. "No. I don't. Had I been here at the moment it occurred I would have lifted my sword in her defence, had she been a shrew of the most revolting kind or a sweet-natured saint. However, the fact remains I was not here to prevent it, and neither were you. And that being so, I don't see there is anything much we can do about it now. The woman is dead and, whoever killed her, that is not going to change."

"There is something called justice," Gideon objected. "There is also the possibility that having killed one person they dislike and getting away with it, whoever it is might decide to kill another defenceless woman. Maybe Zahara."

Lord sighed and stepped away from the table to go over to one of the windows. He spoke with his gaze fixed on the view over the kitchen garden, his arms folded.

"We come to the crux of it all. Where your heart

touches the heart of the matter and beats more swiftly—for fair Zahara."

Gideon ignored the snigger from Mags.

"I know you consider the possibility of such a threat real enough to have Shiraz keeping an eye on her," he pointed out.

"Anders Jensen has a lot to answer for," Lord said. Then turning on his heel went back to the table. He picked up a piece of charcoal and added two broad lines beside the rectangle that represented the kitchen garden on the plan. "Tell me, if this murder had happened a week or even a day before we got here, would you be giving it a second thought?"

"No. Of course not. I wouldn't have known it was murder. But that's not the case. I do know."

Lord shook his head as if tired of trying to explain some simple facts of life to a stubborn child. "Very well, if you wish to spend your free time scurrying around Wrathby looking for a murderer, be my guest."

Gideon was nettled. "Free time? You have yet to allocate me any specific duties here."

"Don't tempt me," Lord said, dropping the charcoal and looking at Gideon with a gaze that was arctic ice. "I don't expect you to tell anyone the death was anything other than an accident. Our presence here is unsettling enough for the household right now. It would not help things if someone else were to trip down the stairs from looking over their shoulders once too often because you had scared them. If you find something relevant, you bring it to me and to me alone. And I will decide what, if anything, is to be done about it. Do I make myself clear?"

Gideon nodded, the resentment bristling inside. "I

shall, of course, do as you require."

Mags broke the tension with a snort of laughter. "In his free time, is it? Well, I hope I get some of that too. The bonny lass, Alice, she told me she would give me English lessons of an afternoon and we could start after dinner today."

Lord's gaze switched to Mags with a frown.

"You can tell her that you have no time at present for language lessons."

"What?" Mags hawked and spat into the hearth. "You think she might fall for my Teutonic charms?"

"I think," Lord said, "that she sees great charm in the land and status you are claiming. I'd not put it past her to try to get a hold on both in the most obvious way. You had better make sure that doesn't happen, nor is there any chance of an accusation of it having happened."

Mags gave another laugh, lacking some conviction. "You don't need to fret, I'd not let it come to that, Máire wouldn't forgive me."

The gazes of the two men locked Mag's face wearing a smile with a provocative edge and Lord's an expressionless marble. It went on for a long time, the silence between them counted in heartbeats. Máire Rider, besides being the widow of the one man Gideon had heard Lord call his friend, was also the driving force of the company's commissary. Mags had made himself the protector of herself and her children following Matt Rider's death and, rumour had it, something else too.

"More to the point *I'd* not forgive you," Lord said, breaking the silence but not the tension.

Mag's smile broadened into a grin.

"Faith! You'd just wave that pretty sword at me. Máire now, she has ways to make a man really regret things."

THE TRAITOR'S APPRENTICE

There was a deep current running like a strike of dark lightning from one to the other and back. It was Lord who looked away first, lip curled in something that, to Gideon, was very like disgust. But it was hidden as he returned his attention to the plan on the table and added a couple more short lines.

Whatever lay between the two men, Gideon had no notion of it and was sure he was better off that way. It was too fierce and feral, and to understand it would be to make himself party to it too.

"If," Lord said, tone mild, "you want to have any free time at all, Francis, you had better make a start on extending the moat."

Francis? Mags had a first name? For some reason that was startling.

Lord lifted his chin to dismiss Gideon and then pointed a finger at the plan. "The gatehouse and the rear of the orchard are our two weakest points. I want them secured before anyone has any time off. It would be a shame if we were thrown out by force majeure before we have started to get comfortable."

Gideon left. Closing the door behind him, he drew a deep breath. The air in the passageway seemed less stifling and easier to breathe than that in Lord's room.

Having gained permission to try and uncover the murderer, Gideon went to the brewhouse. He looked around the upstairs area for anything that might have been used to deliver a killing blow. There was nothing with blood on it and Gideon was forced to conclude that whatever had been used had been removed or cleaned. Then he went to see Anders. Gideon wanted to ask if he would be willing to help uncover the murderer and having brought the wrath of Philip Lord upon him, to both apologise and forewarn him.

He found the Dane in a room that was part of an outbuilding along from the brewhouse. Anders had equipped it with a small table that held his open physician's bag and two stools one of which he sat upon. He gestured Gideon to the other, brushing aside the apology and insisting on rewrapping Gideon's injured ankle.

"I am sure I will survive the tongue-lashing," Anders said, unperturbed. His competent hands rewound the binding. "I am too useful to our patron in his battle to win the goodwill of this household."

"You are offering your services here?" Gideon asked, thinking how unlike the plush physician's consulting rooms he had seen in London the little room was. Anders sat back as Gideon replaced his boot.

"Our Lord and master has charged me with the task of making myself available to treat the ills of any here who might require it at no cost to themselves. While that will help generate the desired goodwill to us invaders, it also means my time is spoken for. My mornings are to be spent here at the disposal of the servants and our own men and my afternoons attending to the needs of the Belamy family and guests."

"It might be you will hear something though," Gideon said. "People often like to talk when they visit a physician, to calm their nerves."

Anders smiled. "You are right, my friend, and you have my word that should I learn anything of interest or relevance to this murder, I will pass it on. It sits badly with me that someone can kill under such circumstances and not be held accountable." Then as Gideon rose to leave, he added, "If you wish to discuss what you discover, consider me at your disposal."

Feeling that he at least had one ally, Gideon walked out of the small room and stopped on his heels to avoid bumping into Zahara who was carrying a tray of small bottles.

She smiled at him and for that moment the world around the two of them dissolved and Gideon stood basking in sunshine. In the last week of travel, he had seldom had any chance to speak with Zahara. She had been much about the Rider family whose younger members were struggling to come to terms with the loss of their father.

"Can I help you with those?" he asked.

She smiled and shook her head. "I am taking them to Dr Jensen. But if you have a few minutes, you could assist me in the still room next door."

Behind her stood Shiraz, dressed in an unassuming servant's outfit of humble browns and beige. His dark eyes missing nothing from under the brim of his hat. Being mute, he acknowledged Gideon's greeting with a terse nod and gestured to the still room.

Gideon followed the direction and found the door standing open. Most still rooms Gideon had seen were little more than storerooms for remedies purchased from apothecaries. But this was as large as the brewhouse and contained workaday devices with which he was not familiar. He presumed they were for the brewing of remedies, the making of tinctures and the creation of oils and poultices. But they had not been used for any of that in recent times. A coating of dust lay over everything. There was also some furniture and other items pushed into the room, filling much of the available space.

"I can make good use of a lot here," Zahara said pointing to various labelled jars and chests at the back of the room. "Dr Jensen would appreciate having a place to compose remedies at need. I would have asked one of the servants to help me, but they are all commanded to dig." She looked up at Gideon. "I would appreciate your assistance, if your ankle permits."

It was, of course, menial work of the kind no one would expect a lawyer to undertake. But Gideon took off his coat and undid his cuffs to roll up his shirt sleeves.

"Where are these all going to?"

II

It had been a while since Nick was last in Durham.

He rode up the narrow street leading from the market square to the Great North Gate with two of the men he had brought from Howe. The massive gatehouse, which held a prison, leant on the castle itself and even the cathedral with its sturdy battlemented towers had a defensive feel.

But the strength of the citadel was an illusion. The once-strong city walls had failed to hold back the Scottish army that had crossed the border two years before. The Scots had forced themselves into the best houses, treating the city and its citizens as they pleased, demanding payment for their keep whilst taking whatever they wanted.

They might share the same king, Nick reflected, but there was little love to be found amongst the people of Durham for England's northern neighbour. Which was perhaps why the attorney he had come to see had changed his name from Scott to Stott.

THE TRAITOR'S APPRENTICE

James Stott was the man both his uncle and his father trusted to oversee the legal side of their dealings. Chosen by Sir Bartholomew Coupland from the brightest of the poor pupils at Durham School, Stott had been apprenticed to the previous incumbent of Coupland's trust at Sir Bartholomew's expense. All he was today Stott owed to Coupland patronage. Nick had dealt with him in the past on his uncle's behalf but was unsure how much the man knew about the Covenant.

He was on the steps outside the lawyer's door when it opened and a woman came out, forcing him to stumble back.

"Oh dear." Her voice was full of apology. "I am so sorry."

By her dress, she was well-to-do, but not wealthy, and by her face she was young. But Nick scarcely took that in before finding himself staring at the jewel-bright aquamarine eyes and the pale wave of white hair that lay loose on her shoulders beneath a lace-trimmed bonnet. His heart stood still in his chest, and he had to remind himself to breathe.

She was looking at him now as if wondering about the balance of his mind.

"Are you all right, good sir? You have turned very pale."

Finding his tongue, at last, Nick managed to stutter something anodyne and polite, whilst his brain struggled to understand what he was seeing. In his mind he was seeing identical eyes and hearing a cold voice of a different timbre speaking with the power of absolute certainty—*You will die.*

James Stott appeared behind the young woman and made a brief bow.

"Sir Nicholas, I have heard the sad news. Please accept my sincere condolences and know that I am at your service for whatever you might need." He straightened up. "Your arrival at this time is fortuitous, however." He turned to the young woman who had been joined by another, whose dress was as a maidservant. "If you will perhaps be kind enough to step inside again, we can make the introductions."

"Introductions?" Nick demanded, then realised he had spoken at the same time as the young woman and with a similar note of confused concern.

"Why yes," Stott said and perhaps realising neither of the two would move, went on, "Sir Nicholas, this is Mistress Christobel Lavinstock…"

Nick didn't hear the rest. He stared at the woman, grappling with the impossibility of what he was seeing. As he did so her expression changed from surprise to a jaw-tight look of determination. If Nick needed any confirmation that the Covenant was behind this proposed marriage, it stood there before him clothed in fair flesh.

It was Stott who managed the moment, arranging that Nick would call on the Lavinstock household later that day once his business in Durham was concluded. Too confounded by the impact of Christobel's appearance to think clearly, Nick said the right words in the correct places and made a formal farewell.

Then he allowed himself to be steered to a comfortable room with cushioned chairs and a warm fire in the hearth. Stott sat down, steepling his fingers and tapping them together.

"I suspect, sir, you will have a lot of questions. Forgive me if I don't have all the answers. I believe it had been expected that your father would have been here should such a circumstance arise. No one anticipated there would be a war preventing him from doing so."

"I am sure no one had," Nick conceded.

"You will have to appreciate that I'm not privy to all that is involved here." Stott unsteepled his fingers and sat back. "Let us say that I'm unable to help you with the 'whys' and the 'wherefores', but I will perhaps be able to answer questions of 'what' and 'how'. I have at hand the documents you need to see. Then perhaps I can try and answer what I may for you."

"Uh—are they in Latin? Because..."

Nick felt the usual stab of shame he had when having to admit to that failing. Whilst fluent in several modern languages he had always struggled to care enough about Latin.

Getting to his feet to fetch the documents, Stott nodded.

"Most is in English. But I can translate anything you need help with, sir."

As he began to read, Nick was glad of the wine as an antidote to the clammy sickness in his stomach. The Covenant was casting its long and inescapable shadow over him. He was as caught in its coils as his father and grandfather had been—victims of the ambitions of men long dead. With trepidation, Nick steeled himself to learn of the path they had determined for him.

Chapter Three

I

At Wrathby, dinner was served at midday in the main hall of the new wing. Gideon arrived there early, having perforce changed his shirt since he had spent much of the morning assisting Zahara in clearing the objects from the still room while she got on with whatever duties her new calling as housekeeper required of her.

His first impression of this wing of the building was of lightness and grace. Unlike the heaviness of the west wing where his bedroom was sited, with its small windows and dark wood, this was modern and bright. Walking through the house from the old wing, he went past the door to a comfortable parlour. He admired the wide entrance hall with an open staircase that rose to a landing and then divided to offer separate access to each side of the upper floor.

There were decorated panels on the walls and an eggshell-blue and white cove ceiling, whilst the floor was flagged in a pale grey stone. The family, Gideon reflected, must have enjoyed some good measure of wealth at some point in the not-too-distant past to be able to afford this.

He crossed to examine one of the more striking decorative panels, one showing what he assumed must be the heraldry of the house, with elements picked out in gold. That was when he heard voices and started, before realising they came from the room beside him on the other side of the wall. A pace to either side and he could hear nothing, but right beside the panel, he heard voices that belonged to an older man and woman.

"...completely insupportable. I knew he was desperate, but I never suspected he would sink so low. How dare he come here and demand that I pay him. After all this time." The woman sounded more hurt than outraged.

"If it doesn't matter then—"

"It matters to me," she insisted.

"We have been over this already. You have paid him?"

"No. Not yet. I know you told me I should, but…"

There was a silence and Gideon realised that good manners dictated he should move away so as not to overhear any more of what was meant to be a private conversation, but despite that, he stayed.

"Do as I say and then leave it to me." The man's voice held a tone that bespoke more than friendship. "I have matters in hand. Well in hand. He will be gone by the end of the week."

"Even with these soldiers here? Do you think he will be allowed to leave?"

"That will make no difference. No difference. I promise you. Now, please, you must compose yourself and then come to dinner."

Gideon took that as a fair warning that he might be uncovered as an eavesdropper if he stayed there any longer and stepped away to go to dinner himself.

The hall was as expansive as the entranceway. There was a marble-fronted hearth and two large windows, facing south to benefit from whatever light and warmth the sun might provide. The walls were panelled, with paintings hung on them—one a view of Wrathby itself and another showing a cluster of people who were presumably family members. A long stretcher table was set in the middle of the room with matching high-backed chairs.

Anders was already at the table and Gideon sat beside him.

"Our Lord and master was here but has gone again, excusing himself and Mags on the grounds that they have much to attend to, so would eat with the men. But I do not think they will miss out on the bounty we are offered," Anders confided. "As I came in through the kitchen door, I saw the late baron's sister taking out some of the choicest items in a basket. So I have a feeling that the two will not be forced to endure whatever more basic rations are being provided for the workforce."

In fairness, Gideon's experience of the food provided for the men of Lord's company had always been good. He was about to say as much when they were joined by Simon Muir, the London-Scot who had challenged them when they first arrived. From his spotless yellow doublet, Gideon assumed that Muir didn't take his commitment to the security of the house as far as helping to dig ditches to defend it.

"Have you been with the graf long?" Muir directed the question at Anders but included Gideon in his interrogative look.

"A matter of a couple of weeks," Anders told him.

"He pays well?"

"I think that would depend on your measure," Anders said. "I find I feel well recompensed for my time and labour. Why? Are you seeking employment?"

Muir shook his head.

"Professional curiosity. I fought on the continent with

the Dutch. But now I am going home. My brother is Laird of Lochcreath. I am joining him there to offer whatever support he might need in these troubled times."

"How did you come to be staying in Wrathby?" Gideon asked.

Muir responded with a cold smile.

"Fox, is it?"

He knows me or suspects he does. Gideon felt a touch of panic. But what did it matter? Muir was heading to Scotland, not London. Besides, as long as Gideon stayed with Lord, he was as safe as he could be from those who wanted him dead for knowing too much about their affairs.

"Fox has been with the graf as long as I have," Anders explained. "We travelled together."

"And that is much the way I come to be here," Muir said, sitting back. "I was travelling with Lady Belamy's sister-in-law, Mistress Alice Franklyn, who was bereaved earlier this year. Since we were both heading in the same direction from London, I offered to escort her here on my way home."

"You should be careful," Anders told him. "Scotsmen are not well thought of the closer you get to the border. I hope you have a strong escort."

"We are not so well thought of in London either. But I will be like Peter and deny my heritage if it comes to it." Muir laughed and lifted his hands in a helpless gesture. "I don't think of myself as Scottish, and it was only through the unfortunate demise of a couple of distant cousins that my brother came to inherit. Before that, he was set to stay a clothier in London, like our father."

"You are the adventurer in the family?" Anders suggested.

Muir chuckled. "I am the youngest of five sons. I *have* to be an adventurer."

The door opened and two older men joined them, taking seats together on the opposite side of the table. At a glance, they were similar, with the same shoulder-length drop of hair, both greying, the same goatee beard and neat moustache. But one had a rounded face with a showing of jowls, his face a healthy pink contrasting the dark green of his coat and the other was hollow-cheeked, sallow complexioned with rings around his eyes. Gideon noticed Anders casting appraising looks at the second man. Muir rose to make the introductions, presenting Gideon and Anders first.

"This is the Reverend William Irving and Sir Arthur Cochrane. Both old friends and guests of Lady Belamy's mother, Lady Grace, who lives here with her daughter and grandson."

The two gave brief nods, then returned to their discussion. From their rather heated discussion and lamentations about the state of the capital, Gideon concluded the two were academic refugees from a London where they no longer felt at home. Cochrane was the quieter of the two, and Gideon wasn't sure who he was or what he did in life. He seemed to be a man with delicate digestion because a special portion of what to Gideon looked and smelt like plain boiled fish had already been set steaming by his platter along with a bowl of syllabub. But Irving had more of Gideon's attention from the first as he recognised the man's voice. It was the one he had just heard talking behind a closed door.

THE TRAITOR'S APPRENTICE

Lady Grace joined the gathering a short time later, clad in an old-fashioned peacock blue robe with a collar that came close to looking like a ruff. Her greying hair was lifted in a high bun. She carried an elderly brown and white spaniel which sat quietly at her feet once she took her place at the table. Greeting her two friends with a simpering smile to which they both responded warmly, she acknowledged the polite bows from Anders, Gideon and Muir. If Irving, whom she sat beside, had been the male voice Gideon had heard, Lady Grace's was the female one.

The baroness herself arrived last. Her dress was in the same practical style she had worn the previous day. She was accompanied by Zahara, who stood beside her chair at the head of the table as Lady Belamy made her apologies.

"Charlie has been restless. Dorcas asked me to help settle him."

"In my day," Lady Grace said, "we left feeding the babies to the wet nurse."

It was clear the baroness was well used to such comments because her gaze dropped, and she said nothing as she took her seat.

Anders spoke in a conversational tone into the awkward silence that ensued.

"Of course, that is the way things have been done in the past. But there are those physicians who maintain that an infant fares better who receives more attention from his mother."

The look of gratitude that earned him from the baroness was warming and she seemed to relax a little as she turned to Zahara.

"We are ready to eat now, please. Alice was insistent

we shouldn't wait for her."

Zahara gave a curtsy and left the room. The conversation had no chance to pick up again before a handful of household servants appeared bearing hot dishes, guided by Zahara.

The meal was good. Gideon heard more than one of the others murmuring that it was pleasant, for once, to have a hot course that arrived hot and was cooked through. He felt a small lift of pride in the certain knowledge that the improvement they noted would be down to Zahara's efforts. Lady Belamy certainly thought so, as more than once Gideon saw her smile and speak a few words of appreciation and gratitude to her new housekeeper. Her mother, Lady Grace, however, made several loud-voiced and sharp complaints about the texture of the sauces and how someone had interfered with the cook to the detriment of the meal. She kept dropping food on the floor throughout the meal and the little spaniel would be quick to eat it up.

It was also impossible for Gideon not to notice the appreciative glances Zahara was getting from the men, only Anders seeming unaffected. Her hair was hidden as ever under a coif and a large lappet cap over that, and her clothing was high-collared and modest. But nothing could hide the sweetness of her expression, the softness of her voice or the kitten-bright green eyes. Gideon steeled himself to ignore it. Giving in to that kind of jealousy when it came to Zahara would be to set himself up for a lifetime of torment. What mattered, he reminded himself, was that she was polite to them all, but when she came to serve him, she turned so she could send him a smile that the others wouldn't have seen.

"Thank you for your help in the still room this

morning, sir." Her tone was respectful and distant, but the smile belied it. "Now the place is cleared, I can set it up again for use."

When she had gone again, it was Muir who commented.

"Pretty little thing that one. Pretty enough to persuade a man of letters to manual labour." He wore a smile as he spoke, but it failed to reach his eyes, which were fixed on Gideon.

"Yes," Gideon responded tersely, realising any attempt to deny it would lead to further conversation about Zahara, something he was keen to avoid. Instead, he replied with an attack of his own. "You are injured or convalescent, perhaps?"

"I think you are confusing me with someone else," Muir said, applying himself to his meal. "This beef is good."

"I wondered why I didn't see you assisting with the improvements of the defences."

"I was too busy being part of those defences," Muir returned. "I was commanding the gate guard."

"The guard seems to be managing quite well without you at the moment," Gideon observed. "Perhaps you should seize the opportunity to allow their initiative to continue once you have eaten?"

"Strip off in front of the men and wield a mattock?" Muir gave a brief laugh. "A good way to lose their respect."

Gideon was finding it hard to warm to Simon Muir. He seemed to have little understanding of people or the nature of leadership. Then it struck him with force that just over two weeks ago, before he had met Philip Lord, he might have acted much the same way himself.

"I would doubt it," Gideon said. "They respect the graf and Blanchard and both of them have been wielding mattocks."

Muir frowned and had his mouth open to reply when Sir Arthur Cochrane leaned forward over the table towards Anders, in the process nearly putting the elbow of his plum-coloured doublet into the untouched bowl of syllabub set beside him.

"I say, are you the physician I have heard mentioned?"

Anders nodded and rescued the syllabub allowing Gideon to help himself to a large portion. It was delicious.

"I am indeed a physician, sir," Anders agreed. "If you would like to see me about some aspect of your health, I would be happy to attend you after we have eaten."

A few minutes later, Sir Arthur excused himself saying he would be in his room and left the hall, looking, Gideon thought, a little pale. Muir turned to look after Sir Arthur as Gideon reached for the syllabub hoping to secure another portion before someone else claimed any. But as Muir turned, he caught the bowl with a careless elbow and sent the contents flying in a sticky mess over Gideon's doublet.

Muir was mortified and apologetic.

"I am so sorry. I was worried about Sir Arthur, he looked unwell to me."

Gideon might have been furious, but seeing as it was Zahara who came to his rescue, taking his doublet and dabbing at a couple of stray splotches of the dessert that had landed on his collar, he was willing to be gracious. He resumed his seat soon after, wearing a borrowed doublet she provided. One he knew to belong to Philip Lord. At least the spaniel was happy, as it got to lap up some of the syllabub before Zahara could set one of the servants to clean it up from the floor.

As he retook his seat Gideon overheard Anders in a discussion of remedies for various common ailments, most of which Lady Grace disagreed with or criticised. By contrast, Gideon found himself caught up in a three-way discussion with Muir beside him and the Reverend Irving sitting opposite. It seemed the other two had an ongoing argument, in which both wanted his support, concerning the legality of the abolition of the Star Chamber the previous year and its impact on the current national state of unrest.

Despite his professional skills in dissembling, Gideon struggled to find the required politely neutral comments to keep the conversation civil. He was close to abandoning the effort when Alice Franklyn burst into the hall, the skirts of her scarlet gown billowing like a battle standard.

"Doctor, you must come. There has been another accident."

II

"Christobel Lavinstock," Stott said, sitting back in his chair, fingers steepled, "is the only child of Blayse Lavinstock, deceased. She was born in French Navarre, where her father held a position in the court of King Henry—father of the present King Louis—before he became king of France."

"She is a Calvinist? Or, God forbid, not a Catholic?"

After all, King Henry had been a Calvinist. He had converted to the Catholic faith to end the religious opposition to his rule, saying that Paris was worth a mass, only to die years later at the hands of a Catholic assassin.

"I have no information regarding the young woman's religious inclinations," Stott told him. "Only that Blayse Lavinstock returned to England and settled in Durham after the death of his French wife in childbirth. Therefore I would suspect she was raised within the Anglican communion."

That was a relief. Although had she been a Catholic, he might have found a way to use that to escape the marriage.

"She grew up in England?"

Stott nodded.

"The child of her father's old age. He died a few years ago."

There was another question, one he needed the answer to, but he was sure Stott wouldn't have it. He needed to know how it could be that she had the same ice-water eyes and white-blonde hair as the man who had vowed to kill him.

"How old is she?" he asked instead.

"Twenty-three."

Two years his senior and until today with no idea she was betrothed. So why hadn't she married, or sought to do so? She was well past the age when women of her station might have been expected to marry.

But Stott, of course, couldn't answer that.

In the end, it was only one of the many questions Nick had burning in his mind as he rode up to Flass Grange with his men.

The house was one Nick wouldn't have glanced at under other circumstances. With well-tended fields, carefully kept barns and woods for coppicing, it was the kind of house the most prosperous tenants of Howe lived in. Not the kind of house he would ever have anticipated visiting to meet the woman he would wed.

Christobel Lavinstock was dressed as she had when they ran into each other. She greeted him politely and made rapid arrangements for his men to be looked after as if it was an everyday occurrence for her to have such visitors, then she led him into the modest house.

The room she took him to was plainly furnished but comfortable. He assumed it was the best room, with a worn tapestry hanging over one wall and a small hearth.

Now he was able to take the time to look at her, he saw that far from being plain, Christobel had a face that held too much strength of character to be considered beautiful—from the pale arch of her white eyebrows to the determined set of her jaw. Hers was not a comfortable face to contemplate in a wife. It flared with challenge and would even do so, he suspected, even in repose. But despite that, he would marry her. He would marry her were she a raddled hag, because in her hands lay the keys to Howe.

Her unsettling turquoise eyes met his appraising gaze, and he realised that as he had been studying her, she had been studying him. The thought made him uncomfortable. It wasn't as if she would get a bad bargain. He was young, strong, healthy and had never had any complaints about his looks—she would like what she might see.

Her first words left him confused.

"You *are* Sir Nicholas Tempest?"

"Of course," he said. "We were introduced, if you recall."

"I recall, but you are much younger than I expected you to be,"

Nick tightened his jaw.

"How old did you think I was?"

She gave a small shrug.

"You must remember before today I had no idea of your existence. All I know of you comes from Mr Stott and the way he spoke of you."

"You thought you were contracted to marry an old man?"

She answered him with a slight shake of her head, sitting with her back straight and her head held proudly. Nick's gaze moved over her body, from her small high breasts, slender waist shaped by the bodice and the skirt concealing all that lay below that. He began mentally undressing her, wondering if the creamy skin was as soft as it looked, if the white hair would be the same in her intimate places. The knowledge that she was to be his excited him and he knew then that he would enjoy her. Suddenly, the completion of his uncle's stipulation couldn't happen fast enough.

"As you can see," he told her, "I am not old, not infirm, not diseased, nor in any way unfit. I will admit I had my doubts before, but now that we have met I can appreciate there was much wisdom in our families' work of matchmaking."

She lifted her chin like an elegant sighthound catching a scent. Something in her stillness, in the clear challenge her expression held, stirred real heat in Nick's loins.

"I am sure there are many women, sir, who would be most flattered to be told so," she said, her voice level and pleasant. "But I have yet to be convinced of the wisdom you perceive. I am not an empty-headed sixteen-year-old, so I would hope for more than *just* a pleasing appearance in the man I marry."

THE TRAITOR'S APPRENTICE

"Of course," Nick said, chiding himself for his impatience. "I understand you would want certain reassurances, what woman would not?"

"Reassurances?" her expression changed as if she doubted what she had heard him say.

"As my wife, you will be living at Howe Hall, of course. You shall have a life much grander than this." He lifted a hand to indicate the room. "I can promise you will want for nothing. You will dine from silver and wear fine gowns and jewels."

Her eyebrows rose and her gem-bright eyes held his gaze, making him feel hot and taut.

"*When a man hath taken a new wife, he shall not go out to war, neither shall he be charged with any business: but he shall be free at home one year, and shall cheer up his wife which he hath taken.* Is that what you are offering?"

The words landed like a bucket of water. Did she devote herself to studying the Bible? Was she indeed a Calvinist? Some canting Puritan? More disturbing still, the edge in her tone was the twin of the one Philip Lord had used. It even sounded mocking.

"Yes," he said. "I mean, no—not like that. I will, of course, do what I may to cheer you, but I shan't stay home for a year. I couldn't even if I might wish it. The nation is at war—I have my duty."

Christobel smiled as if he had said something amusing.

"And how would you seek to cheer me in the time that you were able to spare to be at home?"

What was it the grandest women were most inclined to do? "We can go hunting, hawking and coursing," he said. "There are both mews and kennels at Howe and a fine stable where I am sure there would be a gentle mount you could ride." Then he thought of his father's present wife. "You can have small dogs for company when I am away, so you wouldn't need to be lonely."

"Hunting and coursing and small dogs for company." She looked as though she were giving his words her serious consideration. Nick began to feel relieved until she went on. "But what if I am not given to hunting and small dogs? What if I love music, art, reading great works and discussing philosophy? What if my sole ambition is to follow in the footsteps of Marco Polo? Or to write a treatise on the science of optics?"

She was talking in riddles. Nick had no idea what she was trying to say or how to answer her.

"You want those things? I—I can get you books, a lute, I believe there is a harpsichord in Howe. But the rest..." He trailed off, the passion of a few moments ago, forgotten.

She was still studying his face with those cold jewel eyes.

"You almost tempt me," she said. "However, I am afraid I must decline. I will keep to my own house and my own hearth and maintain my own integrity."

"What do you mean by that?" Nick demanded.

Christobel rose to her feet in a single seamless motion.

"I mean that it has been fascinating to meet the man my father wished I should wed. Thank you for taking the time to visit, Sir Nicholas." The curtsy was swift but polite.

Uneasy now, Nick got up from the hard chair he had been offered. She was playing some game with him, some foolish female game. He bit back the surge of anger that thought provoked.

THE TRAITOR'S APPRENTICE

"I came to discuss the arrangements necessary for our spousal, as your father and my uncle wished."

She smiled, a distant smile of the sort one might offer to an unwelcome acquaintance importuning at a dull social occasion.

"I fear you have not understood me, sir." Her voice was sweet, if cool, and her gaze a flash of blue diamond. "Although your offer is kind and flattering, I must refuse it."

"Refuse? You mean you won't...?" Nick tried and failed to grasp the idea. "You cannot. We are bound by the betrothal and—"

The sweetness was gone from her tone as she cut across him, leaving only the cold hard edge.

"I can and will. Tomorrow I shall speak to Mr Stott about how this betrothal may be dissolved. Now, I am sure you must have many matters you need to attend to as do I, so I bid you good day, Sir Nicholas."

Stunned into immobility by her audacity, Nick struggled for a response.

Christobel frowned and lifted her hands in exasperation. "Oh, go away. And close your mouth, you look as foolish as a village halfwit."

Chapter Four

I

Sir Arthur Cochrane lay at the bottom of the stairs in the entrance hall Gideon had been admiring less than an hour before. The odd angle of his neck left no doubt that he was dead.

Gideon was behind Lady Grace who put her hands over her mouth staring at the Reverend Irving in appalled horror. Irving glared back at her, brows pulled low over his eyes then pushed past Gideon to walk back into the dining hall and sit, whey-faced, staring at nothing. Zahara placed an arm around the baroness who looked as if she had forgotten how to breathe, and, talking to her in a firm, gentle voice, drew her away from the scene towards the parlour.

Philip Lord must have been close by because he was suddenly there as Anders knelt beside the body. Lord was looking far from his usual immaculate self and Gideon had the distinct impression that not only had he been wielding a mattock, but he had also been showing many of the others how it should be done. Lord raised an eyebrow at Gideon then shot a brief interrogative look at Anders, who gave him a frown and head shake in response. So Anders saw nothing in this death that might suggest it had been a murder. Lord turned back to meet Gideon's gaze, his expression expectant, but of what Gideon had no idea.

THE TRAITOR'S APPRENTICE

"Did anyone see or hear anything?" Lord asked, his French accent coming to Gideon as an odd reminder of the playacting they were all involved in here, which clashed with the cold reality of a corpse. And then he realised what Lord had wanted of him. It was Gideon's place to ask such questions as he was the one supposed to be discovering what he could about the murder of the housekeeper. It was a struggle to muster his thoughts and he decided he had somehow tired himself out helping Zahara.

"I was coming through to dinner and saw him lying there," Alice Franklyn said, her gaze on the dead man with morbid curiosity. Gideon had a feeling that given a chance she would be kneeling by the body herself. "I'd only just left you, monsieur, and… there he was."

Anders got to his feet.

"I think the unfortunate gentleman must have fallen right after he left dinner. We were all distracted, no doubt by the commotion with the syllabub, and missed the sound of his fall as a result."

"Commotion with a *syllabub*?" Lord's voice lifted to a note of puzzlement.

"It's an English dessert dish, monsieur," Alice Franklyn said, helpfully. "Made from the curds of cream mixed with the white from eggs, wine, honey and spices."

There was a short silence following her revelation.

"The bowl of syllabub was knocked from the table and wound up over my doublet in large part, on its way to the floor," Gideon explained.

Lord's gaze moved back to meet his own. Gideon saw it held hard-restrained hilarity and had to swallow down his anger. It was all he disliked in Philip Lord made flesh. A man lay dead from a tragic accident at his feet and Lord was struggling not to laugh at the notion of Gideon covered with syllabub.

It must have shown on his face as a hand clapped onto his shoulder from beside him.

Anders.

"That would explain," Lord said, no trace of that inner amusement in his voice at all, "why you are wearing part of my wardrobe, *n'est ce pas*? This was a tragic accident. Sir Arthur was not a well man by his appearance."

Anders released Gideon and looked sombre. "I should have been more careful and offered to escort him to his chamber."

"He wasn't well. Not well at all," Lady Grace stood with her hands grasped together. "He had problems with his digestion—he could only eat certain foods, the fish…" She swallowed hard and blinked. "I'd asked for the syllabub to be made for him as he needs—needed to endure such plain fare in general. The poor, poor man."

"A tragic accident," Lord said. "Monsieur Jensen, perhaps you would be kind enough to attend the ladies who are in distress. Monsieur Muir, you had an efficient approach to the matter of untimely death yesterday, perhaps you can be as efficient again today, and Monsieur Fox…" The diamond-hard gaze recaptured Gideon's own. "If you would be so good as to return to me my doublet and find something of your own, I shall be in my room."

Then with the confidence of a man who knows his orders will be obeyed, Lord made a brief bow to Lady Grace and left through the door that led past the parlour to the peel tower and the other wing.

THE TRAITOR'S APPRENTICE

"I cannot leave the poor man here," Lady Grace objected when Anders tried to persuade her to sit in the parlour and have her maid attend her. "Someone must be sent to the church to ring the Passing Bell. He was a gentleman, you know."

It took Anders, supported by Alice Franklyn, a couple of minutes to persuade Lady Grace that Sir Arthur would be laid out and all the requirements met, including the tolling of the bell. Alice vanished, promising to find Lady Grace's maidservant, but even then, Lady Grace was still fractious.

"Where is Dido? I need Dido. She must be so worried without me."

It was Gideon who came to the rescue seeing the blank look on Ander's face.

"That would be your spaniel, Lady Grace?"

"Yes, of course. Who did you think I meant? Oh, this is too terrible. The poor, poor man."

"I will find Dido for you as soon as you are settled in the parlour," Anders promised, which persuaded her to go with him. Gideon stayed to offer his assistance to Muir who shrugged and shook his head.

"I'll do what's needed. It's not as if he can't be left while I make the necessary arrangements. Besides, your commander seemed very keen to have his coat returned, so perhaps you had better see that he gets it." The look he gave Gideon was almost sympathetic, which left Gideon with the impression that Simon Muir had already felt the cutting edge of Philip Lord's tongue himself.

Leaving Muir to his task, Gideon went through the house and up to the room he was sharing with Anders. He found the only other garment he could wear which was the red coat he had been given by Jupp. Pushing aside his growing fatigue, Gideon brushed down the borrowed doublet, so it looked as clean as it had when he received it from Zahara. Then he made his way along the passageway to Lord's room. As he did so the church bell began tolling the death knell for Sir Arthur. It made for a sombre atmosphere. He rapped on Lord's door.

"*Entrez!*"

When he went in, Lord was by the table where he had been that morning. He had donned a fresh linen shirt and was scribbling some notes on a sheet of paper. He straightened up, quill in hand, and made a gesture towards the bed when Gideon held out the doublet.

"No need to thank me," he said. "I'm happy to have been able to help out in the grand syllabub crisis."

"You seem to find it amusing," Gideon said, putting the garment where indicated. His anger had reignited, given emphasis by the reminder of the tolling bell.

"Amusing enough to not mind that you were wearing my doublet," Lord agreed.

"Zahara offered it to me."

"I had presumed as much since she had it this morning to make some minor repair. But you will, being quick of wit, have realised it was not for the return of a garment that I wished you here."

"I had wondered," Gideon admitted.

"I wanted you here to discuss your present task." Lord moved to the hearth where a covered jug of wine stood to warm and poured himself a measure. "There has been a second death. What do you make of it?" He held up an empty goblet and gestured at it as he spoke.

Gideon shook his head at the offer of wine. He felt tired and his wits were slower than usual. Adding more alcohol would make that worse. The tolling bell was wearing on him as well now. "Anders Jensen seems to believe it was what it appears—a tragic accident."

"*And there is in this business more than nature,*" Lord said. He took a drink of the warm wine and set the goblet on the mantle. "I am aware of Jensen's view; I was enquiring about yours."

Gideon wondered what his own view was. He had seen how unwell Sir Arthur had appeared to be when he was at dinner. It didn't require too much imagination to see him collapsing on the stairs and falling. But there was the odd conversation he had overheard between Lady Grace and William Irving. Could that have been referring to Sir Arthur?

He was ambushed by a yawn and Lord shook his head.

"I must have been working you too hard. Or is it that the topic of conversation bores you?"

"No. Not at all. I apologise." Gideon was annoyed with himself and fought to stifle another yawn.

"Then come now, it's not that hard a question." There was an increasing edge of impatience to Lord's tone and Gideon felt as if he were somehow failing a test. He had to muster his thoughts before he replied.

"It seems to stretch chance to its limits for there to be two deaths, both involving a fall down some steps, but a day apart, in the same house. If one were a murder the other might well be too."

Lord rewarded him with a brief nod of agreement.

"This morning I told you that the murder of yesterday was no concern of mine. I was willing to indulge you in the hope that were we to find the killer it might do something to perhaps quash these tales of there being a curse. This today, has made it my concern. I want you to find out if it was a murder and if so, who is behind the killings. No one is as superstitious as a soldier of fortune and our own men are far from immune to this talk of curses."

"There is always the possibility it is indeed a curse," Gideon pointed out. "Such things are attested even in the Bible."

Lord's lips pulled into a tight line as the last toll of the death bell faded into a merciful silence.

"And if ye be born, ye shall be born to a curse: and if ye die, a curse shall be your portion. Oh yes, let us not forget it could indeed be a curse. But let us first assume it is not and look for more mundane possibilities. I assume you are willing and able to do so?"

"Of course, in fact before dinner I heard—" He broke off as there were yells outside.

Lord had already pushed himself away from the wall beside the hearth and was by one of the windows looking out. A moment later he was through the door at a run. Gideon didn't wait to look out of the window, he followed, wondering if he was about to have a third killing to add to his list of possible murders.

In front of the brewhouse, a lot of angry shouting came from three of the male household servants. The target of their ire was one of Lord's company. Gideon didn't know the man's name, but he had seen him keeping company with those who were given to over-indulgence in gambling and drink. He was sure he had seen this man slink out of Lord's presence looking very subdued on at least one previous occasion. Right now, he was the worse for drink and held struggling by Shiraz, spitting French obscenities back at the men who were shouting at him.

THE TRAITOR'S APPRENTICE

"*Legrand, que diable qui se passe ici?*" Philip Lord's voice rolled over the tumult. Something of its tone must have penetrated both those who didn't understand the words and the man in Shiraz's grip at whom they were aimed because a sudden silence descended.

"What the hell is going on, Legrand?" Lord repeated, keeping to French, his voice as sharp and hard as a sword cut. "You're drunk."

Legrand said nothing, his breathing heavy. He no longer struggled, but he kept his gaze on the ground. At a nod from Lord, Shiraz pushed the man from him, and Legrand wound up on his knees in front of Lord. He looked stricken, his skin sallow.

"That bastard was demanding wine," one of the male servants said. "When we refused him, he drew his sword and if that mute hadn't been there, he'd have skewered someone with it like as not."

Lord glanced at Shiraz who lifted his chin in a brief nod of confirmation. Even Gideon knew drunkenness wasn't tolerated amongst Lord's men unless he had licensed it.

"You are not so drunk that you do not remember what I said yesterday." Lord's expression showed no compassion as he glared at Legrand and his hand moved to his sword.

Legrand gulped his Adam's apple moving in his throat.

"Flogged," Mags' voice, a shout in broken but clear English, came from behind. "He'll be flogged."

Lord's hand froze, eyes flaring with an odd blue-green fire.

Gideon turned to see Mags walking towards them from the direction where the new earthworks could be seen taking shape. He must have been putting in some of the spadework with the men and looked worn and dishevelled from the effort. He was flanked by two men Gideon knew. One was Jupp and the other Olsen, a brawny Swede.

Mags strode up to Legrand, who opened his mouth to say something, but Mags hit him hard across the face. Then he turned to the men with him and snapped at them in German. Neither moved.

Lord had stood like a marble statue, but now he made a small, taut, bow which was little more than the stiffening of his body, towards Mags.

"Whatever you command, *monsieur*."

It was then—and only then, Gideon noticed, that Jupp and Olsen moved to obey.

"Fifty lashes," Lord said before Mags could speak again. "And if he survives that he is to be turned off."

His gaze locked with Mags who gave a sudden and inappropriate grin, which only Lord and Gideon would have seen.

"Whatever you say," Mags murmured.

They bound the Frenchman by his wrists to a tethering ring and pushed a leather gag into his mouth to both stifle the screams and stop him from biting through his tongue. Lord stood watching and many of the company stood silent, together with some of the household. Gideon had little appetite for such brutal violence administered in cold blood and departed as the first blows fell.

He was left with the distinct impression that, regardless of his crimes, Legrand was being used in whatever dark game Mags and Lord were engaged in with each other. The notion turned his stomach.

Mags caught his arm in a steel grip as he walked by.

"You should stay. You're a lawyer after all, and this is justice in action." The only people close enough to hear him belonged to Lord's company.

"This is not justice," Gideon said, making no attempt to keep the bitterness from his voice. "There has been no fair trial. I have no wish to associate myself with it."

Mags' voice dropped even lower, now only for his ears.

"I saved the life of that man," he said, gaze intent. "Lord would have run him through for being drunk. You don't know him very well, do you?"

Gideon felt the same cold shiver of danger he had felt before when the two men had been talking in Lord's room. Like Legrand, he was being pulled into the path of the dark lightning that ran between them.

"I neither know nor want to know him well," Gideon said. Mags stared at him for a few moments longer, then released his arm and gave a brief harsh laugh before saying something loud in German. That got a few grins from those around him and a sudden sharp look from Lord.

Freed, Gideon made his escape into the sanctuary of the house, angry and exhausted. Anders was coming out of the house carrying his medical bag looking grim-faced.

"I need to speak to you as soon as I may," he said. "I think I have some information that will interest you. But for now, you must excuse me, I have been sent for to do what I can for this man when our Lord and master has finished having him flogged." He took two paces then turned back to add: "Sara was asking for you."

Despite his fatigue, Gideon would have been willing to search the entire house after that, if needed, but he found Zahara in the hall clearing up from dinner with two of the household maidservants. She smiled when she saw him and gave quiet instructions and words of encouragement and praise to the women, then led Gideon through the door opposite the parlour and into a room he hadn't seen before.

It was a delightful room. A library with a bookcase, a reading desk and a settle against one wall. There was also an old, fat-bellied lute in a stand in one corner set next to a spinet virginals, with a stool beside it. The window overlooked a small garden which had a low, decorative wall beyond which was the orchard. He realised this must have been the room where Lady Grace and Reverend Irving had been when he overheard them.

Gideon would have been drawn to the bookcase like metal to a lodestone, but because he was with Zahara, she held his complete attention. She sat on the settle and after a moment of hesitation, he sat beside her.

"I wanted to speak to you," Zahara said, "about what is happening with Legrand."

"You mean why a man is being brutalised and likely to die?" It came out more bluntly than he would have wanted.

"Yes." Zahara looked up at him then and he saw the hollow shadows around her eyes. "A week ago, before we arrived here, Legrand got drunk. He started a fight. It is what he always does when he drinks. The Schiavono was going to turn Legrand off, but he pleaded to stay. He gave his word he would not drink again without permission. The Schiavono accepted that, and he was allowed to remain on the roll."

"Then if he got drunk, he should be turned off but not—"

Zahara reached over and gripped Gideon's wrist, her expression intent and urgent.

"Listen. Please."

He nodded and she rewarded him with the ghost of a smile.

"When we arrived here, after you and Doctor Jensen were shown to your room, the Schiavono spoke to the company. To all of us, except you two. He reminded us that this is not the German wars. That this is not an enemy holding we occupy. He told us that we must treat this house as if it were his house and the people here as if they were his people, even the servants. If we did not, we would answer to him for it. Personally."

Gideon was heavy with fatigue, and it felt as if someone had been using his nerves to play tunes, like the strings of the fat-bellied lute in the corner.

"What did he mean by that?"

"The Schiavono meant that he would kill them. You must understand, it is the only way to protect the house and the people in it."

Even though this was Zahara, Gideon felt the familiar leap of anger. Mags had been right. It had been he who had saved Legrand's life. Or at least tried to.

"But why? He makes himself, judge, jury and executioner."

Zahara looked as if she were in physical pain.

"Legrand committed the one crime the Schiavono cannot forgive, cannot afford to forgive. He gave his word and broke it. The Schiavono had no choice." She released Gideon and sighed. "You must understand, these men have nothing to bind them. They are not family by blood. They are not all friends. Money alone can never be enough to hold them. So, they bind themselves by their honour. If that is lost, then there is nothing. They all know that."

It was the kind of wild justice he had seen in the mercenary company before, and it left him feeling empty and sick.

"Why tell me this?

"Because the Schiavono will not," she said and got to her feet. "I need to get back to work. Perhaps you will think about it."

She closed the door behind her, and Gideon was left struggling with those thoughts, before perforce abandoning them and the music room for the greater, and now quite irresistible, need for his bed and sleep.

II

If Christobel Lavinstock had plans to return to see James Stott the following day, Sir Nicholas Tempest was less inclined to wait. His men trailing behind him like the spreading cloth of his riding cloak, he set a vicious pace back to Durham.

This time he made little effort to be careful, his horse's hooves sounding sharp on the twilight cobbles of the steep climb. He led his entire escort into the small stableyard to the rear of Stott's house. Warned by the commotion, Stott came out to greet Nick as he dismounted and threw the reins of his horse to the first man he saw.

The ride had done little to soften Nick's mood, but he had enough awareness not to allow the lawyer to become the quintain at which he pitched his wrath. To do so, he knew, would result in less cooperation from the man than he could gain by biting his tongue.

"My apologies for disturbing you again," he said.

THE TRAITOR'S APPRENTICE

"I am your servant as always, Sir Nicholas," Stott assured him with a bow. "If you would care to come in, I shall do what I may to assist you."

Trusting that his men would manage well enough, Nick followed Stott to the same room he had sat in earlier that day. Stott had a servant bring a taper to light the candles and to build up the fire against the cool of the evening.

When the door finally closed behind the man, Nick dropped into a chair.

"You told me," he said even before Stott had taken his own seat, "that I must espouse Christobel Lavinstock to inherit all the non-entailed aspects of my uncle's estate."

Stott nodded. "That was what is stipulated in the will."

"And if I refuse and the proceeds from those are not mine to dispose of, who has them?"

"I understand they would go to a group of gentlemen whose names I would not be at liberty to disclose even were I to know them. If such were to occur, I have sealed instructions to send to a man in London."

That took little to work out. It would be those who remained of the Covenant. Two of whom he had met on attaining his majority and who had questioned him in depth before declaring themselves satisfied. Gentlemen who Nick was sure he would be encountering again now he had become the master of Howe. But perhaps he could hope they might be put out by this present war.

"And what if Mistress Lavinstock is the one to refuse? What happens then?"

Stott steepled his fingers and tapped the bottom of his chin with the tips, looking thoughtful.

He was silent for so long that Nick couldn't contain himself. "That wasn't considered as a possibility in all this planning?"

Shaking his head, Stott leaned forward a little.

"Am I to assume your meeting with Mistress Lavinstock did not run smoothly?"

Nick had no intention of repeating his humiliation.

"You may assume what you will. I want to know what would happen if such a situation arose?"

Stott got to his feet.

"I regret I do not have an answer for you this evening, much as I wish I did. I have to assume from what you have said that this might become an issue, so you will need to allow me the opportunity to investigate what I may."

Nick's impotent frustration and fury returned in full force. He bounded to his feet, aware he had enough height advantage over the lawyer that the man had to look up to meet his gaze.

"You expect me to accept that? There *must* have been provision." He could hear the snarl in his own voice and found his hand had curled around the hilt of his sword. Stott drew in a sharp breath and his eyes widened. Nick realised how he must appear and released his sword again.

"Whether this is resolved or not," he snapped, "I am still lord of Howe, and it is still in my gift to keep with my uncle's choice of attorney, or to seek another. If you don't oblige me in this matter, you can be most certain that however this falls out I will assume you are not my man and not someone I can trust with my affairs."

Stott drew a couple of harsh breaths, his face losing colour.

"As you well know, sir, I was your uncle's man. I would be as loyal to you, but in this matter of the will, your uncle's wishes—"

"My uncle is dead," Nick said, putting into his tone as much of the cold and imperious note he had often observed in Sir Bartholomew as he could muster. "That means he won't be about to appear and claim you have in any way broken faith with him. I, on the other hand, am very much alive and have it in my power to continue with you or divest my legal affairs elsewhere." He paused and tried to think how he could offer a sensible way through this that the lawyer might accept. "I'm not asking you to set aside his wishes or intentions, only to share with me, in confidence, one detail which it makes no difference one way or the other that I know."

There was a strong silence and Stott stood very still. Then releasing his breath in a small sigh, he sat down again, gesturing to the other chair as he did so. "You are indeed your uncle's heir, Sir Nicholas. He was never one to brook any delay or obfuscation. Let me tell you what I know."

Nick sank back onto his seat with a warm glow of success and paid close attention to what the lawyer told him.

Chapter Five

I

Someone shook Gideon's shoulder and called his name.

It took a lot of effort to drag himself from sleep and the call and the shake were repeated a few more times before he woke up. He opened his eyes, still struggling against the cloying tendrils of slumber, to see Anders' face lit by a candle and wearing a look of relief.

"You are all right?" There was real concern in the Dane's voice.

Sitting up groggily and wondering how it had got to be dark when he had thought only to nap, Gideon blinked a little and nodded.

"I was very tired," he said. Then realised he still was.

"I am not surprised," Anders said, placing the candle on the small table beside the bed. "I could kick myself for not recalling what you ate at dinner. I remembered well enough that you got to wear the syllabub, but I forgot at that time that you had also eaten a good amount of it." He took hold of Gideon's wrist, his fingers pressed on the inside.

"I had a bowl of it," Gideon agreed. "I was contemplating a second one too, but I think Lady Grace's Dido had that one when it landed on the floor."

Anders said nothing for a few moments, then released Gideon's wrist.

"What is sweet in the mouth is not always good in the

stomach and in this case that is the truth. But I think you are fortunate that our murderer laid his plans with care."

Gideon would have shot to his feet were there not a firm restraining hand on his shoulder.

"What do you mean by that? Someone tried to poison me?"

Anders shook his head. "No. Not at all. No one tried to kill you."

Gideon recognised the careful physician's tone of reassurance for a nervous patient.

"Then what are you saying?"

Anders sank down to sit on the bed.

"It was what I wanted to tell you earlier. That little dog you mentioned died peacefully in her sleep. She was elderly and Lady Grace seems more devastated by her loss than by that of poor Sir Arthur, but the two are connected in my view. Your yawning and almost falling asleep on your feet confirmed that for me. I failed to make that connection until I remembered what you ate."

"There was something in the syllabub?" Gideon hazarded.

"There was, I believe, something in the syllabub, something designed, perhaps, not to kill but to induce fatigue. You must recall that it was one of the two dishes that had been prepared for Sir Arthur due to his delicate digestion."

"But anyone could have had some of the syllabub," Gideon protested.

"Indeed so, but most would have taken just a small portion I am sure," The Dane smiled. "As I recall you helped yourself to a large amount, did you not? Which was why I noticed enough to remember."

Gideon opened his mouth to protest. Then recalled

that he had indeed thought that as no one else seemed interested in eating the dessert it would be a shame to leave it in the serving bowl.

"I was even thinking of having some more when Muir sent it flying," he said.

"A greedy man is his own enemy, but in this case, you were saved by the carelessness of another."

Gideon was thinking back to the meal.

"You are saying you now believe that Sir Arthur was murdered?"

Anders considered for a moment.

"I believe someone tried to make sure he would fall or, failing that, pass away peacefully in his sleep like the little dog."

"But he didn't touch the syllabub, he ate most of his fish dish."

Anders nodded. "Indeed so. A puzzle, is it not?"

"Unless," Gideon's mind was working again. "Unless there was the same substance in the fish dish as well. They were the two dishes made for Sir Arthur, but our murderer couldn't be sure only he would eat them. What if they divided the dose between the dishes? One portion might make someone feel tired, as if they had a cup too much wine with the meal, but two being enough to make a sick man sleep too deep and never wake."

He half expected Anders to tell him he was letting his imagination run wild. Instead, the Dane was nodding.

"I had thought perhaps he had eaten some of the syllabub and I missed him doing so, but what you suggest makes more sense. Or even that there was something else in the fish that would act if mixed with whatever was placed in the syllabub. Either way, it means there was no real danger of anyone else being affected even if they did chance to have some, although no one else did, except you."

"And Dido."

Anders nodded. "Although I think perhaps, in that case, it was a kindness. Lady Grace had been concerned for her dog's health and was consulting me about it when I noticed the little one had died. From what she described I think Dido had reached the end of her time anyway and this will have spared her suffering." Then he looked up at Gideon. "And little Dido had been allowed to finish the last of Sir Arthur's fish too, so she stood no chance."

Gideon found his skin feeling cold as he realised how close to mortality he had skated.

"I was fortunate, as you say. Had Muir not been so clumsy I might have been in the same state as Sir Arthur and Dido."

The Dane got to his feet. "The greater the knave, the better the luck, so you must be a very great knave indeed, my friend." He grinned and slapped Gideon on the back. "If you are hungry, then say so and I will bring you something to eat with my own fair hands, but if not, you should be safe enough to sleep off the rest of your syllabub overnight."

It wasn't a hard decision.

"If you are certain it is no danger for me to do so, then I will sleep."

"It is no danger. Now," Anders assured him. "But I am a poor physician, and a poorer friend, to have failed to realise sooner when the danger *was* real."

He began to undress and set his clothes out to air in the warmth from the embers in the hearth.

"And Legrand?" Gideon asked.

Anders paused in undoing the points on his doublet and gave a small shrug.

"I have done what I may. The rest is what God wills or nature allows. At least I persuaded our patron that Legrand could spend one night here before being made to leave, not that the man could walk even if he were expelled."

There was little Gideon could think to say to that, so he lay back in the bed and gave in to the urge to sleep. But Mags' words were still echoing in his head—*You don't know him very well, do you?*

Gideon wasn't surprised to wake alone the next morning. Anders was already dressed and gone even though the daylight outside was thin and still brittle with the dawn, but he returned as Gideon was doing up his shoes.

"Good to see you are up and around," Anders said in greeting. "How are you feeling?"

"Refreshed but hungry," Gideon admitted

"That is to be expected. Sara said she will give you something to eat if you find her in the hall when you are ready. I need to get on. I shall leave you to inform our patron that we now have two murders, not one." The Dane turned away heading back to the door.

"How do you do it?" Gideon asked. "How do you keep working as hard as you do? Since you joined Philip Lord, you've barely slept through a single night. It must wear you down."

Anders hesitated, hand on the latch and looked back.

"As the master is, so are his men. I do no more than the man I serve. In fact, I do less. Our commander, you may not have noticed, works tirelessly and ceaselessly, the first up and the last to bed. How can I do less when he took me on after others have spurned me?" Anders looked thoughtful, then shook his head. "Perhaps it is not something easy to understand—it is as if I have been told by others I may use my left hand or my right, my knowledge as a physician or my skill as a surgeon. But our patron tells me to use both or either as I see fit. It is a liberating and fulfilling experience. So I am happy to do what he asks of me."

"He asks a lot," Gideon said and could hear the bitter tone in his own voice.

"Why do you stay? Every man has his lot, and the wide world before him. You are not bound here. And unlike poor Legrand, you are privileged in that you are free to decide for yourself." Anders held his gaze for a moment more then gave a small nod to show he had expected no reply and left.

It was an uncomfortable question. He finished dressing and went in search of Zahara in whose presence the question lost all meaning and found its answer. He was late for breakfast, but he was sure she would find him something. He would need to talk to Lord about what Anders had discovered and he had no wish to do so on an empty stomach.

As he walked into the newer wing of the house, he was surprised to hear someone picking out a tune on the lute in the music room. It seemed an odd thing for anyone to be doing so early in the morning and simple curiosity made him push open the door.

William Irving sat on a stool, the lute resting on his lap against his own fat belly as he picked out a slow tune with precision. Gideon was sure it was one he had heard before but couldn't think of a name.

"Dowland, of course," Irving said, without looking up.

"In darkness let me dwell; the ground shall sorrow be, the roof despair, to bar all cheerful light from me... He loved Dowland. I always thought it odd." Irving spread his fingers sharply creating a sudden discord and then stood the lute back in its stand.

"You speak of Sir Arthur?" Gideon hazarded.

"Of course. It seems unbelievable that when I got up and went into the hall to break my fast that he was not there, snippy as always because his stomach caused him pain." Irving stopped speaking and blinked a few times, his sunken eyes overbright. "What I wouldn't give to have him moaning at me about politics one more time."

Gideon sat on the settle, ignoring his own stomach's insistent demands for food. This was too good an opportunity to pass by.

"You were friends for a long time?" he asked.

Irving nodded, his jowls wobbling. "Man and boy. Man and boy. Neighbours. Then school together and after that Merton. Odd to think how that changed us both in such different ways—me, joining the clergy and him…" Irving trailed off.

"What did he do in life?"

"He taught at Merton for many years. Mathematics. He had a marvellous mind. Marvellous mind." Irving stopped speaking and stared into the middle distance, caught up in some reminiscence.

"And you were both friends of Lady Grace?" Gideon asked.

Irving nodded.

"Yes. I met her through him. She was a lovely woman back then. Lovely. There was talk of them getting married at one point, but her family would never have it, of course. Nothing like good enough. After all her father had been an earl, albeit a disgraced one. I don't think Arthur ever recovered." Irving sighed. "It can happen like that, you know. A young man ruined by falling in love with a woman he can never have. I always wondered how things would have turned out if he had managed to forget her."

For a moment Gideon had an image of himself in the portrait Irving drew. Himself forever tied to Zahara and she forever unobtainable.

"And Lady Grace hardly had a happy time of it," Irving went on. "Wed to a man who put the welfare of his horses and dogs ahead of her. Horses and dogs." He stopped as if realising he had an audience for what he was saying. "Long time ago now, of course. Very long time." He got to his feet and gave a stiff bow to Gideon. "If you will excuse me, I have some letters to write."

Gideon followed him from the room and waited to be sure he was up the stairs, before making his way to the hall. It was difficult to reconcile the cold anger of the conversation he had overheard the previous day between Irving and Lady Grace and the obvious grief of the man today. He had wondered if what he had overheard was the admission of a murder plot. What had Irving said? *I have matters in hand. Well in hand. He will be gone by the end of the week.* Sir Arthur had been 'gone' perhaps an hour later. And if they had indeed been friends in the past, then perhaps what Gideon had just witnessed wasn't grief but remorse. However, that wasn't the impression he was left with.

Zahara was not in the hall, which had been cleared in preparation for dinner, so Gideon abandoned his pursuit of breakfast and went in search of Lord instead. The excavation work had started at first light, and it took

Gideon a few minutes to find Lord along the growing channel that would soon extend the moat. He was at the end of the trench, hatless, stripped to shirt and breeches despite the cold, breaking the ground with a pickaxe. He swung the pick in a way that showed him to be well used to such work.

Seeing Gideon, Lord called one of the men from further along the trench and gave him the pickaxe together with careful instructions to follow the line marked. Then, hat and coat restored, he joined Gideon.

"Have you eaten?" he asked in greeting, leading the way towards the outbuildings where the company had established their quarters.

Before Gideon could reply his stomach made a loud noise.

Lord laughed. "Answer enough," he said.

A short time later they were sitting at a table, in what probably started life as a barn but was now made into the main accommodation for the men of the company. Straw-filled pallets were piled up around the walls and trestle tables had been set out for daytime use. Having taken a seat Gideon was served a thick pottage by the heavily pregnant Gretchen.

Lord sat and watched him eat.

"I'll eat later," he said, waving Gretchen's offer away with a smile. When she had gone and they were alone, Lord refused to let Gideon talk until he had finished most of the bowl. "I do not have the fine detail, but Jensen left me in no doubt that you were not in a good way yesterday."

"Better than Legrand, I am sure," Gideon said.

Lord shook his head, his expression hardening. "*Res dura, et regni novitas me talia cogunt Moliri.* I take it this is a Lennox and Jensen combined venture?"

That was news. It warmed Gideon to know that Anders, too, had attempted to protest Lord's brutality.

"I can understand Anders might stint at having to put back together—at your command—someone you ordered ripped apart," Gideon said. "But I've not spoken to him about it at all."

"You have not?" Lord leaned forward over the table toward him. "Then I will give you the same answer I gave to Jensen. The day I try to tell him how to treat a patient or you how to pursue a legal case, then I will be willing to have the pair of you instruct me on how to lead a mercenary company. Until that time, I suggest you consider the matter closed because I will not discuss it further with either of you." Lord held Gideon's gaze for a few moments then sat back again, his expression mild. "Now as I recall, you sought me out. If you meant only to berate me then I will get back to my work, or was there something else you needed to talk about?"

"Yes. There is something you need to know relating to the task with which you charged me." Gideon resorted to formality to avoid allowing his emotions any latitude. "Anders now also believes that there is every sign Sir Arthur Cochrane was murdered."

That brought him Lord's full and focused attention.

"Tell me," he said.

So Gideon did, from the events at the meal the previous day, through the death of Dido and including his own extreme fatigue which Lord himself had witnessed and commented upon. He went over the conclusions that he and Anders had drawn from what had occurred, explaining the brief conversation he had overheard between Lady Grace and William Irving, and his own conversation with Irving that morning.

Lord listened and asked a couple of pertinent questions to clarify what Gideon was telling him. Then, when it was told, he said nothing for a short time, looking thoughtful.

"*I fear'd as much: murder can not be hid*," he said. "You have your work made plain then. We need to uncover this man. Jensen seems to have already placed himself at your disposal and if you need my aid, ask for it. But have a care. This murderer may know you are close to hunting him down. I would prefer not to have to break off from my present task because I need to discover who killed my lawyer." Lord got to his feet. "You might be wise to bring Zahara into your confidence. She could be of much help with the women of the household."

After he had gone, Gideon sat for a moment. Lord had given him full licence to seek out Zahara, to share thoughts and ideas with her, to have good reason to spend time with her. Despite the gravity of what he needed to do, his heart sang at the thought, and he took the time to thank Gretchen for the meal and to ask how the company was faring in its new quarters, even managing to say polite nothings as she enthused about the accommodation and how they were being well provisioned.

Then he headed back to the house intending to ask Zahara if she would help him uncover a murderer.

"Fox!" Mags' voice called him across the yard and since to the eyes of the house this was the man in command, Gideon had little choice but to answer the summons. Mags was with one of the handful of mercenaries who he often kept about him, and a determined-looking Liam Rider. The boy was holding a sword in his hand as if he wanted nothing more than an excuse to use it to draw blood.

"Aleksandrov explains." Mags, voice disguised as that of a native German speaker struggling in French, gestured to the sturdy dark-haired man beside him.

It took Gideon a little patience to untangle the Russian's heavily accented French and discover that Mags wanted him to partner with Liam in some sword practice.

One of the expectations placed on all in Lord's company, as Gideon knew well, was that no matter someone's role, the ability to join in an effective mutual defence was essential. But due to his injured ankle, apart from a lesson from Roger Jupp on the fastest way to load and fire a wheellock pistol—holding it with the lock to the sky to reduce the chance of a hang fire or misfire—he hadn't been taking part in any such training.

"My ankle—" he protested. In truth it was almost completely better unless he overused it.

Mags waved a hand dismissively.

"You do a little," he said. Then grabbed Gideon's arm and pulled him a few steps away before speaking into his ear. "The boy has been given his father's sword. He needs to use it and not with someone who he knows can defeat him with ease."

Mags gave him a conspiratorial smile and slapped him on the back.

"*Gut. Gut,*" he said loudly as if Gideon had agreed.

Left with little choice Gideon drew his own sword and after they had both gone through some practice moves, as instructed and corrected by Aleksandrov, he engaged with the boy.

Mags had judged well. Liam was fast and determined although Gideon knew himself the better swordsman. In the end, tiring and his ankle aching, Gideon gave the bout to the boy.

"That is a fine sword," he said, sheathing his own.

Liam nodded and held it up glowing with pride.

"My father's. I will do him honour with it. The graf is one of the best swordsmen ever and he has said I have a talent for it. So now I can fight with the other men."

"The Schiavono has said you may?" Gideon was surprised. The last he had heard Lord had made it clear he still thought Liam too young to be taken on the muster roll as a fighting man.

"*I* have said so." Mags smiled at the boy and put a hand on his shoulder. "I am as proud as if you were my own son."

Liam grinned back at the mercenary with pure delight and Gideon felt an odd apprehension. He picked up his doublet and hat from the post where he had hung them and managed a smile.

"If you are joining the men, then you had better learn how to dig," Gideon said. "I am sure Aleksandrov or the graf himself will be pleased to give you lessons."

It was the wrong thing to say to the child for a thousand reasons. But then the words were not for Liam who looked a bit confused but kept smiling. Mags' smile faltered. He spoke in a low, urgent tone that no one more than a pace away could have heard.

"I would like to talk with you, Fox. Find me later. In my room. It will be to your advantage."

Gideon made a curt bow for the benefit of anyone watching and walked away. He had no wish to speak to Mags, but it would be impossible to avoid doing so if the man was set on it. But that was for later. Right now, he wanted to find Zahara.

She was in the kitchen having a quiet but firm discussion with the cook about some esoteric aspect of food preparation that Gideon let wash past him. He was too captivated by witnessing a side of Zahara he had suspected but never witnessed before. Taking firm control of a situation, instilling those around her with a feeling of confidence and making her reprimands firmly felt without ever raising her voice.

He didn't interrupt her as she moved on from the cook to one of the other servants to show them how they could do one aspect of their task better and then praised them for their improvement. It was only when she had remonstrated with one of the boys about letting the fire get too low, but left him smiling at some quiet jest, that she noticed Gideon where he stood waiting by the door.

Her smile, when she saw him, was brilliant and his world shrank to the compass of her face, and the warmth within him was as if he had been graced by the summer sun.

"You should be the lady of your own house," he told her as she reached him. "With your own servants to do your will."

"Perhaps," she said. "One day. But you are here for a reason."

"Do you have time to talk? I wouldn't ask, but it is important, the Schiavono—"

She didn't let him finish, just nodded and turned back to speak to one of the women, who had arms that looked as capable of wielding a mattock as any of Lord's men might be and a face as red as a cherry. A few moments later Zahara was leading Gideon to the still room, past a watchful Shiraz who sat mending a piece of harness outside the kitchen door.

"We can work while we talk," she said and pointed to a tray of empty bottles. "I will fill each one and you can seal it. These are all for Dr Jensen."

Gideon found the wax and tongs and used a taper to light the heavy-wicked candle needed for the task. He had to concentrate on the first couple of small bottles placing the wax seal before he felt able to shift his focus to include any conversation.

Zahara nodded her satisfaction with his work.

"What was it the Schiavono wanted you to say to me?"

It was hard to know where to begin. But it would be hard to ask for her help without letting her know what was going on.

"I don't want you to be afraid," he said, "but it seems as if both Ruth Whitaker and Sir Arthur Cochrane were not accidental deaths. Anders believes both were murdered."

Zahara gave an unperturbed nod as she held out another bottle for him to seal. He stood without taking it.

"I mean someone in this house is killing people," he said wondering if he hadn't been clear enough with his explanation.

She nodded again, expression puzzled. "I had wondered," she said. Then lifted the little bottle to indicate he should take it. He did and began to heat the wax to seal it. "The Schiavono has told you to find out who is killing people and said that you should ask my help?"

Gideon nearly dropped the tongs.

"You knew? He told you?"

THE TRAITOR'S APPRENTICE

Zahara reached over and took the tongs from his nerveless fingers and began completing the seal. "No. No one told me. But I saw the wound on the back of Mistress Whitaker's head when I helped to lay her out and I know that Lady Grace's little dog died yesterday having eaten poor Sir Arthur's food and you ate his syllabub and were falling asleep so much Dr Jensen worried for you." She put the bottle down. "So, when you tell me these are murders and the Schiavono wanted you to speak to me, it is not so hard for me to understand why."

Gideon realised his mouth had fallen open. Something moved deep within his soul. Where first he had seen a beautiful woman, captivating his senses, then recognised she was someone of both courage and kindness that knew few peers, now he saw a human spirit and intelligence brighter even than the beauty that contained it. Before he had thought he loved, but he had been wrong. Before he had been drawn to her like a moth to a gorgeous flame, fascinated and entranced. But in that moment, he knew he had fallen in love with each and every intricate aspect of her being.

Without knowing what he did he took her hands as she put the bottle with the rest, leaning across him to do so, and drew her close. She didn't resist or try to pull away and her face turned up to his held a look of gentle curiosity as if she wondered what he might do. Deep in her kitten-green eyes, he was sure he could see something more. And it that something led him to lower his lips to hers.

For a single moment, as their lips no more than brushed, he felt as if he had ascended above the clouds and looked down on himself with the woman he loved held in his arms. Nothing in his life before had ever felt so perfect, so right. Then, like a flock of ravens darkening the cloudless sky, he realised what he was doing. His head came up and he released Zahara, stepping back, a cold horror running through him where the warmth of bliss had been a moment before.

"I—I'm sorry. I—"

Christ! What had he done? This was a woman under the personal protection of Philip Lord, who had already warned him never to cross this line and had ordered the barbaric flogging of Legrand for a much lesser crime, yet Gideon had grabbed hold of her and would have kissed her as if she were his to—

Her fingers pressed on his wrist as she held it for the briefest moment before withdrawing her hand and he realised she wasn't looking outraged. But whilst he could see that, try as he would, he couldn't read the strange emotion that shaped her expression.

"There is a story I know," she said. "Told by a very wise man. One night an angel heard God answer the prayers of a man, but the angel could not find the one who prayed, even though he knew the man must be good and pure to have his prayer acknowledged. So he asked God who it was who was praying devotedly enough for their petitions to be answered and God told him to look in a certain monastery that followed the ways of Rome. And there the angel found a man in devoted worship before an idol. The angel was shocked and asked why God answered the prayers of an idol worshipper and God told him that the man erred from ignorance, so he was pardoned, and the way was opened for him."

In the silence that followed Gideon struggled to make sense of that and how it related to what he had just done.

"You could not know, so you erred in ignorance and are pardoned," Zahara said softly. "It is against what I believe in to have something like that with any man unless I were wed to him."

Gideon, heart still pounding, torn between the glory of one moment and the devastation of the next, felt as if he were being asked to read runes cast in darkness. Was she saying she wished for marriage? Or simply that he should never take such a liberty again? Or was there a key in the story of angels and idol worshippers?

He drew a breath and cast himself onto the altar of his own idolatry.

"And if I am pardoned… is there a way open for me?"

She smiled then, a smile so sad it was as though he were watching the world itself dying before his eyes. "If there were a way for any man on this earth, it would be for you."

She looked away then and busied herself with filling the next bottle and a few moments later turned and pressed it into his hands. Numbed inside and out, Gideon took it and tried to focus on attaching the seal.

"I will help you find out who has killed those people and the little dog," Zahara said, her tone as serene as ever. "But first we must finish these. Then I need to serve dinner and you need to eat it. After that is cleared away, I must pray and then we can talk again, and I will tell you what I know."

It was one of the hardest things Gideon had ever done in his life to meet her gaze and nod in agreement. Only when he turned to put the newly sealed jar with the others did he notice Shiraz by the door, leaning against the frame, dark eyes watching him, expression unreadable.

II

When Christobel Lavinstock returned to Durham the following morning, Nick was already sitting in James Stott's parlour. The door had been left ajar so he could, if he wished, overhear the conversation which she would have with the attorney in his cabinet.

He did wish. He wished it very much.

However, the arrangement meant he couldn't see what was going on in the other room, only hear, as Christobel was shown in and seated. He heard the soft sound of her gown—no doubt the same one as yesterday—as it brushed against the chair, the occasional chittering from the logs on the fire, then the door opening again and the slight clink of glass and pottery as refreshments were served. Beyond that, like a backcloth on a stage, the sounds of a busy day in Durham, hooves on cobbles, shouts, the burr of voices.

There was little said between Stott and Christobel until the door that had admitted the servant had been closed again.

"I came to say that having met the gentleman to whom my father thought fit to betroth me without my knowledge, I have no intention of marrying him." Christobel's voice, so close in tone if not pitch to the one Nick both hated and feared, sent tiny daggers of ice through his veins. "I find myself well suited with my present life and have no wish to accommodate anyone else in it." Cool, collected and confident. He imagined her in her sighthound pose, head lifted, elegant, composed and aloof.

"You wish to break the betrothal?"

He pictured Stott, steepling his fingers and tapping the

tips against each other.

There was a short pause.

"I don't see why I need do so," Christobel said. "I have no other matrimonial plans. No one I wish or intend to marry. The betrothal can stand, by all means. I merely wish to inform you—and through you Sir Nicholas—that I will not complete it. He is, therefore, free to withdraw whenever he wishes to bestow his hand elsewhere."

The cunning little vixen.

By doing nothing at all she would trap Nick in limbo.

He was on his feet and would have thrown open the door, but Stott's voice, calm and professional, cut through the roar of his inner fury. The tone of a man who needed to explain the ways of the world to one who lacked the full capacity to comprehend them. That halted Nick in his tracks and made him resume his seat.

"And have you studied the terms of your father's will?" Stott asked, professional and polite, but with a touch of condescension suitable for dealing with a woman.

"In what regard?"

Another pause. Nick could hear Stott getting up and moving to his writing desk, the creak of wood and then the slight rustle of paper on parchment and parchment on vellum. Then the smooth scrape of a document being unfurled and flattened.

"Can you read Latin?"

"Of course," Christobel said, "and Greek and Hebrew if you require it of me. But why? Is the will not written in plain English?"

Nick wondered why anyone had allowed that poisonous, barbed mind access to education.

"It is, but this deed contains some. If you care to look, you will see your father was granted a lease on Flass Grange and its lands to last until his death, or three years after you attained your majority should he predecease that point in time."

There was a harsh creak as she pushed herself up from the chair and then the soft sound of her quick steps to the writing table. Nick could imagine the pale skin drawn over her brows first in concentration, then in consternation and realised he was smiling. Even if Nick hadn't considered she might try to exploit this particular loophole, other—wiser—heads had anticipated it well in advance.

"This means that the day after my twenty-fourth birthday I lose all right and title to Flass Grange." She didn't phrase it as a question but as a cold statement of fact.

"The house and land never belonged to your father. They were granted to him upon his return to England—"

"With the express intent of rewarding him for some service rendered. I can see that. It says so here. And whilst I can understand that it might be granted to him for his lifetime, what it doesn't explain is why it is tied to me, to my age, in any way at all."

Nick shifted in his chair. There was something wrong with her reaction. She should be devastated at the knowledge that all she held dear—her house, her lands, all the people she knew—could be ripped away from her. Instead, she sounded more curious about a legal nicety. He heard her step back from the writing table and could picture her confronting Stott with the same cold, blue-diamond gaze she had bent upon himself the previous day.

"I wonder if perhaps it has less to do with *my* age than that of another. Tell me, when does Sir Nicholas attain his majority? When is his twenty-first birthday?"

Nick's hands formed into tight fists. Did she think him a child? Well, she was a bitch, but Nick was wise in the ways of leashing bitches and bringing them to heel. In that moment he made himself a promise that he would do so.

"Sir Nicholas is already of age. His birthday was earlier this year."

"So he is a man?" The contempt in her voice cut at Nick's pride.

"Of course, but—"

"Then if he is a man, why does he hide away like a little boy listening in when the adults are talking about matters that might concern him?" That was all the warning Nick had, but it was enough that he was on his feet when she flung open the door, Stott's arm vainly attempting to prevent her. Her fury was shown only in two bright points of colour on a face that was white as her hair.

"I hope," she said, her voice as ice, "that you are satisfied with what you have learned, sir." Then she turned to Stott who quailed under the force of her glare. "I am done playing these games. I will remove myself from Flass Grange before the date I am required to relinquish it. And you two 'gentlemen' may make whatever alternative arrangements you might feel are required to allow for the fact that I will *not* be consenting to the marriage."

Nick strode forward, but Stott was in his way, and she was gone before he could reach the door. Shoving the attorney aside, Nick would have followed but Stott gripped his arm, pulling him back.

"Sir Nicholas, please—I would beg you to listen. Seizing her *here* in front of witnesses is not going to serve your best interests. She will call for help and half the men of Durham will rush to her aid."

Nick had lifted his free arm to strike Stott down but froze mid-movement as the meaning behind the lawyer's words sank in. He lowered his arm and turned back from the door.

"Seizing her *here*? What do you mean to imply?"

Stott stepped back and gestured to the writing desk.

"I am obliged to serve the wishes of Sir Bartholomew, which were also the wishes of Mr Blayse Lavinstock, not to mention those of your father and yourself."

"Yes. Yes, of course," Nick snapped. "But how can this be accomplished if the bitch is willing to give up everything to avoid marrying me?"

Stott cleared his throat.

"The young woman," he said, "need only be present at the spousal and speak her agreement before witnesses who will avow, if need be, that she did so. There is nothing more needed than that by law. *Sponsalia per verba de praesenti.* No church. No priest, although having one would add weight in the unlikely event the matter should ever be challenged in a court of law."

Nick thought about that, then a slow delight spread through him.

"I have witnesses who will swear it," he said. "A priest also. She lives alone and travels poorly guarded so I can ensure she attends the spousal."

Stott let out a breath that sounded like a sigh of relief.

"Then let us arrange where and when it will happen,

and I will leave the details of how the Mistress Lavinstock will be brought to attend up to you."

That notion suited Nick very well indeed.

Chapter Six

If he had been given the choice, Gideon wouldn't have endured a meeting with Mags whilst his emotions were still storm-tossed. But he had no choice. When he left the still room, before he could reach the house, he was intercepted by Aleksandrov.

"The graf wants to see you, Fox. Sent me to find you."

The Russian stood with his arms folded in a way that implied he would ensure it happened if Gideon decided to refuse.

"Of course," Gideon said, and changed his direction.

Aleksandrov followed him all the way to Mags' bedroom which was at the opposite end of the old wing to Lord's and offered a view over the earthworks. The bed and the hearth were much the same but there was little furniture aside from a couple of dark oak wainscot chairs, a side table and a large chest. Lord had his room established as a place of work. This was more of a social space with two jugs of wine on the side table and several goblets.

"Take a seat," Mags said, pouring himself a drink from one of the jugs. "I'd offer you wine, but I think you'd say no, am I right?"

"I prefer not to drink, right now, thank you," Gideon agreed.

Mags looked past him to where Aleksandrov still stood in the doorway. He waved the hand holding his cup towards the Russian. "Go down the passage a way

THE TRAITOR'S APPRENTICE

and make sure no one comes close."

When Aleksandrov had gone, Mags took the other chair and sat staring at Gideon, a slight smile on his face.

"You know what he's after don't you?"

"Who?" Gideon asked, dissembling with an ease he found surprising.

Mags pulled a face. "Oh, don't let's play that game. You saw what was in Howe, didn't you? All of it. And I'm sure he told you the tale to go with it." Gideon said nothing. A prickle of cold threaded its way between his shoulder blades. In a secret room in Howe Hall, he and Lord had found what Lord had hoped might be proof of his heritage. Proof he was descended from a child born to Queen Mary and Philip of Spain, the man Lord believed he had been named after. All they had found were blank pages placed where any such documents might once have been.

Mags shook his head then hawked and spat into the fire.

"Yesterday I did my best to save the life of a man who got drunk because he learned some bad news. Today I'm trying to save yours."

This was what Gideon needed to avoid. Being drawn into the dangerous shoals that lay between Mags and Lord.

"From the Schiavono?" he asked.

Mags just stared back at him.

"The rest of us here, see, even the Danish doctor, we can walk away if we choose. But you're in deep, and it seems to me only fair you should know what he's about because he sure as blood won't tell you."

"You sound like you want to turn me against him. Which would be rather pointless as I'm not his partisan.

I would say the men here who follow him are much more so than I am."

Mags gave a harsh laugh.

"Oh, I'd not speak to you one word against the wonderful, the glorious, the celebrated Schiavono, but I think you should know what he's about because as I see it, whether you can thole the man or no, you are getting pulled close into his affairs without knowing what the stakes are of being so."

"I think I have my own ideas on that," Gideon said, but the stirring of curiosity kept him from dismissing what Mags was saying.

"Every man in Wrathby has their own ideas about the Schiavono," Mags said. "But none of them know him as I do."

"You fought together?"

Mags got up and refilled his goblet, then poured a second and crossed to Gideon, pushing it at him so he had little choice but to hold it.

"You might need this after all when I'm done." Mags resumed his seat and took a drink from his cup before he went on. "I don't think I ever fought alongside Philip Lord before. However, we have a few things in common. We both grew up at Howe. He grew up with books, music and feather beds, fine mounts and tutors in everything. Whereas I grew up like a rat in the stables. Tolerated. Beaten. Kicked around. Then thrown out when I was no older than Liam Rider, with nothing but the clothes on my back."

It was said with an old anger, but little resentment and Gideon drew the obvious conclusion.

"You are illegitimate?"

"So they say. I say not. I say my parents were

promised and my birth proved the marriage. They were in love and impatient. But my father died of a fever before they could get to church. And my mother was all but cast out by her people for being unwed and with child and then she died soon after having me." His gaze shifted to the cup in his hands. "They were both sixteen."

Gideon tried to tack through what he was being told.

"Your father was a Coupland?"

"He was the heir to Howe. Francis Coupland, Sir Bartholomew's older brother, and my mother was sister to Sir Richard Tempest. It was no secret to any. Except Sir Bartholomew would prefer it not known. I was an inconvenience to his inheriting Howe. My grandfather had never favoured his true heir, so he made no move to see justice done for me. I wasn't even allowed a proper name—the servants called me 'Francis's child' and that stuck. Sir Bartholomew thinks I bring disgrace to the family by existing." Mags leaned forward in his chair. "But I'm not telling you this to get your sympathy. I've not spent my time hankering after Howe. I've made my own way in the world and I'm proud of it. I'm telling you so you can see I know what I'm talking about."

Unsure how to respond, Gideon shook his head "You must have left Howe when Philip Lord was still very young."

Mags laughed. "How old do you think I am? I've maybe eight years over him. If you think it looks more then that's what life has done. I was old enough to know him as he was then. From the first he was primped, pinked, stuffed full of more education than any twice his age ever had any need of, taught to believe himself a prince of this world. If you think him arrogant now you should have seen the puffed-up infant he was then. Soon as he could walk, he was taught to use a sword by the likes of di Zorzi and Svetnam. I could tell you stories that—" Mags stopped and shook his head. "He has changed, mind, to give him his due. Changed some since then. But you need to know what he has behind him. It's that has shaped him."

Somehow Gideon didn't doubt what he was being told. It matched too well with the man he knew Lord to be. He could believe that the glittering carapace of erudition, the razor-honed intellect and reflexes, the coldness and superlative self-possession came from such a place. Indeed, it was difficult to think how else they could have been formed.

"What is it you want to warn me about?" Gideon asked. Fascinating as it was to get this glimpse behind the mask Philip Lord wore like armour, he did not trust Mags' intentions in sharing it.

Mags sat back and took another drink, holding the cup in both his hands when he was done.

"He'll have told you, I'm sure, about what he wanted to find in Howe—what we both know he didn't find, though he's never told me so." Mags lifted a hand from the goblet as Gideon opened his mouth. "Hold your peace. I'm not going to ask what he said it was, I'm going to tell you. He was there looking for proof of his birth, proof he was the princeling they kept telling him he was. And I think he'll keep looking until he finds it— if it exists. And if it doesn't, there may be men who can make it exist if they're paid enough, because that's but the first part of it all for him."

"If it exists?" Gideon echoed.

"If. Aye. Who's to say? I don't doubt Coupland and

Tempest would swear it does, or why else trouble themselves with him? But that doesn't make it so."

Gideon let that go.

"What is the second part?" he asked instead.

"The second part is why he's come now. With all England torn apart and men not knowing where to look for leadership or rightful rule. He's brought the makings of an army, just needs to recruit for the ranks. And he's more men coming. It's easy enough to see what he would do with his ancestry proven—ancestry that makes King Charles an interloper."

Gideon saw the impossible thought to which Mags was driving and baulked.

"What are you saying?" he demanded.

"He wants to be king."

"What?"

"He wants to be king," Mags repeated. "There's not much to stop him as far as he can see. France, Spain and the Empire have their own wars and no men to spare to save the throne of a protestant heretic. If he has a claim to the throne stronger than Charles Stuart, gives a strong lead and offers the people what they want, he'll take the nation. Least, that's how he sees it."

Had Mags been talking about any other man Gideon had met he would have laughed long and hard at such a suggestion. But echoing in his thoughts was something Anders had said a while ago about Lord's company—*whichever faction our employer decides to favour, be it the king's or that of his parliament, will find it holds a fearsome weapon in its hands*. It had occurred to neither of them then that Lord might be planning to use the fearsome weapon for himself.

"How do you know this?" he asked at last.

"Because I know him," Mags said. "I knew the child, I followed the career of the man and now I work beside him every day. I see what he does, and I watch what horizon his eyes are lifted to—and if ever you think I do things that look petty or out of place, ask yourself how else you keep such a man in check except by that?" Mags got to his feet and put the cup back on the side table. "I've said my piece. You'll take from it what you will. But I warn you that you'll be riding on the devil's own coattails if you cleave to the man."

Gideon rose also, mind churning and stomach close to revolt. It was too much to believe. Even if Lord wanted to do such a thing, surely there was no way he could achieve it, despite an England thrown about and so disordered? He took a reluctant swallow of the wine in the vain hope it might help settle his tumultuous innards, then set the cup down. "You believe he can do it?"

Mags gave a brief laugh. "Oh, I think he could. But he's as like to wind up on the scaffold as the throne—him and all who side with him."

"Yet you stay with him."

"I might be one of the very few who can keep a hand on that bridle. I'll stay as long as I can see I'm doing some good." He gripped Gideon's shoulder and steered him to the door, then paused fingers resting on the latch. "If you ever want to leave, don't try alone. Come to me. That's just advice but bear it in mind if—when the time comes."

Then Gideon was outside the room, stepping aside to let Aleksandrov pass, as the Russian was summoned by Mags from where he had been standing at the top of the staircase.

The last thing Gideon wanted right then was to go to

dinner, force food between his lips and sit beside the plain-speaking Anders, whilst making polite conversation with men like Muir and Irving. But he had given his word to Zahara, and he would rather slice flesh from his own body than break any promise made to her.

Pushing Mags' words away to the back of his mind, Gideon made his way through the house to the dining hall. By the time he reached the main stairs in the new wing, he had managed to pack the troubling conversation away, much as he had learned to pack away difficult legal cases when he wasn't working on them. It was something he would have to come back to, but for now it was better left so he could deal with the other issues he had to face.

He was the last to arrive for dinner. Today he was surprised to see Philip Lord where Sir Arthur Cochrane had sat the day before. He was overdressed for the occasion in a grey, pinked doublet with tiny sapphires in the points and his hair pristine. Alice Franklyn occupied the place on Lord's left, with William Irving to his right. Gideon's seat, between Anders and Muir and opposite Lord, had been kept for him. Lady Belamy sat as was her due, at the head of the table.

Mumbling apologies for his lateness, Gideon slid into his chair hoping to avoid undue attention. But Lord broke from his conversion with Alice Franklyn as Gideon took his seat.

"How is the graf, *Monsieur Renard*?"

Gideon felt his guts tighten.

"He was well when I left him. But I don't think he intends to join us,"

"*Pas de surprise.* It is no surprise. He was saying his old wound was hurting him, so he didn't join the work this morning. I assumed he would be otherwise occupied. He is always a busy man. But as they say, *on n'est jamais si bien servi que par soi-même.* I think in English that is, you are never so well served as when you are self-serving."

Gideon's French was more than adequate to recognise both the proverb in its original meaning—doing a job oneself to be sure it was well done—and the twist Lord was putting on it in translation. So he said nothing and was rescued a moment later by Alice Franklyn asking Lord his opinion on the tart.

Glad to escape further interrogation, Gideon kept his answers to Anders' conversational sallies mediocre and bland. After a few such the Dane leaned in towards him.

"If you require a tonic, my friend, I am sure I have something that can help. Every man must indeed carry his own sack to the mill, but sometimes another may help shoulder the burden."

The temptation was one Gideon felt pummelled enough to give in to, but he met the look of concern in Ander's non-judgemental eyes with a slight shake of his head. The burdens he carried were either ones he felt unable to share, being too personal, or ones it would be unwise and unkind to lay upon the shoulders of others, being too dangerous.

"I appreciate the offer, but I think it might be that I am still a little fatigued from yesterday."

Gideon realised his mistake when the concern spread from Anders' eyes and across his face into a frown.

"Then as your physician, I will insist on a consultation with you at the earliest opportunity."

Gideon opened his mouth to try and deny the need, but Lord's voice cut over him.

THE TRAITOR'S APPRENTICE

"If Monsieur Fox is unwell, I ask that he indeed have your attention, doctor and since the graf is also indisposed, I am sure he would appreciate your care also."

Anders made a small bow across the table.

"The requests of great men are as commands. I shall see it is done, sir."

This meant that as the meal was cleared away, where Gideon had hoped he might have the chance to talk with Zahara, he was instead taken back to the bedroom he shared with Anders and put through a thorough examination. As Anders was rebandaging his ankle, he subjected Gideon to an in-depth interrogation on everything from whether he had noticed any shortness of breath, to when he last achieved a bowel movement and the colour and texture of the result. At the end, Anders sat on the small stool which was the only place provided to sit in the room aside from the bed itself and studied Gideon's face.

"I think your humours are indeed unbalanced, but the cause, I am much relieved to say, is not whatever you consumed yesterday. It is something that weighs upon your heart and that I think you feel the need to keep locked there. It is nothing of this hunt for a murderer, is it? I already told you I am happy to talk with you about that, should you wish it."

Gideon couldn't bring himself to lie. Anders was the one man in the company who had offered him friendship and sought nothing else in return.

"I did want to ask you one thing," he said, taking the path offered instead. "Has Lady Grace talked to you about Sir Arthur Cochrane? I know you said she seemed more distressed by the death of her dog."

Anders thought for a moment.

"I cannot say she spoke about him at all. She was indeed much too concerned by her little dog. Which is strange, as my understanding had been that Sir Arthur was visiting here on her account, as is the Reverend Irving."

"She seemed shocked by his death when we found him," Gideon recalled.

"I think it surprised her if that is what you are asking," Anders said. "You don't think she…?"

Gideon let a breath out and lifted his shoulders. "Not alone, that is for certain. But perhaps she was involved. I overheard her speaking to William Irving yesterday, about someone demanding he pay her. Irving assured her that whoever would be gone by the end of the week."

"I am glad you added a caveat," Anders said. "I don't believe Lady Grace would have the strength to subdue Ruth Whitaker. Though Irving might. But why the housekeeper might be wanted dead by Lady Grace, I cannot imagine."

"Sometimes," Gideon said, "those who stoop to murder are willing to try and muddy the waters by killing a victim to distract from their true intent. I know of at least one example in London where that was true."

"That could work the other way too," Anders observed. "Perhaps Sir Arthur was killed to try to place more people under suspicion—or to 'muddy the waters' as you put it, by stirring up talk of the Curse of Wrathby."

Which was something Gideon hadn't considered.

"I was hoping to speak to Lady Grace, provided as her physician you think she will be able to manage that. I would have Zahara with me too."

THE TRAITOR'S APPRENTICE

"Lady Grace," Anders told him, "has the emotional constitution of a yoked pair of oxen. She was upset and is grieving, but she is not, as her daughter is, held down by distress. She is, by nature, sanguine and her daughter melancholic. I think she will come to no harm from any questions you may wish to ask her." Anders got to his feet. "And now I have fulfilled our patron's command as regards yourself, but I still need to see to the captain."

Gideon stood up and delayed the Dane with a hand on his arm.

"You must have a care then," he said, wishing to warn Anders of the dark morass that lay between Lord and Mags. "Mags is…" he trailed off, unable to think what words were needed to warn and yet not precipitate the very involvement he wanted to avoid.

"Mags is not someone to regard as we might our patron?" Anders suggested.

Gideon nodded. It was not that simple. Anders' words implied that Mags was less advisable to listen to than Lord, and at that moment Gideon was far from certain that was true.

Anders studied his face for a few moments more.

"You should have no concern, my friend. I am paid to treat the ills of all members of our patron's company. It is my *professional* duty."

There was no more Gideon could say to it without the Dane becoming as enmired as he was himself. But he was still uneasy as he watched Anders head along the passageway to Mags' chamber, past Muir's room which was beside their own. He was challenged by Aleksandrov outside the door. Wondering if he should have said more, Gideon made his way through the house to find Zahara.

Zahara had been given accommodation in a small room in the peel tower. The sight of its heavy door with a strong latch and even a bolt on the inside made Gideon a bit happier about her security. He reached the room just as she was slipping inside. She paused before closing the door.

"I need to pray," she said, her smile warming him.

He didn't hear footsteps on the stairs, but he felt a presence behind him and turned fast. Shiraz stood there, surveying him with dark eyes that held some emotion Gideon struggled to comprehend for a moment. Then he realised what it was.

Pity.

He stood silent as Shiraz moved past him and into the room and the door closed. The sounds of the house seemed removed to another world. The distant shouts as the digging work went on, the clatter of pottery and pots, the sound of a hammer hitting metal and the occasional short burst of laughter. Time seemed to suspend so Gideon had no idea how long he stood there.

There was an urgent shout and hooves approaching. The texture of the soundscape changed in a moment. Lord's voice raised without effort, giving clear precise orders in French. Mags' voice, harsher, the German seeming to echo rather than contradict. Torn between waiting for Zahara and knowing he should be responding to the commands, the decision was made for him when someone came running up the steps. Roger Jupp.

Pushing past Gideon, he banged three times on Zahara's door. He was carrying a musket that looked to Gideon more like something a gentleman might go hunting with than a military weapon.

THE TRAITOR'S APPRENTICE

"Mr Fox, sir. You can use a pistol. With me." Then Jupp was heading up the spiral stairs taking them two at a time, to the top of the tower. Left little choice, Gideon followed. Which was why he had a good view of what was happening.

It was impressive to see Lord's company move into a defensive posture so quickly. One moment the men were wielding spades, picks and mattocks, the next they were armed with swords, pistols and muskets. Beside him, Jupp was loading the gun he held and seemed to be having a bit of trouble forcing the bullet into it.

"We are under attack?" Gideon asked.

"Grief no. This is more to impress some visitors."

"Then why are we up here?"

Jupp finished loading and rested the long barrel of the elegant flintlock on the stone of the tower.

"If things were to turn nasty, I can make sure they lose their commander." He patted the flintlock's barrel. "This beauty shoots straight and true. Here," he handed Gideon one of the two pistols he carried. "It won't be needed, but it is how we always do things. If by ill chance it happened to turn bad, anyone comes up who isn't one of us, you shoot them."

Gideon's heart thumped.

"Zahara."

Jupp grabbed him as he turned. "Sara is with Shiraz, sir. If there's trouble, she'll be even safer than us. You should watch this." He nodded towards the gate. "It'll be good, I think."

Gideon watched.

He counted twenty men who rode up to the gate. They were well-mounted and wearing buff coats. Even Gideon's untutored eye could tell they moved in a way that suggested military discipline. At the closed gate, they reined and called a challenge.

"I think they have little idea of our strength here," Jupp said. "And the Schiavono will be careful to make sure they get none." He pointed to one of the ditches. "See there? How many men?"

Gideon counted the men whose muskets showed over the bank.

"Twelve."

Jupp grinned and held up one finger.

"One man, eleven hats and twelve muskets." He jerked a thumb back at the men who were by the gate. "By that and other little tricks, they will be convinced we have more than twice the numbers we do and even if they guess the Schiavono is playing a game, they will still not know for sure what is real and what is not."

Whatever the result of the conversation at the gate, those outside seemed reluctant to force the issue.

"They are going to run away back to whoever sent them and declare we have a garrison even bigger than they think they saw," Jupp predicted.

But he was wrong.

Three of the men dismounted and the wicket gate was unbarred to allow them inside. Jupp kept his weapon trained on them, but Gideon had little chance to get an impression of the three before there were footsteps on the ladder and Bjorn Olsen pulled himself onto the roof.

"The Schiavono wants you, Mr Fox, in the dining hall."

"Me? Why?" Gideon could have bitten back the words the moment they were spoken.

"I forgot to ask him for you, sir," Olsen said. "You think you should wait here while I go and find out?"

THE TRAITOR'S APPRENTICE

Jupp was grinning and Gideon, face burning with embarrassment, hurried down the stairs. He was surprised to see Anders with several of the company's women in the room below. A couple of muskets were propped up to poke through the shutters. He got a brief nod from Anders then went on down the stairs and into the new part of the house.

Shiraz was in the entrance hall at the bottom of the staircase, bow and quiver on his back, sword at his waist. In his servant's garb, he looked like a forester—or poacher maybe. The door to the dining hall was also guarded and the man there must have been told to expect Gideon because he opened the door as Gideon reached it.

The scene inside was far from how it had been at dinner. The salt no longer dominated the table, there were no dishes or settings. The room appeared austere, the faces on the family picture stared down, judgemental and uncompromising, the landscape of Wrathby beside them, bleak and grim. To Gideon, it had more the feel of a courtroom, the same expectant tension, the same possibility of life or death.

If it was a courtroom, then Philip Lord was the magistrate. He stood with his back to the imposing fireplace, flanked at a discrete distance by two of his men, both wearing gleaming breastplates and holding partisans. Lord was still wearing the grey doublet he had worn at dinner, but now the grey seemed transmuted to a metallic gleam and the fire was enchanting the sapphires with a living flame. Lord's white hair glittered silver and, as ever, he wore his cat's head sword by his thigh.

The three men who had arrived with the cavalry

detachment were standing before Lord, facing away from Gideon as he entered the room. All three were well-armed. Two were in thick leather buffs with pot helms, but their commander's apparel equalled Lord's for fashion and style. It was golden orange, slashed with cream with gold braid on his breeches. He wore a stiff-brimmed hat, from beneath which cascaded an exuberance of dark curls. He alone turned to see who had been admitted and Gideon had the impression of a well-proportioned face, with a fashionable goatee and moustache, above which was a long, prominent nose.

"My lawyer, Monsieur Fox," Lord explained.

Gideon made a polite bow but wasn't rewarded with a counter introduction. The man turned back to Lord.

"You need a lawyer?"

"I have assumed you are here to invite us to join your father's Treaty of Neutrality, *n'est ce pas*? We cannot commit without a full study of the terms and for that, I do indeed need a lawyer"

The dark-haired man was frowning.

"You know of the treaty?"

"The whole county knows of it," Lord said with a careless lift of his shoulders.

There was a cold pause.

"You, sir, are not a baron, knight or gentlemen of this shire, by what right would you expect to be included?"

Lord looked as if he were confused.

"*Mais non,* Monsieur Fairfax. You misunderstand me. I thought *you* would wish that we join."

The implications of that silenced Fairfax for a few moments.

"I came to speak with Lady Elizabeth Belamy," he said. "I was assured by those I assume were your men at the gate that you are her garrison."

"*C'est vrai*. It is true. We are indeed here at the invitation of the baroness herself. We have the privilege of being her guests and as such, it is our duty to ensure the defence of her house."

"Then perhaps I—"

As if by stage direction, the door opened and Lady Belamy swept in, attended by Zahara. She smiled at Fairfax with obvious delight and crossed over to him.

"Sir Thomas, this is an unexpected pleasure. Had I known you were coming I would have delayed dinner. Please have your men brought in. I will see them fed. You must have come a fair distance." She turned to Zahara. "Sara, please fetch refreshments for Sir Thomas and his companions here." Zahara bobbed a brief curtsey and slipped from the room.

Sir Thomas seemed taken aback.

"My lady, this…" his hesitation made it clear he was unhappy to use the word. "This *gentleman* tells me he and his men are in occupation of Wrathby at your behest. Is that true?"

"Of course," she said. "The Graf von Elsterkrallen was a good friend to Charles. He came to ensure that Wrathby is well protected in these troubled times. He is training our men and strengthening our defences, although I hope there is no need for either to be tested. We are most grateful to him and to Monsieur Blanchard de Coeurlain here."

There must have been refreshments already prepared because Zahara returned at once bearing a tray. With her was Máire Rider's eldest daughter, Brighid, who was in her late teens. Gideon wondered why it was that one of the company's women was assisting Zahara rather than any of the regular household.

Fairfax ignored them.

"I would speak with you alone, Lady Belamy. If you would allow me."

Lord's voice lifted before she could reply.

"You fear the baroness is being held prisoner in her own home, Sir Thomas?"

The dark-haired man glared.

"That is what I suspect, sir. You see, I have served as a soldier abroad, under Sir Horace Vere, and I am familiar with tales of a white-haired mercenary commander. A man they call the Schiavono. A man well known for his opportunism and brutality."

"Then," said Philip Lord, "you should be glad I am not that man. For if I were, I would not be permitting you and you men to leave as you came. If Lady Belamy asks us to depart, we will do so. I have given her my word on that, as has the graf himself."

"That is true," the baroness agreed. "Both Monsieur Blanchard and the graf have given me such personal assurances. But I find I feel more secure with them and their people here. I don't know what rumours may have reached you, but I assure you their men are well disciplined and neither I nor any of my household feel under threat." She turned to Lord. "Monsieur, if you will excuse us, I will speak privily with Sir Thomas as he asks and perhaps we may resolve this."

Lord made a gracious bow.

"*Mais naturellement*, if that is what you wish, madame. This is your house. It is not for me to say what you may or may not do here."

Fairfax's expression held both suspicion and surprise.

"Let us repair to the library, Sir Thomas." The

baroness took a couple of steps towards the door, then turned. "Sara, please bring some refreshments." Zahara gathered what was needed on a tray and followed the two from the room.

It could have been an awkward and embarrassing wait, But Lord didn't allow the tension to settle, engaging the two men who had come in with Fairfax in easy conversation, drawing them to take seats at the table and seeing them served with wine. Gideon understood then that he had been no more than a property in Lord's staged production. *My lawyer, Mr Fox.* Keeping in that role, he would have stayed where he was, except another memory pushed itself into his thoughts.

Avoiding eye contact with Lord, so as not to be refused permission to leave, he opened the door beside him and slipped out. The door guard made no move to stop him, but he got a curious look from Shiraz as he crossed the entrance hall. It was not too hard to find the place beneath the staircase that allowed him to overhear conversations in the room beyond.

As before the voices were not loud, but he could hear them well enough.

"...I know they seem well disciplined, but these men are like curs. They could turn and rend where they now build and defend."

There was a slight pause before Lady Belamy spoke.

"Thank you, Sara, you may go now." Gideon heard the door open and close along the passageway before she went on. "Tom, you are sweet to be so careful of me. But the graf is an old friend of Charles—"

"You only have his word for that. You can't even talk to the man, and I promise you, this Frenchman, whatever he calls himself—"

"Philippe Blanchard."

"Whoever. He is the mercenary commander I spoke of, and that man has the most unsavoury reputation you can imagine. Just the thought of you and your mother—"

"Mother manages very well as do I." She said stiffly, then sighed. "What will it take to persuade you to let me be? I assure you that Wrathby hasn't felt so alive since poor Charles died. We have our own physician here now. The still room is back in use. I have had help with all the tasks of maintenance both inside and outside the house. Sara, my new housekeeper, is wonderful at her work. If the graf is here with criminal intent, he is investing greatly."

Gideon was distracted as Zahara, curious to see him standing in the corner of the hall came over. He held up a finger to his lips in warning, in case what was heard from without might be heard from within also.

"I see you will not be moved by words," Fairfax said, sounding exasperated.

Zahara's eyes widened, and she turned her head a little to hear better.

"I see no reason to be left undefended in these troubled times," Lady Belamy said. "I ask again, what will persuade you to leave us alone?"

"Do you even know if these men stand for or against the king?"

"Tom, I don't even know whether you do. I've been assured they wish only to keep the house safe from all comers and, as I see it, that is my first duty to Wrathby and my son."

"And my first duty is to ensure there is no stronghold in these lands that might harbour those who support the

THE TRAITOR'S APPRENTICE

king."

"Even with this treaty of neutrality in the making?"

There was a cold silence.

"Let me leave a man with you at least."

"To spy on Wrathby?"

"No. To try to keep you safe."

"I am safe enough," Lady Belamy sounded impatient. "And even if I were not, what could one man do?"

"What of these accidents? People falling downstairs? The village is full of talk about it."

Gideon could picture the puzzlement and outrage that must have formed on the baroness' face as her tone betrayed both when she spoke.

"I have no idea what you are trying to imply. They were accidents, nothing more—and since one occurred before these soldiers even arrived, you are making too much of nothing. Or must I hear you speak of the so-called 'Curse of Wrathby' as much as my most unlettered servants?"

There was a weighty silence, heavy with Fairfax's impotent frustration.

"Very well. I will let you be since that is what you ask. But if things turn out other than you seem to expect, if your visitors decide that they prefer the ill-guided king over his right-minded parliament, then you may expect me to return—and with more than a small escort."

"I promise you that as long as I am the lady of Wrathby, this house will keep to the neutrality your father wishes. If you will allow us to be a party to it."

"All in the county will be subject to it unless they individually renege," Fairfax said. "But it requires all musters of troops to be dispersed."

"I have mustered no troops. These men came as

guests."

"A point we could debate, but I can see I would make no headway."

"Then I believe we have the matter decided unless there was something else?"

"Elizabeth, I wish—" Fairfax sighed. "No. Never mind. These times are destroying everything. Even old friendships. Let us rejoin your Frenchman."

Gideon ushered Zahara away and stood by the stairs with her and Shiraz as the baroness and Sir Thomas walked back to the dining hall, before following them in close enough for the door guard not to shut the door again before he and Zahara reached it.

A burst of laughter welcomed them back into the room, Philip Lord, one foot on a chair and an arm leaning on the raised knee had succeeded in both relaxing and entertaining the two Yorkshire gentlemen left in his charge whilst their commander was absent.

He turned a smiling face to Fairfax.

"Ah, Sir Thomas, I can see you are satisfied that the lady is not being held hostage in her own house. *Tout est bon, n'est pas*? All is good, is it not?"

"*Tout n'est pas bon,*" Fairfax said. "All is not good, sir. But this is the lady's house and I have accepted her word—for now."

"And you will give us notice of the terms of this treaty we need to abide by?"

"I shall ensure a copy is delivered," Fairfax conceded.

"Then it *is* all good," Lord took his foot from the chair and crossed to Fairfax and embraced him, kissing him on each cheek. "And now we are all friends, you will stay and eat, *naturellement*? Your men outside, also?" He stepped back, his smile warm leaving Fairfax standing as a frozen statue, a man in shock.

"I thank you for the offer of Lady Belamy's hospitality," he managed stiffly. "However, I must take my leave."

Gideon made a polite bow as Sir Thomas left the room accompanied by an effusive and ebullient Philip Lord. Then he followed behind, summoned to do so by the merest eye flick from Lord in passing. In like manner, Lord added Zahara and Shiraz to his train.

"Let me show you something that will impress you, Sir Thomas," Lord said as they walked towards the gates. He held out a hand, gaze still on Fairfax and Zahara placed a linen cloth in it, large enough, perhaps to cover his hand, fingers outstretched. Fairfax stopped, frowning.

"What do you—?"

Lord had slipped a ring from his hand and looped the corner of the cloth through it, then in the same movement cast it into the air right above the other man's head. A shot rang out as he did so, and a flurry of weaponry appeared in the hands of Sir Thomas and his men.

Ignoring that, Lord bent and retrieved the cloth, pulling it free from the ring and holding it up to show the hole where a bullet had passed through. Bowing he offered the cloth to Sir Thomas.

"I can see you are impressed, monsieur," he said.

"God damn you, sir," Fairfax said, pushing his sword back and walking away towards the gate.

They were through the wicket and the three men were mounting when it happened.

A shout from the tower.

Gideon caught a glimpse of a figure running with

awkward speed to the wall where it was at its lowest. Once over that, he would be amongst Fairfax's men. But he wasn't moving very fast when he clambered up the wall, as if he were in great pain.

That was when Gideon realised who it was.

Legrand.

Lord said one quiet word.

"Shiraz."

Shiraz slipped the bow from his back and in the same movement took an arrow from the quiver, so the two came together in his hands in a moment. Drawing and loosing with no apparent time to aim, Shiraz sent a single arrow over the entire width of the courtyard and the stableyard beyond to slice with accuracy through the throat of the man on the wall. Legrand staggered backwards in a small spray of blood, and dropped away from the wall, lost to Gideon's sight as he did so. Shiraz was already running, following the course of his arrow.

Lord stepped forward and made a theatrical bow through the open gate towards the departing Fairfax, like a player acknowledging his audience.

Sir Thomas must have seen him bow but gave no return salute. He rode off oblivious to the real and deadly drama that had just played out hidden from his sight by the wall.

Chapter Seven

I

As Lord straightened from his bow any trace of good humour vanished.

"Who in hell's name let that happen? Legrand was supposed to be under lock and key." Lord glanced at Gideon. "Find out, fast, and let me know." Then he strode off giving brisk orders to restore the house, get the defensive works restarted and to send a small scouting group to be sure Fairfax had left the area.

"Legrand was being held in a small room behind the bakehouse," Zahara said. "I'll find someone to join you before I attend upon Lady Belamy."

Gideon gave her a grateful smile and hurried to the bakehouse. A small room, little more than a store cupboard, backed onto it on the opposite side from the brewhouse and the still room.

The first person he saw was Simon Muir, crouched on the ground beside a prone man. Muir held a knife covered in blood. Without thought, Gideon found he had drawn his sword.

"What are you doing?" he demanded.

Muir straightened up, the knife still in his hand as if he had forgotten its existence. The figure on the ground was one of Lord's men whose name Gideon had yet to learn. He lay still in a pool of blood.

"He might still be alive," Muir said. "Can you fetch Dr Jensen?"

Gideon hesitated but Shiraz had appeared beside him, stepped forward and took the knife from Muir's unresisting hand. Keeping a wary eye on the man, Shiraz stooped to make a rapid check of the prone form. He lifted his head in a brief upwards nod and Gideon put up his sword and headed back to the house at a run.

By good fortune or God's grace, he didn't need to go further than the corner of the building. Anders was walking across the yard towards the still room and changed his direction at Gideon's urgent call.

When they got back to the store cupboard, Shiraz moved aside to let Anders work.

"It's his own knife," Muir said. "Someone stabbed him with his own knife, from behind."

Gideon took in the small room where Legrand had been kept. It held only a pallet mattress with a blanket. There was no lock to the door, although there was a bolt on the outside. But the door had been open.

"Why are you here?" Gideon demanded. To his thinking, Muir had just become the prime suspect for this assault.

"I was in the bakehouse with Novak, my appointed position for the supposed emergency defence. Novak said he'd heard something. He told me to stay put, so I did. Then he went to investigate and didn't come back. By the time I got here..." Muir trailed off. "Damnation, Fox. You can't think that I—" He stopped talking and shook his head. "Do you think I'd be stupid enough to stay there holding the knife if it had been me?"

It was a good point.

"So this man opened the door to Legrand and was killed by him?"

"Not killed," Anders said. "At least, not yet. Help me

here."

Between the four of them, they manoeuvred the stricken man onto the pallet. Then Anders ordered them to leave him be and send a servant who could be trusted.

Aware that Lord would be expecting an immediate report and he had been the one charged to provide it, Gideon headed back to the house, taking Muir with him on the well-founded excuse that Captain Blanchard would want to hear his account of events. Shiraz remained with Anders. Having no idea who of the household servants might be reliable, Gideon sent the first he came across to take a message to Zahara to tell her what Anders had asked for.

Philip Lord was back in the dining hall giving a brusque debrief to the handful of his men who officered the company. As soon as Gideon entered the long room, he made a sharp gesture to silence Jupp who was recounting what he had observed from his high perch atop the peel tower and strode over towards the door.

"You. Wait here," he said to Muir and Gideon knew that would be taken as an order by his men even if Muir chose to ignore it. "Fox, *avec moi*."

Lord strode across the entrance hall and opened the door to the library.

"No," Gideon's voice was too sharp, and Lord turned to him, frowning. Gideon dropped his voice. "There is a place by the stairs where conversation in this room can be overheard."

"Then we make music," Lord said. "Do you play?" He didn't wait for an answer but took a seat by the virginals and opened the case, running his fingers down the keys and then striking a succession of chords, before breaking into a pavane.

"I would hope this might cover our conversation, although there should be none of the household close enough to hear." The tempo switched to a galliard. "How did Legrand get out? He was held behind a bolted door."

"I don't know. Someone must have unbolted the door. But there is more—your man Novak was knifed from behind with his own knife, presumably by Legrand." He explained how he had found Muir and Novak, Muir's explanation and Novak's current condition.

"I will speak with Muir. If Novak survives, we may learn more." Lord continued playing as he spoke, switching back to the more measured pavane. It was as if his fingers knew the music without the need for his mind to engage with it. Gideon realised this was a further tribute to the intense and eclectic education Mags had described. "This is your priority now, over and above the household murders. I will make my own enquiries, of course, but you may do better. Let us all be happy that Shiraz is an excellent shot. If Legrand had gone with Fairfax, we would be looking at a very short tenure here indeed."

Gideon thought about that for a moment.

"You mean that he would have betrayed all he knew of us?"

"The problem with mercenaries," Lord said, "is they tend to be mercenary. Fairfax would have seen his chance and taken it. Legrand would have been given a fat purse and we would have been put in much hazard. I suspect there would have been a move to evict us before the treaty of neutrality came into effect. The bigger issue is, who wanted that to happen?"

"Someone who wants us gone from here?" Gideon

suggested. "I overheard Lady Belamy talking to Sir Thomas. I got the impression they might be closer friends than they were appearing in public."

Lord met his gaze and then looked back at the keyboard, fingers moving effortlessly. "You heard something to make you suspect Lady Belamy was keen for us to leave?"

"On the contrary. She seemed keen to make it clear that she wished us to stay. My point being that if Sir Thomas is known here there may be those who are partisan to him and his cause."

"You could be right," Lord said after playing a few more bars. "It is always a mistake to believe that because one disaster embroils you others will stay away. But I was thinking it was something much more simple and straightforward."

"Simple and straightforward?"

Lord stopped playing.

"*This is of purpose laid by some that hate me.* I want a trusted guard on Novak. Tell Shiraz to stay with him for now, I'll send someone to relieve him." He closed the virginals' case and stood up, moving across the room to open the door, Blanchard restored. "*Monsieur Renard*, attend upon me this evening with a report of your progress. I am expecting much."

Following him back to the entrance hall, Gideon heard Lord address Muir in cold Gallic tones as he walked back into the dining hall before the door closed behind him.

Gideon hurried back to where he had left Anders tending Novak. Shiraz, standing outside the storeroom, inclined his head to acknowledge the instruction from Lord and moved aside so Gideon could go in.

Somehow Gideon was not so surprised to find Zahara there rather than one of the servants and with her was Brighid Rider. Considering that the Riders as a family seemed to hold Anders responsible for the death of their father, Gideon was surprised to see one of them there and willing to work with the Dane. But then Brighid was, from what he had seen, the closest to a friend Zahara had in the company, so perhaps her influence had prevailed.

Anders glanced up as Gideon entered.

"He will not be talking for a while if that is why you are here," the Dane said. "I will send word when he can, or if he says anything you need to hear. For now, you can serve matters best by not blocking the light, my friend." The criticism was modified by a brief smile, but Gideon took it as the dismissal it was and left the small room. Zahara joined him.

"Brighid will do what is needed for now," she said. "I still have to see Lady Grace. If you wished to ask her anything you could come with me."

It wasn't, he would have thought, the most appropriate of times to ask the lady about her relationship with Sir Arthur Cochrane and it wasn't following the letter of his latest instructions from Lord, but Gideon accepted anyway because Zahara suggested it.

"Were any of the household out and about whilst Sir Thomas was here?" he asked as they walked back to the house. "Apart from Muir and Lady Belamy, of course."

"They were all told to stay in their rooms, and as Lady Belamy was requesting it, Lady Grace and the Reverend Irving agreed. Alice Franklyn said she would not, but the Schiavono told her he would lock her in one of the outbuildings if she refused."

THE TRAITOR'S APPRENTICE

Gideon was sure Alice Franklyn would have taken that suggestion ill.

"And Mags?"

"He would have gone to the men on the earthworks."

"Who would have been with him? Someone reliable?"

Zahara looked at him with sudden understanding. "I will find out for you if he left that place."

"He or Aleksandrov."

That earned him a sharp glance before she nodded. "I will find out if any of his men were absent."

Gideon hadn't yet been upstairs in the new wing of the house and found it as tastefully designed as the lower floor. There were, he counted, five bedrooms with the nursery being set on the same side as the baroness's suite and the guest rooms on the other side.

Irving must have heard footsteps on the stairs as he put his head out of a door.

"Am I to be permitted to leave my room yet?" He sounded pettish.

Zahara smiled at him. "If you would be kind enough to wait a little longer, sir, the soldiers are still about the house. They will be gone soon."

Gideon suspected it was her smile rather than her words that subdued him. But Irving nodded and closed the door again. Zahara shared the smile with Gideon then tapped on the door opposite.

Lady Grace had worked hard to shape the chamber to her taste. There was a frieze above the wainscotting which showed delicately painted birds on interlaced branches that blossomed with an unlikely variety of flowers. Hangings displaying the same theme surrounded her bed. It was also on embroidered cushions and on a high-backed settle which served also as a storage chest. An empty dog bed was set beside that.

Lady Grace herself had a well-cushioned chair by the window to catch the sun. She was wearing a gown in black velvet, with long open sleeves revealing embroidered black silk beneath. A fan-like collar spread out from her shoulders to frame her head in a style that Gideon suspected must have been the height of fashion three or four decades before. She made no move to disturb herself when Zahara dropped a curtsey and explained that Mr Fox would appreciate a few moments of her time.

"A few? I can spare him more than a few. There is precious little else to do when we are told we cannot even walk about our own house." Lady Grace sounded piqued, so Gideon adopted his best smile and the attitude he kept for the most difficult of his legal clients. He bent over her hand as he bowed in greeting and offered a smooth blend of compliments, together with condolences for both her human and canine loss.

It worked to at least some degree because she gestured to the hard stool beside the bed and suggested he brought it a little closer and sat down.

"Sara, you do not need to linger, girl," she said as Gideon moved the stool. "Unless Mr Fox would like some refreshment? No? Well, in that case, I am sure you have work to do. I am much too old to need to worry that being alone with a man would cast any kind of a pall over my reputation." Bobbing another curtsey, Zahara sent a quick look of reassurance to Gideon and then withdrew, closing the door behind her.

Lady Grace turned to Gideon. "Now young man, I am sure you didn't come here to offer platitudes, so you might as well say what it is that you do want."

THE TRAITOR'S APPRENTICE

Gideon wondered how direct he should be. He was certain she had no knowledge of something being added to Sir Arthur's food or she would have been careful to keep Dido from eating any of it. But that didn't mean she wasn't to some degree a party to the murder or an instigator of it.

"I wanted to ask you about Sir Arthur if that wouldn't be too painful for you."

She treated him to a gimlet stare through narrowed eyes.

"Sir Arthur is deceased. He will be buried tomorrow, far from his home. He was a friend. I am not sure what more I can say that either good taste or decency would merit at this time."

Gideon thought about that as he shuffled his weight on the uncomfortable stool and wished he had refused the offer of a seat.

"I have no wish to upset you, of course, Lady Grace, but I understood that you and Sir Arthur had a disagreement."

"A disagreement? Is that what he told you?"

Gideon wondered who the 'he' mentioned was supposed to be, Sir Arthur himself? Or had William Irving mentioned to her that he had spoken to Gideon?

"Something about you paying him some money. I was uncertain—"

Lady Grace almost spat with fury.

"How dare he tell you about that? Did he also mention *why* I was supposed to pay him? I suppose he called it 'an old debt', but anyone could see it was a ludicrous attempt at extortion."

"Ludicrous," Gideon echoed, using a technique he had often found worked to draw his clients out when they were reluctant to speak of some matter affecting their case.

"Yes. That is the only word I can use—except perhaps ridiculous. Trying to claim that a book which had been a gift was, in reality, a loan and that so long after the event."

"A loan?" Gideon prompted.

"Of course it wasn't a loan," Lady Grace snapped. "The book was his gift to me, over fifteen years ago, yet he seemed to think he could somehow hold me to account for it today. It was very hard to stomach even though I understood his plight. The foolish man. He resigned from his university post on the promise of becoming a private tutor only to have that offer rescinded. Someone spoke of his beliefs to his would-be patron and they declined his service as a result. If I had the wretched book, I would have returned it, but I passed it on to William years ago to sell for me."

"This book…?"

"It was a valuable tome but something more fitting for a bookshelf in Geneva or perhaps Amsterdam, than anywhere here in England. I didn't have the heart to tell poor Arthur at the time, but I was not willing to have something so incendiary in my keeping. It was a gift, but it was also dangerous. He had even inscribed it so as not to incriminate either of us, '*To my dear friend*'. But that inscription was clear proof it was a gift."

"Clear proof," Gideon echoed, nodding.

"Yet he still came here insisting I either returned the book or paid him its worth. William counselled me to pay him and consider the matter closed and our friendship over. But I was unwilling to bend to such demands. And in the end, I was right."

THE TRAITOR'S APPRENTICE

"You were right?"

"Just before that fateful dinner. Arthur called me into the parlour and told me that he regretted he had spoken to me as he had, that he had no wish to trouble our friendship by laying upon it such a burden and he apologised for having done so. William was with me, and we were both quite surprised."

Gideon realised that must have been just after he had stopped listening to their conversation.

"He said you didn't need to pay him after all?" Gideon found himself more than a little confused. Why would a man go to the extreme of alienating an old friend with some rather desperate claim of debt owed and then retreat from it?

"I can only assume he received a letter that morning with some hopeful news regarding his financial circumstances. He had been such a good friend before—well before all this."

A tap on the door announced the return of Zahara. She told Lady Grace that she was free to go where she would in the house again, as all the soldiers had left, and that some food would be served for the family in the parlour. Declining a graciously made invitation to join the gathering, Gideon was glad to make his escape.

Lady Grace caught his arm in a strong grip as he rose to do so.

"I'm not sure why he confided in you," she said. "Was it as a lawyer?"

"It is a confidential matter," Gideon lied.

She nodded and released him. "Typical of the man," she said. "Typical." And glancing back as he left the room, Gideon noticed that her eyes were bright with unshed tears.

As much of the household headed to the parlour, he made enquiries and found that no letters had arrived at the house for Sir Arthur in over two weeks. He caught Zahara on a repeat journey from the parlour to the kitchens and asked if she had the key to Sir Arthur's room on the ring on her belt.

After trying a couple, it appeared she had, and Gideon was able to enter the room. It was small and austere, much as the man himself had been. He spent an unedifying time until it grew dark, looking through what papers and documents Sir Arthur had with him. There was nothing of any use. Just personal documents, letters and a half-written book on some obscure aspect of mathematics which Gideon found incomprehensible. There was no helpful diary with an entry naming someone who had offered him money.

Fighting back a headache, Gideon realised that even if Sir Arthur had told Lady Grace and William Irving of his change of heart, if either of them had doctored his food it would have been too late to do much about it—unless they had tipped the lot on the floor before he could eat much…

That thought was blossoming into a rather profound realisation when he was disturbed by someone at the door of the room.

"Sara told me you would be here," Anders said. He was carrying a candle and Gideon realised then quite how dark it had got. He had needed to hold the last few papers to the window to read them.

"There is something wrong?"

"Sara said to tell you she has asked, and no one was absent, whatever that may mean. But I came about Novak."

"Novak is dead?"

"No. Novak is alive," Anders said. "I expect him to remain so. The injury was not so deep. What laid him out was a blow to the head. He was awake for a short time, but he needs the rest, so I questioned him on your behalf."

"He was stabbed after he was hit?"

"Yes, but the wound was superficial. Whoever made it was either in too much of a hurry or not meaning to do real harm."

"Then whoever attacked him wasn't trying to kill him?"

"Any cut that deep could kill if he had been left bleeding. If his blood becomes poisoned, or the wound festers, he could still die. But I would agree that the purpose of the attack was not to kill, or if it was it was ineffectual."

"A man in a hurry?" Gideon suggested.

"That could be. Novak himself claims that the bolt was drawn, and the door closed when he got to it. As he was reaching out to open the door to see if Legrand was still inside, he was attacked from behind. He said he has no idea who it was. He thought it was Legrand and that perhaps the bolt had not been secured. It has not even occurred to him that there might have been another party involved and I did not make such a suggestion to him." Anders gripped Gideon's shoulder for a moment. "It is getting late, my friend. We were both up with the dawn. I would suggest you leave these things until tomorrow now. If you need food, go eat, then sleep."

Anders' words made Gideon realise how tired he was.

"I need to report to Lord first," he said. "If he is available."

"He will be." There was no doubt in Anders' voice at all.

And of course, he was.

Gideon found him in the buildings occupied by the majority of the company, those who were not admitted as houseguests. Laughter flowed out to betray his presence in the same room where they had been served by Gretchen that morning. *Was it only that morning?*

Lord sat at a table sharing a jug of beer or ale and a game of dice with a handful of his men, more clustered around the table watching. At first glance, Gideon was tempted to beat a retreat and leave the matter until morning, he was too tired to face the inevitable badinage. Before he could step back out of sight, Lord glimpsed him and rose.

Pulling a watch from the pocket of his breeches, Lord held it, so the candle illuminated the dial. "Gentlemen, that is all. We should go to our beds." For once there were no additional barbed words chosen to slight and draw humour from Gideon's presence.

As Lord crossed the room, the men were already pulling out the pallet mattresses that had been stacked against the walls and turning the room from a place of leisure to a place of rest. Lord reached the door and, meeting Gideon's gaze, inclined his head towards it in silent summons, then he was gone.

"I will not keep you up," Lord said when Gideon caught up with him. Then nothing more until they reached Lord's room, and he unlocked the door. Someone had been in it to keep the embers of the hearth warming the room and the covered lamp lit. Gideon suspected that would have been Zahara. Lord seemed short on trust when it came to such things.

up some documents and started looking through them as he spoke.

"You must not forget the king was here in the summer and his presence did much to encourage his supporters—whilst stripping them of men. At the same time that served to harden resolve against him in the hearts of his ill-wishers who saw in his attempt on Hull an act of tyranny." Lord put the documents down, keeping one in his hands. "I know for a fact that many of those who favour the king's cause, whilst mouthing niceties about neutrality, have already written to the Earl of Newcastle asking him to come south and protect them, and neither Hotham in Hull nor Cholmley in Scarborough seem much inclined to follow Sir Ferdinando Fairfax's lead as regards not pressing their cause."

"And what do you see happening?"

"I hope," Lord said, "that no one takes too many active steps at all, and the treaty holds for a time at least. If Newcastle moves south that will make our lives uncomfortable. But if we have a small break of good fortune things will hold as they are until spring."

"You expect to stay here until the spring?"

"Unless circumstances change." Still holding the document Lord strode over to the door.

"And then?" Gideon asked.

"And then…" Lord drew a slow breath as if giving the matter his deepest consideration. "And then we will go to war."

He opened the door and held it, so Gideon had little choice but to leave.

It should be simple enough, Nick decided, to intercept Christobel Lavinstock on her way back to Flass Grange from Durham. He had ten men with him, and she was travelling escorted by her maid and one man, who Nick was sure would be a household servant or farm hand.

What he was doing was not illegal. It wasn't an abduction. It was a man taking control over his wayward but lawful wife. Even her late father had wished to see her wed to Nick, and both his own father and uncle had been insistent upon it. Who was she to thwart the will of such men?

Her lack of ability to make measured and sensible decisions was proven by her ridiculous statement that she would give up her entire means of support, rather than make what any woman in the land of her station would consider a good match.

The messenger reached him as he was riding out from the stableyard of the house that had accommodated him and his men overnight. Had the man been but a few minutes later he would have missed Nick. The messenger would have ridden for Howe and Nick until could have completed his intention.

But by the damndest twist of fate, he was delivered the message before that could be accomplished. It was a summons from King Charles' Commander of the North, Sir William Cavendish, Earl of Newcastle, ordering the immediate attendance of Sir Nicholas Tempest as a captain of cavalry within Newcastle's own regiment.

There was no getting out of that.

Had Nick given the matter any thought, he should have anticipated it as an inevitable consequence of the death of Sir Bartholomew.

The messenger was adamant. "The earl said

immediately. Anything you need from your house can be sent for."

He had no choice.

Christobel Lavinstock would have to wait.

Howe Hall would have to wait.

Like it or not, Sir Nicholas Tempest was going to war to fight for his king.

Chapter Eight

I

Nick had hoped that joining the army might at least allow him the chance to question his father about the terms of the will. But no sooner had he arrived in Newcastle-upon-Tyne, in the early afternoon, than he was summoned to speak with the Earl of Newcastle.

The earl was in his planning room where he was meeting with other officers, half a dozen men clustered around a large table on which maps and documents were spread out. A man close to fifty, the earl wore his light brown hair well above his shoulders. He radiated an aura of focus and energy, his gaze dark, intense and intelligent. Acknowledging Nick's bow with a nod, the earl exchanged glances with one of his colonels and shook his head.

"This war is making children into soldiers."

Nick tightened his jaw.

"I might be young, my lord, but I promise you will not find a more loyal man or one braver in your service."

The earl looked pleased. "So your father has told me."

He reached over and tapped one of the documents on the table.

"I have a job for you. We have received a request from Yorkshire for support and the information I am getting is, to say the least, incomplete and varied." His hand moved to the map and over it, finger-pointing. "Hull,

THE TRAITOR'S APPRENTICE

Scarborough, Leeds, Tadcaster, Bradford, and Halifax, all held against the king—and York itself threatened by Ferdinando Fairfax."

He straightened up and turned back to face Nick.

"The loyal men of the county seem to stand between pleading terror of being overwhelmed and sending loyal assurances that they are strong and will hold true. They ask me to come and secure the county. But at the same time the Honourable Henry Belasyse, knight of the shire, is away to Leeds to sign an agreement on behalf of those 'loyal men' in which they agree all should disband their troops, to muster no more and to keep the peace." The earl shook his head as if in disbelief. "It is, you must admit, a perplexing situation."

There was silence and Nick wondered if he was supposed to speak.

"Perhaps they seek to buy time for you to bring the army south?" he suggested.

The earl looked at him and then nodded as if it was a new idea.

"Perhaps indeed. A strange stratagem to seek to be forsworn."

"Can one be forsworn to traitors and rebels?" Nick asked. It was the catechism of his youth.

The intense brown eyes studied his face and then nodded.

"I think you have the right of it, Sir Nicholas. I need a man who so holds, to visit the houses of those in the north of the county declaring themselves loyal to the king and assess what they feel. I will give them assurance I will march, and you may do likewise, but I need to know how strongly they cleave to this treaty and how quick they will be to support any movement I might make. I also have a short list of houses we are as yet unsure where they stand and those need to be reminded of their true loyalty and encouraged to contribute to the war effort."

Someone beside the earl cleared his throat. "My lord, might not a more—um, mature individual be a better choice for a mission of such delicacy?"

The commander who spoke was certainly mature. Nick decided he was even older than the earl.

"I think not," the earl said. "We need to demonstrate that we have the vigour to support them, and we need a show of strength to persuade those who waver, not sweet words and gentling. Can you do that, Sir Nicholas?"

"I can," Nick said. "Although I would need sufficient men at my back to make it clear I am not speaking empty words and have the resources to enforce your will."

"You see?" The earl turned to the man who had spoken before. "He thinks he can do it and he knows the means required to do so." Then he turned back to Nick. "You have your orders, sir. You may take fifty men and add to them with any you may recruit as you go. I will provide you with a warrant to take what you might need for supplies from our loyal supporters. Any who seem reluctant, offer them a paper they can bring to me for recompense. The harvest is newly in so there should be no shortage."

Nick bowed and the earl gave him another brief nod.

"Go to your work and God go with you."

Later that afternoon on a fresh horse and armed with pen, ink and a list of names as well as fifty cavalrymen, Nick headed south.

THE TRAITOR'S APPRENTICE

II

Gideon was summoned early to Lord's chambers the day following Fairfax's visit. He was greeted with a pile of documents and an irascible commander.

"I have at present, no clerk whose services I can trust," Lord said. "I also find myself swamped in paperwork, but I lack the resource of time to discern the wheat from the chaff." He gestured to the chair set by his portable desk and must have seen something less than enthusiastic in Gideon's expression. "I am not esteeming any less your lawyer's skills, nor do I take you for some melancholic under-scribe, but a special gentle, the sole hope of your grandmother, one who writes in six fair hands."

For once Gideon was able to respond in kind. "*A fine clerk, and has his cyphering perfect. Will take his oath o' the Greek Testament, if need be, in his pocket; and can court his mistress out of Ovid.*"

"And one who patently does consort with the small poets of his time, though perhaps Ben Johnson would not be accounted small," Lord said, then smiled. "Keep it up and you will be heir to much more than forty marks a year."

Then he was gone, and with no more instruction than that, Gideon found himself confronted by a pile of some twenty or so letters from various correspondents. They came from many corners of Europe and beyond. Many were travel-stained and battered. Some were written in neat and educated hands, some in hard-to-read scrawls. Most were in Latin and French, a couple in English and one was indeed in Greek, which he had to set aside as he couldn't read it.

It took Gideon little time to realise that this was more

by nature of a test than a task. He was willing to lay whatever money he might yet possess that Lord had already read each one of these letters. So, sharpening a quill, he prepared a fresh page and started reading.

"...should know that Cinq-Mars has been executed in Lyon. The king seemed unmoved and was heard to say, 'I would like to have seen the grimace he made on the scaffold'. Thus do royal favourites fall..."

"...saying that O'Neill has made himself master of the better part of Ireland but is struggling to keep his people under control. Lord Forbes is sent by Parliament to waste the coast of Ireland and has invested Galway..."

"...inevitable as Torstenson is in Saxony with perhaps twenty thousand, and the Archduke with Prince-General Piccolomini have five thousand more but near half as many guns. However, it ends will shape the war to come profoundly..."

"...is known true power here is now in the hands of Kösem Sultan. Her son, who they call Ibrahim the Mad, starts at shadows and is unfit to rule, which is perhaps not surprising as he grew up in the Kafes. His days are spent sporting with women whilst the reins of the Ottoman Empire are held by his mother and the Grand Vizier..."

"...appears Formosa is finally taken by the Dutch after Sebastián Hurtado de Corcuera, who is Governor of Manila, recalled the majority of the Spanish force there for another campaign, leaving the fortress unable to mount a proper defence..."

"...since Parliament has now voted to close and suppress all theatres here in London. It seems not only must we have war, but we must also have war with misery and canting too..."

THE TRAITOR'S APPRENTICE

The digest he composed and wrote included references to the relevant letters so Lord might pursue the matter outlined in more detail, where such was available. He tried to put the events in chronological order and date them consistently, which meant calculating where necessary the difference between the calendar used across the rest of Europe and the old-style calendar still employed in England that lagged ten days behind.

The breadth of information flowing in with the letters was impressive, and Gideon wondered how and in what coin it was all paid for. He was sure some of it would be deemed as confidential in the nation where it originated, although most was simply gathering together many threads of news, rumour and informed conjecture.

It was clear to him now that Philip Lord was much more than a simple military commander, going here or there to fight as instructed by his paymaster. Mags' words came back to Gideon sounding much less hollow: *He wants to be king.*

Making sure all the documents were placed back inside the travel desk with his digest on the top, Gideon locked the case, pocketing the key with care. A glance outside showed he had spent the morning working and it was past time for dinner.

Deciding to stretch his legs a little, he took the way around the house rather than through it and was thus, by chance, in the yard when there was a disturbance at the gate. Seeing an approaching force, his heart froze. Fairfax? Returned? In greater numbers and with a force designed to occupy Wrathby?

But there was no alarm, no sense of urgency, no rapid-fire orders and scrambling men. Instead, when Philip

Lord came out of the house he strode to the gates and called for them to be opened. Cheers rose from the handful of Lord's company who were in the vicinity as the new arrivals came into the stableyard. The two men at the front rode through the gate and swung down from their horses, their reins taken by willing hands.

Having a good reason to seek out Lord to return the key, Gideon went forward and saw, with some surprise, that he recognised the large man who was driving the first wagon. It would have been hard to forget the gargoyle features, although the last time they had met the man had been choking Gideon with one of his brawny arms. Gideon recalled his name was Thomson.

But the two who left their mounts and walked over to greet Lord were not men Gideon knew. One was tall, slim, of an age with Lord, but looked his opposite in colouring, with clear olive skin and lustrous black hair. He was immaculately dressed despite the vagaries of travel. He made a formal bow, and the language in which he greeted Lord, made Gideon think him a Spaniard.

The other man was shorter, a little closer in age to Gideon and had a mass of tawny curls, a face that sprouted freckles in profusion, and a carelessly kept beard which framed a cheerful smile. Far from greeting Lord, he stood there looking attentive as the conversation proceeded in rapid Spanish. Then he glanced at Gideon and grinned, before saying in a stage whisper.

"It is like standing beside Jachin and Boaz. Have you noticed how those two make us all look as if we gave our tailors the wrong dimensions?"

His accent was English and his grin infectious. Gideon

found himself smiling back.

"In my case," he confided, "the dimensions were those of other men to begin with. My present wardrobe is made up of borrowed or donated clothing."

"Ah, a man of wit always has a ready excuse. And since our elders and betters seem unlikely to take the time, allow me to introduce myself." He gave a small bow. "Daniel Bristow. Or Danny—although I answer to most hails from 'Oy!' through to 'You prurient bastard!' and sometimes just a despairing look."

"Gideon—" he drew a sharp breath in time as he remembered to use his assumed name. "Gideon Fox."

"Not 'Sir Gideon of Whateverplace' or 'Lord Gideon of Somewhere-or-Other'?" The other man sounded surprised "Just plain Gideon Fox?"

"Just plain Gideon Fox, attorney at law."

"Ah," Danny Bristow said and waved a finger in Gideon's face. "You are not *just* plain Gideon Fox."

"Fox." Lord's voice cut across their conversation and Gideon realised first that the intense conversation in Spanish had ceased and also that, from the smirk adorning Danny Bristow's face, he had known and ignored the fact.

"You may continue your conversation with Lieutenant Bristow as you show him to your room. He will be sharing with you and Monsieur Jensen."

Gideon knew better than to point out the obvious lack of accommodation. Lord would be aware of that. Instead, he gave a neat bow.

"Of course, Captain Blanchard. I came to report I have completed the task you required of me and to return your key." He held it out and Lord took it, turning away as he did so to attend to installing the new arrivals.

"Lieutenant?" Danny Bristow sounded surprised. "Wonderful to see you again too," he observed to the retreating figures, but there was nothing of unpleasantness or resentment in his tone and he turned back to Gideon with an enquiring look. "Known him long?"

"Nearly three weeks," Gideon admitted.

"So little time?" He shook his head. "And already he trusts you with that key? Yet you must be barely past the stage of wanting to smack his teeth down his throat every time he opens his mouth at you. Consider me intrigued."

Gideon laughed as he led the way towards the house.

"And you? How long have you been acquainted with—" He hesitated, uncertain which name was best to use, then took inspiration from Anders. "Acquainted with our patron?"

"Longer than he'd like, I'm sure," Danny said. "He hates me."

"Hates you? That wasn't the usual reaction he has to people he hates."

"It would depend on why he hates them. Me, he hates because I am better at mathematics than he is."

Gideon thought about that.

"You are a military engineer?"

Danny paused mid-stride to make a flourish. "It is one of my hard-learned skills and talents, the other for which he employs me is in the use of artillery as master of ordnance, the rest—well they are ones that I keep under a bushel. It never pays to outshine others, I find. In fact, I believe—"

The shout of fury rang across the yard and Gideon turned fast, his hand resting on his sword, only to find

THE TRAITOR'S APPRENTICE

Danny already had his sword in hand, prepared to attack or defend.

"*¡Bastardo!*"

The shout had come from the Spanish officer. His rapier was drawn, and he ran like a greyhound after a hare. His unmistakable target was Mags who was walking across the yard from where he must have been supervising the digging.

"Oh Christ!" Danny muttered. "He's useless with a sword."

Mags had pulled his own sword free but barely broke his stride as the Spaniard lunged towards him with the elegance of a fencing master and the grace of a dancer.

Lord's raised voice was hard and harsh. "Put up your swords."

He was too far away, having already walked part of the way along the train of the new arrivals, and the fury on the Spaniard's face knew no bounds. Beside Gideon, Danny swore and started running. Gideon drew his sword and followed.

They were too late.

What the Spaniard possessed in elegance and grace, he lacked in speed and competence. His blade failed to make any impact on the careful guard, Mags threw up, parrying and moving in fast to disarm. That should have been what happened. Even Gideon could recognise the move, and a few paces ahead, he saw Danny hesitate. Lord had vaulted a cart and sprung forward along the same path the Spaniard had taken.

But the disarm was not completed, Mags stumbled as he brought his hand up to finish it—and the Spaniard struck. Mags had no other possible defence. His own blade slid into the body of the Spaniard catching him mid-thrust. The impact deflected the force of the Spaniard's blade, so it sliced into the leather of Mags' buff coat.

Arriving too late to make any difference, Gideon could do nothing as the Spaniard's face froze in a gasp of shock. He staggered, then collapsed. Mags straightened up and pulled his blade free, stained red, as Lord reached them.

Mags said something loudly in German, then he switched to French and said more quietly. "I had no choice. I was trying to disarm him—you saw."

Danny, sword still in hand, crouched by the fallen man.

"He's dead."

"I saw," Lord said, his gaze fixed on Mags as if he hadn't heard the pronouncement.

"The man was mad." Mags sounded defensive. "I swear I've never even seen him before. Who was he?"

"Manuel de Torres," Danny said, his tone regretful but without any trace of grief. "I didn't know him for long, only met him two months back. He was good with artillery, but he had a temper he couldn't govern." Standing up, Danny sheathed his sword shaking his head, and then looked at Lord. "I take it I have just inherited his job in addition to my own?"

The Baltic eyes didn't shift their focus from Mags' face.

"You might come to wish otherwise, Captain Bristow," he said, sliding his sword home. "You will need to forgo the home comforts I mentioned, for the time at least as we have ordnance and supplies to unpack and stow."

Danny doffed his hat, but Lord ignored him, striding

off shouting orders to have the dead man removed.

Mags watched as the body of Manuel de Torres was carried away.

"Four corpses in the four days since we arrived," he said in English. "It's like there is a curse on this place." His tone was speculative as if the last death had nothing whatsoever to do with him.

Danny, hat restored, shot him a puzzled look. Then when Mags gave no reply, lifted a brow at Gideon.

"Two of the household suffered fatal accidents," he explained. "Then one of our men broke the rules—and now this."

"That sounds a bit unfortunate."

"It's all being investigated," Mags said and jerked his head at Gideon. "Fox is on the scent. If there is anything untoward to unearth, I am sure he will discover it." Then he stepped past Gideon and slapped Danny on the shoulder, propelling him towards the gate. "Congratulations on your promotion. Danny Bristow? I think I've heard of you. Breda, was it? Now, as I am the one who is supposed to be in command, you can show me what you've brought us. You speak German?"

Danny did, so the rest of the conversation that took place in his hearing was lost on Gideon. Perhaps if he stayed with Lord he should try and learn more languages.

The thought jarred. Did he want to stay? How was it these men could be so unconcerned over the death of de Torres? Yet again he felt the aching gulf which separated him from their understanding of the world. Theirs was a world where death walked with sword drawn at all times. It was not a world he ever wanted to understand or accept, and yet each day he remained with

Lord it seemed he was ever more enmired in it.

He beat a hasty retreat, by instinct seeking the peace he knew he could only find with Zahara. He even had an excuse as he had missed dinner attending to Lord's correspondence. Zahara was happy to find him something to eat and sat with him in the dining hall as he did so.

"Who is Daniel Bristow?" he asked.

She smiled at his mention of the name and a small sliver of jealousy slipped under Gideon's skin.

"He is a good man, and he is a friend of the Schiavono. I hope you will like him."

"He seems likeable," Gideon said, stabbing at his food.

Zahara's smile faded a little.

"You should not think that way," she said. "I have already told you what you wished to hear. It was the truth."

The heat of shame burnt his face and sought a way to change the topic.

"Have you heard any more from the household that could help me uncover the murderer?"

She frowned and lowered her voice so only he should hear.

"Perhaps, but I am not sure it is something that helps you find the murderer. Lady Belamy's sister-in-law, Alice Franklyn, and Simon Muir—I believe they are together in their hearts, even though they allow no sign of it to show to the world."

"Alice Franklyn," Gideon observed, "plays up to anyone with wealth and status. Which means I am mercifully excluded from her attention. If any here, she seems to be setting her sights on the Schiavono, or maybe Mags."

Zahara nodded.

"It is as I have told you. What you say, that is how she wishes things to appear. I have seen them alone together. I have heard whispers from other servants too. It is something that might be important for you to know."

Gideon didn't doubt for a moment that Zahara spoke the truth, but he wasn't sure how it could relate to what he was trying to find out.

"Why would they keep it secret? Alice Franklyn is a widow and free to bestow herself as she wills, and Muir has no impediment."

"No impediment," Zahara agreed. "But also no money. He is a younger son, is he not?"

"Youngest of five," Gideon recalled.

"Did you not tell me yourself that without money a man cannot hope for a wife?"

It had been one of their first conversations and despite himself, Gideon recalled it with embarrassment. And then recalled something else that made him sit up.

"It was Muir who spilt the syllabub over me."

Zahara's brow wrinkled into a small frown.

"I don't see…"

"If he knew it was treated with something, he would want to stop me eating it. He had seen me eat a big portion and I was about to help myself to more. If I had passed out—or, God forbid, died—it would have betrayed that Sir Arthur's demise, far from being an accident was indeed a murder."

"Then that would mean that Muir is…" She looked around, then leaned closer in. "But why would he have any reason to kill Mistress Whitaker and Sir Arthur?"

And that was the problem with the theory. Gideon shook his head in defeat.

"I've no idea. Even if we assume Sir Arthur was going to get the money he sought through blackmail, that couldn't be Simon Muir. We know he is without resources."

"As is Alice Franklyn," Zahara agreed. "I could see this making sense were it Lady Belamy that Muir was involved with. She at least has some wealth she can speak for. After all, it is her infant child who owns all of Wrathby. Lady Belamy has control of the property and all its wealth until he comes of age."

"Which makes it even less likely to be Muir," Gideon agreed. "Perhaps it was chance that he elbowed the syllabub after all."

"Perhaps," she agreed. "But if he was the murderer, he would also have grounds to want us gone from Wrathby."

Which was another very good point. The last Gideon had heard, Novak was making a strong recovery and had his upcoming pay docked for the next three months for failing to ensure the bolt on Legrand's prison had been secured. The only other person who could have been responsible for the bolt being open was Muir. Presumably, he had satisfied Lord he was not. But then Lord would have seen little reason to consider Muir as a serious suspect.

"I must go," Zahara told him. "I have my work and it seems you have yours now too."

She left him then and Gideon sat for a while trying to imagine any reason Simon Muir might have had to kill either Ruth Whittaker or Sir Arthur Cochrane. He decided to take the problem to Anders, but as he crossed the courtyard he was hailed from the far side.

"Fox, *avec moi*." Philip Lord changed into black garb, waited by the gate. He was flanked by two of his men, also in black. Gideon crossed over to join him. The church bell was tolling. "With me, Fox. I have a funeral to attend, Sir Arthur's. I think you should be there too."

Gideon held out his arms to display the red coat he wore.

"Like this?"

Without a word, Lord undid his black cassaque and held it out. Gideon took it and donned the garment. His breeches were dark blue and with the cassaque done up, he looked almost respectable. As he walked with Lord towards the little church close beside the house, he decided he needed to obtain his own wardrobe.

They were the last to arrive and the service was already underway. As patrons of the church, the Belamys had secured a place in the crypt for the remains of Sir Arthur to be interred. Gideon must have missed seeing the escort of men from Lord's company who had borne him to the church.

"Ruth Whitaker's family took her to the village to bury her there," Lord said as they stepped into the sonorous gloom of the church. "But I offered what I could for a family friend."

No doubt it was all part of the considered effort Lord was making to be amenable to Elizabeth Belamy. Gideon wondered as they stood at the back of the church, what Lord would do if she changed her mind and asked him to leave. He had a strong feeling that might be the point at which the mailed fist was withdrawn from the bejewelled and embroidered kid leather glove.

Lord stood beside him, silent and with every outward show of respect. Aside from Lord's two men and a handful of local people, all attending were those of Wrathby's household. The funeral was being conducted by the Reverend Irving in a low but powerful voice.

Lady Grace and Lady Belamy sat together with Alice Franklyn beside them. Muir was also seated at the front and glanced around as Gideon and Lord walked in. He was restless and fidgeting as if counting the moments until he could leave. Watching him Gideon decided that his gaze, if it lingered anywhere, visited Alice Franklyn more often than anyone or anything else. It was the natural way a man's gaze would slip to the woman he loved, and she returned his looks now and then.

When the service was over Lord didn't delay. He restored his hat and gave Gideon a brief nod. "As you were, Monsieur Fox."

Then he strode away to intercept the man Gideon assumed, from his dress, was the incumbent of the church. He heard Lord secure the priest's assistance in conducting the burial of the two men of his company who had been killed. Lord had clearly already contrived to secure a place in the graveyard behind the church for the purpose.

He missed the end of the conversation because Muir was about to leave a few paces behind the three ladies. Gideon dropped into step with him.

"I was wondering," he asked, "when you intend to continue your journey to your brother's house in Scotland?"

Muir frowned at him. "This is not the time to talk of such things. The ladies—"

"Lady Grace," Gideon said, "has the support of the

Reverend Irving. Lady Belamy has the support of her mother and sister-in-law." He paused and when Muir said nothing, was gratified to note the man wasn't that quick-witted. "Or am I wrong in assuming it is Alice Franklyn you wish to remain for?"

Muir sent him a sharp look.

"You assume too much, sir. I have spoken to the graf and asked to sign up with his men as long as they are in quarters here. I want to do what I may to ensure the security of Wrathby and *all* the women here."

Muir extended his stride and Gideon let him go. He was still waiting on the path from the church when Philip Lord returned along it a short time later and greeted Gideon with an inquisitive look.

"Were you aware Simon Muir has joined your company?" Gideon asked.

Lord laughed.

"No. But I am not surprised. It seems of a piece. The graf, I suppose?" Then the humour was gone from his face. Lord rested an elegant, gloved hand on Gideon's shoulder and his voice was too low to carry even to the men escorting him. "I warned you before, Lennox, and I repeat it now—have a care."

Then the hand was gone, and Lord walked away, back towards the house. Gideon waited until he had reached the gate before following. He wondered where Lord was trying to tell him he thought the real danger would come from—Muir or Mags?

Chapter Nine

I

The funerals of Legrand and Captain Alonso de Torres took place that evening. Most of the company attended and Lord took on the role of chief mourner. Gideon hadn't planned to be there, but he was still in possession of Lord's cassaque so decided the fact he hadn't been asked to return it was a way of implying he should go. It was a cold autumn evening, and he was glad of the cassaque's extra warmth before he was able to turn away from the churchyard and walk back to the house. A hand clapped him on the back before he had made it halfway.

"Sorry about earlier," Danny Bristow sounded as if he meant it, but it was now too dark to see his expression.

"As a friend of mine said recently," Gideon told him, "the requests of great men are commands. You didn't have any choice."

"True. But it means I must now request that you show me where I'm to sleep and, since I'm not a great man, you might refuse me." He pulled at the fabric of the cassaque. "You miss a wardrobe but have mourning garb?"

"I was lent it by our patron."

There was no answer to that for a few paces.

"He must think highly of you." Danny's tone was reflective. "He's not in the habit of lending clothes to anyone. The man is fastidious."

THE TRAITOR'S APPRENTICE

"You read too much into it," Gideon said. "He wanted my company for a specific occasion and for that to happen in the required respectful manner he had to lend me this." He could have added that this was far from the first time Lord had perforce lent him clothing.

There was another silence, shorter this time. Then a laugh.

"Yes. That would be it."

As they reached the house Danny turned, hand to sword, facing the shadows. A moment later he relaxed. "Christ, you should be glad my pistol wasn't loaded."

Philip Lord stepped into the pool of light offered by the lantern at the door.

"Not loaded? You're slipping." He spoke with no trace of the now familiar French accent. Instead, his tone was light but there was an edge to it, and he shifted his gaze to Gideon and held out a hand. "You have my cassaque." Gideon eased the garment from his shoulders and held it out. Lord took it and put it over one arm. "Thank you. And as soon as you have found your bed for the night, Danny, I want a word. Lennox here will show you where to find my room."

Then he was gone, striding across to the outbuildings which now accommodated close to a hundred of his men

"Yes, my lord. Of course, my lord," Danny made a deep bow to his departing back, only speaking once he was out of earshot. "Anything you say, my lord." Then he straightened up. "Lennox? I thought it was Fox?"

Gideon shook his head.

"It is a long story," he said and led the way up to the room.

It was clear Lord had been making a statement about Danny Bristow's trustworthiness for Gideon's ears.

There had been another message too. Except when mocking Gideon's name, he had only ever heard Lord call one of his men by their given name. The late Matthew Rider, a man who Lord had held in friendship. Everyone else, himself and Anders included, were addressed by their surnames.

Reaching the room Gideon found someone had provided a truckle bed, equipped with a straw pallet and a flock mattress for extra comfort. Danny eyed the truckle and pushed it with his foot. It moved over the wooden floor.

"This man we are sharing with, Johnson, is it? Is he tall and heavy?"

"Jensen. Anders Jensen and he's not particularly tall or broad. Why do you ask?"

"Because," Danny explained, "I want to know how easy he will be to intimidate into taking the servant's bed here."

Gideon shook his head. Much as he didn't want to sleep on the less comfortable truckle himself, he wasn't willing to allow the man for whom sleep was a frequently interrupted necessity to be denied the more comfortable place.

"Anders is our physician-surgeon. He gets the good bed. The truckle falls to you or me."

Danny sighed.

"I was concerned it might come to that. It's an unfortunate problem."

"Why is that?"

"The problem is I hate having to intimidate people I like."

Gideon looked at the other man, shorter than himself if well set, a half-smile on the freckled face, stance relaxed. There was little about Daniel Bristow that could be described as intimidating. It was hard not to smile and Gideon, taking the comment as a joke, couldn't help doing so.

A moment later the room upended around him, and he was flat on the ground. Then Danny was holding out a hand to help him back to his feet. Gideon took it cautiously. He had grown too used to the horseplay of the company to take any offence.

"I thought you said you were a military engineer?"

"I am," Danny agreed. "As I have no wish to intimidate you, let us think of another way to decide the sleeping arrangements." He reached into his doublet and pulled out a pouch the size of his hand, then opened it and set the contents on the one small table, looking at Gideon. "Cards or dice?"

Before Gideon could explain that he was unpractised at either, the door opened. Danny spun round, stepping between Gideon and the entrance with his sword drawn.

Anders surveyed the sword and then the man who held it with a slight frown.

"You must be Daniel Bristow. Our patron asked me to remind you that he wished to see you at the earliest opportunity, and I believe that meant immediately. His room is at the end of the passage on this side."

Danny restored his sword and bestowed a freckled grin on Anders together with a brief bow. "Thank you." He turned to Gideon. "The battle for the bed must await my return. I shall have to trust you not to assume victory through possession."

Then he left.

"Battle for the bed?" Anders echoed. Gideon gestured to the truckle.

"That one is easy to solve," Anders declared. "I shall have it. I am afraid you two will just have to share." And with that, he pulled the truckle closer to the hearth. "But I would have a care sharing with that man, my friend, he seems the kind who might find sleep an unwilling companion, and his dreams ones he would prefer to avoid. I have seen it before in men who have such haunted eyes and over-fast responses. Confused by dreams, they may imagine assault where none is intended."

It wasn't a comfortable thought and when, sometime later, Danny returned, Gideon still hadn't got to sleep even though Anders was deep in slumber.

"You intimidated him?" Danny asked, speaking softly and jerking a thumb at the sleeping Anders.

"No. He chose it for himself."

"Lucky man. What it is to have a choice. Myself, I am as one drawn out on tenterhooks and beaten with hammers."

"You have been given orders you dislike?" Gideon guessed, sitting up.

"Yes. Indeed, and most certainly so. I have been given orders that I find make me wish to scrub my skin and shrive my soul. 'Go, Danny,' he said, 'wallow in filth and ordure, but keep smelling of roses whilst you do so.' A simple enough thing." He looked suddenly exhausted and there was something raw at the edge of his expression that Gideon couldn't recognise but felt was the sign of a profoundly troubled man. Then Danny grinned again and picked up the cards. "Let's play then for who has the side of the bed closest to the fire."

Gideon wanted to say he didn't mind either way, but somehow, he knew the game was nothing to do with the bed. It was to do with something Gideon struggled to understand but could perceive—an inner wound for which there was no true salve but only temporary easing. So, from compassion, he consented and spent half the night learning to play Primero and being beaten mercilessly at Piquet.

By the time he got to sleep he had also learned that Danny had started out in life as the son of a wealthy merchant in Manchester—"Christ, you would think fustian was the Holy Grail itself the way his eyes lit up at the word. I had to get out before I turned the same"—and how to curse in five unusual European languages. Gideon's last conscious thought of the night was that he did, after all, recognise that drawn look Danny had worn on his return from Philip Lord. It was fear.

II

Gideon woke to the sound of Danny and Anders becoming acquainted. They were discussing the functioning of Danny's bowels and Gideon wondered if he should pretend to be asleep a bit longer. But even as the thought crossed his mind Danny broke off mid-sentence and laughed.

"We are embarrassing Gideon. Perhaps we should conclude this some other time."

"Indeed so," Anders agreed. "However, you should remember it is care, and not fine stables, makes a good horse. If you want your body to behave well, you should treat it well."

"Chance would be a fine thing," Danny sounded rueful. "My body has to take what it can get when it can get it and be happy."

Gideon got up and dressed as the other two were still

talking. It occurred to him that not since his student days had he shared accommodation in such a way. In London, he had enjoyed his own rooms, with his own servant.

"It is good to meet you, Danny," Anders was saying. "I must to my duties and I will leave you to yours. Find me later if you need me—and you too Gideon, my friend."

Gideon looked up from putting on his boots to nod in acknowledgement.

"What a very, very, *very* nice man," Danny observed some moments after the door had closed. "And a few more verys. I can see why you were so tender of his sleeping needs." He had been sitting on the far side of the bed in shirt and breeches, but now rose and stretched. "I, too, should be working, but I am curious, what tasks does a lawyer have in this company?"

There was something in the way he asked that made Gideon sure it was more than a casual question. Lord had implied Danny could be trusted, but he still hesitated to offer full confidence as to why he believed he was kept on.

"I am an overqualified copyist and a verifier of contracts, mostly. Though I think I might also be kept as a mark of our commander's prestige like the jewels on his clothing. He paraded me as such when we had visitors here. But, in part, it is for my protection also. He has enemies whom I inadvertently offended by not being killed at his hands when we met. As I said before, it is a long story."

"Now that sounds like a good tale to go with some fine ale one day," Danny said, pulling on his doublet and working the buttons and points. "I'll have to hope we have the opportunity." He finished his fastenings then picked up and pushed his hat onto his head. "But for now, I have a moat to extend, a possible hornwork to design and locate, gun carriages to assemble and any number of calculations on fields of fire, elevations and other such to compute." He paused by the door. "I shall leave you to your lawyering and suggest you see if any specific services might be required of you today."

From which Gideon understood he was to seek out Philip Lord first thing. Then Danny was gone. It was strange, therefore, when a short time after, as Gideon left the room and looked along the passageway, he saw the door to Mags' room being closed by the omnipresent Aleksandrov on the unmistakable figure of Danny Bristow.

Lord wasn't hard to find. It seemed the newly dug moat was ready to be filled and he was supervising the last cutting. But from the voluble curses that reached his ears as he neared the group of men working there, Gideon decided there had to be a problem. Lord looked up at his approach.

"Just what we do not need, *un homme de loi*. I regret this obstruction is not of the variety a man of law can assist with. *Mais*, have you, by chance, seen *Capitaine* Bristow?"

Had there been less mockery in his voice, Gideon might have been more wary, but that stung.

"I believe he is with the graf."

Something shifted in Lord's gaze at that.

"Indeed?" He sounded cold. "Then you may go and request the graf to spare me *Capitaine* Bristow's presence so he can advise us upon the best placement and quantities of powder to remove the footing of this stonework which is preventing us from enlarging the moat."

Gideon's jaw clenched.

"Of course," he said and turned away.

"Come back with him," Lord added. "You will find this educational."

Danny was walking out of the house wearing a thoughtful expression when Gideon encountered him. But his face lit up like a schoolboy being offered a bag of apples when he heard what was required. He clapped his hands and rubbed them together in glee, grinning.

"This is what makes it all worthwhile."

Word must have spread that something was going to happen because the group of men around the moat had doubled in size by the time Gideon and Danny got there. For once, Simon Muir was taking an interest in the work being undertaken and most of the children from Lord's company had found themselves a place at a safe distance.

Danny commanded the scene like an actor on the stage, or a pagan priest performing a ritual invocation. He spent a few minutes studying the stone and then made some brief calculations on paper before asking for two cracks to be made deeper with a hammer drill. He insisted on testing the quality of the powder, running it through his fingers and even tasting it, before making up packages from oiled linen himself and setting them in the deepened cracks.

Through it all, Lord looked on, leaning on the wall, arms crossed, like a tolerant uncle indulging a favoured nephew.

"You might want to get people to stand back, sir, if you would be so kind," Danny said from the trench.

THE TRAITOR'S APPRENTICE

Lord straightened up.

"*Mes hommes, battre en retraite!*"

Gideon joined the scramble to get a decent view of what would happen from a safer distance. Lord stayed by the ditch, holding a length of lit match ready in his hand, which he passed to Danny, now visible only as a hat below the sides of the excavation. And it was Lord who reached down a hand to speed Danny's ascent up the short ladder and pushed him, running, away from the trench.

The explosions, when they came, were a lot less impressive than Gideon had expected. A series of loud sounds, with mud, clay and stone erupting in flashes of flame and smoke. When that cleared Lord, peered into the newly cut channel.

"Where is the water, Captain Bristow? There is no water. Your careful explosions have not worked."

Danny, who had flattened himself when the first of the charges went off, got to his feet and stared at the empty trench. Gideon moved forward to look, and sure enough, the wall of mud and rock was still there.

A low murmur went through those who had come to see, with a mixture of disappointment and disbelief.

"Perhaps Captain Bristow is not so skilled as he has led us to believe," Muir's voice lifted above the rest.

Danny said nothing. He stared at the place where the explosions had been, a slight frown on his face.

Then a small trickle of water began running through the clay from the remains of the old foundations. As Gideon watched, the trickle grew in strength. Water seemed to spring in miniature rivulets from other places in the bank. A moment later the whole bank collapsed, earth and stone together and water rushed along the trench. A ragged cheer went up. Lord was banging Danny on the back and wearing a grin almost as broad as Danny himself was.

It took a few minutes for the celebratory mood to fade, Lord allowed it time, talking to those whose hard labour had dug the moat extension, giving praise and congratulations. Then he lifted a hand and his voice at the same time.

"Gentlemen, we still have plenty of work that we need to do. Let us get to it."

Like frost on a spring morning, those who had gathered dispersed, and Lord gestured Gideon over with a beckoning hand to where he was still talking with Danny. They were far enough from the rest not to be overheard.

"...the graf intends to lead some of the patrols himself," Danny was saying. "He wanted me to ride with him."

"Patrols or reconnaissance?" Lord's French accent had vanished.

Danny shrugged. "A bit of both is my guess. I'm sure I'll find out."

"And the graf had not intended to tell me? Or…?"

"He told me to inform you. He says he will choose the men himself."

Lord was looking thoughtful.

"*And they that are with him are called, and chosen, and faithful.* You are one of the chosen. How do you feel about that?"

Danny considered.

"I'll be glad to take a look around. I'm interested to see what passes for fortifications around here. What I saw on the way left me weeping into my beard." He then broke into a grin. "I will draw up your designs between times. You don't need me measuring every inch and degree of the excavations and constructions as they are done, I'm sure."

"*My* designs?"

"That was how the graf described them. He seemed confident I would have time for both tasks."

Lord clapped him on the shoulder. "I am sure you will. As I recall it was you who once told me that sleep serves no end save the passing of nighttime hours more quickly."

Danny nodded and looked pleased. "I did say that didn't I? I can be quite the philosopher sometimes. I must work on it."

He stepped back and gave a deep bow to Lord and a much slighter one but with an extension of his previous grin to Gideon before striding off in the direction of the stableyard.

"I wanted to thank you for the digest you provided me with yesterday," Lord said when they were alone. "You have a good grasp of what matters in world events and what is mere gossip. *And certainly, the more a man drinketh of the world, the more it intoxicateth.* I will have more use for you with that in the future." He started walking along the new moat, so Gideon had to walk with him. "How goes your hunt for our murderer?"

It took little time for Gideon to tell what he had learned from Zahara and his own thoughts and observations regarding Simon Muir. "But you suspect Muir already," he concluded. "You warned me against him yesterday."

Lord's lips drew into a tight line.

"Perhaps. But my warning was because Shiraz told me

Muir has been taking a lot of interest in you."

Gideon drew a breath. It was an unpleasant sensation to feel he was being watched and studied.

"That could be because he recognises me—or thinks he does. We are both London-Scots."

"Ask him."

"That would mean—"

"He has been recruited to our company. Your true name will not remain hidden from him for long. He probably already knows." Lord stopped and prodded at the bank of the moat with his heel as if it had offended him. Then he looked up at Gideon with his disconcerting, brilliant gaze. "Danny likes you. If you are wise, you will nurture that into friendship."

Gideon wondered what to say to such a comment, but before he could think of a suitable reply Lord had looked away and was walking off towards the fortifications. He turned, French persona restored.

"Let me know if you discover anything more, Monsieur Fox."

Dismissed, Gideon made a brief bow and was halfway back to the house when a group of eight armed, armoured and mounted men led by Mags and including both Aleksandrov and Danny Bristow, rode past him. Gideon stood still as they went by then watched as they cantered along the track that led up to the road.

"Mr *Lennox*? Gideon Lennox"

Gideon turned, unsurprised to see Simon Muir.

"I thought I recognised you," Muir said, looking pleased. "You are Minister Lennox's son?"

There was no point denying it. It wasn't too surprising that Muir would know him, even if it was not mutual, considering the place Gideon's father had held in their community. Even now Gideon only had to close his eyes to see his father preaching hellfire and telling his congregation to fear the wrath of God. It had been his mother, thirty years her husband's junior, whose more gentle faith had taught Gideon to believe in a God who loved the world and forgave it.

"I am," he acknowledged. "But here they call me Fox. Names seem to change amongst mercenaries sometimes."

Muir nodded.

"Names are earned," he agreed. "I find myself curious, how did you wind up with the graf's men?"

It echoed the question Danny Bristow had asked but felt as if it came from a very different place. Gideon offered the same answer.

"It's a long story. I'm sure you will hear it one day if you decide to remain with the company."

"I am sure I will, from you—or others." He made it sound like a threat.

They had gained the courtyard by then and Gideon saw Anders walking across it to his crude consulting room. Anders must have caught something in Gideon's look because he glanced at Muir and then changed direction to intercept them.

"Mr Muir," he said, after giving Gideon a brief nod of greeting and a look that held something more. "I was hoping I might take a moment of your time."

Muir, compelled by politeness to honour the request, let Anders draw him away. Freed, Gideon was almost running as he went into the house. He nearly bumped into Zahara just inside the door. The emotional impact was as sharp as if he had. For a moment he could neither think nor breathe.

She smiled and gave a small curtsey.

"Mr Fox, I was just coming to find you. Lady Belamy would be most grateful if you were willing to allow her to consult you regarding a legal matter."

Wondering at that, Gideon followed Zahara upstairs to the rooms occupied by the baroness and waited as she tapped on the door and went inside. Zahara returned a minute later and showed Gideon into the room.

It was light and airy with a soft carpet over some of the floor, light wood wainscotting and apricot-coloured walls, matching the embroidered curtains held back from the windows by heavy loops. As well as a tall linen chest, there was an elegant writing desk in one corner, and cushioned chairs one of which supported a sewing basket and on another was curled a small tabby cat.

Elizabeth Belamy, herself small and brown-haired, was sitting in the chair beside the cat, wearing a neat russet gown with a wide lace-edged collar over her shoulders. Her hair was put up in a simple style. She rose as he entered, and Gideon adopted his most gracious manner for dealing with wealthy clients and made an appropriate bow.

"I apologise for summoning you so peremptorily, Mr Fox, but I find myself in need of legal advice and Sara—" she broke off and smiled at Zahara with evident fondness. "Sara tells me you can offer such. It concerns a matter of inheritance." She sat again and then gestured to a chair. "Please, be seated."

Gideon sank onto the chair as directed.

"If I can be of any assistance, I am happy to be so, Lady Belamy. Was there a document you wished me to examine?"

She shook her head.

THE TRAITOR'S APPRENTICE

"I don't think so. I wish to know if there is any way I can ensure Wrathby passes in the male line should anything happen to my son?"

Gideon hesitated, trying to think what might be behind the request.

"I would need to review the terms of your husband's will to be able to provide you with an answer."

"The terms are those his father wished. That Wrathby would go to Charles and his son after him."

"What is your concern here, my lady?"

She drew a breath and reached out a hand to stroke the cat beside her.

"That were anything to happen to my son, then the Belamy name will be lost to Wrathby. My husband was always so proud that there have been Belamy's here for five hundred years."

"There is another male heir?"

"To the name, yes. Richard, my husband's cousin. But Wrathby would not go to him. The baronry is an ancient one, created by writ. It is inherited in the female line should there be no male heir. Alice is the heiress of Wrathby."

For some unaccountable reason, Gideon felt a shiver pass over his skin as she spoke. He cleared his throat.

"I will need to look at the will to be able to answer you, but I should say I would doubt that there is a way to change that without great legal difficulty, if at all. But surely, Wrathby is secure in your hands until your son comes of age?"

"There have been unexplained deaths in the house. Accidents," she said. "I fear for my son. I try to protect him. I have him watched all the time. But there is no guard against illness or accident."

With a shock of surprise Gideon saw tears well up in her eyes—tears she blinked away.

"You believe your son, the baron, is in some kind of danger?"

"Mr Fox, I do not believe in the Curse of Wrathby, but I do believe that such tales carry with them a kind of impetus. That, say, should my son fall ill, there would be an expectation of his demise so he might not be treated as if he were expected to survive."

"Dr Jensen would never—"

"Yes." She gave Gideon a small smile. "You see, that is why I am so pleased to have him here. To have Sara, Monsieur Blanchard, the graf and all his men, you included, here at Wrathby. It is as if the defences that are being built around the house are being built around my son, defences against superstition and the expectation that he will soon die."

Gideon wondered if that was any less of a superstition than a belief in the curse might be, but perhaps if it brought her comfort...

"Would you show me the will?"

She gestured to the writing desk. "Sara? Would you please find the document I was reading earlier so Mr Fox can see it?"

Zahara moved to the writing desk and, opening the doors, took out a document which she laid on the desk, before stepping back so Gideon could see it.

It wasn't hard to find the relevant passages and check through some addendums. Gideon studied it for any loopholes that might offer Elizabeth Belamy the way out she wanted, even hoping for some careless wording, but after prolonged scrutiny, he straightened up.

"I regret, my lady, that there is no clear legal path for

what you wish."

"There might be one though—even if it is less clear?"

Gideon found it hard to meet her demanding gaze. There were, of course, the tricks and trims that his colleagues played with to line their own pockets and hold scant hope out to their clients and maybe one time in twenty succeed in somehow proving the will was invalid through some technicality or manufactured falsehoods.

"None with which *I* could assist you," he said.

She studied his face, frowning as if trying to understand what was behind his words. Then she did and her lips tightened. She released his gaze and looked at her hands now folded together on her lap.

"I see."

"I'm sorry, my lady," Gideon said, and he was. Zahara looked between them and then moved past Gideon, her words spoken to him as she did so were no louder than her breath.

"Ask about her husband."

Zahara continued her way across the room to reach Lady Belamy and crouched beside her, one arm reaching around her slight shoulders in comfort.

Gideon's every instinct was to withdraw. He had performed the task he had been asked and given his answer. But he trusted Zahara's instincts more at that moment.

"May I ask what happened to your husband? He died recently?"

A bit to his surprise she answered without any hesitation.

"Yes. It was in the late spring. Alice's husband had died in March, and she had some problems sorting his affairs, so Charles went to London to help her." She broke off as her words seemed to catch on her breath. "He was only to have been gone ten days, he did not want to leave me as I was with child and my time was drawing nigh, but I had been assured there was close to another month at least and Alice sounded so desperate in her letter, pleading for his help."

Gideon regretted asking now, her distress was so evident. He would have said so, but a fierce look from Zahara silenced him.

"Charlie was born five days after he left. The midwife said he was somewhat early, but he was strong and a good size despite that, and God blessed me in making his arrival not too hard to endure. I sent word to London the next day, but the following evening a messenger arrived. There had been an accident on the river when Charles was travelling. The river around the bridge, I understand, can be perilous and he somehow wound up in the water." She broke off and drew a steadying breath. "When they found him, he had hit his head and drowned. It is so sad as it could have been no more than an hour or two after Charlie was born. They told me it was after dark when he took to the river and Charlie had been born in the afternoon. They were in this world together for such a short time."

Gideon drew a sharp breath. He could see the grief was getting beyond Lady Belamy's power to control, but in her words he had the answer to this mystery. He was sure now that he knew who had killed Ruth Whitaker and Sir Arthur and why it was done. But proving it in any way which would allow the law to act or sway a jury was something he couldn't yet see how to do, so he said nothing of that. Instead, he spoke the needed polite, sincere and compassionate words, then leaving Elizabeth Belamy in the comforting embrace of Zahara, took his leave.

Chapter Ten

I

The weather had changed that morning bringing heavy rain and a brisk, blustery breeze from the north which was attempting to pluck his hat from his head as Gideon left the house.

He was uncertain now of how to proceed. Of course, he had to take what he knew—what he thought he knew—to Philip Lord as instructed, but he couldn't support any of it with more than conjecture. There was nothing he could lay before a court, or even before Elizabeth Belamy herself, only a sick certainty in his stomach and a pile of possible speculation. The fact that each fitted to each like hand to glove still didn't mean that it amounted to anything more than surmise.

He found Lord, freed from his French persona, in the building beyond the stables where he had eaten breakfast the previous day. There was a guard on the door who nodded him through. The room seemed to have been turned into some kind of courtroom with about twenty of the company gathered there, two guarded and with hands bound. Philip Lord, standing at one end, was dispensing rapid and ruthless judgement in what struck Gideon as a grotesque parody of a magistrate. Here there was no law except the whim and invention of the man applying his own creative version of justice.

THE TRAITOR'S APPRENTICE

"You took the shirt without permission. Since you lack the means to purchase it, your pay will be docked for the cost of the shirt twice over and the monies paid to Mistress Rider."

"You were both fighting, I don't care who started it. It seems obvious that the two of you must have more energy to spare than you are using to work for me. Double shifts in the excavations for the pair of you for the next week."

"No one lays a hand on any woman in this company unless she allows it. Be grateful she slipped your grasp before you went far enough to forfeit your life. Ten lashes and you will have no pay for the next three months."

At which point, as the offender was being taken outside by Jupp and one of the other men, Lord caught sight of Gideon.

"The law of the Lord is perfect, converting the soul: the testimony of the Lord is sure, making wise the simple. The statutes of the Lord are right, rejoicing the heart: the commandment of the Lord is pure, enlightening the eyes. I assume you have some business here, Mr Fox?"

As always, Gideon felt sharp indignation at the way Lord made light of scripture and had to bite his tongue on a retort.

"I am here at your command, sir," he said instead.

"I regret," Lord said, "I am occupied, so unless whatever you have to report endangers life or our security, it will have to wait."

Gideon decided he had no wish to witness any more of this handing down of wild justice, like a farce playing out under the thin veneer of legitimacy.

"It can wait," he said. "Sir."

"I shall send for you as soon as I may." Gideon dismissed, Lord turned his attention to the next man awaiting his verdict.

Gideon walked back across the stableyard. The rain was being blown into his face and he used that as an excuse to put his head down and ignore the fact that there was a man tied where Legrand had once been. But his attempt at avoidance failed when Jupp called over asking him to tell Anders he would be needed. Feeling a tightness in his stomach, he nodded acknowledgement.

Anders was in his consulting room. One of the household servants was scuttling out at speed as Gideon reached it. He bobbed a bow at Gideon and ran off clutching a remedy bottle in one hand. Keen to get out of the rain himself, Gideon went inside without waiting for an invitation to do so. Anders greeted him warmly.

"You need me to rewrap your ankle?"

"That wasn't why I came. I came to tell you that Roger Jupp asked for you to attend a flogging—and to thank you for distracting Muir earlier."

Anders made no move to get up.

"You are most welcome, my friend, and I am already under orders from our patron to attend on him for that purpose you mentioned, but only after I have completed my work here for the morning. I think he would not be pleased were I to arrive early. I have time to examine your ankle. Sit."

Gideon sat and submitted to the examination and answered questions about its mobility and what pain it was still giving him. He was wondering if he should share his thoughts and concerns about the murder when

Anders spoke.

"What do you make of our new companion?"

"Daniel Bristow?" Gideon wondered how to answer. He was still uncertain whether the real Danny Bristow was the man with whom he had spent an entertaining night playing cards, the man who had seemed unperturbed by the death of Alonso de Torres, the man who had placed explosive charges with such technical precision, or the man who had gone to speak with Mags. "He appears to be something of a force of nature. Lord seems to think I should cultivate his friendship."

Anders nodded and having finished with Gideon's ankle, began to pack things away in his bag.

"I think he is someone who would make a good friend and a bad enemy. Myself, I shall work to be friendly, but not a friend. Such men demand blood for their friendships. The problem is," Anders concluded, thoughtfully, "if you live with wolves, you must learn to howl."

"I am not sure about Danny Bristow, but I don't think I would want to be a friend of Philip Lord," Gideon said.

"Which is my view also," Anders agreed, getting to his feet and collecting his bag. "However, you might well want to bear in mind that Mr Bristow does not feel the same way. I think he considers himself a friend of Philip Lord."

"I had the impression it was mutual," Gideon said.

Anders looked thoughtful. "Perhaps. But I would not be too sure. I sometimes wonder if our patron is a man who is capable of true friendship. After all, to have true friendship means admitting another as your equal." He put an enveloping cloak over his shoulders to keep off the rain then opened the door and stood aside to allow

Gideon to leave before following him out. "Your ankle is nearly mended, but you should try to rest it a bit more. I hope to see you at dinner."

It was that residual weakness of his ankle which meant Gideon narrowly avoided disaster as he hurried back into the house. It gave way, his foot turning a little on a wet cobblestone, so he had to throw out an arm to catch himself against the wall. At that same moment something impacted with the sound of a shot on the cobbles less than a hand's span away, where he would have been had his ankle not pained him.

Stepping back and away from the building, he stared at the missile and realised it was a piece of old stonework, twice the size of his fist. He looked up at the tower. Perhaps if it had been loosened by Jupp when he rested his gun's long barrel on the wall and then been brought down by the weather. Offering a brief prayer of thanks that he had been half a pace to the side when it landed, he went into the house and out of the rain.

He'd hoped to find William Irving in the library, thinking it possible that Sir Arthur might have said something to him which could cast some faint light on what he had seen or discovered that made him the victim of murder. But the room was empty. This time the bookshelf was too inviting and, unable to resist the opportunity, he went over to investigate the books. He had only intended to do so for a few minutes, but he was still there, lost in a copy of Roger Ascham's *Toxophilus* when he received a summons from Lord and realised the rest of the household was already called to dinner.

So, instead of joining Anders in the dining hall, he found himself knocking on the door to Lord's room and being invited in with a terse French command.

THE TRAITOR'S APPRENTICE

Lord was alone and eating as he worked, reading through what appeared to be a long, itemised list. Without looking up from it, he gestured to Gideon to help himself to the dishes provided.

"You will forgive me, I hope, for denying you a proper meal. I have a lot to do and little time to complete it."

"But you had time to hold a mock court."

Lord put down the paper he had been reading through and gave Gideon his undivided attention.

"There was nothing in it of mockery," he said. "Perhaps you should ask those who received justice if they thought it so?"

"And am I subject to your 'justice' also?"

The uncomfortable gaze held his own.

"If you steal from one of my men, touch one of my women or try to kill someone in my company, then yes, you will be."

Gideon felt a stab of guilt. The memory of that one moment when he was with Zahara in the still room was sharp in his mind. He looked away.

"I suppose it is part of the contract," he said.

"No. It is part of how I choose to command. An essential part, in that it provides restitution to those who are wronged, which I thought was the purpose of any court of law. I think I'm as well qualified to tell right from wrong as a justice of the peace, many of whom have no more legal training than one of their hunting dogs. Unlike such men, I am not driven by favouritism, malice, greed or lust for power." He stopped talking and shook his head, then went on, tone changed. "I already told you that you must leave the running of the company to me. It is not something I am willing to rehearse again and again with you each time something occurs which offends your sensibilities."

"If I see—"

"Then you keep your opinion to yourself. It is not a matter that concerns you or on which you can have an informed opinion and it is extremely galling to have to keep saying so."

Gideon closed his mouth hard on the retort he wanted to make.

"Despite that," Lord went on, "I am glad you survived the attempt on your life earlier."

Gideon's mouth opened again in a gasp.

"What are you talking about?"

"Shiraz told me someone tried to drop a lump of masonry on your head from the tower."

Lord moved to the table where the food had been placed and poured a goblet of wine, before taking it over to Gideon.

"Drink this, you look pale."

Gideon took the cup but held it in fingers grown nerveless and as Lord went on talking his voice seemed to come from a great distance.

"Shiraz was too far away to see much more than a shadowy outline against the dark of the clouds and by the time he got to the tower whoever it was had made their escape." Then: "For God's sake sit down and drink, man, before you fall."

Lord must have guided him to the chair by the portable desk because Gideon had no conscious memory of reaching it. In his mind, repeating, again and again, was the moment he heard the sharp report of the stone hitting the cobbles. He managed to take a mouthful of the wine and the room came back into focus, Lord in the foreground looking down at him with a frown of concern. Drawing a steadying breath and then another, Gideon found thought and speech restored to him.

"Someone tried to kill me?"

"I believe I warned you several times that you could expect to become a target for our murderer. I assume that whatever you have learned has become apparent to whomever it affects—or they fear you know something. Had the attempt been successful I am sure the dreaded Curse of Wrathby would have been blamed, and had Shiraz not witnessed what he did there would have been none to say otherwise." Lord straightened up and crossed back to the table. "It would put me to no small inconvenience to have to recruit another lawyer and after what happened to Sir Arthur, I am reluctant to allow the killer any further opportunity with poison. I find I require your clerking to my dictation as I eat. You will take all your meals here in my room henceforth until this matter is resolved." He paused then to pick up his own cup. "I am hoping you may have some news towards that?"

Gideon gathered his scattered wits and nodded.

"I believe I know who the murderer is and why he has been killing, but I have nothing of proof, and it could still be that I am mistaken."

As he spoke, Lord poured a cup of wine for himself and drank some of it before replying.

"Tell me your who and your why, and your reasoning and let us see if I concur."

Gideon drew a breath.

"The 'who' is Simon Muir. The 'why' is because he wants Wrathby and the—"

"Muir?" Lord's voice was sharp. "I could see him as the tool of another, but I can see no way Muir might secure Wrathby to himself." He looked as if he was going to say more, then gestured at Gideon with the hand that held the cup. "But you promised me your reasoning and I should hear that first. *The fisher hath a bait deceiving fish, the fowler hath a net deceiving fowls* and what, pray, does Muir have?"

"He has the love of Alice Franklyn—and a like passion for her in return. But he knows she wouldn't marry without money, so he works to get that for her." Gideon sat up, warming to his theme, now more confident in what had seemed mere conjecture. "I believe he began in London. The last baron went there to assist his sister in organising her affairs following the death of her husband. I know nothing of how Mr Franklyn died, although it is even possible that he was the first of Muir's victims, but the baron was drowned following a boating accident after dark."

"An accident that you believe was no accident, I assume?"

"It was a convenient accident for Muir if so. He would have known he had little time to act as the baron's wife was with child. It would have been a great temptation for him. If the present baron had been born three weeks later at the time expected, then Alice Franklyn would have inherited Wrathby. Even if he had been born three hours later, indeed. The key point here is that an unborn child has no right of inheritance. Alice would have gained the wealth and position she craved. She would then be free to bestow her heart as she willed. Muir thought where that would be was in no doubt."

Lord was frowning.

"He finds he has failed because of the early birth, then he brings Alice to Wrathby, you believe, and stays to finish the task to which he has set himself." Lord tapped the side of his cup with a finger in thought. "But surely we would be looking at a case of infanticide if so, not of a housekeeper and a house guest?"

"What would be most important would be for the child's death to appear also as an accident—the Curse of Wrathby striking the firstborn son as everyone here half expects that it will."

"He seems a hale and hearty infant to me," Lord said. "I had the dubious pleasure of being presented to his lordship and can attest he has a fine set of lungs and even the first showing of a tooth."

"I don't think a curse takes account of such things," Gideon said, irritated by the evident lack of concern in Lord's voice.

Lord laughed.

"I don't suppose one would," he agreed. "Explain the two murders to me then."

"Muir has limited access to the child. We know Ruth Whitaker was venal and not very compassionate as a human being. It might well have seemed to Muir she would be willing to do the deed for a price. If she refused him, he would have had to ensure she couldn't speak of it to any other. Or maybe she even accepted then changed her mind."

Lord nodded, but more in acknowledgement than agreement. "And Cochrane?"

"He must have witnessed something, or overheard, or guessed. He told Lady Grace that he had another source of finance—a source of which he was so certain that he stepped back from a desperate, friendship-ruining move. To me, that would suggest blackmail, on the promise of payment once Wrathby was secured, and that would be something Muir would have no tolerance for. After all, by that time if I am right, he had killed two, maybe three, people already in his planned ascent to become Wrathby's lord. I doubt he will stop at anything now."

Lord nodded again, this time with more sense of acceptance in the gesture.

"I think I'll have Mr Muir watched at all times. Since he believes he has joined the company I will endeavour to keep him under my eye as much as possible. That way we can ensure there are no more murders. If he is unaware he is being watched, he may even betray himself by his actions. And you," Lord paused. "I think you need to cease your role in this. You have done well to bring it this far, but Muir is trained to arms and you, whilst learning fast, are not."

"Someone needs to warn Lady Belamy that there is a real threat to her infant son," Gideon pointed out.

"I don't think that will help matters." Lord sounded adamant. "I have no wish to promote any kind of maternal panic. Zahara can arrange for some of our women to be always about the child, assisting the nursemaid." He picked up an apple from the food on offer and polished it on his doublet. "Stay here. Eat. I need to make some arrangements." He bit into the apple and left the room.

From then on Gideon found his freedom and activities curtailed. It wasn't just his mealtimes that had to be spent in Philip Lord's chambers. There seemed to be a sudden, unaccountable amount of work which Lord required of him that involved sitting at the portable desk in Lord's room. He wasn't fooled though. These were tasks he was being set so Lord had an excuse to keep him out of Muir's way.

Gideon wondered how long that was meant to go on.

II

The work the earl had demanded of him was more fitting for a usurer than a soldier, Nick decided.

At least it was not slow.

Once the reason for his presence had been made clear, whether he was received with relief, delight, chilly politeness or pathetic eagerness to please, there was always a desire to see him leave as soon as possible. They made promises and provided men and payment. In return, Nick reassured them that the earl would be coming to their succour and that their offerings would speed that process.

The money he dispatched under guard to Newcastle, the men he added to his escort and soon had close to a hundred even after sending thirty north with the coin and plate. There was no resistance, and on his second day out he decided to divide his force to cover the ground more quickly. He sent half the men with his lieutenant, Robert Cummings, who was a distant relative by marriage to the earl.

Cummings made no secret that he resented serving under a captain five years his junior and that, despite Nick's higher social status, he believed it should have been himself promoted and entrusted with this task. Nick got the impression many of the men with them thought as much too. Cummings was cheered when Nick told him that he was being given an independent command. Taking half the list and the troop's quartermaster, they agreed on a rendezvous two days hence, by which time the entire list should have been substantially completed.

A couple of hours after they split up Nick's force encountered a body of horsemen ahead of them on the road. It appeared to be a small lightly armed unit and if they kept to their path they would ride into Nick's larger force. There was nothing to say which side they might support so Nick had his men make ready. He hoped this would be a Parliamentarian force. The thought of returning to Newcastle with prisoners and word of a successful skirmish was one to savour.

The smaller troop must have been aware of them but did not attempt to avoid, evade or flee. It continued in good order and stopped in hailing distance. Puzzled, Nick halted his troop and waited.

Two men rode forward to a point halfway between the two forces. Both were well dressed. One was well groomed, the other with a small explosion of tawny hair escaping from under his hat.

"It's yourself then, sir," the well-groomed man called.

Nick blinked. It was a voice he had last heard having been dragged to safety through a wood not far from Howe after escaping from a failed ambush. An ambush which should have led to the end of Philip Lord but had, instead, resulted in the heavy loss of Howe's manpower.

"Mags?" he called back. "What happened to you?"

Mags took off his hat to show the thin line of puckered flesh where hair no longer grew and made a small bow. "May I suggest we step aside a little, sir? I promise it will be to your advantage."

Nick hesitated. His force outnumbered this small troop five to one and Mags had saved his life.

Twice.

He issued brief orders to the cornet he had kept with

him, then rode forwards to meet the two horsemen. Close to, he was amazed by Mags' transformation. The last time they had met he had been dressed worse than the least of Nick's own soldiers. Now he wore a doublet with silver points.

"It is good to see you, sir," Mags said and smiled, gesturing to the man mounted beside him. "This is Daniel Bristow, he's a solid man, someone you can count on."

The man with Mags made a brief bow, as much as he could on horseback, doffing his hat.

"And this," Mags went on, "is Nicholas Tempest, heir to Howe Hall."

Nick shook his head. "*Sir* Nicholas Tempest *of* Howe," he corrected. "My uncle has died. A tragic accident."

Mags' face showed nothing of grief.

"I'm sorry for your loss," he said.

"You will know that I am not."

"Sir Bartholomew was a difficult man to like." Mags shrugged, dismissing the topic. He gestured to the troop of horse behind Nick. "You're with Newcastle?"

"Of course. Who employs you now?"

Mags moved one of his legs, freeing his foot from the stirrup and pointed to it. "I still have the boots you gave me in place of pay, so I suppose I am still your man."

"But not in my troop?" Nick said, unsure where the conversation was leading.

"No. But only because I can serve you better where I am."

Nick found himself frowning.

"Where is that?"

"I'm with Philip Lord. He's in a house not far from

here, fortifying it against all comers. He thinks to stay there until spring."

Nick's fists clenched on his reins.

"What house?" he demanded.

Looking at the horsemen on the road behind Nick, Mags shook his head.

"No point saying. You'll not move them with those."

"Would be good shooting practice for Lord's men," the man Mags had introduced as Daniel Bristow observed. "Ordnance and earthworks can make a mess of horses and they don't look the kind who'd be happy to go in on foot."

Nick glanced at him, wondering if he was being insulting or ignorant. He looked back to Mags and made a brief nod towards Bristow.

"And whose man is he?"

"Mine," Mags said.

Bristow inclined his head and smiled. He looked ignorant. Too much of a fool to offer a deliberate insult with his open freckled face and the kind of beard that a boy in his teens might grow. Dismissing the man as irrelevant, Nick returned to the point that mattered.

"And if you're with Lord, why is he still alive? It can't be beyond your wit to find a way to kill him?"

"If it were that simple then it would've been done already, I promise you. Besides," Mags said, his tone shifting to something more conspiratorial, "I plan to bring you more than the head of Philip Lord. If we do things as I say I will bring you his men as well. Loyal and ready to fight."

Beside Mags, Daniel Bristow gave a sudden impish grin. "Now that would bring you favour with King Charles. Maybe more than Newcastle has for all his wealth."

"Or whoever you chose to take them to," Mags said.

Nick seized his meaning and bridled.

"Are you suggesting for a moment that I would be anything other than loyal to the king?"

Mags held up a placating hand.

"No one would ever doubt your commitment to the king and his cause, sir. But sometimes such loyalty can be best served in strange ways."

It was the kind of enigmatic speech Nick loathed. He had endured too much of it from his youth onwards. Hinting at secrets but never telling them.

"As strange as the way you say you serve me?" he snapped.

Mags didn't even look uncomfortable.

"It is not so strange when you think of the prize."

"The prize?" That brought Nick up short. "You mean an end to Philip Lord?"

"Oh, that would be just the start of it." Mags lowered his voice even though they were out of earshot for either group of horsemen. "These are troubled times, sir. That means there is an opportunity for a man of vision to rise—if he has the means, the men and the determination. As I see it, at the least the Lordship of Howe could be raised to an Earldom or more. The Lord of Howe could become one of the most powerful men in the country. These men would be the keenest bladed sword in the hand of whichever side you chose to bestow it. They could win this war and bring their commander place and power."

It was a tempting vision and sounded as if Mags had put some thought into it.

"Is this a chance meeting?"

"Chance. And happy chance too," Mags assured him. I was thinking to send Danny here to Howe to get word to you to meet with me, but now we see that had I done so it would have been a long and wasted ride for him."

"What you offer would demand much of you. More than just a hard ride." He nodded at Mags' companion. "What would be in it for you and Daniel Bristow here?"

"Wenches, wine and wealth?" Bristow suggested, sounding hopeful.

Mags laughed. "You see, sir, we are modest men with modest needs. For me, it would mean much to be acknowledged in my heritage by your good self as your uncle and mine would never do."

Nick knew he must have turned pale as he could feel the breath halt part way from his lungs. There had been talk in his childhood, of course. An infant born out of wedlock to the long-dead Coupland heir, the older brother of Sir Bartholomew, and his Tempest bride-to-be. Nick's own aunt and uncle. It was the kind of thing any family of repute would suffer now and then—and seek to keep quiet.

"*You?* You are Francis Child?"

Nick was shaken to the core.

Mags bristled and his horse danced beneath him.

"Francis Tempest, by my mother's name or Coupland had my father's wishes been acknowledged." He breathed out a heavy sigh. "Is it too much to ask for what I offer—cousin?" Then he lifted a hand. "No. Save your answer. Think on it. I can see by your face that this is not easy for you to learn." He pulled his horse around and summoned Bristow to follow him with a jerk of his chin. Then he looked back at Nick once more. "You should stay well away from Wrathby in Ryedale until I send word by Danny here."

The two men rode away and rejoined their troop, then wheeling it around, took off at a brisk pace.

Nick watched them go then returned to his men, his mind full of new possibilities.

Chapter Eleven

I

Nick had just reassembled his expeditionary force having met up again with Cummings two days later on the Saturday evening when word from Mags reached him. Cummings had arrived a day early, with over a score of recruits and a good amount of plate and coin, reporting a string of rapid successes.

How the devil Bristow had known where to find Nick in the whole of Yorkshire was a mystery. He appeared like a sprite sometime after dawn at the drover's inn Nick had commandeered overnight to provide shelter and sustenance for himself and his troops. Nick had quartered Cummings and his men in a village nearby.

Bristow was escorted in as Nick was attacking the remains of a cold pigeon pie, which was all the host of the inn had been able to offer by way of breakfast. Nick was in a bad mood because Cummings had secured more contributions and better-equipped recruits than Nick himself. The lieutenant had been arrogant about that, so much so that Nick was beginning to regret having sent him off alone.

Scooping off his hat, Bristow made a low bow.

"I bring word from a mutual friend, Sir Nicholas, from his lips to your ears through my mouth."

Had he not been a messenger Nick would have ordered him beaten for his impertinence.

"For a discreet man, you talk a lot," Nick said,

wondering what qualities Mags found in Bristow that made him suitable for this task. As well as being impertinent, he seemed presumptuous and a little simple-minded.

Bristow glanced at the men who had just escorted him in and then looked back to Nick. "Being a discreet man, I would deliver this message privily as I was asked."

Nick gestured to the men and as they left there was a strange noise from Bristow's stomach.

"Sorry, sir. That food looks good, and I've not eaten since yesterday afternoon."

Nick continued demolishing the pie, wondering how much of the glory Cummings might try to claim for himself when they returned to Newcastle. He already had the support of Quartermaster Bayliss who, coming from the ranks, was the one the majority of the troop respected most. If he was not careful, Nick might find all credit for the success of this task would fall to Cummings and not himself.

"Never mind," Nick said. "What is it you were sent to tell me?"

There was an odd pause before he was answered.

"I was to tell you that Sir Thomas Fairfax will be riding with a handful of his men to Wrathby to ask the garrison there to disband under the terms of the treaty of neutrality for Yorkshire which his father has just negotiated, and if you were able to move quickly you could intercept and capture him. It would be something to please your earl, I think." Bristow's stomach made another horrific noise.

"On a Sunday? And why would the man appointed as Lieutenant-General of Horse for the Parliamentarian Army of the North be riding with such a small escort?"

It all sounded unlikely to Nick.

"In my experience, sir, war takes no account of the day of the week and my understanding is that Sir Thomas sees himself as a friend and protector of the lady of Wrathby and her infant son. Although I am sure he would also be keen to secure Wrathby to his cause as much as you would."

"Despite this treaty of neutrality?"

Bristow shrugged. "Any man who thinks that will last so long as it takes the ink to dry is either a fool or a hopeless idealist. I have a feeling that whatever his father may be, Sir Thomas is neither."

It was only then that Nick realised this man was doing something more than just repeating a message.

"So, Fairfax seeks to use this treaty to cozen Wrathby to disband its men so he may then use it himself?"

Bristow smiled.

"I would never have thought of that myself, but it could be you are correct sir. After all, to achieve such a thing it wouldn't work if he were to arrive at the gates in full force. That would make his intentions too clear. I think you have solved the mystery, sir."

By God, he was an irritating creature.

"And how have you come by this intelligence regarding the movements of Fairfax?"

Bristow pulled himself up to his full height, somewhat below Nick's own and pushed out his chest, an attempt at pride spoiled by the basso rumble which emanated from his midriff. "I am but the mouthpiece of the Graf von Elsterkrallen, sir."

It wasn't a name that meant anything to Nick. "The Graf von—?"

"Elsterkrallen," Bristow provided helpfully, then

lowered his voice. "I think you know him better as 'Mags', sir."

II

For two days Gideon had lived in Lord's room, its regular occupant only occasionally coming in to consult the plans for the fortification of Wrathby or add to them.

In the evenings, Gideon was banished to the room he shared with Anders and Danny. He at least found some warmth and company there. Danny had taught them a three-handed Spanish card game he called *L'Hombre*. To Danny's pained discomfort and Gideon's great amusement, Anders proved good at the game and held his own, winning almost as many of the hands as Danny himself.

"How do you do it? You're too lucky in the way the cards fall for you," Danny protested.

"Not at all," Anders assured him. "Luck will stop at the door and inquire whether prudence is within. It is that I take far fewer risks than you do. You are a far better player of cards but much more of a gambler than I am. If you were one step more prudent in your calls, you would defeat me all the time."

By the time they went to bed on the Saturday night, Danny had vowed he would never play cards with a Dane again.

The following day was the first Sunday in October and a week to the day since they had arrived at Wrathby. Gideon was permitted to leave the house to attend church. Anders went with him. Danny had ridden out well before dawn but for what purpose he did not confide.

The women of the family—except for Alice

Franklyn—and their household guests Irving and Muir, were seated in the front boxed pews. Space had been left in the row behind for those of Lord's officers who attended the service. Behind them were the household's servants and some villagers, but the back of the church was occupied by a large number of Lord's company. The entire Rider family was there, as were Jupp, Olsen and others who Gideon knew. Despite the nervous backward glances from those in front of them, they were decorously dressed, the men all with hats and the women without. Mags and his favourites were marked by their absence as was Lord himself.

Gideon was surprised to see Zahara sitting behind Elizabeth Belamy. When he realised he would be seated beside her, he stopped so fast that Anders would have collided with him had he not been agile enough to avoid doing so. Zahara gave him a brief, sweet, smile as he took his seat, but then she rose as Lady Belamy turned and spoke to her.

"Sara, I forgot my purse—the one I had prepared to give Reverend Glover for those in need in the village. Would you be kind enough, please...? And whilst you are there, make sure Alice is all right, she must be feeling quite unwell to miss Sunday worship."

Zahara bobbed a curtsy, gave a quiet reassurance and left the church. The service began, but Gideon found it hard to concentrate on prayer, knowing Zahara was going to return.

But she still hadn't come back when the sermon started. The Reverend Glover had chosen to write around a verse from Isaiah: *And he shall judge among the nations, and shall rebuke many people: and they shall beat their swords into ploughshares, and their*

THE TRAITOR'S APPRENTICE

spears into pruninghooks: nation shall not lift up sword against nation, neither shall they learn war any more.

There had been time enough for Zahara to walk to and from the house three times over by then and even Elizabeth Belamy had cast a glance back towards the door. An irrational uneasiness began to seep into Gideon's thoughts. Then the door opened, and he felt a brief rush of relief until, turning, he saw it was Philip Lord standing there.

"*Mes hommes, à moi.* To me, gentlemen. Monsieur Glover, I apologise, but regretfully the learning of war is still needed, or at least its practice by those of us who have already learned it."

His final words were drowned by the sudden eruption of men from the back of the church Gideon saw that whereas he and Anders had come unarmed to church, Lord's men had been wearing swords and pistols under coats, cloaks and cassaques as if expecting such a call to arms. Their women and children watched them go with brief words of farewell, but one or two closed their eyes as the men filed out, lips moving in silent prayer. Even Muir responded to the call and followed the others out.

Anders gripped Gideon's arm.

"We should go too."

Gideon followed Anders in the general exodus and tried to ignore the disapproving glares of the reverend and the villagers that bored holes in his spine.

By the time he got outside, Lord was already mounted and with his men forming up around him. Their horses must have been made ready before the service. Gideon heard Lord answering something Anders had asked.

"Your offer is appreciated, Jensen. But if there is a

need for a physician it will be on our return. I am not anticipating there will be too much of a problem."

"Where are you going?" Gideon demanded, expecting to be ignored.

Lord was already turning his horse but replied as he did so, his voice loud enough for all around to hear.

"Word is that Sir Thomas Fairfax is on the road to visit us, and I would speak to him first. I will be back shortly."

Then Lord moved away shouting brief orders. The whole body of cavalry, between forty and fifty men in all, sorted itself into some semblance of order and headed out through the gate, which was then closed behind them as they headed off at a canter.

"I wonder what that is all about?" Anders asked as they vanished from view.

Gideon shook his head and was about to express his own puzzlement when a movement caught the corner of his eye and glancing around, he saw Muir running towards the house. A sudden sick sensation expanded in Gideon's stomach. He had seen Muir on the edge of the mounted men. Lord must have planned to take him with the rest, but for some reason Muir had not gone and now he was clearly not being watched by anyone. Without conscious thought, Gideon followed at speed, ignoring the half-heard question called after him by Anders as he took off.

Before he was halfway to the house, he could hear the baby crying through an open window. When he reached the door of the house, Muir was already inside and thundering up the stairs. Gideon could see him gripping his sword to stop it from impeding his climb and realised that he had no sword himself.

THE TRAITOR'S APPRENTICE

By the time Gideon got to the top of the sweeping stairs, there was no one in sight, but the door to the nursery was open. The wailing of the infant baron was louder and the sound of hammering, of fists on a door.

"Open the door, you evil wretch." The voice was that of Alice Franklyn.

He reached the nursery and flung himself into the room. There was a woman Gideon recognised as being the baby's nurse, lying unmoving by the empty crib, blood soaking her clothes. Alice had blood on her dress too and stood by a closed door that led to a small side chamber where the nursemaid might sleep. The door had a lock, and despite Muir's best efforts appeared to be made of solid stuff as it didn't open.

"She killed poor Dorcas and has taken the baron," Alice shrieked, her blood-covered hands dragging through her hair. "She worships demons, I've seen her doing it, and she will give him to them. You must stop her."

It took Gideon a moment to realise that the evil woman being described was Zahara and that she was shut in the side chamber with the screaming child—and Muir, sword in hand, was trying to break through the door to kill her. Before he could cross the room, Muir put a solid flat-soled kick right onto the lock plate and the door burst open. Gideon launched himself in a flying attack aiming to bring Muir down, anything to keep his sword from Zahara. But Muir saw his attack and turned hard to meet it, sword in hand, his back to the wood of the open door, forcing Gideon to try and catch himself or be impaled. Gideon managed to turn his leap into a rolling dive and finished on one knee out of range of the sword and held Muir's attention.

"Leave him, you fool," Alice hissed, her voice no higher than a whisper and the previous hysteria absent from her tone. "Get in that room now and finish this."

Muir hesitated, unwilling to leave an enemy, even an unarmed one, to his rear. Gideon took full advantage and was on him in a moment. He grabbed and hefted an upholstered, gate-legged chair, using it as both weapon and shield. Swinging it round at head and chest height, he forced Muir away from the inner room. Muir dodged to avoid it, his sword hacking at, but not through, the solid wood. The legs of the chair made it hard for Muir to bring the blade of his sword up for a proper attack.

It couldn't last, of course. Once the impetus of the swing was spent, Gideon was left reaching to one side across the doorway and had to throw the chair in a desperate attempt to parry the now mobile Muir. He was lucky and the chair caught Muir in the shoulder so he staggered back a couple of paces before he could recover.

But at least Gideon had put himself between Muir's sword and Zahara and for a moment that was all he cared about. He cast about for anything that could make a weapon, grabbing at some loose cloth, a woollen cape left on a settle by the door.

"Here," Zahara's voice, behind him, was calm even above the wails of the infant and something metallic was pressed into his palm. It was a poker from the hearth, with no ability at all to cut, but at least it gave him something he could parry with. He took it in his left hand, his right still holding the cape. It was awkward, but there was no chance to change hands since Muir was already attacking again. Gideon sidestepped trying to foil the sword in the thick folds of cloth. It brought him a free hit with the poker, and he crashed it onto Muir's other wrist and had the satisfaction of making him draw a sharp breath.

Where was Shiraz? Surely he should have been here? His key task, Lord had said, was to protect Zahara.

Muir had caught the cloth and pulled it free, now he flung it back in Gideon's face. Momentarily blinded, Gideon stepped back with an instinct to try and avoid the blade he could no longer see. But for some reason, the expected blow didn't come. As he caught the cape again, he saw Muir, with a slight cut on his face, bringing up a hand to defend himself from something that was flying at him from over Gideon's shoulder. The small lotion pot was aimed with accuracy and made Muir dodge back allowing Gideon to swing the poker. Zahara, from behind him, had gathered some small objects to serve as missiles which she was throwing hard and deftly in his support. The lotion pot was followed by a brush and a hand mirror.

Even so, it was a fight that Gideon knew he couldn't win. He was outmatched and had only invention, grim determination, Zahara's missiles as long as they lasted, and his own limited natural agility. He had no sense of time or of anything outside the perfect focus needed for keeping the deadly blade from his body.

"Stop this!" Anders' voice was loud even above the caterwauling of the infant but sounded on another continent to the one where Gideon stood. Which was when the sword slipped through his desperate defence and he felt the pierce his flesh, weakening his arm so the poker dropped from his grasp. Muir's eyes held his knowledge of victory, and the sword came up to deliver the killing blow.

Except it didn't. Somehow a sword, ringingly, brought up the blade aimed for his unprotected chest even as it thrust. There was a brief flurry of movement and Muir was disarmed.

"Did your fencing master teach you nothing?" Danny Bristow addressed Muir and sounded as if he were telling off a student. He was holding two swords gripped in his leather gauntleted hands. His own dipped and ready to use, and Muir's, its blade stained with Gideon's blood. Beneath his freckles, his skin looked a little pale, which was, perhaps, a sign that Danny was aware a single heartbeat of time had stood between life and death for Gideon in his intervention.

Muir was restrained by one of Lord's men and Alice Franklyn was shrieking.

"She killed Dorcas. She is going to kill the baby."

Then Anders was beside him holding his arm and urging him to sit.

Gideon pulled himself away and turned to Zahara. She had blood over her clothes and in her arms, she now held the squalling infant.

"Zahara..."

"I am all right. It is not my blood. The baby is fine. He was cut, but not badly. Gideon, please, let Dr Jensen look at your wound." There was something beneath her usual serenity, a real concern that he took a moment to realise was on his account.

It was only then he collapsed into the chair that Danny had pushed across the room to catch him. He felt nothing as Anders removed his arm from his coat, then gave up on the doublet and, using a small-bladed knife, sliced through that and his shirt, now saturated red from where the sword had stabbed into the flesh of his upper

THE TRAITOR'S APPRENTICE

arm below the shoulder. He was dimly aware of it happening, but all he could think of was that Zahara was alive and unhurt, and she had called him 'Gideon'.

Danny, back from whatever he had been sent to do that morning, had taken control of the situation in the absence of Lord or Mags, whose whereabouts no one seemed to know. With an authority and efficiency Gideon wouldn't have suspected him of possessing, he heard Danny send a runner to the church to tell the parson there had been an accident and that Lady Belamy was needed and issue a stream of orders to the remaining members of the company.

As Anders worked to staunch the flow of his blood, Gideon saw the body of the nursery maid being removed and Danny had Alice Franklyn escorted to her room, saying she should be placed under the watchful gaze of Máire Rider. Muir was removed to his room also and kept under guard. Gideon realised that both himself and Zahara were to be equally segregated and held.

As soon as Anders allowed it, Gideon was helped to the side room and made to lie on the dead nursemaid's truckle. He lay there as Anders unwrapped the baby and confirmed that aside from a small cut which Zahara had treated, the baron was unharmed. Zahara had already been taken to her own room by Brighid and Gideon heard Danny issuing the same strict instructions as he had for Alice Franklyn and Muir—for a guard to be placed on her door and no one to be allowed in or out without his permission.

Under orders from both Anders and Danny not to move, Gideon lay on the bed in the side chamber and heard the sounds of activity in the room next door. The cry of distress from Elizabeth Belamy as she saw her baby no doubt bewrapped in bandages and Anders' soothing tone, quieting her, then she, in turn, quieting the child at last by feeding him.

It was sometime later when the door opened to admit Danny. He crouched beside the truckle and placed a hand on Gideon's uninjured shoulder to prevent him from struggling to sit up.

"You'd better tell me what happened. Alice Franklyn is accusing Sara of murdering the maid and trying to sacrifice the baby to her infidel god and you of being a minion under Sara's thrall. Muir is saying he was trying to save the baby. Sara says she found the nursemaid dead, Alice Franklyn distraught and she snatched up the baby to protect it, locking herself with it in this room. Anders assures me she made a fine job of caring for the infant's wound, which he believes was inflicted by a knife. And though I really do enjoy playing God as much as the next man, this is not something I want to make any kind of a decision on without a lot more information."

Gideon wondered if he had the strength to retell the tale.

"I'm sure you won't need to," he said, realising then just how weak he felt. "You just have to keep a lid on the pot until Lord gets back and you seem to have achieved that already."

"I wish it was that simple. I've got Lady Belamy demanding that I deal with the situation—by which she means that I dispatch you and Sara to eternity right away. I couldn't prevent her from sending a servant to find the graf, who might consider her view of events and her solution to them the one he prefers."

Gideon felt a sudden chill in the air.

THE TRAITOR'S APPRENTICE

"Where is he?"

"Out on reconnaissance. Not back yet. And hopefully not back before Philip. But if he is, this moves out of my hands and into his." Danny drew a breath and let the air puff out his cheeks as he expelled it. "So, you would make my life a lot easier and yours a lot safer, if you could give me the truth so I stand some chance of mollifying the lady of the house who wants your head on a platter alongside Sara's."

It was too much for Gideon to absorb. He was trying to marshal his thoughts into some kind of coherence, to take on board the realisation that he had been wrong about the murders and think how to lay the tale out to make sense when Anders pushed his way into the small chamber.

"For the love of God, you must let him rest." The Dane stood behind Danny, studying Gideon's face, his own frowning with concern. "He has been injured and lost a lot of blood."

Danny straightened and threw up both hands in despair.

"There will be worse than that to come if he doesn't speak to me and the graf gets back before Ph— Blanchard does."

Anders shook his head.

"If you think the company would allow any harm to come to Sara on the say-so of—"

"I am sure it wouldn't. But you mistake me. It's Gideon I fear for more."

"And you would stand by and allow it to happen?" Anders asked, his voice cold and edged with disgust.

Danny said nothing, his lips tightening. Then he turned on his heel and left the room. Gideon watched him go, stomach sick and thoughts bleak and uneasy.

"I think that is a dangerous man," Anders said, lowering his voice. "But whatever he says, you need to rest. Meanwhile, I will talk to Lady Belamy. It is obvious to anyone that had Sara wished any harm to the infant she had time enough to do so and that far from doing so she has tended to his injury with great care. I will also explain you have been investigating the deaths. Once the baroness is over her shock, I am sure she will see reason."

Gideon wanted to say that he was happy to talk, to tell what he now knew about the murders, but somehow the words were not there when he reached for them. Instead, there was a soft blanket of darkness which engulfed the last vestiges of thought.

III

Before setting out on the road which, if Bristow was correct, would lead him to encounter Fairfax completely unawares, Nick took the precaution of sending the plate they had collected under a strong guard back to Newcastle. He kept Cummings with him and nearly eighty men. An ambush, Bristow had said and detailed the place so well that Nick didn't need to consult the small sketch that had accompanied the explanation. The man himself had refused to ride with them, saying he had other pressing commissions he was under orders to see to for the graf.

Graf. That was a revelation Nick had not expected. Graf was the German equivalent in rank to an earl, meaning Mags was already equal in status to Newcastle and, by the same measure, a man of greater importance than Nick himself. Yet he still craved to be recognised as a Coupland.

That was something Nick struggled to understand. In his view to be such a man, made by oneself, freed from the long shadow of family and all that placed upon you, must be a great thing. Greater than to inherit the ties and duties and irksome restrictions of the kind Nick had to endure.

The skies were grey overhead as they rode and now September had given way to October a colder breeze tugged at his hat and blew his hair over his face. The roads were mud-churned from the recent rains and the horses found it heavy going at times. It took longer than he liked to get to the location Mags had directed.

Once before Nick had taken the advice of Mags on an ambush and that time, through no fault of his own or Mags, the result had been a disaster as the ambush was turned against him. This time Nick was careful. He had men scout the area before committing himself, and if he followed the plan he had been given it was only because that was the one that made the most sense given the lie of the land. Even Cummings had no objection to the dispositions made and took his part of the command away at a brisk trot.

Only something happened to spoil the plan.

There was an unexpected eruption of shots and shouting on the wing of his force where Cummings' men were concealed. Nick had placed them furthest along the road from the direction Fairfax would approach, wanting the glory of the capture for himself. But somehow Fairfax must have got wind of the plan. A belated messenger from Cummings arrived then saying there was a body of some forty men approaching. At which point Nick did the only thing he could do and called in his men to support Cummings.

It was obvious to Nick that these were not Fairfax's men. It was just cursed bad luck and Cummings' stupidity. Had he let these men ride by all could yet have been salvaged. Now Fairfax would be warned by the shots and having but a small escort would turn back and the whole plan was ruined.

Whoever the troops belonged to they seemed well-disciplined and unperturbed by his sudden appearance even though they were surprised when Nick brought his men in at a brisk trot. To give their commander his due, he was quick to see the danger and was taking the best action he could to avoid being trapped. Ordering his men to withdraw.

Such was their swordwork and shooting—most seemed to carry more than one pistol—Nick's force was reluctant to pursue them.

Their commander had held back to cover the retreat, with one other man at his side—a man firing a bow from horseback, dropping lethal shafts onto those who tried to close with them. Then there was a shout from the commander and the archer turned his mount on the spot, still firing backwards over the creature's rump, covering his captain's retreat.

It was impressive to see and had one of the arrows not killed the man beside Nick, driving through his neck and splattering blood, like red rain, over those around him as he fell, Nick might have even admired it. As it was, a sudden sharp fury made him lift his pistol, tilt it and aim towards the commander of the enemy force.

The distance was much too great, and the chances of hitting were minute. In a few moments, the rider would be safe away with his men, but even so he pulled the trigger.

He missed the man, of course, but by some miracle, the magnificent horse he was riding threw up its head, dropped and rolled. It was as its rider fell, trying to kick himself free, that he lost his hat and Nick saw the betraying white hair. Then he knew a moment of exultation so intense that as cheers went up from his men when the first of them closed around the fallen horse, he let himself give voice with them.

The archer, Nick saw, was now well out of pistol shot. He had reined, hesitating, then turned and raced away after his comrades.

Chapter Twelve

I

For a few glorious moments, Nick had believed Philip Lord was dead. When he found otherwise, he would have done his best to make it so, but Cummings seized his bridle, pulled his horse away and yelled at him to put up.

It would have been straightforward had not Cummings reached Lord, trapped by his dead horse, before Nick himself, and claimed him as his prisoner. The lieutenant believed it had been a shot from his pistol that had felled Lord's horse. By the time Nick reached him, Cummings had nearly been cozened into freeing Lord, who was claiming they had taken each other for an enemy force when he was, in fact, also a supporter of the king.

"He is a liar, lieutenant," Nick said between gritted teeth, having to fight the urge to use his sword to slice the hand gripping his horse's bridle. "He serves no one but himself. He is a man called Philip Lord, a criminal—a traitor—and no servant of the king."

Lord had needed help to stand, his ankle having sustained some injury when his horse fell.

"I think you mistake me for someone else, sir," Lord said, his breath short but his tone impeccably polite although the cold glitter of his gaze as it gripped Nick's own was saying something very different. "However, I am sure the matter can be cleared up by the Earl of Newcastle."

Then with an evident effort that must have cost him pain, he made a bow to Cummings and carefully unbuckled his sword belt, holding it out to the lieutenant who already had his sword. "It seems I am your prisoner, sir. Please treat that sword with the greatest of care and respect. I shall redeem it as soon as this matter is resolved by the earl."

It was sickening to see Cummings falling for the ploy as if it were a hundred years ago and Lord was a person of noble rank to be held for ransom. The lieutenant was for sending Lord as his prisoner back to Newcastle with only a small guard. It had taken all of Nick's crumbling authority to prevent that and buy some time to consider how he could redeem the situation.

At least Lord himself had undermined his cause with Cummings somewhat by refusing to say where he was from or what his name might be. He kept repeating that he would speak with the earl on the matter and no one else. That had at least driven the lieutenant to agree that if he wouldn't supply his name, he could not be a man of honour so he should be kept bound.

Then men started vanishing.

They might be stepping out to relieve themselves at night or they might be those sent as advance scouts, but on the second day and with eight men gone, even Cummings was willing to listen to Nick who was convinced it was some of Lord's men set on freeing him.

He had, of course, challenged Lord with the missing men.

They were staying that second night at a prosperous farm, his men with decent shelter in the barn, Lord under guard in the corner of a solid stone-built cowshed.

Lord laughed at his question. "Has it not occurred to

you that they might be deserting? Not every man is fond of war, and some have sweethearts, families and homes to go to."

"I saw your man. Shiraz, you called him, the Moor who is an archer. I think you have him out hunting my men."

"That would be hard as I am here and unable to order anyone to do anything," Lord said, shifting his position on the floor of the byre as best he could with his wrists and ankles bound, to avoid Nick's boot. "It must be difficult for you. You cannot kill me outright because I am Lieutenant Cummings' prisoner. These who guard me are not Howe men, they are Newcastle's so you would risk facing a charge of murder."

Nick wanted to strike the smirk from his face. It was, at least, satisfying to see there were already a number of bruises there from where Lord had been manhandled. His fine clothes were spoiled by the mud of the road when he fell, not helped by the far from salubrious accommodation he had since been afforded. Satisfying himself with another kick, Nick took satisfaction from the sharp inhalation of breath that caused.

"It makes no odds. By your orders or not, it is your man out there killing."

"Then perhaps you should find him and stop him," Lord suggested. "Or you could release me and I could do so. No? Because that is not your real problem, is it? Your problem is once I get to Newcastle, you have no certainty that the good earl will not embrace me as he might a long-lost brother and appoint me to his staff. Then it might be you cast into outer darkness with much weeping and gnashing of teeth."

"The earl will condemn you as the traitor you are,"

Nick said coldly.

Lord seemed unconcerned by the thought.

"And if he does, won't that be embarrassing for some people? He would send me to the king, of course."

"Why would he do that?"

Lord leaned back against the hard stone of the wall and closed his eyes, declining to continue the conversation. Furious Nick knew from previous experience that he would only make a spectacle of himself before the men if he tried to compel Lord to further speech.

He left and an ironic voice followed him from the cowshed.

"It is new but a foolish way you have found out, that whom you cannot equal or come near in doing, you would destroy or ruin with evil speaking; as if you had bound both your wits and natures 'prentices to slander, and then came forth the best artificers when you could form the foulest calumnies...."

But his point was made and the uncomfortable truth of it was becoming unavoidable. Nick had completed the work the earl had tasked him with. They had now visited every name on the list except for Belamy of Wrathby. That was a place he had been assured by Mags was a nest of Lord's men, so Nick had no intention of risking himself or his prisoner anywhere near it.

The next day, Tuesday, Nick woke to the news that they had lost two more men in the night. Furious, he snapped out the order to head back to Newcastle.

II

It was a time of confusion for Gideon, during which he was never sure if he was conscious or not. If he was experiencing the present in some semblance of wakefulness or the past in vivid and disturbing dreams. Shouting. Steel on steel. The sharp crack of a pistol shot—or of stone hitting stone. Someone crying—a woman—sobbing as if her heart was broken. The wail of an infant. Footsteps coming close, then someone shaking him.

"Come on, Gideon, wake up." The voice was low and urgent.

He tried to open his eyes and eventually succeeded. It was dark, cold and there was a candle somewhere nearby. He thought at first two figures were crouching beside him, but as he blinked a few times they resolved into one.

Danny Bristow.

"Are you awake?"

His head throbbed in unison with the wound in his left shoulder and he felt as weak as a new-born. He tried to speak, but his mouth was dry, and nothing came out. Swallowing a bit desperately, he managed to make a sound of acknowledgement.

"Then listen. I shouldn't be here, and I don't have long. Philip and Shiraz have not returned. Mags is going to put you on trial. If he can prove the case against you then he will do the same with Sara. But it isn't about you, or Sara, or who is the murderer, it is about Mags establishing his authority in the company. You *must* understand that and use it. I will make sure Anders gets to see you beforehand, but that is all I can do. You are going to have to fight this yourself—and you damn well *have* to win." There was a short silence, then "Did you understand all that?"

Gideon wasn't at all sure he did, but he heard the

urgency in Danny's voice which seemed to border on desperation. He managed to make some kind of reply and then the footsteps receded, the candlelight was gone and somewhere a door closed. He lay awake in the dark for a time, wondering where he was, where Zahara was and how he was going to manage to speak up to defend her when he couldn't even sit up. Then thought stopped again.

His next awakening was more gentle, almost as if he was stirring from a natural night's sleep. Almost but not quite. The smell of lavender was sharp in the air and his eyes opened to soft autumnal sunshine. He had a pounding headache and there was still a dull soreness where his wound was invisible beneath the careful bandaging.

"Thank goodness," Anders said. "You are awake at last."

He was supported by pillows, so he was able to see that the room he was in wasn't one he had been in before. He assumed from the old stone of the walls, the lack of a hearth and the narrow windows that this was a room in the peel tower. Anders held a cup to his lips which smelt of honey and rosehips and something altogether more astringent. It tasted less than pleasant although the honey made it palatable at least.

"That was just a mild tonic, but you should feel a bit better soon, and I will give you something more potent when you do." Anders sounded more confident than Gideon felt he should. By the time Anders had redressed his arm wound and declared it to be healing well and wrapped his ankle with firmer bandaging than usual, the pounding in his head did seem to be receding a little. He was able to drink the water he was offered by himself and ask for more. When some frumenty was brought soon after, he devoured it under the approving gaze of his physician.

But he couldn't fail to notice that when the door opened to allow Anders to take the bowl from one of the household servants, there was an armed man outside the door.

It was then he remembered Danny had been there at night—or had that been a dream?

Hunger and thirst slaked somewhat, he began to feel his strength returning and felt able to ask the questions he needed to.

"Is Zahara all right?"

Anders took the bowl from him and set it aside.

"She is well. You need not worry."

"How long have I been—?"

"It is Wednesday morning, so this is the third day since you were injured. I am pleased to say you seem much restored."

Three days…

"Thank you for your care," Gideon said and managed a smile. If Zahara was fine, and Anders had been tending him, then that strange incident with Danny must have been a dream.

"It is your robust good health that deserves the credit, my friend," Anders said, his face sombre. "Despite all my attempts to do so and my continual protestations, I have not been allowed near you until this morning."

A sudden tightness, close to cramping, gripped Gideon's guts.

It had not been a dream.

He closed his eyes to let the dizzying impact of that spiral through his mind, aware of the weakness of his body and the need for it to be strong.

"What has happened?"

"I am afraid it is not easy for me to say or for you to hear. I only know what we are being told, and where truth ends and falsehood begins is beyond me to judge."

"I would hear it anyway," Gideon insisted.

Anders drew a deep breath. "Very well. As you know, Philip Lord took a body of cavalry to meet with Sir Thomas Fairfax, who had been planning to visit. He was to summon Wrathby to abide by the treaty his father had just signed on Thursday. That would, Fairfax hoped, oblige us to disarm. But from what I have heard before our patron encountered Sir Thomas, he was attacked by a much larger force sent by the Earl of Newcastle, which was waiting in ambush on the road, presumably also having somehow learned of Sir Thomas' intentions and hoping to seize him."

Gideon felt the cramp worsen. He could tell already from Anders' tone and demeanour that there was no good ending to this. He just wanted it told.

"And Lord's men?"

He thought of the cavalry force Lord had led from Wrathby, the men fresh from church. *I am not anticipating there will be too much of a problem.*

"They say they were outnumbered more than two to one. We've lost two men, though there were another five injured and of those, I am not sure one will survive."

"Two men?"

That wasn't so terrible from a skirmish against a much superior force, surely. It was the risk all here took making their living from trade in war.

"Yes. Just two men," Anders said. "They all returned,

except Philip Lord and Shiraz."

Gideon felt as a drowning man must feel when the rope he had been thrown slipped away through his fingers even as he grasped at it in hope.

"Mags...?"

Anders nodded. "Has taken command of the company." The Dane looked as if he was wrestling with an inner decision then gave a short sigh. "And Captain Bristow is now his right hand, enforcing his will in all things. It saddens me to say it, but he is not the man we thought he was."

But Danny had been there last night, what had he said? Something about a trial, and something Gideon had to remember... but at that moment he could only think of Zahara, no longer with Shiraz to protect her, and of the impossible thought that Philip Lord was dead. That last was so immense he had to step away from it. He couldn't let himself walk through the door to the despair it represented. Instead, he focused on the moment, on what Anders had said and on how he had spoken the words.

"There is more," Gideon said, certain he was right. "You haven't told me the worst yet, have you?"

Anders dipped his head in acknowledgement and went over to where he had an array of bottles set out on a small trestle. He took the cup he had given to Gideon when he woke and began to pour careful measures from two of the bottles into it.

"I will not be staying with the company much longer," he said, his voice heavy. "Ambition and revenge are always hungry, and I will not be devoured by another man's weakness. I have remained so far because of you, my friend, and as long as I can be of some help to you,

you have my word that I will stay."

Gideon had no idea what to say to that.

"It seems too little but thank you."

"Well, gold is tried in the fire, friendship in need. It is my sincere hope that the two of us will soon leave here together, with Sara and those who remain of a mind not to sink in the mire that this man, Mags, is making."

"I can sit on a horse," Gideon said. Even as he spoke, he wondered if that was more bravado than truth, but if it would get Zahara to safety he would manage it somehow.

Anders poured some still steaming water from a pewter jug into the cup he was preparing and picked up a pot of honey.

"If that were possible, my friend, I would have horses ready. But you are held here under guard, as a prisoner. No one has been allowed to see you since Sunday until I was told I might help prepare you this morning."

"Prepare me?" Gideon floundered. "Prepare me for what?"

But even before Anders could answer him the words Danny had said by the light of a flickering candle filled his mind. *Mags is going to put you on trial. If he can prove the case against you then he will do the same with Sara.*

"There is to be a trial. Or rather the travesty of one, with Mags as the judge. He said that as there are no regular courts, he would convene a military one to secure justice for the household." Anders sniffed the cup and added a couple of drops from another bottle. "It was a good speech. Amazingly he seems to now be fluent in English and French and yet none have remarked that."

"I am to be the one arraigned, I assume?" Gideon

asked, trying to keep the bitterness at bay.

"Yes. You are accused of plotting to murder the infant—you and Sara between you." He stirred some honey into the cup as he spoke. "I tried to speak for you to Lady Belamy, but her sister by marriage has poured poison into her ear, and I fear my words are discredited. Unfortunately, our new commander finds what he calls my 'interference' an inconvenience and for the sake of my health, I have had to desist from trying to oppose this madness. There is more going on here than some irrational dislike of you and Sara, but I cannot see what." Anders tipped half the contents of the cup into a bottle and sealed it. "God help the sheep when the wolf is judge."

Danny's voice echoed in Gideon's thoughts. *It isn't about you, or Sara, or who is the murderer, it is about Mags establishing his authority in the company. You must understand that and use it.*

He opened his mouth to tell Anders about the strange night-time visitation, then hesitated. For whatever reason Danny had taken the risk to warn him, but with Anders so convinced of Danny's enmity, telling him so wasn't going to help matters.

"When is this so-called trial to take place?" he asked instead.

Anders turned back to him, the cup in one hand.

"Later this afternoon. They are at dinner now."

Gideon knew then that he was defeated before he even began. He couldn't stand, let alone walk and talk, cajole or persuade. He had learned the skills of a barrister to some degree in his training, but his mind and body were too weak.

"Surely I can be granted a day to prepare?"

THE TRAITOR'S APPRENTICE

"Roger Jupp suggested that and was told by Captain Bristow that the graf had already decided what was to happen and if he valued his place, he would guard his tongue. You are not without sympathisers, my friend, but Daniel Bristow is not one of them. He is the whip our new commander wields to keep the rest in line." He held out the cup. "Drink this."

Gideon smelt the cup and recoiled.

"What is that?"

"It is something from the Spanish colonies that I have seen given to soldiers before battle and would keep a dead man on his feet for a few hours. I have mixed it with what I may to balance your humours so you may think more clearly. There is another dose in this bottle for later, but only take it if you need it. Too much places a great strain on the body and can kill. When it wears off you will feel ill, but if all goes well, I can then give you something so you can sleep through that."

If all goes well…

If not, then it wouldn't matter, of course.

With a silent prayer that whatever might happen to himself, Zahara would somehow be safe, Gideon swallowed the contents of the cup in two gulps, then let Anders act as his body servant and help him dress. By the time he needed to stand, he had the strength in his limbs to do so and he picked up and put on his red coat himself.

He was trying to persuade his hair and beard into some kind of decent state when there was a sharp verbal exchange outside the door.

It was opened a few moments later to admit Aleksandrov and another of the soldiers, one Gideon didn't know. Aleksandrov fixed Anders with a stare and jerked his head towards the door.

"You. Out now."

Anders inclined his head in distant acknowledgement and began to pick up and pack into his bag the bottles and pots he had out on the trestle. Aleksandrov took a step towards him making it obvious Anders wasn't going to be given the time needed to do so. Instead, he swept them with one hand into the open bag.

"Remember, my friend," he said, bestowing a brief, warm smile on Gideon, whilst scooping up the bag in his arms with its straps still undone, "lawyers and painters both can change white to black when it is needful."

Then he was gone, and the door slammed shut. Gideon was left alone with his troubled thoughts to try and prepare a defence for his life and that of the woman he loved, in a court whose rules were going to be set by whim and wild justice.

Less than an hour later they brought some more food.

"Captain Bristow's orders," he was told by the sullen Aleksandrov as if the man wanted to distance himself from any act of humanity directed towards Gideon. But by that time Gideon was feeling surprising strength and energy. His mind had become clear and fast. Although he had little appetite, common sense told him to eat what he could. It crossed his mind that the food might be poisoned, but he doubted it. If Mags wanted to make an example of him, he wouldn't be killed before it could take place.

For that was what he was sure was happening here.

It was what Danny had warned him about in the dark. With Lord and Shiraz both gone, something Gideon couldn't let himself dwell upon, Mags needed to assert

THE TRAITOR'S APPRENTICE

his authority to pull the company together. He needed a scapegoat—someone for whom he had little use but who had been marked by the favour of his predecessor.

Gideon ate and thought.

As it transpired, he had more time to think about it than he expected. It was late afternoon, when the first stirrings of a possible way forward were taking shape in his mind, nebulous and unformed, that the door opened again, and he was out of time.

He had assumed he would be taken to the dining hall, but instead, Aleksandrov and his companion escorted him out of the tower. They crossed the courtyard under heavy grey skies with spitting rain, to the same place where Gideon had witnessed wild justice being served up before.

The room was set up much as it had been when Lord was there dispensing justice. It seemed to Gideon impossible to imagine that the man wasn't just about to stride in and take control of the situation with a few brief words. Instead, Mags was in the place Lord had occupied. But where Lord had stood, as did the rest of his company, Mags had brought one of the larger and more impressive chairs from the house. A high-backed, dark oak edifice of a chair, which gave the impression of being a throne. Mags slouched at an angle across the seat, legs wide and one elbow on the arm so his hand could support his chin.

Most of Lord's men were there, standing around the walls. Chairs had been brought from the house for Alice Franklyn, Lady Grace and William Irving. Muir was standing beside Mags to his left and to his right, stood an unsmiling Danny Bristow. Behind Mags were Aleksandrov and another of Mags' supporters who

Gideon recognised as a man called Turk. Amongst the company men were Anders and Jupp, both of whom gave him nods of support, and here and there he caught sympathetic glances from some others. But the majority were curious to see what would happen. He was nothing to most of them and they were hard men by nature.

Gideon struggled to believe that any of the company would feel that way about Zahara. She was one of their own. Which was no doubt why Mags was making Gideon the principal in the drama and not her.

He couldn't see Elizabeth Belamy with the others of her household, although there was an empty chair in the middle where she might sit. There was no sign of Zahara either. Only a couple of the company's women were standing with their men, most were not present. The space in the centre of the room remained empty, like some kind of cockpit or baiting arena. And that was, of course, what this was.

Gideon's heart constricted, as he realised that no matter what he did, no matter how well he argued his case, the man sitting on the impressive oak chair had already decided what the outcome would be.

As he was escorted through the centre of the room and brought to stand in front of the seated Mags, part of his mind was speculating on what form of execution Mags might favour. Standing as straight as he could, he waited as Mags lifted a hand. Silence consumed even the low murmur of speculation in the room. When it was quiet Mags leaned forward a little in his chair.

"So, Fox—Lennox, whatever name you profess, you claim to be a man of law, is that so?"

Gideon found his mouth dry and had to wait for a moment before he could speak. "I have been trained, qualified and registered as an attorney in the Inns of London, so yes, I would consider myself a lawyer."

"Then I'm sure you will have much to say in your defence." Mags sounded amused. Then his tone hardened. "As a man of law, you must accept that by serving with this company you become subject to our justice."

Wild justice.

Gideon drew a breath. He wanted to say that justice wasn't the whim of one man in one moment. It was the considered body of law and precedent, the very structure of civilisation itself. But from beside the heavy oak chair, he saw Danny Bristow staring at him.

...it is about Mags establishing his authority in the company, you must understand that and use it.

Gideon had no reason to trust that Danny hadn't said that to make the job of demolishing him easier. But then again, whether he accepted it or not, *force majeure* meant that he was indeed subject to the jurisdiction of this so-called court and its judge. And regardless of what Danny had said if he acknowledged that brutal reality, he might at least be given a hearing.

"If you are asking if I accept you have the power to sit in judgement on me, then yes, I acknowledge that you do."

"And the right?" Mags insisted, eyes narrowing.

"And the right," Gideon said, "*because* you have the power."

Mags smiled then and sank back in his chair.

"Tell us, why did you lend your aid in a plan to murder the baby baron?"

Danny Bristow cleared his throat and Mags shot him an irritated glance. But that wasn't enough to discourage him from speaking.

"With respect sir, the first question should be to ask if Fox admits doing it or not. If he is pleading guilty or not guilty."

Mags snorted then waved an arm in a broad gesture towards Gideon and including the entire room.

"Then if you know the questions, Danny lad, you ask. I'll listen." He lifted the hand he had just gestured with as Danny opened his mouth, looking unhappy. "No excuses. That's an order, Captain Bristow."

Danny gave a brief bow, acknowledging the command, and moved forward of the throne, stopping at enough distance from Gideon that he didn't have to tilt his head to meet Gideon's gaze. He stood feet apart and arms folded, sword and pistol worn on crossed baldrics.

"Do you wish to admit that you were involved with the murder of the nursemaid Dorcas Lucas and the attempted murder of the infant baron, Lord Charles Belamy?" Danny asked. "It would save us all a lot of time and effort were you to do so." He looked around the room, implying that too many people were having their time wasted.

"Is this a trial?" Gideon demanded. "If it is not, then it makes no difference what I plead. You will execute me anyway."

"It is a trial, of course," Danny said, making it sound as if he were indulging Gideon rather than according him any fairness. "The graf wouldn't execute a man without good cause. So far we only have the words of your accusers. But if you don't contest the accusations, you would speed the conclusion. That is a matter of fact."

Gritting his teeth, Gideon shook his head. Danny, for

all he looked like a freckled schoolboy with a beard, had a mind as quick and capable in a battle of wits as his body was in combat. Bearing that in mind, Gideon drew a breath and launched his own attack.

"I contest the accusation," he said, lifting his voice to be sure it would carry the length of the room. "I did not murder Dorcas Lucas, or Sir Arthur Cochrane, Ruth Whittaker, or the fourth baron or Mr Franklyn, the late husband of Alice Franklyn. But someone in this room did and if left undiscovered they will also murder the fifth baron and blame it, as they have the rest, on the Curse of Wrathby."

As he spoke, he moved his gaze to Muir who glared back at him with venom, and before he finished there was a rumble of confusion and disbelief from the assembled men. Mags sat up in his chair, frowning.

"I didn't ask you to share your wild fantasies," Danny said, his tone dismissive. "I asked if you wanted to admit you tried to murder the infant."

"I did not," Gideon repeated. "I am innocent of the charges you bring against me and what you call my wild fantasies will stand scrutiny even here."

Danny adopted the look of a long-suffering adult indulging an importuning child.

"Of course." He nodded a couple of times. "Of course. However, my questions are not going to touch on your stories but keep to the facts—what actually happened."

And what had happened, Gideon wondered, to this man who had seemed so loyal to Philip Lord and offered the tentative first shoots of friendship to Gideon himself? Was he a weak man clinging to the new font of power?

"Ask your questions," he said and pushed all

speculation about Danny out of his mind. Whoever he might have been before he was now Mags' creature. The only way Gideon stood a chance of surviving this himself and of protecting Zahara, was to regard Daniel Bristow as his enemy.

Chapter Thirteen

I

The glowering autumnal sky seemed uncertain whether to make an effort to rain properly, whilst allowing small spits to escape from the clouds. Nick led his men through the drizzle at a ground-eating pace, heading north. It wasn't so much premeditation as inspiration that led him to choose the destination for his troop that night. In theory, he could have pressed on to Durham at least. But as he rode through the deteriorating weather, he could hear the bursts of ungovernable laughter that marked where Lord was in the close-pressed ranks, well surrounded by Newcastle's men. Irritated, Nick realised that he had an opportunity to slay a second bird with the same stone he had cast at Lord.

By the time the day was falling into twilight he was bringing his troop into the yard of Flass Grange, filling it with men and horses. Leaving Cummings and Bayliss to organise what was needed to ensure the men would sleep dry he made for the house.

A cold voice greeted him with words that held little of welcome.

"Oh, it is only you. I thought for a moment that someone of note had arrived." The tone and pitch were such a perfect reflection, in a feminine register, of what he had put up with from Philip Lord that he turned to face Christobel Lavinstock with his anger already strong.

But the moment he saw her, the ire shifted key. She looked aloof and beautiful, dressed in a soft grey bodice and skirt with a plain collar that sat on her shoulders. Her hair was caught up under a lace-edged cap and fell from that to around her face framing it with a haze of pale silver. Her intense fury was contained in the stillness of her frame and the twin points of red which flushed her cheeks below the Baltic cold of her eyes.

Something moved in his chest and spread downwards through and past his guts and upwards through and past his throat, uniting his brain, his heart and his loins. At that moment Nick knew he wanted Christobel for his own. He would master her and bring her to his side, but on his own terms and not because she was the foundation of his hopes for Howe. He made a brief but gracious bow and met her bristling hostility with a smile.

"Mistress Lavinstock, I find myself and men in need of shelter. My men will find accommodation, I am sure, in your farm buildings and I will ask for hospitality in your house for myself and Lieutenant Cummings. We will need, however, food and firewood to be provided for the men or I will have to permit them to take wood from your outbuildings and some of your animals to roast and feed themselves."

It was a threat that had worked well in the houses he had visited in Yorkshire.

Christobel stood with her back straight and her head lifted, making Nick think again of a beautiful greyhound.

THE TRAITOR'S APPRENTICE

"Your men will be fed," she said. "And you and your lieutenant. If you wish to enter the house, you already know the way to the parlour. You will need to excuse me as your demands mean I have much work." She turned and would have gone but Nick reached out a hand. She froze and stared at the leather gauntleted fingers which encompassed her arm.

"If you detain me, sir," she said, "I cannot make the necessary arrangements for your food and accommodation."

"There was one more thing," Nick told her, realising he was enjoying the moment. "I have a prisoner who needs secure holding. Do you have somewhere appropriate?"

She looked up and met his gaze. Visible even in the sparse light that came from the open door, the burning contempt in them shocked him.

"I have no places of secure holding. This is a farmhouse."

"There must be somewhere," Nick insisted, his annoyance returning.

Her eyes narrowed for a moment.

"I have a cellar. but that can only be reached from inside the house. I don't want your men traipsing in and out at will."

"My men will go where I need them to go," he told her. "But if the cellar is secure there would be no necessity for them to remain in the house."

The thought of removing Lord from the company of the men who were being suborned by his ready ability to make them laugh had a definite appeal. Discomfort and isolation were the least he deserved.

"Then if you release my arm, I will show you,"

Christobel said.

He let her go and she turned and ran up the few steps to the door of the house. Nick was surprised she moved so fast and had to take the steps in a bound himself to catch up. Following her through the house, they reached the kitchen where she made him wait as she apologised to the two middle-aged women who were preparing a small meal. She explained to them what they would need to use from their stores to provide basic provisions for a large number of men. From what Nick could gather it would amount to a pottage of vegetables and barley with some small taste of bacon. He hoped whatever he and Cummings would be served might be both tastier and more substantial.

Then, still ignoring his presence, she continued through the kitchen into a small, shelved chamber where boxes, bags and bottles were stored. On the far side was a sturdy wooden door which she unlocked with a key on the ring of household keys at her belt. Pausing to take a candle she opened the door and went down the stone steps beyond.

Nick followed, admiring the way the light caught her profile as the steps turned to the side and she glanced back. For a moment, with her hair and clothing touched to silver and her smooth pale skin, she looked like a living statue. Then she turned away and reached the bottom of the steps, lighting a sconce there.

The cellar was a small room that had some boxes and sacks by the steps and there was a table pushed against them. It was dry and clean, and along the far wall was a rack of small barrels. Curious, Nick took a candle from the table and lit it in the sconce then crossed the cellar in a few short strides and studied the barrels.

THE TRAITOR'S APPRENTICE

"My father had one passion which he indulged," Christobel explained. "He loved fine French wine. He had friends in France who would send him gifts. But as the wine wouldn't last long, these are distillations he had made from them."

"Brandy?"

"Yes."

"And you are going to leave these when you leave this place?" Nick found that hard to believe.

"No. I am going to sell them," she said. "But if you would like to try some, I will have it served with the meal."

Nick's mood improved still further at the prospect of fine brandy.

"That would be an excellent idea."

"Will this do to secure your prisoner?"

Reminded of why he was there, Nick glanced around. There was no way out except the door, which was stout and had a strong lock.

"That is the only key?" He gestured at the keys that hung from her belt. She lifted them and with a few deft moves removed one and held it out to him.

"This is the only key. I trust you will return it. If you will excuse me, I need to finish instructing my cook and then I will need to prepare the guest rooms."

He watched her go, enjoying the way her hips moved as she went up the stairs. Then he grounded his thoughts and took care to make sure there was nothing in the cellar with which Lord could cut himself free. Were he to manage to do so he would not make it through the door. And with no lit candle in the sconce, the cellar would be darker than a moonless night anyway.

Satisfied, Nick went back up the stairs, ignoring the

bobbing curtsies the servants gave as he swept through the kitchen. Outside, his men were being organised by Cummings and Bayliss. Nick made sure they knew food would be provided and was even now being cooked for them. As he had hoped it led to a quieting of protesting voices and a more focused determination to see to the horses and argue less about sleeping arrangements.

He found Philip Lord by a sudden shout of laughter from the far corner of the yard. Nick pushed his way past the horses and men that filled the small yard. By the time he reached Lord, the two men guarding him had schooled their faces to appear attentive and efficient. Lord, hands bound, perched with one haunch on a fence rail, looking at ease.

"Ah, is it Dogberry or Verges?" Then he straightened up as Nick approached, favouring his injured ankle as he made a brief bow. "My apologies, it is *Sir* Dogberry or *Lord* Verges."

Riled beyond endurance by the cold mockery delivered in the match of voice and intonation he had just suffered from Christobel, Nick lashed out hard. But Lord's head was somehow not where it had been and the gauntleted fist that should have smashed into lips and broken teeth, flailed into the air and came close to impacting the man behind who was working hard not to laugh. Recovering himself, Nick snarled orders at the two men to bring their prisoner into the house.

Christobel was in the kitchen supervising one of her servants who had brought two of the small barrels up from the cellar and was arranging them on the kitchen table. Lord was hustled through the door in the grip of his guards, and they came face to face.

It wasn't something he had planned to allow, but when

it did, Nick realised he had been hoping it might happen in just such a way—by an accident of fate for which he need feel no responsibility. Nick would never forget the moment no matter how long he lived. The two faces were so similar and yet so different. The identical turquoise eyes widened, reflecting each other in a mirrored gaze. The same white hair framing matched expressions of shock quickly concealed on both sides. If there had been any doubt in his mind before, Nick was now certain that these two had no previous knowledge of the existence of the other before this encounter.

"Will you look at that?" one of the two men guarding Lord murmured with something approaching awe.

Lord lowered his head in a gesture as close to a bow as he could achieve with both his arms held.

"*Whether we fall by ambition, blood, or lust,*
Like diamonds, we are cut with our own dust."

Christobel's eyes widened and she drew a sharp breath.

"*Like to calm weather at sea before a tempest,*" she said with the slightest of hesitations before she went on, "*false hearts speak fair to those they intend most mischief.*"

"I am no Ferdinand, I promise you," Lord said and smiled.

"That is as well since I am not a duchess." Christobel didn't return the smile, but her colour had risen.

Nick had enough. They were talking nonsense.

"This way," he said and pushed Lord towards the cellar door. Once he had made sure Lord was bound securely, the door locked and the key in his pocket, he went back to the kitchen with something to think about. Word was soon going to be around the entire troop about the incredible similarity between their prisoner and the lady of the house. No one who saw them together could fail to remark on it.

Christobel was still in the kitchen and stood demurely waiting for him. Whatever the impact meeting Lord had upon her there was no trace of it in her face.

"Let me take you to the parlour, Sir Nicholas," she offered. "There you can sit in comfort and enjoy one of my father's brandies until supper is served."

Leading him through the house, she took him to the old-fashioned room where she had once been so rude to him. This time she served him the drink with her own hands. But when she turned to go, he caught her wrist.

"What did he say to you—that about ambition and diamonds?"

She didn't try to pull away and met his gaze with the same cold, incalculable look as always.

"They were just words from a play."

"What did he mean by them?"

She shook her head. "You would need to ask him. I answered with some words I knew from the same play. It seemed fitting. Who is he?"

Nick had wondered how long her female curiosity could be curtailed and he released her wrist with an odd sense of satisfaction.

"He is a criminal, a traitor. Not a man you need to concern yourself with."

Nick had expected she would be defiant or demand to know more, but instead, she lowered her gaze with meek decorum and nodded.

"If you will excuse me then, Sir Nicholas, I still need to see to the necessary preparations for your meal and accommodation."

THE TRAITOR'S APPRENTICE

He let her go, pleased she was no longer the vitriolic harridan she had seemed to be in Durham. Perhaps the realisation of her position, the looming loss of her home, had changed her and made her more willing to see him as her saviour.

II

There was a short delay before Danny Bristow could begin his questioning. The shades of twilight were creeping in through the windows earlier than usual due to the bad weather, and Mags decided more light needed to be provided. As they waited, the door opened, and Lady Belamy came in accompanied by a maidservant. She was shown to her seat with the rest of the household and sat, her eyes downcast, looking, Gideon thought as if she sat alone in an empty room.

"I want this finished quickly," Gideon heard Mags say to Danny as the tapers were carried about. There were large lanterns set hanging from the rafters, which illuminated the centre of the room. But around the edges were only candles here and there, giving small pools of light in the growing shadows.

Whatever reply Danny made to Mags, Gideon couldn't hear as it was too low-voiced, though his words made Mags give a bark of laughter. But Danny's expression when he turned back held nothing of humour and much more of grimness. And then by the inconstant flicker of flame, Gideon faced trial.

It lacked any professionalism a barrister would have brought to the task, but Danny proved perfectly capable of setting out the key facts that could damn Gideon in a way that made it seem plausible he was indeed guilty.

"Let's look at what happened. You were the first

person to suggest that the accidents which befell Mistress Whitaker and Sir Arthur Cochrane were in fact acts of murder and to ask permission from Captain Blanchard and the graf to investigate them as such. No one else seemed to regard them as murders before *you* decided they were."

Anders stepped into the arena, at the edge of the lantern light, his amiable face darkened with a wave of uncharacteristic anger.

"That is not true. I was the one who identified both—"

Danny spun on his heel.

"Ah yes, of course, you would say that in support of the man who all here know to be your friend. You can't expect anything you say in his defence to be taken seriously. If you wish to be believed we need more than just your word. Did you tell anyone else of your suspicions?"

"Yes. Of course." Anders was frowning. "I told Captain Blanchard."

Danny nodded a few times.

"But not the graf, who should have also been informed. It is a great shame you didn't think to do so, because as we are all aware Captain Blanchard isn't with us anymore, so there is only your word, which as I already pointed out is tainted when it comes to this man."

"But you are—"

Mags made a low sound that was close to a growl. "You have been told you can't speak up for Fox, so hold your peace."

Gideon could see the immense effort it took the Dane to gather his self-control and step back. It struck him then that the only way he could win this, if indeed it could be won, was through the words of his ill-wishers and not his allies. That, and somehow leading Mags to believe that his authority was shown better by seeking the truth than by allowing a scapegoat to be sacrificed. Even a scapegoat who was, for most there, the symbol of all they had disliked about Philip Lord.

Danny turned back to Gideon. His expression transformed by the lantern light to something menacing.

"You will admit that you claimed Ruth Whitaker and Sir Arthur Cochrane were both murdered?"

"I did because they were."

"And yet you didn't share your concerns with any of the household, those who were the most at risk from this putative killer?"

Gideon felt his jaw tense.

"I was told not to say anything to anyone to avoid there being a panic."

"Told? Who by?"

"By Captain Blanchard."

Danny didn't say anything to that. He made a show of looking around at those present, peering into the shadows, as if seeking a familiar face. Then he shrugged.

"The graf didn't know of your investigation?"

It took all Gideon's willpower not to look at Mags. This was the point at which he had to decide whether the words spoken in the night by Danny Bristow were meant to help or harm. There was nothing to guide him in Danny's steady gaze. But he realised it made no difference whether Danny was right or not because to announce that Mags had known of the murders and allowed Gideon to continue his investigation would be to undermine the basis of this trial and so would be denied. Though had he known then how Mags would choose to reward his discretion, he might well have spoken out regardless.

"No. Unless he was informed by Captain Blanchard."

There was a shift in Danny's expression and a brief glimpse of what Gideon thought might be relief.

And now the farce was complete.

"Did Captain Blanchard encourage you to investigate?"

Gideon decided it was time to move things further onto his own ground, to demonstrate the restrictions being placed on his ability to defend himself.

"There is no point in asking me what Captain Blanchard did or did not say since as you already observed he isn't here to confirm or deny it. You have made it clear my word alone is not sufficient on the matter."

Mags was not happy with that.

"Whether the man is here or not, you can tell us what he had you do," he growled.

Gideon took a half step forward, then pulled himself up to his full height and met Mags' gaze.

"Either my word on its own is good or my word on its own has no value. It cannot be both. And in the latter case anything I might have to say, unsupported, about any private conversation, is irrelevant."

"Spoken like a true lawyer," Mags said, then he hawked and spat on the floor at Gideon's feet. "I'm your judge, so how about you answer what you are asked and leave it to me to decide what's true in it and what's false? Even in the assizes they do that, so I hear."

There was some laughter from around the room. A

dozen rebuttals leapt to Gideon's tongue, and he swallowed them all, together with his pride. He had made a mistake. Whatever his motive in saying so, Danny had been right to warn him. Mags cared nothing for this except in how far it left him with more authority—more *appearance* of authority. Playing the clever lawyer would only lose Gideon what small amount of sympathy he might yet have from the company.

He drew a breath and bowed his head.

"You are right, of course, my lord. My apologies." When he looked up the surprise, though quickly hidden, was evident in Mags' expression. Gideon turned back to Danny. "Captain Blanchard asked me to investigate once it became clear that the death of Sir Arthur was not an accident, that he too had been murdered."

From the chairs where the household sat there was a small commotion. Sir William had got to his feet.

"You claim Sir Arthur was murdered, sir? Why would you think that?"

Gideon said nothing and looked towards Mags. If he was permitted to speak now…

Mags waved a dismissive hand.

"He wasn't, except in one desperate man's imagination. Let's just get to the point, Captain Bristow."

Danny gave a slight bow towards the chair. "Then perhaps, with your permission, my lord, I might ask Mistress Franklyn to tell us what happened."

Even before Mags had agreed, Alice Franklyn had risen to her feet, letting the cloak she had been wearing fall to the seat behind her. She was dressed in bright red, with gold points, her collar heavy with lace and low enough to reveal the creamy flesh of her swelling breasts. She held the eye of every man in the room. Gideon's heart sank as he saw Mags' look was as lustful as the rest.

Danny made a slight bow towards her.

"I must apologise. I know you will find this troubling. To speak of a murder witnessed, and a child—your own nephew—nearly so."

Alice Franklyn lifted her head nobly, her shadow dancing behind her as a draft caught the candle flame. "It must be said. I may only be a weak woman, but I know my duty."

"We can all see you have great courage," Danny assured her. "Please, tell me how it was you came to miss going to church with the rest of the household?"

She hesitated and Gideon knew from long experience it was a question she had not expected to be asked. He felt a sudden stir of hope, but that was crushed when she lowered her head as if embarrassed and a little colour flushed her cheeks.

"I was suffering from a woman's problem," she said, in a quiet voice. It was an answer guaranteed to ensure that she wasn't asked to offer any explanation or account of herself. There was an uncomfortable silence in the room.

Even Danny looked unsettled.

"You were—uh—resting?"

"That's right. Then I felt better and had risen and dressed when I heard a scream from the nursery. I rushed there and found poor Dorcas bleeding on the floor and that vile witch was picking up baby Charlie." She put both her hands to her face as if the memory was too shocking. "I tried to stop her, of course, but she ran

THE TRAITOR'S APPRENTICE

into the nursery maid's chamber and shut the door and locked it. I shouted for help and Mr Muir came running. He had just managed to kick the door down when that man," she pointed an accusing finger at Gideon, "came in and attacked Mr Muir."

"He drew his sword and attacked Muir?" Danny asked.

"Yes." There must have been something in Danny's expression because she flushed. "I—don't remember. It was all such a rush." Now her hands were clasped together over her heart, her expression one of appeal. "Oh, now I remember, he was hitting poor Mr Muir with a chair and Mr Muir was so brave and endured it whilst trying to rescue Charlie. I was full of fear for Mr Muir was sorely pressed." She turned her wide and vulnerable gaze on Danny. "But you were there. You saw. You rescued Mr Muir."

"I was there," Danny agreed. "Thank you for your account, and my apologies for the need to remind you of such distressing events."

Gideon felt the fragile fabric of hope that had been sustaining him fraying away at the edges. Danny turned to him, expression unreadable.

"And your account?"

Muir shuffled behind Mags' chair.

"Excuse me, my lord, but is that necessary? It isn't as if anyone here would think for a moment that Mistress Franklyn might be lying and I for one can vouch for the truth in what she says, I am sure Captain Bristow will do the same."

Mags glanced at Muir and then at Gideon before leaning back in the chair, his arms resting on the ones it had.

"You make a good point. We all heard what happened. I think we can—"

"No." The voice was quiet and firm and every eye in the room moved to its owner. Elizabeth Belamy stood up. "It was *my* son who was nearly killed and those others who have died were a guest in *my* house and *my* servant. I would ask then, as this affects me more than any, that we hear from Mr Fox why he did what he did. I want to know."

Had it been anyone else who objected to his riding roughshod over the most basic principle of justice, Mags could have silenced them with aggressive bluster or subtle threat as he had all others who had so far tried to do so. But as Gideon knew, Mags needed the approval and tacit support of Lady Belamy, just as Philip Lord had done, to provide the fig leaf of propriety for his occupation of Wrathby.

Were she to withdraw her permission, the company would of course remain, but as an occupying power not as welcome guests. That would doubtless bring Fairfax with as many men as he could muster, if not the Earl of Newcastle with his much larger northern army of the king.

Mags inclined his head after a moment of thought.

"If that is your wish and as long as it is brief."

Still on her feet, Elizabeth Belamy turned to Gideon.

"Then tell me why? Why did you want to kill my son?"

Gideon swallowed hard. In any other place, it would have been the opening he could use to state his case. But in this corrupt gathering dominated by the whim and will of a man who cared nothing for guilt or innocence, for the lives already lost or those that would be through

THE TRAITOR'S APPRENTICE

his injustice, that wouldn't be enough.

Chapter Fourteen

"It's obvious why he wanted to kill the baby," Alice Franklyn insisted before Gideon could speak. "I already told you, Elizabeth, he is enthralled by that vile creature you let into the house, and *she* wanted to sacrifice my nephew to her demons. She sneaks off to worship them several times a day, her and that Moor who follows her around like a guard dog." She spun to face Gideon, her cheeks almost as bright as the colour of her silk dress. "And *he* is her thrall and paramour. Anyone who has seen him when she is around will vouch for that."

Gideon's head was beginning to ache. He made himself step aside from the torrent of abuse and spoke to the baroness, answering her question, as if Alice hadn't intervened.

"Lady Belamy, I swear before God that I have never and would never seek to harm your son or allow any other to harm him. I do, however, know of one who does seek his death, and if I am condemned and they go free, then I fear that your son won't live to see his first birthday. All I ask," he continued, over the rumble of outrage his words instigated, "is that I am allowed to present my case. After that, even if I am condemned at least you will be forewarned and able to guard yourself and your child against his real enemy."

Elizabeth Belamy swayed on her feet and her skin, even in the softness of lantern light, looked ashen. She swallowed a few times as if fighting back nausea and there was a brief fluster of movement at the far end of

THE TRAITOR'S APPRENTICE

the room which Gideon realised was Anders being restrained from going to her aid.

"I don't think Lady Belamy wants to hear your tall tales," Muir said as he crossed from the shadows beside Mags' chair and helped her to sit down.

"The graf summoned this trial to get to the truth." Danny Bristow's voice was sharp. "The graf wishes the truth to be known, don't you, my lord?"

Gideon glanced at him, wondering why he spoke up. Then realised far from being in support of himself, it was no doubt to bring the initiative back into Danny's grasp.

Mags moved on his chair. "The graf," he said, "wants this cursed trial over and done and the murderer dealt with so we can get to other things."

Danny made a small bow of compliance towards Mags, then turned his attention back to Gideon, a brutal intelligence glittering in his eyes. "Do you believe you can help us with that, Mr Fox, without ranging into the realms of wild fantasy and conspiracy? Concise and precise?"

Gideon had to take a breath before he could speak. The tightness in his chest increased as painful hope threw out tender shoots to wrap around his heart. Perhaps he was wrong, perhaps Danny had been speaking in his support. But he was far from sure. His hands felt clammy, and it was getting harder to concentrate.

"If Lady Belamy and the graf will allow," he said.

Alice Franklyn was whispering something into her sister-in-law's ear, but the baroness drew away. "I want to hear him speak."

Gideon turned to Mags, who glowered at him and lifted a hand granting permission. Gideon responded with a bow, wondering what mix of emollience and praise would work and hoping he could judge the blend aright.

"My lord," he said, straightening from the bow and meeting Mags' disgruntled gaze. "It takes a great man to bring justice to those who are wronged and a wise man to know that only by holding up its counter can true justice shine."

It was enough to confuse him at least and Gideon didn't allow him the time to frame a response, turning to Elizabeth Belamy.

"There is only one person in this house who has anything substantial to gain from the death of your son, my lady. The same person who was present also at the death of your husband when it was thought his child was not yet born. The same person who tried to suborn Ruth Whitaker to murder an innocent babe and murdered her when she refused. The same person who killed the man who had been witness to something that would have betrayed the murderer and who was, from desperate need, attempting blackmail. The same person who was alone in the house, with everyone else of the household in church, when your nursemaid tried to defend your son from being stifled and died heroically in the attempt."

Gideon stepped back a pace, so he was illuminated more by the candlelight and pitched his voice to reach everyone in the room. It was becoming more difficult to do. The miraculous surge of strength that had carried him so far was ebbing now. His hands were trembling, so he clenched his fists as all eyes were fixed on him, awaiting his revelation.

"My lady, let me be condemned if you will, but I beg you, do not allow Alice Franklyn or her lover, Simon

THE TRAITOR'S APPRENTICE

Muir, anywhere near your son or yourself when you are alone or unguarded." He had to raise his voice to be heard over the inevitable outcry. "Whether I live or die, I beg you banish them from Wrathby that your son might live."

Alice Franklyn was on her feet and shrieking, Muir, sword in hand, threw himself across the few feet separating him from Gideon and met the steel of Danny Bristow's drawn blade, before he could complete the cut he had intended.

"He dishonours the lady," Muir snarled. "I'll slice his lying tongue from his mouth."

Gideon kept very still. His head was throbbing, sweat had begun beading all over his body and a feeling of weakness spread through his limbs. Danny, sword still a barrier between Muir and Gideon, took a step to the side and looked at Mags. Gideon followed his gaze. Mags hadn't moved but was wearing a thoughtful look.

"What would you, my lord?" Danny asked.

Mags spread his hands in a gesture of benevolence.

"Give Fox a sword, Danny, eh? Let's settle this the old-fashioned way."

For a moment Gideon couldn't understand what that meant. The collective sigh of expectation followed by speculative murmuring and even the chink of coin made no sense to him.

Then it did and the walls of the room seemed to close in.

Trial by combat.

It still existed unrepealed in English Law, Gideon knew, but it was archaic. Someone had tried to invoke it ten years before and the king himself had squashed that. But this was a court acknowledging no law except that decided by Mags. To him and his men, it must seem a natural way to settle their differences.

Except this wasn't an internal dispute between two mercenaries, this was the fate of the household of Wrathby. Zahara's life and the life of a child hung in this balance and justice for those murdered by the greed of one callous woman. Gideon's guts twisted with anger and frustration. He stood unmoving as Danny ordered Muir to back off, before stepping in, reversing his sword and offering the hilt to Gideon.

Then reality hit home.

This could only end one way.

Gideon's stomach revolted into nausea and his entire body now was shivering.

"She is a good blade," Danny said. "If you let her, she will fight for you." His voice had dropped to a low and urgent tone covered by the excitement around them. "Muir counts on aggression for his guard, prefers to go high and left, and his swordmaster must have wept tears trying to remind him not to overextend on every other lunge. Make him angry, get him off balance and he'll be easy to spike." Then something shifted in Danny's eyes. "Christ, Gideon, you look dead already. I had hoped Anders—"

Then Gideon remembered and instead of taking the proffered sword reached into his breeches pocket. Danny gripped the hand that held the bottle before he could lift it to remove the cork.

"Give me that." He took the precious bottle before Gideon's trembling fingers could even attempt to stop him and it vanished from his hand. "Faint. Now. Just drop."

Gideon wondered at what point he had decided that

THE TRAITOR'S APPRENTICE

Danny was someone he could still trust but took a step back and did his best impression of a collapse. It must have been convincing as he heard Anders call his name. The kick was unexpected, but he managed not to respond.

"Get up Fox," Danny sounded cold. Then he lifted his voice. "Jensen, get over here now, I want Fox on his feet."

Anders must have run because it was a moment later Gideon felt his hand feeling for a pulse.

"He is ill. He can't fight your vengeful duel." Anders was struggling to contain his anger.

"He has no choice," Danny said, his tone callous. "The graf requires it. If he can't stand and fight, Muir will just skewer him where he lies. Your choice."

"That might be kinder," Anders said. Then he drew a sharp breath of surprise and Gideon realised Danny must have slipped the bottle into Anders' hand.

"Just get him up," Danny snapped, and the sound of his boots retreated.

A powerful and pungent smell filled Gideon's nostrils and he started coughing. Anders helped him to sit and studied him with concerned eyes. Then he opened his bag and taking the small bottle added something more to it, shaking it before holding it out.

"This might kill you, my friend, but that is 'might'. Without it, in your state, Muir will for sure, so better small beer than an empty jug."

Gideon looked at the bottle and hesitated. The bitter truth was that Anders was right. Muir was a trained swordsman, and he was a professional lawyer. The outcome would be in little doubt even if Gideon had been at full strength.

Anders must have misunderstood the reason for the hesitation because he shook his head. "You are young, and your heart is strong. I would not offer this if I thought you could not withstand it."

Hand still trembling, Gideon took the bottle and drank the contents to the dregs. As he did so the doors were thrown open at the end of the room and one of Lord's— no, Mags' men came in, the gargoyle faced Thomson, escorting another prisoner.

Zahara.

Clad in her housekeeper's clothing, she walked uncompelled and unafraid, head lifted and expression as serene as if she were going about her usual business of the day. She radiated calm. Her gaze met Gideon's and as it did so, she smiled. Gideon felt as if he had received a blessing. Then she was pushed into the corner of the room, and he lost sight of her.

Perhaps it was whatever simple Anders had added to the bottle, or perhaps it was Zahara's presence and the smile which carried her belief in him, but he felt his strength and energy returning and got to his feet, unaided.

Anders clapped a hand on his unbandaged shoulder, his expression lifted into a wry smile. "I hope you've had more sword practice than I have found time for."

Belatedly Gideon realised that Anders' own life was being placed at risk by showing himself so partisan.

"Thank you and I am so sorry that you have been pulled into this through me." It sounded inadequate.

Anders' smile became a little more defined.

"If you die, I forgive you, my friend. If you live, we shall see."

There was no time for more. Danny was already

striding over. He eyed Gideon.

"You've done your work, Jensen. You can go."

Anders gave Gideon a final nod and then made his way to the back of the room. Danny slid his sword free of its hanger and offered it with the lattice-like basket grip first. Gideon closed his hand on it and noticed the replica of the pommel shape Philip Lord had on his blade, although this was in unpolished brass where Lord's looked silver. Like Lord's sword, it had a double-edged blade with a serviceable point and could be used to cut or thrust with equal facility. The curving quillons extended to the top, bottom and back of the blade, and the thumb was protected by a looped guard.

As he took the sword, he knew that it was as different as night and day from any other blade he had held, even set against the well-made backsword he had been given since joining the company. Just the movement to lift it from Danny's grip showed how easily it could be recovered. He now understood what he had been told about the importance of quality in a sword.

"Don't forget what I said before," Danny murmured. Then he turned away as Mags summoned him.

Gideon moved his hand to feel how the cat's head pommel countered the weight of the blade and tried to remember all he had learned about preparation for a fencing bout. Except, this was not that. This was a duel and would be to the death. The enormity of that settled on his shoulders like a heavy cloak.

Letting the blade dip, Gideon folded both his hands around the hilt and careless of the eyes of all upon him, he dropped to one knee in the middle of the room that would soon become a duelling ground. Then he closed his eyes to prepare in the way he knew he should. He was going to die in this room and there was nothing he could do to stop that from happening.

But even prayer seemed beyond him. When he tried to pray, the only words that came were those from his heart—not for himself, not for forgiveness, not for any of the things he knew a man facing death should consider when confronting his final chance on earth for repentance and making peace with his maker. There was one sincere prayer he could utter. *Dear God, whatever happens to me, please place your hand over Zahara and somehow keep her safe.*

"Fox!" Mags' bark broke into the prayer. "Get up man, I want this done."

Gideon opened his eyes and got back to his feet. The same surge of strength that had carried him through the verbal jousting had returned in full. There was no pain from his shoulder and his mind was lucid and sharp. Perhaps it was an answer to his prayer. Suddenly Gideon felt there was even hope...

Muir stood ready and waiting. He looked collected and confident, treating Gideon to a look of contempt.

Someone had found a Bible and it now lay on a small table in the middle of the cleared area of the room which was lit by the ceiling lanterns. One at a time, to give the fight some semblance of legitimacy in the eyes of the company, if not the law, they each avowed their belief in the rightness of their cause.

Gideon went first as the challenger and then as Muir spoke the words of an oath that should have burned his tongue to ash and choked in his throat, Gideon caught sight of Elizabeth Belamy. She sat behind the row of company men, her face pale. Gideon wondered at what point she realised that any notion of attaining true justice had been thrown out the moment she placed her trust in Mags to deliver it. That she had unleashed something dark, savage and well beyond her power to control.

The Bible and table were removed, and Danny gestured Gideon and Muir to stand on either side of himself, facing each other with perhaps three sword lengths between them.

"Simon Muir," Danny said. His voice was solemn, lifted to reach to either end of the room where the company had disposed themselves, leaving the lantern-lit centre as the field of honour the combatants had to fight in. "Do you swear before God that you have this day neither eat, drank, nor have upon you, neither bone, stone, nor grass—nor any enchantment, sorcery, or witchcraft, whereby the law of God may be abased, or the law of the Devil exalted, so help you God?" He must have done this many times before as he knew the words by heart.

"I so swear," Muir snarled. "Alice Franklyn is innocent, and I will prove it in the blood of this upstart lawyer just as soon as you let me."

"Gideon Lennox," Danny had turned to him now, "do you swear before God that you have this day—"

"For the love of God, Danny, enough of the swearing. Just let them at it before we all die of old age waiting."

Mags' voice cut through just as Gideon was wondering if the potent medication Anders had given him counted as drinking some such enchantment and if he could therefore even take such an oath without placing his soul in jeopardy.

Danny made a curt bow towards the throne-like chair and then turned to look between Gideon and Muir.

"This is to the death, gentleman. May God favour the

righteous."

He stepped back and Muir attacked.

Gideon had forgotten the ferocity of the man, but now he had a length of sharpened steel at least to defend himself, not the short blunt stub of a poker.

It was a feint, Gideon knew, because he went low and right. Danny had said Muir favoured high and left. So instead of defending he sidestepped and had his sword ready for the follow up which could have ended the fight had Gideon tried to block the feint. It was far from a perfect defence even so. The length of Muir's rapier slid over the steel of Gideon's weapon and caught on the basket lattice of the hand guard.

But the fact Gideon had managed to predict and deflect his attack with such apparent ease had shaken Muir's nerves a little. After the scuffle in the nursery, Muir clearly believed he had the measure of Gideon as a fighter and was expecting to make short work of him. Seeing that, Gideon's confidence boomed, and the last vestiges of his fear vanished. He found an inappropriate smile was tugging at the corners of his mouth.

The next few attacks from Muir were probing more than serious attempts and with a sword in his hand that moved like an extension of his own will, Gideon turned them. Then he realised he had been so focused on his defence that he had neglected any opportunities to attack or riposte himself.

What had Danny said? *Muir counts on aggression for his guard. Make him angry, get him off balance and he'll be easy to spike.*

Flowing with a new certainty and an odd sensation of invincibility, Gideon pushed himself onto the attack. He knew he had the advantage in holding the superior weapon with the flexibility to cut or thrust as the opportunity offered. He blocked a thrust from Muir's rapier high and left and used the basket to catch Muir's blade and the quillons to turn it so he could cut in at the other man's head, forcing Muir to duck away and disengage.

There were some protesting calls from the watching men at that point. Not surprisingly, as the clever money was on Muir, and they were protesting their investment. For the first time, Gideon realised he might have a chance to win.

So as Muir retreated, he pushed hard, blocking the next thrust and trying to repeat his head cut. But this time Muir was ready, and Gideon had cause to offer silent gratitude to the few men of the company like Jupp and Olsen who had taken the time to teach him some of the more common dirty tricks and their counters. He saw the move Muir was trying and turned his body sideways, lifting his blade to catch the incoming point just as it reached his chest and then bringing his own to cut upwards so he caught the leather of Muir's thick buff coat.

Which was when he realised the advantage that layer of armour gave the other man. But the shout that went up from those watching was some reward. A voice Gideon thought he recognised as Jupp called out.

"Not such a big brave man, now are you, Muir. Cut up by a paltry lawyer with a borrowed sword—fresh from his sick bed too."

The effect on Muir was immediate and the man started attacking again with a renewed ferocity that put Gideon off balance, and for a time it was all he could do to keep the probing blade at bay from his torso. Sweat was running down his face and his heart was beating so fast he wondered if it could sustain itself for much longer.

He tried to find an opening to counter, but the rapier moved with incredible speed. Each attack pushed him back and each parry seemed impossible to turn into a riposte. He realised that Muir was now in his stride and enjoying himself. Whatever confidence he had lost by Gideon's first response was now restored and more. There was a certainty of victory in his intent gaze. Gideon was forced back under the onslaught, giving ground and giving ground.

He heard a voice shouting his name as if in warning and then there was nowhere to retreat to. The wall was right behind him, and he was about to be pinned to it. A bubble of panic welled from deep in his stomach. Despite the fire and ice that reigned through his body from whatever Anders had given him, he knew he was struggling now.

The lunge when it came was fast and lethal. Betrayed by a movement of Muir's shoulders and hips, then his front foot shifting forward. It should have pierced Gideon's heart and left him nailed to the wall like the sconce beside him, but somehow by blind instinct, he had his hand in the way—the hand protected by the basket hilt of the sword. He turned his wrist and deflected the blade away along the topmost quillon. The rapier blade slid past his ribs instead, the point pierced cloth—and wall. Muir tried to recover the blade, but it was held, gripped in the wood for a moment too long.

Muir's body was open, but Gideon's blade was locked in place by the rapier.

From somewhere in his mind came Danny's voice. *He overextends on every other lunge.*

THE TRAITOR'S APPRENTICE

Gideon had no idea if Muir had overextended this time, but kicked out, full force, with his booted foot into the side of Muir's front knee.

Unable to defend as his weight was too far forward, Muir staggered and fell, his desperate grip on it for some point of balance pulling the rapier free as he went down. Gideon kicked him again, then realised the danger and cut down hard with the sword.

In his fear and anger, he sliced at the arm that held the rapier just as Muir tried to roll out of the way. Gideon's blade cut through the leather and cloth of Muir's right arm a little above the elbow and bit into the flesh beneath, stopping only when it hit bone. Muir gasped and the rapier clattered to the floor. Without thinking, Gideon kicked it away.

Muir was trying to push himself back, unable to get to his feet as his knee had been too damaged, his right arm broken and useless. Gideon brought the blade of his sword up Muir's blood sheening its silver with a blush of red. There was a sudden silence in the room as if the entire company was holding its collective breath, waiting for him to give them the catharsis of another man's death. Gideon could see Mags leaning forward in his chair to see better, not to miss a moment of what would now be an execution.

Muir's eyes fixed on Gideon along the length of steel in his hands, waiting, body tensed against a weapon designed to sunder life from flesh. From somewhere it came to Gideon as certain knowledge that if he completed this act, he would cross a line. He would no longer be the person he knew himself to be. He had killed before in hot blood. In defence of his own life and another's. He would have killed today had the blow he inflicted been fatal rather than incapacitating. But to take the life of a crippled and unarmed man was something different.

"Just get it done, Fox." Mags' words were echoed by an ugly murmur from around the room. Not surprising as those were the ones now going to be poorer by whatever they had wagered against Gideon, and he was denying them the only compensation they could expect.

"No." It was a moment after the word was spoken that he realised he had said it. Then lifting the blade away from Muir, he stepped back. "I have won the fight. I don't need to take his life to prove it." He had to raise his voice to be heard over the swell of protest. "God almighty has given witness through my victory that I spoke the truth. That Alice Franklyn and Simon Muir plotted the deaths of all those who stood between her and Wrathby and they cared nothing for killing anyone, innocent or otherwise who might seek to prevent that."

Mags made a gesture to the men near him and nodded towards the household, where Alice Franklyn sat in her chair, face chalk white against the red dress, like a lily in a bouquet of roses. She didn't even resist as she was pulled to her feet and brought to stand in the cleared area of the room.

"What to do with them then, Fox? They are murderers, but you won't kill them. Yet the law you claim to serve condemns murderers to death. Why so squeamish?"

Gideon lowered his head and bit back the words he wanted to say. That this wasn't any kind of court of law and that it had no jurisdiction to order the death of anyone.

"I am a lawyer," he said, his voice hoarse. "Not an executioner. Find someone else to do it."

THE TRAITOR'S APPRENTICE

The sword was still in his hand and a part of him wanted to fling it away, but he couldn't bring himself to do that. Wielding this sword, he knew, had saved his life. If he had fought with another blade, even his own, he would be the one lying there on the floor.

Mags stared at him for a moment as if not believing what he had just heard. Then he laughed and, getting to his feet, slapped Danny on the back.

"You'd better see to it then Captain Bristow. It's your sword that started the work after all."

Danny straightened up and inclined his head.

"As you wish, my lord."

He crossed the room, and a low murmur of speculation broke out. Gideon heard voices debating if the wagers were still valid if Gideon failed to complete the kill himself. He ignored them. He was feeling the first signs of returning weakness. As before, his hands had begun to tremble. He had expected Danny would come and take the blade from him, but instead, he went straight to Muir, who was denying, protesting, begging. Danny stood astride him and in a single movement, drew the knife from his belt and despatched the fallen man as if he was killing a stricken dog.

Straightening, the knife in his hand, fresh with blood as Muir died, Danny looked over to Alice Franklyn and took a step towards her. Her eyes went wide, and her mouth opened as if to scream, but no sound came. Instead, she collapsed unconscious against Aleksandrov who had been holding her and now scooped her up in his arms. Danny, reaching them, grabbed a handful of Alice's hair and exposed her throat.

"Leave her be, Danny. That would be a waste," Mags said. "I'll see to her myself. Aleksandrov." The last word was an order and Aleksandrov carried the unconscious woman out of the building."

Gideon felt nothing. Not even relief. It was as if the part of his being that was capable of feeling had been numbed. He had won. He was alive. Zahara was safe. And nothing else mattered.

Chapter Fifteen

I

As the door closed behind Aleksandrov, bearing the unconscious Alice Franklyn to Mags' chambers, Gideon realised whatever Anders had provided to keep him on his feet was beginning to lose its ability to do so. Although he was still standing, sword in hand a few paces from the body of Simon Muir, he lacked the will or ability to move and feared if he tried to do so by even a step he would collapse.

There was a small commotion on the other side of the room. Elizabeth Belamy stood up. She pushed her way past the men to command attention in the space that had been cleared for the fight and which was only now being reoccupied as the company began to relax.

"You are barbaric monsters. All of you." Lady Belamy's voice, shaking with fury, carried over the growing volume of conversation and quietened it. "I want you all gone from my house. You must leave tomorrow. Every one of you."

Behind her, her mother Lady Grace had taken shelter under the arm of the Reverend William Irving, who looked to Gideon as if he had been thunderstruck. They had come to witness a trial and learn the truth about the death of a friend. Instead, they had been forced to take part in a parody of justice ending in a bloody fight to the death, directed by the will of a man for whom it was a tool to advance his dark ends.

Mags laughed.

"That is precious little gratitude for what I just did for you," he said, his tone hard. "I've saved the life of your puling infant. You should be thanking me for it. But as it happens, my lady, your wishes and my intentions align for the now. Captain Bristow—" Mags looked over to where Danny was cleaning the blood of Simon Muir from his knife and glanced up hearing his name, "will escort you and yours back to the house. I'd suggest you stay in your rooms tonight."

Danny acknowledged the order with a brief bow, then crossed to Gideon and reached for the sword before, instead, grasping the wrist that held it.

"Jensen," he called. "This man needs your attention." Then in a different tone and under the cover of taking back his sword, he spoke so softly it was hard to hear. "Well done. I wasn't sure you had it in you, but by God, I am glad you did."

Gideon glared back, a toxic mix of emotions stirred by the words. Part of him wanted to acknowledge that more than anything it had been Danny's sword and Danny's advice that had given him the upper hand over Muir in the end. For that Gideon owed him a debt of gratitude and his life itself. But the choking anger at this man who seemed to be playing some strange double game, friendly one moment and brutally callous the next, deprived him of words.

Danny stepped away, wiped the blade of his sword clean and sheathed it, before he approached the baroness with a polite bow and escorted her, her mother and the Reverend Irving through the room, two of his men following behind. Those of the company in their path moved aside at a sharp word from Danny.

THE TRAITOR'S APPRENTICE

Then Anders was there, his face wearing the same suppressed look of concern as it had before the fight.

"I need to get you out of here. Can you walk?"

In reply, Gideon took a step and staggered, held up only by Anders' arm. He realised his whole body was shivering and a sheen of sweat had broken out over his face. His shoulder ached and the place where Muir's rapier had grazed his ribs was smarting.

"Zahara?" He had to know but shaping the word was hard. His mouth was dry, and a bitter taste lingered on his tongue.

"She is safe. You, on the other hand, my friend, are not out of danger yet. I know we all have either to suffer a lot or die young, but you seem set on a course to do both."

With Anders' help, Gideon was more than halfway towards the door when it opened again to readmit Danny Bristow. At which point Mags lifted his battlefield voice over the noise.

"Bar the door, Captain Bristow. I have something to say to the company and I wish no one to leave until it is said."

Anders growled a word in his native tongue that Gideon assumed was exceptionally virulent. They were saved by Jupp who was now beside Gideon with one of the chairs the members of the household had been sitting on.

Gideon sat, feeling nauseous. The pace of his heart was making his chest tight with the effort of containing it. He wanted to lie down somewhere quiet, but instead, he had to sit and listen as Mags spoke the doom of Wrathby.

Mags stood in front of his chair flanked by the men

Gideon had marked as being most often in his company, men who, like Aleksandrov, had made no secret of their allegiance to Mags above Lord. Eight of them stood with him. Their eyes raked with hostility the faces of those they had called comrades or friends earlier that day. Glancing back, trying to find Zahara, Gideon could see six more of Mags' men standing by the door, with Danny Bristow, hand on sword, before them.

Gideon shivered with something that had no kind of physical cause. He couldn't see Zahara and could only hope she had managed to slip out with the other women, none of whom seemed to be in the room any longer.

"You all know now, don't you?" At Mags' first words the room became silent. "You know the Schiavono isn't coming back. He's the best way to Newcastle and they'll hang him there as a traitor—that is if he lives that long. He's been taken by a man that hates him enough to slit his throat for him a good time before that. Whatever happens, he's a dead man."

The idea that Philip Lord was still alive, even if a prisoner, brought a sudden breath of hope back to Gideon. The low rumble that greeted this pronouncement told him it wasn't news to those here. He wondered why Mags didn't just say Lord was already dead, then realised that too many of the company wouldn't believe it.

"That means," Mags said, "we need a new commander."

The rumble of voices grew louder then fell again as Mags held up his hand.

"Now you all know me. You know I'm not an arrogant man. I'm not a man who assumes things. So even though the Schiavono himself made me his second, and command of the company here should therefore fall to me by right, I want it to fall to me because you and you…" He pointed his finger at the assembled men and moved it to point again and again. "And you and all of you approve that right."

"How you going to pay us then, Mags?" someone called from the back of the room.

"Did the Schiavono pay you? I've not seen any man here receive his pay these last three weeks."

Which Gideon had to admit was true. He had been promised pay but had so far received none.

"The Schiavono paid us in the first week of each month," the Swedish man, Olsen, put in, "and a bonus after any fight he took us to. I was paid on time last month. He's not been here this and I've not been fighting since so I've no complaints."

"Been digging though," another voice said and that prompted laughter and more calls.

"Too much bloody digging."

"My hands are turned shovels, I swear it."

"Christ, my back knows all about it. He had us at it like Pharaoh with the Israelites."

Mags nodded. "Yes. We've been digging, all of us, on the Schiavono's command. Like day labourers. Or slaves." He broke off and looked thoughtful. "And what for?"

There was a sudden silence. It was hard for Gideon not to feel a grudging admiration for Mags' technique. He was a clever man, more so than Gideon had realised before.

"Why have we all been scabbling in the dirt?" Mags asked again.

"Because the Schiavono ordered it?" one voice

suggested.

"To provide a secure base for our winter quarters," Jupp said. "We all know that."

"Secure?" Mags made a sound like a disgruntled horse, then spat on the floor. "Danny, you tell these men the truth. Is this house going to be secure if Newcastle comes south or if Fairfax brings men in force?"

There was a strained silence and all eyes moved from Mags to Danny, who shrugged.

"As we are now, with a bit of good fortune we could make a decent fist of defence for a week or two," he told them. "Enough to put off a smaller force, make them think us not worth the effort. We need another month, some decent weather, a supply of stone and a lot more digging to change that. Even then, we've not got adequate ordnance so it would be a scrappy kind of make-shift. And it's not like we've declared for one side or the other so if it came to a proper siege, we'd have no hope of relief. We'd have to break out sooner or later."

His words were met with silence and Gideon realised that each man in the room knew he spoke nothing but the simple truth, as they were all familiar enough with such matters to have drawn the same conclusions already. But they all knew Danny, more than any of them, was qualified to state that truth.

Of course, what he didn't say was that Philip Lord himself would have provided the true strength for their defence. Using diplomacy, subterfuge or force according to circumstance and keeping the goodwill of Elizabeth Belamy—something Mags had lost them in the space of an hour.

"So much for secure winter quarters, eh?" Mags nodded and walked from one side of the room to the other as he went on. "I have a better plan. I say we leave the digging to the farm labourers, and we remember who we are—what we are. We're soldiers, not peasants." He made a gesture, snatching at the air in front of him. "We take what we need, we don't break our backs grovelling in the dirt for it."

"The Schiavono always paid for our supplies," Jupp said. "Unless there was none to be bought or no gold in the coffers and that was rare."

"He did," Mags agreed, nodding his head. "He did indeed. And do you know what that meant?" he paused and looked around. "No? No one?"

"The goodwill of the local people?" one man suggested.

"And what is that compared to the loss of gold used to buy it? They'd still provide whether paid or forced. We've all seen that in the German wars." Mags made an expansive gesture. "You, all of you, could be rich men by now if we had full and proper shares of the money the Schiavono has spent on buying what he could just take."

"He took enough in the German wars," someone muttered.

"Aye, and he had no problem taking ships in the narrow sea and the Mediterranie—even English ships," one of the men beside Mags said.

"And you would know, eh, Turk?" Mags clapped a hand on his back.

The mood in the room was getting ugly as old resentments aired and when Jupp and some of the others tried to counter the talk, Mags made a gesture to Danny, who with two of the men at his back pushed Jupp to the middle of the room. Gideon's skin bristled with goosebumps as they brought him to stand before Mags, who stood up and called for silence. When it was quiet, he laid a hand on Jupp's shoulder.

"You're a good man Roger, we all know that. A loyal man. A man the Schiavono counted on. But he's gone. You can't be disloyal to him whatever you do. He's not here anymore. Can't you see the best way you can serve him now is by doing what's best for the company?"

It was clear what Mags was trying to do. Jupp was Lord's man through and through. He was also the one who commanded the respect of his peers more perhaps than any other, one they would listen to and follow.

"I was waiting," Jupp said, "to hear your offer to the company, before deciding."

Mags started a smile that broadened into a wide grin. He slapped Jupp on the back. "As I said, you're a good man—and a wise one." Then he jerked his head to Danny and Jupp was taken to one side, leaving Mags his stage once more. Gideon had a sudden cold fear that Jupp, the leader of the disquiet at Mags' coup, would be dealt with by the same cold dispatch as Muir had been.

"I say we don't stay here one more day," Mags continued. "We've been living on top of a gold mine and making do with scraps. My offer is simple—we take this house, take its bounty and then tomorrow morning we ride out with all we have, and we find someone who will pay us good money for our skills. You know I can do that. It's what I've always done for my men. I'll negotiate the best deal you ever had with shares for all, not just miserly pay."

There were murmurs of agreement and approval around the room. Mags smiled.

"You've all seen this land—rich and lush, like a virgin

sprawled with her legs open. All we have to do is take her." He pushed his hand into a tight fist and punched the air. "But tonight, this house—the wine, the women, the wealth—is ours, boys. Now, who is with me?"

The cheer was so loud the roof seemed to vibrate with it and most of the company were stamping their feet and clapping as if Mags were an actor at the end of a play. Gideon's mind reeled. He had been so sure Mags had been planning to stay, why else would he have treated Elizabeth Belamy with such respect?

Mercifully, he could see the enthusiasm for Mags' plan was not universal. Here and there a few faces looked grim and as Mags ordered the door opened, saying that beer and wine should be brought to celebrate, some men slipped out. In the chaos Gideon sat, helpless on his chair, like an island battered by high seas.

"The peel tower. Get all the women out of the house." Danny's voice was low and urgent. Gideon doubted anyone except himself and perhaps Anders could have heard, though the Dane showed no sign of having done so as he seemed to be looking around for someone. Then Danny was gone again shouting orders into the maelstrom. From nowhere, Jupp, still surprisingly alive, was beside them.

"Let's get you out of here," he said, his face ashen.

With Anders on one side and Jupp on the other Gideon found himself being half dragged and half carried through the thinning crowd and out of the building. Outside the night air was cold, its peace broken by shots, and a woman's scream came from nearby.

"The peel tower," Gideon gasped.

Jupp halted, wrenching Gideon's shoulder painfully in

the process.

"He's right. Can you get him there, Jensen? I'll gather who I can, and we'll hold out there. Mags and Bristow will wreck the house, but the tower should stand despite that. We can defend it with but a handful. It's what it was built for after all." Jupp didn't even wait for any reply and was gone at a run.

"Come on," Anders said, clearly making an effort to sound encouraging. "Let's get to the tower. You can do this."

But Gideon had something more important than his own safety to think about.

"Zahara," Gideon said. "I've got to find her."

"She will be with the company women and safer than we are," Anders said. "We need to go. It won't take much to have those who are supporting Mags turn on those who are not, and he has the numbers by far."

The logic of it didn't help much. Despite his weakness Gideon tried to pull away, driven by a new desperate fear. Then unbelievably, she was there, with Brighid and Gretchen and two more of the women.

For a moment she reached up and pressed her palm against his face and the expression in her eyes made him wish he could sweep her into his arms and hold her forever.

"I was afraid for you and prayed you would live," she said. "God is kind to have kept you safe for me." Then she was gone and the women with her.

The next few minutes were lost in a blur, Gideon was aware of being violently sick and then the next thing he knew he was lying on the pallet in the room he had been in before the trial. But this time the room was more crowded and poorly lit.

THE TRAITOR'S APPRENTICE

He could hear shouts, screams and shots but it was as if they came from a vast distance away. There was pain and his mind seemed to wander into fantasies, but through it all his heart and lungs struggled within, harsh and strained. Zahara was there again, her face swimming in and out of his vision and then Anders' anguished voice.

"I am sorry Sara, I was sure he could withstand it, but I think I may have given him too much."

II

Nick was mellowing in the parlour with his second brandy waiting for supper to be called when Cummings joined him. The lieutenant downed his drink with less appreciation than he might a tankard of small ale and refilled the glass.

"I needed that. Cuts the dust of the day from your throat, doesn't it, sir?"

For some reason, that choice of words set Nick on edge. It took him a moment to realise why and then he swallowed what remained in his glass just as fast. That had been one of the strange things Lord had said to Christobel—*Like diamonds, we are cut with our own dust.* What was that supposed to mean anyway?

Christobel appeared in the doorway to summon them to the dining parlour just as the last of the brandy had been drunk. It was obvious Cummings had missed out on the gossip because his jaw fell open. If he had been holding a drink still, it would have slipped from his grasp.

"By God," he said. Then to Nick's annoyance gawped at Christobel as if his wits were scattered in her presence.

The dining parlour was a cramped room at the back of the house. The table was small, and Nick decided that it might just fit six people if they sat close together. There were only three chairs set around it at that time—one at the head of the table and the other two placed opposite each other in the middle on either side.

The room was decorated in the same rustic and old-fashioned style as the parlour. The hearth was tiny and inconvenient, and a box settle ran along the wall beside it. Nick doubted the fire would heat the room well on a cold day, which was perhaps why the windows were swathed in heavy curtains.

Pride of place had been accorded to a lantern clock, set on the wall at the far end of the table, with its weights hanging below. The square case that contained its workings and the dial were brass. The pointing finger that showed the time was dark, like steel, as were the pillars supporting the bell fixed on top of it. The regular click of the balance wheel turning was like a drum tuck.

Christobel offered the seat at the head of the table to Nick. He was about to accept when he realised that to do so would place Christobel much closer to Cummings than to himself. So he graciously declined.

"It is your house, so of course, that is your seat."

"Except, of course, it turns out it isn't my house at all," she said, her tone uninflected as if she were commenting on the weather. "It is a dwelling place loaned to my father. I have no right to remain here beyond the end of March." She took the chair and nodded towards the clock. "I see you admiring that, Lieutenant Cummings. You may have it for ten pounds. The building may not be mine but all within it is. After March, since I am no longer entitled to be here, I will have nowhere to keep my possessions, so all you see around you is for sale, should you wish to make an offer. Ah, and here is the first course. Thank you, Judith. Baked hare. Do you like hare, lieutenant?"

Face turned puce, Cummings nodded his head as if a string had been attached to it, seemingly incapable of speech.

"Then you will recall what Juliana Berners had to say, I am sure," Christobel said. "*Now wylle we begynne atte hare, and why? she is most merveylous best of the world and wherefore? that she bereth grece and grotheyth, and Roungeth, and so doth non other best in thys lond; and at one tyme he is male and other tyme female...*"

Her meaning wasn't lost on Nick, and Cummings choked on his brandy.

"Who is he, the other face of our changeable hare?" Christobel asked as she served the baked hare in its pastry coffin.

"You don't know?" Cummings asked, confused. "Surely, you must be—" Then he broke off.

"*An apple, cleft in two, is not more twin?* You should enjoy this." She handed him a plate loaded with the hare. "It is cooked with apples. And I know less than you, Lieutenant Cummings, although it seems I should. Can you tell me, at least, the name of your prisoner?"

"He wouldn't give it, but Sir Nicholas said…" He glanced at Nick as he spoke, who returned the coldest glare he could manage, and Cummings faltered. He went on sounding subdued. "I am sure we will find out when we get him to Newcastle."

"One way or another?" Christobel suggested.

"I—"

"You look a little pale, lieutenant. More brandy,

perhaps?" She indicated the tall necked jug and Cummings reached for it as Christobel turned her attention to Nick. "Who is he, Sir Nicholas? If I have a stray relation, whether conceived within wedlock or out of it, I am entitled to at least know his name."

Nick shook his head. The last thing he wanted was to tell her that. But then two thoughts occurred together. The first, and most pertinent, was that if he didn't tell her she would continue to probe and dig until Cummings broke and gave in. The second was that the name was unlikely to mean anything to her anyway. She wouldn't know much about the mercenary commanders of Europe and even if she did, she might have heard mention of the Schiavono, but not that of the name it concealed.

"If he is your relation, I have no knowledge of it," Nick told her. "His name, though he denies it, is Philip Lord."

But of course, what he had not foreseen and should, was that she wouldn't be satisfied with just a name.

"And who is Philip Lord?"

Nick felt his jaw tighten.

"You said he was a criminal," Cummings put in. "A traitor, even."

"A traitor?" Christobel leaned forward a little. "How exciting. To think I find myself with a bastard brother and in the same night discover he is a traitor. What did he do?" She sat back and stabbed at her hare.

Nick wished now he had said nothing, but to withhold would serve no purpose except further to encourage the woman's venom. It would all come out as soon as they reached Newcastle anyway.

"He was accused of being complicit in selling state

secrets to the Spanish and plotting against the life of King James. He fled the country before he could be arrested and questioned, so he was declared a traitor."

For once his words silenced her and she paused with the piece of hare lifted from the plate.

"When was that? King James died nearly twenty years ago."

"It was around the time that King Charles—Prince Charles as he was at that time—went to Spain to pay a surprise visit to the Spanish Infanta in the hope of attracting her as his bride."

Christobel's face had frozen and even Cummings was staring at him.

"But that man in my cellar—he could have been no more than a child at that time."

"He was fifteen, and I am told he was a man in stature and with a mind well beyond his years. He had already been at court for many months. No one accounted him a child—King James least of all.

There was an awkward silence then as the implication of that made even the forward Christobel colour and Cummings had a brief coughing fit, which served to cover the moment.

"If you have any pity for him, it is misplaced," Nick said. "The pity is he has been able to maintain his vile ways as a mercenary for so long on land and sea. He has spent his life since then looting, killing and ravaging his way across Europe. He fought for the Spanish, the French and the Emperor, and sailed with the Dunkirkers and the Mediterranean pirates. If you have any pity save it for those who have suffered because of him."

"But he insisted he is not this man you name," Cummings protested. "He says that you mistake him for another."

Christobel had recovered herself and ate the morsel she had cut. "Perhaps," she said after a moment of thought, "I have two brothers. My, how productive my father's loins must have been in his time, and how glad to settle down with just one regular wife. Do you have one regular wife, lieutenant?"

At least that allowed for a topic change with Cummings waxing eloquently and with a sentiment that Nick found maudlin, about his wife and their two young children. But Christobel's acerbic tone and flow of erudite commentary seasoned the entire meal and, unable, because of Cumming's presence to respond to that as it deserved, Nick ground his teeth. He took increasing refuge in the brandy and a second jug was brought to the table.

Cummings himself seemed to veer between incredulity and admiration for Christobel. As if there were anything admirable in a woman whose head was so full of books that she could wield their words like weapons.

After one particularly scathing comment, it became too much, and Nick found himself unsteadily on his feet snarling.

"Your rudeness to your guests knows no bounds, it seems."

"My rudeness?" she echoed. "You dare to speak of *my* rudeness when you come here, bringing your men rampaging into my farmyard and insist I provide for them with no notice. Then you offer me no gratitude but take as you please."

"These are the king's men, not mine," Nick snapped. "You should remember that before speaking slightingly

THE TRAITOR'S APPRENTICE

of them. It is an honour for you to entertain them."

"Then I would like to think his majesty won't mind that I take some entertainment from entertaining his men."

At which point Nick reached for the brandy and found Cummings had just emptied the jug for a second time. Or was it a third? Christobel got to her feet.

"Please excuse me, I will ask Judith to bring some more with the dessert. A compote of apples and pears and other fruit I believe."

Christobel's absence from the room lifted a weight from Nick's shoulders. Why was such an attractive woman filled with so much spite and malice? It was only when Cummings replied he realised he had spoken the thought aloud.

"Education. That's the problem. You see the same thing in men of lesser birth as well. Educate them and instead of keeping to the place in life God granted them and being happy with it, they start thinking themselves above that station, so become churlish and arrogant." He waved the knife he held in his hand towards the empty seat where Christobel had been. "That one's been spoiled by it. She'll be nothing but a mean and bitter shrew now all her life, mark my words."

It was a judgement Nick didn't want to agree with.

"Even the wildest filly can be broken to bit and bridle."

"Oh, I'm sure, it could be done," Cummings said. "But is it worth the time and effort when a man can find a good woman born and bred? Like my Arbella, for instance, sweet as a rose."

Nick said nothing to that and let Cummings go on about the many virtues of his wife. Besides, he wasn't sure of the answer anymore. Christobel Lavinstock both attracted and repelled him, but the attraction was stronger. He couldn't get the thought of her out of his mind. He realised he'd had a little too much to drink, but that wasn't surprising with the woman goading him all evening.

She came back into the room with a servant who carried the compote and, moving the salt, placed it on the table in a pewter bowl.

"I regret, Sir Nicholas, that if you wish for more to drink you will need to go yourself to the cellar to fetch it—or at least unlock the door."

Nick frowned at that. He was sure he had seen at least two of the small barrels brought up and on a table in the kitchen.

"There is more than enough," he protested.

"There was," Christobel said, nodding a thank you to her servant as she left the dining parlour. "However, it seems your men have the same taste for this brandy as you do. All I had in the house is now gone."

"What the devil?" Cummings was a few moments ahead of Nick in grasping the significance of what she had said. "You let the men have—?" He groaned and then buried his face in his hands. "Good God."

"You did not say they were to be denied. Indeed, I recall you prevailing upon me to offer them the full hospitality at my disposal."

Nick staggered to his feet.

"Then I hope you have no care for your outbuildings and that your maidservants are locked in the house."

Christobel, still entirely sober having only sipped at her drink to Nick's knowledge, met his accusation with a mild gaze.

THE TRAITOR'S APPRENTICE

"They are not my outbuildings after all, and my cook and housekeeper are safe enough. Though by all accounts your men seem more inclined to song and gambling than rapine and burning at the moment. But it remains that if you want to have brandy with your compote you will need to send someone into the cellar."

Cummings was still sitting with his face in his hands. He looked like he could do with a stiff drink and with disaster already unavoidable Nick saw no reason to deny himself.

It seemed further to the kitchen than he remembered, and the floor was uneven in places which he hadn't noticed before. He missed his step and stumbled a couple of times. Because of that he thought it much the wiser course not to be the one who went down the steps and into the cellar so waited as Christobel and her man descended and came up again a couple of minutes later bearing another small barrel.

Jug refilled, he returned to the table and found Cummings still looking pale, happy to accept the offer of another drink. Christobel, though, hadn't resumed her seat and now made them both a brief but elegant curtsey.

"Please forgive me if I retire and leave you to finish your meal. It is much past my usual time to sleep, and I will be busy before dawn arranging matters for you and your men. When you are done, Seth will show you to your room."

Cummings drained his drink and stood up at once.

"I must check on the men and then get to bed myself. Thank you for such a fine meal, Mistress Lavinstock."

Nick found himself sitting alone in the dining parlour listening to the slow tick of the clock, fruit compote untouched, savouring another brandy and wondering if he should mount the stairs and establish his legal right to the body and being of the woman who was his already in all but the deed.

Chapter Sixteen

I

Nick woke up feeling as if he had been beaten with cudgels all over his torso and that his head had been turned into an army drum. He opened his eyes to be dazzled by thin grey daylight pushing through the windows and realised he was lying on the settle in the dining parlour of Flass Grange. Someone had thrown a blanket over him and there was a bucket on the floor by his head. The contents of that showed he had needed it in the night, although he had no memory of it. Or of anything much else after he had been left alone.

His clothes were a mess, and when he sat up, he realised he had vomited over his arm. Cursing, he got to his feet and found a bowl of warm water, with a cloth, on the cleared table. He used both in a belated attempt to retrieve his dignity. Having washed, he used the cloth to sponge his arm clean.

As he finished, there was a sudden commotion outside the door, shouting and feet running, then someone calling his name and a moment later a pounding on the door which made his head throb. Furious, he strode over and flung it open. Quartermaster Bayliss stood there, which made him glad he had at least improved on his waking appearance, but from the look on the man's face, Bayliss was too preoccupied to notice.

"What is it?" Nick snapped.

"It's the prisoner, sir." Bayliss looked distraught and fell silent. Nick's heart stood still. He grabbed the quartermaster by the shoulders and shook him.

"For God's sake, speak man, speak. What about the prisoner?"

"He's gone."

"Gone? He was locked in. I did so myself. How can he—?"

Nick saw only confusion and fear in the quartermaster's face so released his grip and pushed past him. The key to the cellar was in the pocket of his breeches still. Deep enough for him to be sure no one had removed and replaced it as he slept, even assuming they could do so without waking him, which he doubted.

The first person he encountered was Cummings who had just run down the tiny staircase and looked as perturbed as Bayliss.

"The sword, sir. Someone stole it."

"Sword?" Nick struggled to find any context where Cummings' words would make sense. "What sword?"

"The prisoner's sword. I had it with me. It was in my room on the table. I was admiring it last night."

The chill of certainty sent a shiver over Nick's flesh.

"With me. I think we have more to concern ourselves with than a stolen sword."

The cellar door stood wide and the room at the bottom of the stairs was empty. It showed no trace of it having had any occupant either.

"God's wounds, the whoreson *is* gone." The words came out as a snarl of impotent fury. He turned to Bayliss. "I want every servant in this household assembled. If need be, I will have them beaten bloody until one of them admits they did this. Whoever it is I will see them hanged for abetting the escape of a traitor."

"Sir." Bayliss turned to go.

"There is a problem?"

Christobel stood in the doorway to the kitchen. She wore a fine worsted robe in a delicate rose pink with silver points and roses embroidered on the stomacher of the bodice. She looked devastating. The soft fall of her white hair over a broad linen collar also edged with tiny, embroidered rosebuds and scooped to lie close over her breasts. For a moment, Nick forgot everything except her presence. Hearing Bayliss give a small groan he knew he wasn't alone in the enchantment.

"I could not help but overhear what you said, and I have no wish for you to abuse any of my servants, Sir Nicholas. Besides, there is no need."

Trapped by Christobel's presence which would have required him to push her aside to get through the doorway, Bayliss cast a rather desperate look at Nick.

"There is every need," Nick snapped. "Someone amongst your servants contrived the release of my prisoner—"

"My prisoner, sir," Cummings muttered.

"—and whoever is responsible for the prisoner's escape will be hanged."

"Stole my sword too," Cummings added.

Nick turned on him. "Will you stop whining about the damned sword?"

"It was a superb blade, sir. If you had held it, you would under—"

Nick's temper, already frayed to its limit and made less steady than usual by the pounding in his head, slipped its leash. He turned and hit the wall an inch from

Cummings face with a hard fist. The pain brought him up and the shocked expression on Cummings' face made him realise how he must look.

"I know it must be very frustrating for you, Sir Nicholas," Christobel said, a note of forced patience in her voice as if she were dealing with a truculent child or a difficult servant. "But the fact remains you have no one to blame for this but yourself."

Ignoring the blood on his bruised knuckles he turned back to Christobel.

"What do you mean by that?"

She smiled infuriatingly and shook her head.

"I told you yesterday that there was only one key to that door, and you have it. Or you did yesterday evening. You used it to open the door so Seth and I could fetch you more brandy."

Nick frowned. He had a vague memory of that.

"Oh yes, so you did, sir," Cummings said. "It was just before I went out to check on the men, I recall now."

"And what of it?" Nick demanded.

"Your prisoner was there at the time. Seth will confirm as much if for any reason you choose not to believe me. Seth took the barrel into the kitchen, and I followed him. You stayed to lock the door behind us. I closed this door." She tapped the one to the kitchen that she was standing beside. "That was after you came through and there would have been no call for anyone to open it again until this morning."

Nick stared at her, trying to decide what she was seeking to imply.

"You are saying—"

She didn't let him finish, stepping back and away from the door as she cut over him, so Bayliss could pass if he

THE TRAITOR'S APPRENTICE

wished, but the damned man just stood there like a puppy with its tongue out.

"I am saying what I observed yesterday evening, Sir Nicholas. You may place upon it what import you will. But before you begin to beat my innocent servants, might I suggest you at least consider the idea that it was you yourself who failed to secure the door?"

The idea was ridiculous, of course. He would have been careful to check the door was locked. But the fact remained that try as he might, thanks to the influence of the brandy he could barely even recall coming to the cellar let alone locking or unlocking the door.

He shook his head.

"Bayliss, find this man Seth. I will speak with him in the dining parlour."

"Perhaps not," Christobel said. "When I left you a bowl of water this morning, having discovered you were asleep there and not in your room, I did notice it needed—" She hesitated, her lips curling before she went on. "It needed a thorough clean after yesterday evening's excesses. And I would like to know which of your men took a blanket for you from the bed upstairs and provided you with a bucket from the kitchen. I don't like to think of one of your soldiers wandering around my house like that."

Nick looked back at her, of a sudden bemused.

"None of my men would—" He stopped, thought, and then went on more surely still. "They were under orders to stay out."

"Well, someone—"

Cummings spoke from behind him. "Perhaps it was the prisoner, sir. He was upstairs in my room to take back his sword, so he might have taken a blanket…"

Nick spun round, anger swallowing up the fear at the thought of Lord bending over his sleeping form. Leaving the blanket and bucket in mockery. A statement of what he could so easily have done instead. Cummings stepped back and muttered something about being mistaken. Getting the best grip he could on himself, Nick drew a steadying breath and returned his attention to Christobel, who he felt certain was enjoying his discomfiture.

"The day parlour then," he said. "I will be there and hope to be served something to eat as well."

"There is plenty of compote," Christobel told him, her expression one of supreme innocence. "And I will send Seth to speak with you." She turned away and was gone in a sweep of rose.

It took all Nick's self-control not to pound a fist into the stone again and he clenched both his hands tightly, his jaw close to cracking with tightness. By God, she was the most abominable creature he had ever met in his life. He fought down the anger and tried to turn his mind to what this meant for his immediate future. Thank goodness he hadn't been so rash as to send anyone ahead with news of his captive. With luck, he wouldn't need to face the humiliation of explaining the loss to those who would know its full import. Cummings and Bayliss would not want it known either, he was very sure about that. It made them look just as bad. Between them they would ensure the men kept silent

"Should I send out search parties?" Cummings asked, seeming more distressed at having lost the sword than the man. "He can't have gone far. He was on foot, and he had an injured ankle."

Which Nick had to admit was a good point.

THE TRAITOR'S APPRENTICE

"Yes. And ask the pickets what they saw or heard. Assuming they were not also making themselves free of the brandy."

"Not when I checked on them before bed, sir."

"Then perhaps, just perhaps we might be able to recapture him. But he must have been away some hours ago and even hobbling he could have covered some ground."

"And we can't be sure where he is heading," Cummings put it.

And that was where Cummings' lack of intelligence in both the meanings of the word showed up and Nick's better ability to hold the place of command stood out.

"I can," Nick said. "He'll be heading south to Ryedale."

"And what if that man of his who was picking off our stragglers is still out there with a horse?"

Nick cursed aloud. How could he have forgotten that? If Lord had a mount, he could be halfway to Ryedale by now and if he was with that cursed Moor and his deadly arrows...

"Make sure those search parties are no fewer than eight men," he ordered.

Cummings went to obey, and Nick took his foul mood to the parlour where a maid servant brought him some frumenty which seemed to his judgement to have had much of the leftover compote added to it in the cooking.

He was just finishing the bowl when the servant, Seth, was brought to him by Bayliss. Seth was a young man, perhaps of an age with Nick himself, dark-haired and swarthy skinned, weathered from the work he must do outside every day. He stood, eyes downcast, gripping his hat in both hands and wringing it with fingers turned to fists. Bayliss stood behind him, an adequate threat.

"Do you remember yesterday evening when you went to the cellar with your mistress?"

He nodded his head but kept his eyes on the floor. Bayliss gave him a light smack on the face.

"Speak when the captain asks you something and no mumbling or lies."

"Yes, sire, my lord, captain, sir. I remember."

The hat was fast resembling a floor cloth from the ill treatment it was receiving. Nick found that irritating to watch and he steeled himself to resist ripping it from the man's hands.

"You went into the cellar with your mistress. What did you see?"

"There was a man there. Tied hand and foot."

"Did he say anything?"

Seth swallowed hard and looked even more afraid.

"Yes, sir. He did."

Nick was getting more impatient by the moment.

"Tell me then."

"Well, I'm not sure 'bout all he said." Seth was almost cringing as he spoke as if expecting another blow. "You see the mistress says to him: 'I hear you are a traitor.' Then he said something short in foreign talk and the mistress said he was taking it very lightly. Then he laughed and I remember the words he spoke then as they were odd, 'Tis destiny, unshunnable, like death.' I don't know if the mistress answered that as I was busy with the barrel but there was nothing more before we came back up."

Even with some of the dialogue missing, Nick had to admit it didn't sound as if there had been any plotting or even any thought that Lord's freedom might be obtainable. He was tempted to have his men beat Seth to see if he changed his tale, but the fear in the man was so obvious he doubted it was worthwhile.

Dismissing both men, Nick sent for Cummings and received a satisfactory report of the search parties he had organised. If those search parties failed, he would have no choice but to return to Newcastle. However, Stott's words came back to him and he decided when he left it would not be alone. He could spare some men to go back to Howe. Smiling at that thought, he went in search of Christobel to tell her that she would need to find more provisions for himself and his men as they wouldn't be leaving that day.

II

Gideon woke to the wail of a baby crying in a room nearby.

It was dark. Not the dark of night, the dark of the early dawn, with thin illumination teasing through shutter and casement creating shadows and shades. Someone shushed the baby, and it must have been offered a nipple because it was soon quiet. Then he became aware of other sounds. The soft and even breathing of people asleep or seeking it, low-voiced conversation nearby. Footsteps, leather on stone and the odd scrape of a hobnail.

His focus came back to himself and the dull ache which seemed to fill his body, the dry, bitter, burning in his throat and the tight throb between his temples. Memory returned last of all, putting together the pieces of perception to make some sense. The trial. The desperate fight with Muir. Mags' ultimatum. The chaos after.

He must have made a noise, or perhaps it was just the change in his breathing because someone moved beside him, and he felt a cool hand on his brow.

"Gideon?"

Zahara's voice. The sweetness of it stole his breath. With the softness of snowfall on a windless day, she leaned forward, and her lips brushed his brow before she pressed her face against his, and he could feel her tears on his skin. Then she pulled away, gently. He didn't attempt to hold her. She had told him: *If there were a way for any man on this earth, it would be for you,* and he hadn't understood what she meant. Now he was beginning to understand, and the pain of that knowledge was almost more than he could bear. But it was what she had to bear every day she lived and if she could, then he would.

"I thought God had taken you from me," she whispered. "Last night, your breath was so low, Anders said…"

And he remembered, then, the last words he had heard from Anders. He lifted his hand to stroke her shoulder, his heart full. She caught his hand and held it in both hers.

"I am always here for you," he said. "For as long as God grants me life, there will be no other." And even as he spoke the words he knew their truth, branded through and through his heart and his soul.

He could still not see her face although the light had grown a little. He could only hear the infinite sadness in her voice as her hands released his with a whisper. "I know."

The door opened and someone, Jupp, came in.

"They are making an early start," he said. "The devil

THE TRAITOR'S APPRENTICE

knows how he'll get them all up, half are still in their cups. But have a care, gentlemen, and make ready, they might yet decide to attack us as a parting gift."

Gideon realised that the room had been full of slumbering figures, all now stirring and rising. Someone made a light and a moment later Zahara had moved aside so Anders could get next to him, the relief on the Dane's face clear in the candle-lit grey of pre-dawn. He held out a cup of water for Gideon to drink.

"I thought you were lost, my friend, that I had given you too much, that—" He broke off and then shook his head smiling. "Thank God. I only wish you were waking to a better day. There is some cause to fear none of us will live to see its end."

Before he could explain further, Jupp, his face drawn from a night with no sleep, was issuing orders to get as much water in every container that would hold it. When one of the men asked why Jupp gripped him on the shoulder.

"This is Mags. It's what he does. What he's always done. He takes what he wants and will burn what is left to deny it to the enemy—that includes us."

Gideon was left wondering whether Jupp meant that they were the enemy to be denied—or, in a more sinister vein, a resource of fighting men to be themselves denied to any enemy. He supposed that the impact on them would be much the same.

"I will have to go and help with the work," Anders said, getting up as Jupp left, followed by the four men who had been sleeping in the room. "I will see you as soon as we are as secure as we can be. You rest for now."

It seemed Jupp had taken command of the remnant of

men who, even if not holding onto an old loyalty to Lord, at least had no taste for the kind of prospect offered by Mags. But there were few which was perhaps not surprising. Those who fought the hardest, the most ruthlessly, were by nature hard men. Men like Aleksandrov and Danny Bristow, who Gideon had seen could slit a man's throat—or even a woman's—with no more compunction than a butcher slaughtering beasts. But where Philip Lord had held these men of blood leashed to his will, through fear, respect and even sometimes a warped variety of affection, Mags was keen to keep them loyal by allowing them full rein in their base instincts for destruction.

Zahara left with the others and when the door closed, Gideon was alone in the room, trapped there by his bodily weakness. He could hear the quiet sounds of movement outside and the odd shout from further away, where Mags was rousing his men from their drunken stupors. It felt wrong that others should be out there preparing a defence and he was left as a liability to be defended, rather than a part of that defence himself.

There was little in the room to hold his attention. Beside him was a tall and narrow window, now glazed but which had once been just a defensive slit in the stone wall of the peel tower.

When he tried to move, he found it easier than he thought. It hurt, but it was less effort than he had expected. Once up, he discovered that with the advantage of height afforded by the tower, he could view the courtyard by the house and over the roof of the brewhouse, the still room and other domestic outbuildings, he could see to the stableyard beyond. To where the company was based in the long barn that had held his mockery of a trial the day before.

In the courtyard below the window under the protection of two men armed with muskets in addition to their swords and pistols, water was being brought into the tower in buckets, pots and jugs.

From the glimpses Gideon could get of what was happening in the outbuildings on the stableyard, those occupied the company, Mags was indeed rousing his men. There seemed to be a deal of activity involving various wheeled modes of transport, which were being manoeuvred out into the stable yard, a couple stood there already loaded with prizes from the house. From previous experience, Gideon knew that the company could be packed and ready to go in less than two hours, but with many of the men still half drunk and most unwilling to haul themselves up, it would take longer.

Looking down, Gideon could see the front of the newer wing of the house which had already been despoiled. Windows were broken and the courtyard had become a graveyard for many of the contents. There was the spinet virginals smashed on the cobbles, the beautiful parquetry cabinet splintered apart. The lute, its fat belly flattened into kindling, lay amongst broken jars and bottles from the still room together with such as remained of their contents. All about the courtyard, books had been cast in the muck, ripped pages fluttering like injured doves, unable to take flight.

The whole house had been ransacked.

He recognised some of the furnishings from various rooms in the new wing—the wooden crib from the nursery, the embroidered hangings from Lady Grace's bed chamber, dragged out and heaped up or left trampled. Even the family picture which had hung in the dining hall was there, half of the family ripped away, its frame broken.

Sickened by such wanton destruction for no purpose, Gideon hoped the baby he had heard was the infant baron and that his mother and her household were all secure elsewhere in the peel tower. At least the ruined things were only objects, mattering little if the people were safe. Then his heart skipped a beat as he realised that there was one thing more precious than any of these items lying broken on the cobbles, something that needed to be secured from destruction and, more importantly, from the eyes of Mags. And he had seen nothing as yet from the old wing where Mags and Danny would still be in occupation, so there was even hope.

With a sudden surge of energy brought on by the pressing urgency, he crossed to the door. Except, having done so he realised the folly of trying to go anywhere himself. A wave of weakness engulfed him, and he only remained vertical by bracing himself on the strong stonework. As it passed, he went back to the narrow window, leaning on it to hold himself upright.

So he was there when a shot echoed from the stableyard and Gideon saw a figure collapse, the betraying cloud of powder smoke lingering a moment longer before dispersing in the still, dawn air. Yelling followed the shot and Gideon could see the man holding the pistol lower it, sword now in hand, and Mags striding towards him shouting. It was impossible to hear the words, but he recognised the man with the sword.

Which was when the door burst open to admit Olsen, who came close to knocking Gideon aside in his rush to get to the window.

THE TRAITOR'S APPRENTICE

"Sweet Jesus! Bristow just pistolled Aleksandrov." The Swede added a selection of expletives in his native language and a few more in French for good measure. "Mags will slaughter him for that."

Weakness forgotten, Gideon was grateful for his good eyesight. It was too far to see expressions on faces, but it was obvious there was some kind of stand-off taking place and where Mags had gathered twenty or more men at his back, only a handful had aligned themselves with Danny.

There was more shouting and someone beside Mags raised a pistol which Mags himself reached over and pulled down. Then there was a tense silence and speech that wasn't shouted, before Danny turned on his heel, slammed his sword home to its sheath and vanished from view as he strode into the shelter of the outbuildings.

"What was that about?" Gideon asked.

Olsen shook his head, still watching Mags, who was now urging his men to more effort in their preparations to leave and glancing in the direction Danny had taken.

"I have no idea, but I hope it means problems for Mags. At the least, it might keep him from giving us too much attention."

Gideon could see the tightness of the Swede's expression.

"Can we defend the tower?" he asked.

"We have twenty-one men and seven of the company women who can load as well as any of us and even shoot at need. Mags has upwards of seventy—and most of the women too."

Twenty-one against seventy. The odds sounded devastating.

"Do we have *enough* men?"

Olsen's eyes continued to study the scene outside as he answered. "That depends. This place could be held by a handful if they had no need to sleep or eat and an endless store of powder and bullets. So, yes, we could hold out a day or two, longer if we have supplies. But I doubt they will press that hard as they seem in a hurry to go. So maybe they will just leave."

"Then what is Jupp so worried about?"

"The way we can hold them is by breaking the wooden stairs to the first floor. Then they can't reach us, and we can shoot at them or hack them back if they try. But we can't keep them out of the bottom floor. It has weak doors that go to each wing of the house and another door to the courtyard. The real danger is fire. They could set a big one beneath us and if it caught, we would be roasted alive. Though more likely choked by the smoke first, which might be a blessing." Olsen shook his head and crossed himself. "Anyway, that is why Jupp is soaking the wood on the first floor with all the water we can…" then his face changed as something he saw outside made him frown. "But what the—? He can't be serious."

Gideon looked and saw Danny Bristow and the five men who had been with him standing by the still room door in the shards of shattered pottery and glass. One of the men had torn a shirt in half and carried it tied it to a broken pole. As Gideon watched Danny took that and walked alone into the courtyard.

"The bastard wants to parley." Olsen sounded incredulous. Then stepped back so quickly Gideon nearly fell and would have had the big Swede not caught him. Unfortunately, it was by his bad arm, and he couldn't contain the moan of pain. Suddenly solicitous, Olsen helped him to sit on the pallet. Anders arrived a few moments later, bearing food. Gideon was ravenous and ate all the bread and cold meat the Dane had brought him. Distracted by the food, it was only as Olsen was leaving that Gideon remembered why he had made the effort to stand in the first place.

"Someone must get Lord's travelling desk," he said, gripping at Anders' sleeve. "It is vital to keep that safe." The thought of the documents locked within it and the inflammatory knowledge they contained being given to Mags was unthinkable. Olsen looked nonplussed but Anders nodded understanding and turned to the Swede.

"Lennox is right. Tell Jupp. He will understand."

Then feeling he had done all he could to protect Lord's papers, if they hadn't already been discovered and rifled, submitted to Anders' concerned insistence that he take some more medication and rest.

Chapter Seventeen

When he woke again, Gideon realised Anders must have put something to encourage him to sleep in the medication offered with the food. From the quality of the light pouring in from outside, he knew he couldn't have been sleeping for too long. Where it had been dawn, now it was perhaps late morning. The sound that woke him was that of the door being thrown open and someone being manhandled into the room and dropped on the floor.

He was still slurred with sleep and whatever had been encouraging him there, but Anders' voice was sharp, like a rapier piercing the soft fabric bundled around his mind.

"If you are turning this room into a torture chamber or butchers' shambles at least have the decency to move Gideon first."

Which was more than enough incentive to persuade his reluctant eyes to open and his muffled brain to fight for focus.

"Rest easy, Dr Jensen, sir. It's neither—just a secure prison," Olsen said, his normally amiable tone taking on an uncharacteristic edge. "We can't spare the men to keep watching the bastard, and Jupp says we might need him as a hostage so won't let me slit his throat—yet. So you get the privilege of enduring his company. If he gives you any trouble, just hit him a few times—hard, or call me and I'll do it. With pleasure."

The door closed as the Swede left and there was a

groan from nearby. Gideon had to turn his head to see. From where he lay there was little he could tell about the man lying on the floor beside him, except that he was in a bloodstained shirt and muddied breeches. The match cord used to bind his ankles had been pulled tight enough above his bare feet to cause vivid purple bruising.

"Anders? And Gideon here too?" The voice, sounding as though it was speaking through damaged lips, was unmistakably that of Danny Bristow. "I fall among friends at least. And please, as my very good friends, help me not to forget in future that Jupp has never read Grotius." He finished on a sharply indrawn breath. "Careful, Anders, I think I have broken a rib."

"I see no reason to be particularly careful," Anders said.

"Didn't you have to take some oath not to—?" This time the breath caught and finished on a shuddering release before Danny could speak again. "Keep that up and you'll be doing Jupp's job for him."

Gideon made an effort then to push himself to sit up and was pleased to find it was much easier than it had been before. He was no longer feeling weak, aside from the pain of his wounds and a persistent headache. Beside his pallet, Danny lay with his wrists bound as his ankles. The damage to his face was visible even through the profusion of freckles and there was blood matting his hair.

Danny caught sight of Gideon from his prone position. "God, Gideon, you look like I want to feel—over the worst and medicated to the eyeballs. Please, Anders, can I have some of what you gave him? I vow to let you win at cards for—ouch."

"You think all this is a joke?" Anders' face had darkened. "Men have died. More will die, because of what you have done."

Danny's reply was evidently as instinctive to him as a riposte with his sword. "And you can say different?"

The binding of temperance that was normally a strong rope on the bridle of Anders' emotions, Gideon could see, was fraying fast. He was certain that he had no wish to discover what would happen if the final threads parted and the Dane gave full cry to his fury.

"Anders," he said. "The night before last Danny came here in secret and warned me about the trial and what Mags wanted from it. It was Danny who arranged for you to see me yesterday, so you could make sure I was in a fit state to manage it. Danny lent me his sword and told me how to use it well to defeat Muir. He even told me to pretend to pass out and then called you to me when he saw I was close to collapsing before the fight— you will recall he gave you the bottle—and it was his idea, not mine, we should come to the peel tower to be safe from Mags. He charged me to bring all the women from the house here too, though I forgot to pass that on, someone else seems to have thought of it thank goodness."

His words were met by a pregnant silence. Anders surveyed him with a frown as if trying to decide how much he could trust what he had heard, the anger in him slow to rise and slow to disperse. Unfortunately, Danny seemed to lack any sense of the needs of the moment.

"Thank you, Gideon," he said. "I shall let you win at cards instead—and that will be a lot easier to arrange than if it were Anders but...." He must have seen the Dane's face. "I'm sorry. I apologise. I—" He closed his

THE TRAITOR'S APPRENTICE

mouth, then as if worried he might say something more regrettable, drew a shuddering breath. "Forgive me. Please. I'm a bit light-headed. With relief, perhaps. Until Olsen dropped me in here, I was convinced Jupp had every intention of dispatching me once he was done."

"He may still," Anders said, sounding as if he would not himself be unhappy with that outcome, but continued his work inspecting the other man's injuries with impersonal compassion. "You are more fortunate than you deserve. The ribs are not broken, I think, but they will be painful for a good while from the bruising and lacerations. Whoever kicked you was wearing hobnails?"

Gideon tried to think, and his head throbbed with the effort. Then seeing the cruelly tight match cord bindings he picked up the knife Anders had been using and shifted his position to reach Danny's feet.

"Hobnails. Yes. And thank you, Gideon."

Anders turned and gripped Gideon's wrist, eyes darkened.

"You trust him that much?"

That forced Gideon to think again. The image sprang into his mind of a sword coming up to block what would have been a fatal blow.

He thought and then he nodded.

"I would be dead if Danny hadn't done his best to warn and ward me."

"You would be too, physician friend," Danny said. "But you only have my word for that, so I don't suppose that counts for much."

Thinking was coming more easily now to Gideon and memory fed it with morsels of meaning. He was remembering what had happened and remembering Philip Lord a few days before saying, *Danny likes you. If you are wise you will nurture that into a friendship.* And the haunted look on Danny's face when he came back from his initial interview with Lord.

"This is what you meant," Gideon said. "That first night when you told me Lord had given you orders you hated and feared."

"I don't recall mentioning anything about fear," Danny protested.

Anders sat back and frowned. "You said you had to wallow in the filth but still keep smelling of roses, I recall that."

Danny gave him a strange look. "You were asleep."

"I was," Anders admitted. "Until you returned and woke me with your talk. Your idea of a quiet chat involves too much of raised voices and laughter. I've slept better in the common room of an alehouse."

"What had Lord asked of you?" Gideon asked.

"Ah, well there lies the problem. If I could share it all with the world, I wouldn't have had to take that beating."

"But Lord is dead," Anders said. "What good can you do him keeping his secrets and serving his ends now?"

"Dead?" There was a sudden and genuine concern in Danny's voice, and he bent his body to lift his shoulders from the floor the better to see their faces. "When did that happen?"

"We all heard what Mags said, he is either dead or as good as and no one, not even Jupp could deny it. Is it not obvious?" Anders asked.

Danny let a long breath out in a sigh of relief and his shoulders eased back to the floor.

THE TRAITOR'S APPRENTICE

"Shiraz hasn't returned," he said as if that explained everything.

Gideon saw his own lack of comprehension reflected in Anders' gaze.

"Shiraz is—"

"Dead?" Danny suggested. "I beg your leave to doubt that, and I would suggest you ask Sara's opinion on the matter too. Shiraz will come back alone only if there is no hope for Philip."

Danny was the second of just two people Gideon had heard call Lord by his given name. It was done with the naturalness of frequent usage that spoke more for the depth of their relationship than a thousand explanations could ever do. He could tell from the widening of Anders' eyes that the Dane had marked it too. But then Gideon doubted Anders had ever heard anyone make free use of their patron's Christian name before.

"And that will unlock your tongue?" Anders asked.

Danny said nothing for a moment, then turned his head to Anders.

"Would it help if I gave you my oath that I am not going to do anything to harm you or the men here and am willing to do all in my power to help, succour and assist you?"

"Eggs and oaths are easily broken," Anders observed. Then he moved to stand up. "It would be better not to cut the match, my friend, then we can retie it if needed to convince Jupp that his prisoner is still restrained. I fear that he will not be in the mood to listen to reason about Danny here at the moment. He is currently occupied trying to deny the tower to Mags."

Anders tried to untie the match cord on Danny's wrists, but after a minute, as Gideon had done before him, he bent and used the knife to cut the tight knot.

Then Gideon remembered. "Lord's desk...?"

Anders shook his head. "No one knows where it is."

"Is safely hidden." Danny's voice clashed with Anders', rubbing at his wrists and shaking his hands as they were freed. "I made sure of that as soon as I realised what had happened. Mags gave me Philip's room. Our room and Muir's went to Aleksandrov and his good friends." Then he laughed. "The irony, if Jupp had killed me and Philip returned to find half his life's work missing because of it. I've managed to hide a few things."

Anders finished releasing Danny's ankles and began to massage below the chafed flesh.

"You shot Aleksandrov," Gideon recalled. Before Danny could respond there was a commotion outside the door, and shots and yells from the courtyard. Anders pulled one of the blankets from Gideon and threw it over Danny, pushing the ropes out of sight under Gideon's pallet. Danny scooted himself into the corner just as the door opened.

Olsen came with a long-barrelled weapon in his hands the same fowling piece Gideon had seen Jupp using when Fairfax visited. The Swede pushed Anders to one side and used the butt of it to break the window beside Gideon. Zahara came in behind him holding a regular flintlock musket. Olsen fired, cursed, then turned to give Zahara the weapon he held and took the musket from her, checking the priming pan as he did so.

"What is—?"

"We lost three more men and Mags has taken the house."

"What is the point?" Anders asked. "He has all of

THE TRAITOR'S APPRENTICE

value from it and there is nothing left now except us."

"Pride," Danny murmured from under the blanket that concealed his lack of bonds.

"You would know," Olsen snapped, his focus being along the length of the musket barrel. Behind him Zahara was reloading the better weapon and struggling to force the bullet down the barrel, then wadding it, the ramrod packing it tightly.

Anders cast a brief worried look at Gideon, moving his head towards Danny. Olsen wouldn't have noticed as he was looking back out at the courtyard, but Zahara, Gideon saw, followed his gaze and she sent Gideon a questioning look. He made a small movement of pulling his wrists apart. Her eyes widened and she nodded.

From below came sounds of shouting. Danny put his head on one side as if to listen better, then winced at the report of Olsen firing the musket followed by some choice words in Swedish as Zahara passed him the loaded gun. Gideon realised he should offer to be the one reloading for Olsen so Zahara could go elsewhere if she was needed, but then she smiled at him, and he realised she knew that also and had said nothing.

The door opened again and a man came in, half carrying another who was pale and gasping for breath with a blossom of red on his chest. Without thinking, Gideon got up and pulled the pallet mattress further away from the window so the wounded man could be laid on it. It was then he realised that if not fully restored, his strength was largely returned.

"What is happening downstairs?" Olsen demanded and the unwounded man paused by the door to answer him.

"They are piling furniture and combustibles through

the two doors from the house. Jupp says Mags plans to set a fire in the new house that will spread below us. It's what he'd do in the same place, he said." Then the man was gone, closing the door and leaving a cold chill of despair in his wake.

His words were a reminder to Gideon that it wasn't even the methods employed that the mercenaries here objected to, merely that they were the current target of them.

"I think he's got beyond the planning," Olsen said a few minutes later as the rumble of wheels began. "I think he's done it. They are pulling out. Just leaving some men to keep us pinned in. But I see no flames or smoke. He must have set a fuse."

"Christ." Danny said with sudden feeling. "Of course, why didn't I think of it? You've got to get me down there. I'm the only one who can stop what's going to happen."

His words were punctuated by the Swede firing another shot, ringing their ears from the stone all around.

"Got one of the bastards," Olsen said, speaking, Gideon realised, of a man he had seen as a brother-in-arms just yesterday. Then the Swede turned to receive the loaded musket from Zahara and looked at Danny. "You are a piece of shit, Bristow. You think Mags would trade our freedom for yours?"

Danny shook his head. "Right now, he'd put a bullet in me faster than you would. If you recall, I helped five of his people defect to you."

"They were coming anyway, with or without your help. They have women or family with us."

"They wouldn't have come if I hadn't made a path for

them," Danny said, sounding weary. It was hard for Gideon to know which of them spoke the truth.

"Yes? Well two of them are dead now anyway. The gain to us is three men and you." He was bitter as he turned back to the window with the loaded weapon.

Zahara drew an audible breath and Gideon saw she had gone pale. He realised that all these were people she knew and most she counted as friends. It must be a hundred times harder for her than it was for himself.

"Gideon? Anders?" Danny's voice held appeal.

"In case you hadn't noticed I have a life to save here," Anders snapped, his attention on the wounded man.

"And I have a score or more to save, yours included," Danny returned, an urgency in his tone. "Gideon?"

Gideon glanced at Olsen whose focus was fixed on the outside. Zahara placed the weapon she had just reloaded into Gideon's hands and moved over to Anders, gently pushing his hands aside and taking over his work, ignoring his grunt of protest and treating him to a severe look and a sharp nod at Danny. For a moment Anders hesitated, evidently torn in his trust. Then he sighed and got to his feet.

"I don't see how we do this," he said looking at Gideon.

Danny was also looking at him now. It was clear what he wanted. Drawing a breath, Gideon moved his position so he could aim the length of the fowling piece at Olsen. He pulled back the snaphaunce. His heart had started hammering again and he was sure the long-barrelled weapon wasn't steady in his grip.

"Do what?" Olsen asked, looking around. He froze when he saw Gideon. "Are you insane, Fox?" Then he shook his head. "You won't pull that trigger. I'd trust

Sara to do so before you." Gideon felt the sweat on his palms and knew that the Swede was right, he wasn't the man to shoot a friend. But he knew with equal certainty that Olsen was exactly that man.

From the corner the blanket erupted, with Danny beneath it, engulfing Olsen's head. Anders moved and grabbed the barrel of the musket, twisting it from the Swede's grip. A few moments later, muffled in the blanket and bound much as Danny had been and with the same match cord, Olsen lay in the corner wriggling like a landed fish. Beside him, Anders returned to his patient.

"I have to get out of here," Danny repeated and looked out of the window then back at them, his eyes dark. "You don't understand. Mags isn't planning to start a fire in the house. He would have lit that already if he was. It's just a feint to hold our attention if we break out. What you don't know is there is an undercroft to this tower. You can only reach it through the old wing, which is why Mags has had us all looking at the new one. The thing is Philip had several barrels of powder stored there as an emergency supply. Mags joked a couple of days ago about setting it off and bringing the tower down—even got me to show how it could be done. Except I'm sure now he wasn't joking. When that black powder explodes it will destroy the tower and we're all dead."

There was an appalled silence. Gideon felt as if the ground beneath him was giving way and had to put out a hand to steady himself against the wall.

"I know what he has done and how he will have done it. I told him how to set it up, how to put the fuses where it would be difficult to discover or get to—or stop it once started. I thought it was just an exercise. I never dreamed he'd…" Danny slumped back. "Christ, what a mess."

"We should tell Jupp," Anders suggested.

"If I'm right it'll take longer than we have left to convince him I'm telling the truth,"

"You couldn't climb down there anyway," Anders said, nodding to the wall below the window.

"You would be surprised," Danny said. "I'd rather not as I would be an easy target for Mags' rear guard, and I am not at my most athletic today. But if I go out that door I'll be stopped in a moment."

"How long do we have?" Gideon asked, his guts tightening.

"He won't want the explosion happening when the draft animals are still close or that could cause chaos. If he stuck to what I suggested, we maybe have twenty minutes more or less. We'll know when we are out of time because he will have set a signal for his men in the outbuildings to get them away just before the main explosion. At that point..." There was a movement behind them, and Gideon turned to see Zahara had got up from beside the injured man and was working at something around her waist.

"I still can't see how you will get out," Anders was saying. "I've seen down there. Even if you could sneak down, the doors to the two wings have been blocked either by us to keep them out or them to keep us in and Jupp would stop you trying to move any of it."

"I will have to go around the outside then." Danny gripped Anders' shoulder. "You don't understand. It's not safe anywhere in the tower. There's no choice. I have to try or we're all dead."

Zahara had turned her back and was pulling at something then a moment later turned around holding out some mulberry wool fabric.

"If you put this on," she told Danny, "no one will know you."

Danny took the fabric, shook it out, looked at it and grinned. Then winced. Stretching his bruised lips must have hurt.

"It is one of my underskirts," Zahara explained, pulling the lappet cap from her head, leaving her hair contained under its coif. "Put this on too and Bjorn's boots—and Anders' hat and cassaque."

It took longer than made Gideon comfortable. He knew, in a distant, intellectual way, that somewhere in the house a fuse was burning towards a barrel of powder and when it reached it, the ground beneath them would explode. He knew it. But the reality of it had yet to take root. More immediate in his mind was the thought that Jupp or one of the other men would walk in.

Zahara helped Danny dress and put his hair into something more feminine in style which if seen from behind, with the lappets hanging down, would cause no comment. Anders had, perforce, gone back to his patient, but like Gideon was glancing to the door now and then.

After what seemed an eternity, though in reality less than a handful of minutes could have passed, Zahara stepped back, looked Danny up and down and nodded. He wasn't a tall man and if he made a taller woman than usual it was not unbelievably so. Hidden by the brim of Anders' hat pulled low, his face was all but invisible, and Zahara had trimmed back his beard, so it didn't betray him from a distance. Close to, he wouldn't fool anyone who looked at him. Which made Gideon wonder how likely it was he would even get past Jupp and the others to reach the blocked doors in the first place.

But before he could ask, Zahara had turned to him, her hands held out.

"I will need that gun. And Anders, can you please give Captain Bristow your sword?"

It was only then Gideon understood her intention. Instead of surrendering it, he tightened the grip on the weapon.

"I will go with him. You stay here. It is safer."

For a moment she looked down, then she lifted her gaze, folded her hand over his where it held the fowling piece and shook her head.

"It's no safer here should the powder explode. If I go with Captain Bristow no one will think to look closely at him. They will assume it is one of the other women. If you go, they will look to see who the woman is with you." She smiled then and tightened her fingers over his hand for a moment. "We women are invisible when men are distracted by war."

"That is sad but true," Danny said and grinned again, this time without wincing. The prospect of action seemed to give him new resources of energy. "But we can use your help, Gideon. Wait a short time, then follow us down with the other musket. If we do get stopped, you can add your ha'penny worth of persuasion. And if we don't you can help me get the door open."

Anders looked up at them and shook his head. "Don't ask me. I have work here. If I leave this man now, he will die."

"And when Jupp comes?" Danny asked.

Anders shook his head.

"If you are not done by then there will be no point in my lying anyway. I will tell him the truth." He stood up and undid the baldric that held his sword, handing it to Danny. "Good luck, my friends. Remember, daylight will still come, though the cock does not crow."

A few moments later Zahara and Danny, sword concealed under the enveloping cassaque, had gone. Gideon waited by the door listening, the musket in his hands. There was no shouting or sounds of a scuffle, just some conversational voices and even a laugh. Footsteps went past and up the stairs. Then all was quiet, so he opened the door. As he stepped through it, a soft "Godspeed and good luck," from Anders followed him out.

The floor below was awash with water and the way down to the ground floor, where there was normally a fine wooden staircase, was now a hole in the floor partly covered by a heavy oak door taken from the only room on that floor. Zahara stood beside it and Danny was crouched looking down through the hole.

"Where is Jupp and everyone?" Gideon asked.

"They are all upstairs," Zahara told him. "Lieutenant Jupp wanted us all on the roof. He seems to think that even if the house is burned the tower may yet survive and the danger is more from smoke. We passed the last of the men going up and I told them we were fetching cushions from the servants' parlour here for Lady Belamy and Lady Grace to sit on." She gestured to the doorless room.

"Sara was proud of me," Danny said and gave a brief laugh. "I resisted the temptation to flirt outrageously."

Gideon looked back at the door-covered hole. "I

would have thought Jupp would want someone to guard the way up here."

"Who from?" Danny asked. "No one out there is going to come in here now. It is a death trap. No one here can go out without becoming musket and pistol practice for our erstwhile colleagues out there. Mags is a bastard. He wants this to be a showcase of his ability for whoever he seeks to sell the company to."

The thought tightened Gideon's guts and sent a wave of nausea into his stomach.

"We need to get on," Danny said. "Sara, you'd better get back to Anders and be ready to cover me from the window."

Zahara nodded and her gaze moved to Gideon, a sensation as physical to him as if their hands had touched. No words could have been enough and neither of them tried to find any. Instead, for the space of a heartbeat time stepped aside and Zahara lent him a small breath of the peace she always carried within her. Then she smiled and was gone.

"That," said Danny, with evident admiration, "is some woman." And it was obvious from his tone that his judgement wasn't in any way based upon Zahara's appearance. Then his expression became more serious. "I'm going to need your help, Gideon. I didn't want to risk Sara. The truth is, if by some slim chance I happen to survive this, I'd rather face Philip with your demise than hers."

Chapter Eighteen

I

"You don't know how hard these skirts are to manage," Danny protested. "Especially when they get wet."

Gideon had seen him struggle to make the descent from the floor above, unable to see where he was about to land because of the obscuring folds of fabric. Now Danny had to hitch up the skirt as they clambered over the untidy heap of broken furniture which sat in a half inch of water.

"My respect for the female kind has risen," Danny said. "How do they live in such things day in, day out? Perhaps they have some feminine instinct we mere males lack which allows them not to be encumbered." He reflected for a moment. "Or perhaps, it was a dire and cunning plan by our forefathers to ensure women would always be unable to evade us."

Gideon shook his head.

"Is everything a joke to you?" he asked.

Danny shook his head. "Not everything, no. But if seeing me wearing skirts isn't funny, I can't imagine what might be."

The doors that led to the two wings of the house were both effectively barricaded with furniture taken from the house. The door that led out of the tower was scantily blocked by comparison. It took the two of them precious minutes to clear it and doing so reminded Gideon of his own weakness. Danny was looking pale under Anders' hat, the freckles on his face standing out stark on his skin, his bruised hands clearly painful to bend to the task. Gideon realised that the incessant humour was for Danny's own benefit, a way to maintain himself. The punishment he had received was taking its toll and he was running on little more than a mix of grim determination and willpower.

Finally, it was done.

"I don't think they will shoot a woman," Danny said, as he reached out to open the door. "However, if they see an armed man, he will get their attention for sure." Danny paused letting Gideon add up the words like a simple sum in accounting. "I am the only one who knows how to stop the explosion, or I wouldn't ask you."

For a moment the unfairness of it struck Gideon with crippling force and his grasp on the weapon he had just picked up again slipped a little. He had survived a duel with Muir—twice, survived the effects of whatever Anders had given him and learned that all he felt for Zahara she returned. But now he was to die acting the decoy. It must have shown on his face because a damaged hand clutched his uninjured shoulder.

"For God's sake don't give out on me now," Danny said, a thread of desperation in his tone. "This is the crucible of courage. You can stand with me, or you can condemn us all to die like dogs." He drew a breath, eyes searching Gideon's face. "I can save Zahara, have you thought of that?"

Perhaps it was the invocation of her name, but the moment of wavering was gone. He nodded.

"What—" The words caught in his throat, and he started again. "What do you need me to do?"

"We have perhaps only a handful of minutes now. If Mags took my advice his men will see the signal set and withdraw at three. I'd wait for that but that won't allow enough time for me to get in and do what I have to. So, I'll go first—they will see a woman and hesitate, and you follow, holding that musket. We run."

Gideon swallowed down the bile that fear released and made himself hold Danny's gaze. Words were beyond him, but he managed to nod.

"Good man."

Danny released Gideon's shoulder, pulled open the door, then turned and grinned back at him before stepping through. It was an invitation to heroism. Or suicide. Gideon tried not to think which. Then he was running, clutching the musket so it could be seen.

The air outside was fresh and cold in the autumnal sunlight and Gideon drew a breath with full consciousness it could be his last. The first two shots came together as a bellow of sound, and he had no idea how close or distant they came to ending his life. All he knew was that they had miraculously failed to do so, and he kept running.

Their way lay along an exposed stretch of the courtyard along the wall of the house for the first twenty feet, then there was a low wall and if they made it past that, there was the promise of protection from the orchard wall by the main door to the older wing.

The next shot was so close that he felt the breeze of the bullet on his face and the sharp sting of stone where it hit the wall a fraction ahead of him. Then there came a loud report from above and a curse from the outbuildings. Zahara had discouraged at least one man.

By then Danny had already reached the orchard wall and a few moments later he vanished inside the house. At that point, Gideon felt no compunction in hurling himself behind the low, decorative wall which edged the path to the older wing and scuttling along in its shelter folded almost double, until he could stand again heart pounding. As he did so there was a flash and a sharp report from somewhere inside and, heart pounding in dread and disbelief, he knew they were too late.

But there was no following explosion and instead, he heard shouts from the far side of the courtyard and shooting from the tower before there was the clatter of hooves leaving the stableyard.

The small explosion must have been the warning Danny had mentioned and now they were on borrowed time. Riding away those men would escape all risk from the blast, but there was no escape possible for those in the tower. Gideon realised that perhaps he alone stood a chance. He could still get to one of the stronger outbuildings and that would protect him from the worst effects of the blast to come. For a moment the drive of simple self-preservation was so intense he felt the sweat spring from his body.

Then he thought of Zahara—of Anders, Jupp and the others, and of Danny, who must have known that he too had the same chance but had thrown it away to go into the house in what had to be a doomed attempt to try and stop the inevitable.

Before his rational thoughts could prevent him, Gideon ran the last of the short distance to the door of the old wing and went inside, his heart with every beat counting the ever-decreasing moments left. How long had Danny said there would be between the warning going up and the main charge? There was a strong smell of smoke lingering in the air.

"Gideon," Danny's voice from the end of the downstairs passage had a sharp urgency. "Thank Christ. I didn't think you were coming. Close the damn door and get in here."

Gideon closed the main door behind him and found Danny at the end of the passage that led to the tower. He had shed the skirt, which now lay, in a heap of charred, wet mulberry wool. Beyond it, two steps down and a pool of water which had seeped under the door. Gideon realised Danny must have soaked the skirt and used it to stifle a fire started by the warning explosion,

Danny had cleared some of the debris, but a heavy oak linen press, as tall as the ceiling and wider than Gideon's arms could span, had been used to block a door to one side, presumably the door to the undercroft. It must have been beyond Danny's reduced strength to pull it free alone, and there was no space to get purchase to push it from behind. Gideon could see he had even tried using part of a tabletop as a lever. It had splintered and Danny's hands already battered and red with burns were now a complete mess.

"We need to move this at least a little," Danny said, the previous urgency subdued now beneath a layer of cool professionalism. He showed Gideon where to grip. "Now, if we both pull…"

Had either of them been at full strength they would have moved it. But both of them had bodies damaged inside and out and muscles that refused to obey, even in extremis.

"That was just for practice," Danny said, breathing

THE TRAITOR'S APPRENTICE

hard. "Now let's do it properly."

This time they managed to move the linen press enough to allow the door to open two or three inches. For some reason opening it at all was a dangerous prospect because Gideon could see Danny tense as he did so. Then, when Danny opened it a crack, he understood why. The breeze from outside rushed in and whatever small amount might remain of the fuse was now going to burn a bit faster.

Inside, looking down into the room a few steps below him, Gideon could see nothing at first. The room was black. He could smell the stench of burning. As his eyes adjusted, the shapes of crates and barrels became visible in the gloom. The three powder barrels crouched in the far corner, against the very foundations of the tower. Seeing them, Gideon's lungs clung to his ribs in terror, stopping his breath. Somewhere in that gloom was the small glow of light that held their doom. Somewhere behind those crates and as inaccessible to them, being unable to open the door further, as if it were on the moon. There wasn't even time now to turn and run back to the door and hurl himself behind the orchard wall.

Danny drew in a breath.

"Can you see that wine cask on the shelf? The far wall." He might have been asking if Gideon could see some feature in the landscape on a country ride. The cask was there, right above where the three barrels of death stood waiting to be woken into their moment of supreme destruction. Gideon's throat was too dry for any words to escape. In his head, a silent prayer began, and his thoughts were of Zahara in the tower. He found himself praying that she wouldn't suffer when it happened.

Danny seemed not to notice there had been no reply to his question. He gestured to the gap in the door, wide enough to accommodate a musket barrel and little more than that.

"Shoot that barrel close to where the wood meets the rim. Don't think about it, just do it now. I can't."

It took a tremendous act of will to pull his mind from its preparation for death to hear and understand what Danny was asking. He glanced at Danny's ruined hands in the dim light of the passageway.

Danny's gaze found his own. There was nothing of fear in it. It was as if what was going to happen was an appropriate and expected ending to all his life had ever been. And it was that very stillness and acceptance that unlocked Gideon's paralysis.

Danny spoke again in the same calm and assured voice.

"Now, Gideon. Just do it. We have less than a minute."

It took about half that time to bring the musket up, and aim it, pushing the long barrel of the gun through the narrow crack. Gideon had never been a good shot and never claimed to be, but this time that couldn't matter. He hesitated, and Danny's voice took over.

"Just relax. Aim. Hold your breath so you don't move your hand as you fire."

He held his breath and pulled the trigger.

The dog-head hammer clicked forward.

Nothing happened.

Gideon froze. He hadn't checked the priming pan, the powder could have become too damp and—

The flash took him by surprise and the explosion echoed in the passageway as the gun fired. A moment later a small waterfall of wine cascaded down from the barrels on the shelf and then, as Gideon, weak with relief and fraught with hope, counted silently to five, the room went completely dark.

Then Danny clapped him on the back.

"Christ Gideon, I didn't think you could do it. I vow I'll never tell another lawyer joke so long as I live." Then his expression changed. "Or at least not in your hearing."

After that, Gideon recalled little for a few minutes except sliding down the wall to sit on the floor of the passageway, with Danny beside him. They were both laughing hard, gasping for breath as if someone had just told the funniest story either had ever heard.

But when the halting footsteps came along the passageway a minute or two later, Gideon was first on his feet, borrowed sword in hand. He stood squarely in front of the unarmed Danny. After what they had just been through, he wasn't about to allow Jupp or Olsen or any of the others near Danny until there had been a chance to explain.

"Here stood he in the dark, his sharp sword out, mumbling of wicked charms, conjuring the moon." The voice and its light mockery were familiar enough that Gideon didn't need to see the ghost-pale hair of the man who spoke to know who it was. "Though I must say I think I heard more of laughter than mumbling, and that sword—unless I am much mistaken—belongs to Anders Jensen. Is that Danny I see hiding behind you?" The voice lost its playfulness and took on an edge of steel. "Perhaps you indeed should hide, Captain Bristow. I recall giving you specific instructions regarding the security of this house and those in it. I shall require an account and explanation of what you

have allowed to happen here in my absence."

Philip Lord had returned.

II

After Danny, whose interview was brief, Gideon was the first to give Lord an account of events. But the questioning only went in one direction. Gideon's enquiry as to where Lord had been, was met with a curt rebuff.

"That is unimportant," Lord said with a dismissive gesture. "It goes without saying I was detained against my will. You may be sure that Shiraz and I returned as quickly as was humanly possible once free to do so."

And before Gideon could ask more, he was being subjected to further interrogation himself.

After that Gideon was sure Lord heard from Jupp and every other man of the seventeen who now remained of the company, not to mention the women, the furious and heartbroken baroness, her mother, houseguest and servants. Lord's first instruction, once he had sent out scouts to make sure Mags was not returning, was that the house should be set in good order before they left.

It was an impossible task and Gideon wondered at first why the attempt was even being made. But as it went on, he began to see the reason. It was returning some self-respect to these men who had fought so hard not to be the destroyers and wasters Mags had commanded them to be. Instead, Lord had them become builders, restorers and creators.

By the second day into the clear up Gideon could see that even those who had protested the task to begin with were starting to take some pride in what was being achieved.

THE TRAITOR'S APPRENTICE

Along with Lord himself, Zahara was the driving force behind the restoration. Mustering the servants as well as the soldiers, like a general commanding an army on the battlefield, she organised what needed to be done. From repairing the structure of the house to mending damaged furniture and hangings. From clearing the debris from rooms and outbuildings to adapting enough of what could be salvaged to provide the essentials for life and comfort. There was a task for everyone from dawn until dusk and into the night. Even Lord himself could be found on occasion carrying something for Zahara or running an errand on her behalf.

Lady Belamy was slow to show any appreciation, but Gideon could understand how she must feel. Her entire world had been destroyed in one night. Even when the tattered remnants of the company had done what they could to make good the worst, she would still face years of work to create in Wrathby even the shadow of its former grandeur. And that was assuming the tides of war didn't rise to pound against her walls again, which Gideon feared was all too probable. But, he reflected, at least she still had her home, her son and her life, which was more than Mags would have left her.

The old wing had been the least damaged since that had been where Mags and his chosen had slept. So Zahara cleaned and furnished those on the upper floor and settled Elizabeth Belamy in the one that had been Lord's—the least damaged, as Danny had taken some care of it during his brief stay. Last Grace was placed in the room which was once given to Mags and William Irving occupied the room Muir had been in. The room Gideon had shared with Anders and Danny became a nursery for the infant baron, so the three of them were now sleeping on pallets in the outbuildings with the remnants of Lord's company.

Once a basic stairway had been constructed on the first day, Lord took over a room in the peel tower. Not that he spent much time there. He could be found sometimes in shirtsleeves doing the hardest of the physical work required, and sometimes with Zahara, supervising the endeavour, encouraging, praising, advising and, at need, reprimanding and punishing.

It was Lord who rode out with a handful of men and their one remaining wagon to purchase whatever surplus of supplies was still to be had in the area so the household wouldn't starve in the winter and to secure promises of more.

Gideon found his own time was spent between working on the clearing up for Zahara and clerking for Lord. The portable desk was set up on a table in the corner of Lord's room in the peel tower. Danny had kept it hidden on a shelf in the same undercroft room where the powder had been stored and joked that his real reason for working so hard to stop the explosion was that he feared the wrath of Lord should he find that Danny had done so.

Inventories were needed of the few supplies and resources the company still had and another of those it now needed, and Gideon was the one turning notes, dictated in the moment or scribbled in charcoal, into ordered, inked lists.

It meant that he was present, sitting in the corner of the room, for many of the interviews Lord had with those of the company. Most were terse, designed to establish the facts of the events. For each, Lord had words of praise, even if he needed also occasionally to censure. Each man was given his pay and an amount of coin in addition. From this, Gideon concluded the desk had been holding more than just a wealth of documents.

He was also present when Danny came to make his full, formal report. It was the afternoon of that second day and Danny had been under Anders' ongoing care for the intervening period.

Gideon sat writing up a list of items that needed somehow to be procured to make the company a viable fighting force once more. It brought home to him the immense scale of the loss to Lord of what Mags had done. So he was in a sombre mood as Danny came in.

Danny's face was livid with purple, black and yellow, against which any freckles were almost invisible, and his hands were swathed in bulky bandages. But he was dressed smartly in a blue doublet and breeches, decorated with silver braid. The sword he couldn't presently even draw, let alone wield, was worn at his hip, leaving Gideon to wonder who had tied his points and done up his buckles.

Lord greeted him with an assessing look and gestured to his own chair.

"You had better sit, I would rather not be having to carry you back down. Besides I'm seeing Anders next, and he has strange notions of gentleness around how those under his care should be treated."

Danny moved stiffly to the chair and sat as if his legs were unwilling to bend.

"Jupp," he said, "is too damn good at his job."

"Better than you at yours."

"Christ, Philip, don't you think I know that?" He held up his bandaged hands. "And if you want my life for it there is nothing I can do to stop you."

"I am more interested in why I found myself riding into a force more than twice the size you told me to expect."

It was hard to read any expression on Danny's face now the bruising had swollen it, but Gideon could see that he closed his eyes, as if in pain.

"Tempest had linked up with Cummings again. Something that was not supposed to have happened for another day at least. I had no way of knowing until I reached him. And they had both been collecting men as they went." He paused and Gideon glanced over to the still mask of Lord's face. "I rode like the wild hunt to get back to warn you, but my horse went lame, and I was reduced to a walk. I got back to Wrathby to find you had just left. I was going to arrange a remount but there was a commotion in the house and Anders was shouting about Gideon being in danger." He lifted both his shoulders. "After that, I found my attention was fully occupied with saving the lives of Sara and your damned lawyer."

Gideon felt his ears grow hot at the words, true though they were. The image of Muir's blade swept up at the last moment by Danny's intervention was still all too clear in his mind.

Lord moved to a side table where he kept a jug of wine and cups to drink from. Somehow it didn't surprise Gideon that where everyone else in Wrathby, from the baroness down, now had to make do with weak, freshly brewed ale, someone had found wine for Lord. The cups, however, were ill-matched old pewter, no doubt uncovered by Zahara in a store of tableware that had been boxed up and retired from use years since.

Lord poured the wine into two of the cups and took

one to Danny, who held it between the padded claws his hands had become.

"Thank you for saving them. You were, of course, correct to assume I was the one better able to cater for my own welfare and it was only through ill fortune and overconfidence on my part that I was not."

"Is that 'you did the right thing, Danny' in plain English?"

"You did the right thing, Danny," Lord agreed, and the mask of his face betrayed a trace of humour, which vanished again just as fast. "But you should have killed Mags."

Danny had been drinking from the cup and some of the wine splashed redly over his bandaged fingers.

"Would you believe I tried? I poisoned the wine in his room before the trial, but he didn't drink it. It killed Alice Franklyn instead. At least it spared her being raped by half the company, I suppose."

"There were other opportunities. If you are anything you are resourceful."

"I had other lives to look after, and I was trying to keep the company together until you got back. If I'd made a stand, there would have been a slaughter—myself and the few I could persuade to oppose him. When it comes down to it, Mags has the power of legend. I'm just Danny Bristow. And once he'd dug his talons into the company the only way I could try and save it was by staying with him. I did what I could. Little things to disrupt his plans, spreading false rumours, confusing his orders, that kind of thing. The fact that we have any horses left at all is because I took some pains to hide them."

"Jupp managed to make a stand." Lord made it a

observation, not an accusation and Danny let out his breath in a sigh that finished with an ironic laugh.

"Jupp only lived to make his stand because of me. Mags had seen how the wind was blowing and gave me the nod to slit his throat. I didn't. Mags' idea of creative punishment for that failure to understand his unspoken order, was to have me locked in my room—your room—for most of the night so I would miss out on all the fun."

Lord shook his head. "After you had rendered him such good service too."

"Indeed so," Danny agreed. "Directly or otherwise, I helped remove a few of his embarrassments. Although I can't claim all the credit for Simon Muir, who incidentally was the one who freed the man we buried with de Torres and attacked Novak, a task I learned too late he was set by Mags to prove himself."

Which made Lord frown. "I questioned Muir myself. I must be losing my touch. But that is good to know since Novak is one of those who have stayed with us." His expression changed. "Did you learn what happened with de Torres?"

"De Torres had a sister once. Mags told me he seduced her with grand promises and then sent her away with a bag of gold when she spoke of expecting marriage. She took her own life and that of her unborn child. Mags didn't see how he held any responsibility for that, after all she had been willing, and he had paid her."

"That sounds much like the man," Lord said, his tone bitter. "I heard you also had the pleasure of relieving this weary world of Aleksandrov."

"Mags wanted it done. Aleksandrov had made the mistake of acting on his initiative a few too many times for Mags' taste. The man, you will have noticed, prefers blind obedience. Besides, it served his ends to convince Jupp of my defection, which was, of course, the purpose of it all. Sadly for him, and for me, Jupp has nurtured some ability to think, and he took me for the Trojan horse I was meant to be, even though I wasn't. He is," Danny added, "a very good man, is Jupp."

Then he lifted the cup awkwardly and drank again. This time when he had finished Lord reached over and took it from his useless hands to return it to the side table.

"He is," Lord agreed. "I'll promote him when we are done here. Matt thought him good enough so perhaps it is fitting he takes on Matt's job."

"But he could never replace Matt, could he? No one could."

Danny, Gideon realised, wasn't talking about military capacity.

Lord moved to the window, still broken where Olsen had smashed it and looked out over the courtyard, face invisible.

"You know Mags killed Matt," he said at last. A statement not a question, the words sounding as if each cost pain.

"I asked around," Danny admitted. "Then I spoke to Sara and added up what I heard."

"You always were the mathematician."

"And you didn't tell me before, because…?"

Taking a drink from his cup, Lord stayed his back to them, by the window. "He poisoned Matt, gave him something that hurt his heart, and tried to blame it on Anders Jensen. Liam tried to kill Jensen and still hates him... hates me…" Lord paused as if even breath had fo a moment become too difficult. When he spoke again it was with more emotion than Gideon had ever heard him let slip before. "Mags murdered Matt and turned his widow and son into my enemies."

"Christ, why didn't you—?"

"Because I had no way to prove it." The control was back, and his voice restored to its usual measured tones. "All thought it a natural death—even Jensen himself missed the signs. Only Zahara suspected and she could not be completely sure. Matt was not a young man… But then why make Jensen look bad if there was no murder?" He drew a slow breath. "There was no proof—is no proof. Only conjecture. At the time it happened everyone was on edge. Mags had halfway turned them against me and that would have been the final straw. If I had accused him, called him out, I would have lost the men and I did not want to lose them to Mags of all people."

"Lost *all* of them?" Danny sounded doubtful.

"Maybe not all, but most. Mags had them gulled, dazzled by his legend. It is my fault. I made a huge mistake in Weardale thinking I could leave him alone with them for even a short time. He had it well planned, and by the time I got back, he had them eating from his palm. I decided to keep him as close as possible until I could muster a reason to call him out or arrange for him to have an accident. It was why we came here. It was why I put him in apparent command, to give him every opportunity to overreach himself. It was why I set you to the task I did. And we nearly had him. We would have if not for my being captured. Proof of his perfidy. Your witness, the word of Sir Nicholas Tempest and that of most of those he had lured to his side who would have turned to save themselves. It would have been over."

Danny laughed, but it was hollow and without humour.

"And Mags believing all along it was a scheme to get rid of you. I think at one point even I believed Fairfax was coming to Wrathby, I had to say it so often."

"Except it nearly ended exactly as Mags intended," Lord observed.

"He always was a lucky bastard. Part of what makes him that legend you mentioned."

Lord turned and crossed the room in two strides to set his cup back on the table. He strode over to where Gideon sat and picked up the list, holding it up so the length of it was visible to Danny where he sat. "This is just part of what I have lost. What I had hoped would provide the needed skill and expertise to produce a force capable of restoring peace to England before this war gets out of hand. Such men as Jupp has been able to preserve for me are too few to make that difference now. Mags has most of them."

He let the sheet drop and Gideon grabbed it to prevent it from slipping to the floor. Then realised he shouldn't have troubled. He had just wasted his morning compiling a list that would never be used.

Lord had already returned to where Danny sat and crouched beside the chair, his eyes on a level with Danny's, holding his gaze.

"I need you to go back to him and finish what you started. Mags has drawn a knife that he will hold to the throat of this nation if left in his hand. I can't reach him now, but you can. He thinks you are still his."

"Christ!" The single syllable of blasphemy was as hard as a pistol shot and Gideon's body tensed as if had been. "You can't ask me—"

"There is no one else."

Gideon found he was holding his breath as the two men locked their gaze. But he wasn't surprised it was Danny who looked away first, his eyes lowering to his damaged hands. "I'll need a couple of days before I can ride. I can't even hold a sword at the moment."

Lord's face held no triumph, only a bleak moment of sadness as he nodded.

"You'll have that, of course."

"And you?" Danny asked. "Where are you going to go?"

Lord stood up and turned away.

"I think you know."

"You'll join the prince?"

"He has made it clear he wants me."

"You will go," Danny said, tone shrewd. "He has Kate."

Lord's expression slipped as if taken unawares by an emotion too strong to conceal and he lowered his head.

"He has Kate," he agreed, then looked up.

"I get Mags and you get Kate. There is no justice in this world."

But Gideon heard no trace of resentment in Danny's words.

"At least you will know where to find me," Lord said. "I hope you will not be long."

Danny got to his feet a little less than smoothly and for the first time since his greeting, turned to Gideon and acknowledged his presence.

"I have not forgotten I owe you victory at *L'Hombre,* although if Anders won't play it may need to be Piquet. Just as soon as my hands can hold the cards again, we will play before I leave." Then he drew himself up to his full height and made a formal military bow to Lord, who responded with a wry smile and a like gesture.

"Dr Jensen asked to see me earlier. If you would please pass the word that I am happy to see him now, Captain Bristow."

Having closed the door behind Danny, Lord retrieved his cup again, emptying it in a single swallow. Gideon wondered for a moment why he had been made a witness to what had passed between them.

"Danny told me," Lord said, refilling his cup, "that you were the one to whom I owe the most—after himself, of course." Then he turned to where Gideon sat at the portable desk and lifted the cup as if in a toast. "We both thought you deserved some explanation of what you had risked your life to save. I hope that you will stay. I am short on friends. However, I will understand if you decide not to do so after what you have suffered in my company."

It was impossible to reply to that glibly and Gideon, feeling both the weight and the warmth of what was being offered, found he had no words. Before any could come there was a knock on the door and Lord turned away.

"*Entrez.*"

Anders came in and glanced past Lord to Gideon, then back to Lord and gave the expected bow.

"Fox is due a break and can leave us," Lord said, gesturing with the cup in his hand. Gideon got to his feet, stepping away from the desk but Anders shook his head and held up a hand.

"Please stay, Gideon, then I need not say this so many times."

Philip Lord crossed to the side table again, put down his cup and filled the two others there before handing one to Gideon and offering the other to Anders, who shook his head. Lord withdrew his hand and drank from the cup himself.

"You have come to tell me you wish to leave," he said, and Gideon nearly choked on his wine as Anders nodded, lips in a tight line.

"I have," he confirmed. "Although I have much appreciation for the opportunities working for you has given me, I find I do not feel so comfortable with the ways of your mercenary company."

"We are not all as Mags and Aleksandrov," Lord said.

Anders nodded again.

"I know that. I have healed the handiwork of you and your 'good' men too. Men like Bjorn Olsen and Roger Tupp. I have walked so tangled in deceit I did not know where to place my feet. Perhaps it is that he is little suited to be a baker, whose head is made of butter. But I am intending to leave, and I hope that Gideon will have the sense to come with me." He finished speaking with his gaze back on Gideon's, holding a silent appeal. An appeal to step away from the world of violence and subterfuge, of wild justice and vile individuals, who paid no heed to the laws of God nor man. And Gideon knew that Anders was right. This was not his world, nor was it a world to which he could ever truly belong.

Lord turned to him, an eyebrow raised in interrogation.

"Are you leaving us too, Gideon?"

A frisson lifted the hairs on Gideon's forearms. Aside from using it in their early acquaintance as a way of mocking him, Lord had never used his given name to address him before. Now he had made it easy to say yes, easy for Gideon to walk across the room and stand beside Anders and leave Philip Lord and all the chaos he represented behind for good.

Before it had been simple: he had stayed for Zahara. But now, though he loved her with his entire soul and knew she felt the same, he also understood that what lay between them, invisible like glass, was a barrier neither of them knew the means to overcome. Being beside her, in her company, day by day, was as much torment as joy—for both of them. And knowing it, a part of him wished to spare her that, even if the cost was a greater loss to the two of them.

For what seemed an age but couldn't have been more than the passing of a breath, Gideon remained undecided. Anders stood there patiently, the man who had only stayed these last few days on his account and who had nearly lost his life for doing so. Then there was Philip Lord, immured in his tower of intellectual isolation, with the bastions of arrogance and indifference to repel all who trespassed close enough.

Gideon lowered his head, unable to meet either waiting gaze.

"I will stay," he said. Then with sudden courage, he looked up at Anders and offered him the only explanation he could. "I think I have work to do here."

Anders' expression barely changed, and Gideon realised that the Dane had expected it. He made no attempt at persuasion, merely nodding again, a mix of understanding and compassion in his gaze. Lord had turned away the moment Gideon spoke and now gave his full attention to Anders. Reaching for one of the coin pouches sitting in the portable desk, he threw it deftly to land in Anders' hands.

"Your pay for the work you have done, together with my gratitude, Dr Jensen. If you are willing to wait a few more days, Captain Bristow, it seems, is also leaving my employ and he will provide you with an escort to wherever you may wish to go before he takes his own path. I am sure I need not say that if ever you were to change your mind, you would be welcomed back."

It was clear from his frown that Anders felt the amount Lord had paid him was much in excess of what he had expected, and he seemed about to protest when Lord spoke again.

"*For the scripture saith, Thou shalt not muzzle the ox that treadeth out the corn. And, The labourer is worthy of his reward.* Thou hath trodden and thou hath laboured. That is the least you deserve for all you have done. Thank you."

Anders made a brief bow. "You are a generous man, sir, and I think a better one than your profession allows you to be."

For once Lord seemed to have no reply or at least none he was willing to offer. Instead, he inclined his head in acknowledgement. Anders nodded to Gideon and left them.

There was a silence after the door closed, and then Lord turned to Gideon wearing an expression he couldn't read. "It seems I must apologise since I have neither earrings of gold nor chains about my camels' necks to offer you, and forty years of peace in my company is, at best, unlikely. But I have a pledge." He lifted the cup he held. "Friendship."

Feeling as if he were taking on a new and strange burden, Gideon lifted his cup, the same that Danny had clasped in his bandaged hands and echoed the word like an oath.

"Friendship."

Ryedale, Yorkshire, Early October 1642

Four days later they left Wrathby.

Danny Bristow and Anders Jensen headed north, and the remnants of the company headed south. In its entirety, the small cavalcade numbered less than thirty people, including women, children and a new-born infant. There were perhaps twenty fighting men, a handful riding horses trained to war, a handful on hacks and the rest on foot. All bore swords that had drawn blood and taken lives. Some had recent injuries speaking, perhaps, of a skirmish which, from their demeanour, was one they had lost. They marched in a disciplined column in escort of a single lumbering wagon, which carried all they had by way of possessions and supplies.

Their progress was slow.

This being England and the season being autumn, the way was frequently rutted and flooded. With luck and only one wagon to manage, they might hope to make twenty miles in a day. They followed a drovers' road with sheltered stopping points, wayside inns and places where they could buy supplies at need, so the journey south wasn't as arduous as it might have been even on the cold and beautiful Yorkshire Dales.

Behind them, lay the partially resurrected manor of Wrathby. Its proud walls still standing and the earthworks that could have given it a strong defence lay unfinished about its skirts like an open grave.

Ahead of them, lay two armies, each convinced of the

THE TRAITOR'S APPRENTICE

absolute rightness of their cause, mustering for a battle to decide the fate of the nation.

Author's Note

This book is dedicated to my father, Dr D.T. Swift-Hook, who was one of the first to read the unvarnished versions and who has given me some truly incredible support when I have needed it over the years. My debt is beyond measure as is my love and appreciation.

Sir Thomas Fairfax and William Cavendish, Earl of Newcastle, both of whom make fleeting appearances in The Traitor's Apprentice are the only characters in this book whose names you will find in the history books. How they behave is my invention. All the other characters you will have encountered are the product of my imagination, as is the conspiracy known as the Covenant.

If you visit Ryedale, North Yorkshire, you will find some wonderful old houses and castles in that beautiful corner of England, but you will not find one called Wrathby.

Peel (or pele) towers, such as that which forms the basis of Wrathby, were built across the north of England and southern Scotland from around 1300 until 1600. With border raids going in both directions and penetrating quite deeply behind the frontiers, these strongholds provided their local communities with secure places to retreat to at need. These towers were also homes and when the need for them as defensive structures reduced, some became incorporated into proper houses. You can find examples of peel towers northwards from Lancashire and North Yorkshire, in England and all across the south of Scotland.

There was indeed a real attempt by the leading lights of Yorkshire to secure peace in their county despite the inexorable march to war. The Treaty of Neutrality was signed on 29 September 1642 between Lord Ferdinando Fairfax of Cameron, the leading Parliamentarian and the man appointed to command the army of Parliament in the county, and Henry Bellasis, son of Sir Thomas Bellasis, Lord Fauconberg of Yarm, representing the Royalist faction. Both men were 'knights of the shire', Members of Parliament for Yorkshire.

Although a noble attempt, it was doomed to failure. Men like John Hotham (one of the Hothams who had denied Hull to the king that summer) saw it as no reason not to continue hostilities. Even as the treaty was being negotiated, he seized Doncaster and with the ink barely dry on the page, he attacked Cawood Castle taking it for Parliament. At the same time, many Royalist sympathisers were in ongoing communications with the Earl of Newcastle. In a letter dated just three days before the treaty was signed, they petitioned him to march south and protect them. The final nail in the coffin of the treaty came on 4 October 1642, when Parliament denounced it saying those who had signed it had no authority to do so.

Another casualty of the onset of war was justice.

The breakdown of the legal system was rapid. At this time the most serious cases, those with capital punishment such as murder, rape, burglary and forgery were heard in the assizes courts. These were organised as six circuits across the country with judges from London visiting the county towns. The outbreak of war saw these circuits suspended and the administration of justice in most places in the countryside fell into abeyance or upon the shoulders of the local justice. Almost inevitably in many places, military commanders became de facto justices and military governors were granted—or took upon themselves—powers to enforce martial law on civilian populations.

If you have enjoyed The Traitor's Apprentice, I would love to hear what you thought about it so please do leave a review. You can also follow me on Twitter @emswifthook or get in touch with me through my website www.eleanorswifthook.com where you can find more about the background to the book including the origins of the various quotations in the text.

Meanwhile, you will be pleased to know The Traitor's Apprentice is just the second of six books which follow Gideon Lennox through the opening months of the first English Civil War. As he unravels the mystery of Philip Lord's past, he finds himself getting caught up in battles and sieges, murder investigations and moral dilemmas as all the while his heart is torn by his seemingly impossible romance with the beautiful Zahara.

Printed in Great Britain
by Amazon